Count Leo Tolstoy (1828 ___) ___ Polyana, Russia. Orphaned ___ an elderly aunt and educa ___ matriculated at Kazan University in 1844. In 1847, he gave up his studies and, after several aimless years, volunteered for military duty in the army, serving as a junior officer in the Crimean War before retiring in 1857. In 1862, Tolstoy married Sofya Behrs, a marriage that was to become, for him, bitterly unhappy. His diary, started in 1847, was used for self-study and self-criticism; it served as the source from which he drew much of the material that appeared not only in his great novels *War and Peace* (1869) and *Anna Karenina* (1877) but also in his shorter works. Seeking religious justification for his life, Tolstoy evolved a new Christianity based upon his own interpretation of the Gospels. Yasnaya Polyana became a mecca for his many converts.

Regina Marler is the author of *Bloomsbury Pie: The Making of the Bloomsbury Boom* and editor of *Selected Letters of Vanessa Bell*. She also writes for the *New York Times Book Review* and the *Los Angeles Times*. Marler lives in San Francisco.

Hugh McLean is Professor Emeritus of Slavic Languages and Literatures at the University of California, Berkeley, where he taught from 1967 until 1994 and served as Dean of Humanities. He edited *In the Shade of the Giant: Essays on Tolstoy* (1989) and wrote *Nikolai Leskov: The Man and His Art* (1977), as well as numerous articles in professional journals.

Leo Tolstoy

THE DEATH OF IVAN ILYCH
AND OTHER STORIES

TRANSLATED BY
Aylmer Maude and J. D. Duff

WITH A NEW INTRODUCTION BY
Regina Marler
AND AN AFTERWORD BY
Hugh McLean

SIGNET CLASSICS

SIGNET CLASSICS
Published by New American Library, a division of
Penguin Group (USA) Inc., 375 Hudson Street,
New York, New York 10014, USA
Penguin Group (Canada), 90 Eglinton Avenue East, Suite 700, Toronto,
Ontario M4P 2Y3, Canada (a division of Pearson Penguin Canada Inc.)
Penguin Books Ltd., 80 Strand, London WC2R 0RL, England
Penguin Ireland, 25 St. Stephen's Green, Dublin 2,
Ireland (a division of Penguin Books Ltd.)
Penguin Group (Australia), 250 Camberwell Road, Camberwell, Victoria 3124,
Australia (a division of Pearson Australia Group Pty. Ltd.)
Penguin Books India Pvt. Ltd., 11 Community Centre, Panchsheel Park,
New Delhi - 110 017, India
Penguin Group (NZ), 67 Apollo Drive, Rosedale, Auckland 0632,
New Zealand (a division of Pearson New Zealand Ltd.)
Penguin Books (South Africa) (Pty.) Ltd., 24 Sturdee Avenue,
Rosebank, Johannesburg 2196, South Africa

Penguin Books Ltd., Registered Offices:
80 Strand, London WC2R 0RL, England

Published by Signet Classics, an imprint of New American Library, a division of
Penguin Group (USA) Inc. Published by arrangement with Oxford University
Press, Inc., who have authorized this softcover edition.

First Signet Classics Printing, February 1960
First Signet Classics Printing (Marler Introduction), August 2012
10 9 8 7 6 5 4 3 2

Introduction copyright © Regina Marler, 2012
Afterword copyright © Hugh McLean, 2003
All rights reserved. No part of this book may be reproduced, scanned, or
distributed in any printed or electronic form without permission. Please do not
participate in or encourage piracy of copyrighted materials in violation of the
author's rights. Purchase only authorized editions.

 REGISTERED TRADEMARK—MARCA REGISTRADA

Printed in the United States of America

If you purchased this book without a cover you should be aware that this book
is stolen property. It was reported as "unsold and destroyed" to the publisher and
neither the author nor the publisher has received any payment for this "stripped
book."

CONTENTS

INTRODUCTION

WHEN word reached Moscow that Count Leo Tolstoy had stolen away from his home and family in the middle of the night, reporters and government agents flocked to the scene. At eighty-two, Tolstoy was a national icon—not only a literary giant but a holy man, moral philosopher, and scourge. Along with his less popular stances, such as vegetarianism and pacifist Christian anarchism, he remained a bitter and unflagging critic of the government and the Orthodox Church in a country where almost every voice of opposition had been stifled. Instantly recognizable in his peasant garb with his aristocratic demeanor, the great man had attracted a steady flow of pilgrims and sandal-wearing "Tolstoyans" from around the world to his country estate at Yasnaya Polyana. Now, in late October 1910, he was missing.

Newspaper editors paid reporters to track him, printing a stream of telegrams with the details of his flight, his attempts to cover his tracks, and his discovery at Astapovo Station, where he had fallen ill with pneumonia and lay feverish in the stationmaster's bed. Who was visiting Tolstoy? What had the invalid eaten that morning? What had he said? Tolstoy's devotees turned away the district governor, then an abbot from Optina Puystin Monastery intent on deathbed repentance. Until the last moments, even Tolstoy's tormented—and tormenting—wife was forbidden access; she mingled with the crowd outside and gave conflicting, highly emotional statements to the press.

The major papers devoted almost half their space to the unfolding drama, which has been described as "the first modern media event in Russia."*

When Tolstoy died three weeks later, a frenzy of grief struck the nation. Students rioted. Demonstrations broke out. Thousands followed his coffin back to his home—a jostling crowd captured in newsreel footage—where his "orphaned peasants," as they called themselves, held up a memorial banner to this champion of the poor. Some fell to their knees in the snow. Church authorities refused to officiate at the funeral—Tolstoy never having recanted the views that had caused him to be excommunicated nine years earlier—but the crowd sang ancient Russian funeral hymns. Something "extraordinary and immense" had happened in Tolstoy's death, as a student in St. Petersburg wrote, and an uprising felt possible: "These are days of life and passion, days of anxiety, days on fire, brimming over with thrilling events."†

Aware that a hero and genius had died, but also one who had hated and reviled the government and might still provoke trouble, the Russian parliament stood in unison to honor Tolstoy's passing. After all, he remained one of them—a nobleman. When a second vote was taken on whether to adjourn for the day, results were mixed. Conservatives mostly declined, and grumbling could be heard as the legislators shuffled out.

A hundred years later, while Europe and America celebrated the centenary of Tolstoy's death with broadcasts, scholarly conferences, new biographies and translations, a feature film about Tolstoy's final months, and a novel parody called *Android Karenina*, the Russian government made no statement, arranged no ceremonies or

---

*William Nickell, *The Death of Tolstoy: Russia on the Eve, Astapovo Station, 1910* (Cornell University Press, 2010). A Russian work with a similar focus is Basil V. Basinsky's *Lev Tolstoy: Escape From Paradise* (2010).

†www.linguadex.com/tolstoy/diary.html.

festivities. There was no official recognition of Tolstoy's death centenary, despite the fanfare recently accorded to the 150th anniversary of Anton Chekhov's birth.* On Alexander Pushkin's death centenary, a town had been named after him.

Similarly, the Orthodox Church rejected requests to reconsider his excommunication, on the grounds that only a living person can repent. "The church's position to Tolstoy has not changed," reported a member of the church's culture committee. "Tolstoy is anti-Christian. He is excommunicated and therefore presents no interest for the church."† In a letter published in a state-run newspaper, the cultural council secretary to Patriarch Kirill II acknowledged Tolstoy's "unforgettable, beautiful works" but complained that he had "purposely used his great talent to destroy Russia's traditional spiritual and social order" and archly pointed out that "the leader of the Bolsheviks [Lenin] supremely valued the aim of Leo Tolstoy's activity."‡

It is worth examining how a writer—especially so exceptional a figure as Tolstoy, "the greatest of all novelists," as Virginia Woolf summed it up—managed to leave such a conflicted legacy. Tenth graders in Russia are required to read *War and Peace*, yet the government would like to forget Tolstoy existed. This testifies to his enduring power to upset people. "He was one of history's great truth-tellers," wrote A. N. Wilson in a recent reassessment of his own 1984 Tolstoy biography:

> the first of the great dissidents, and their patron saint. In a world dominated by crooked rulers, unjust wars, malice and corruption, and, above all,

*The city of Moscow—home to two Tolstoy museums—declared 2010 "The Year of Tolstoy."
†Quoted in Miriam Elder's "Russia Snubs Tolstoy," www.GlobalPost .com, 12 October 2010.
‡Quoted in Ellen Barry and Sophia Kishkovsky's "For Tolstoy and Russia, Still No Happy Ending," *New York Times*, 3 January 2011.

lies, Tolstoy became what Dante called a "one-man party" and struck out to right and left.*

It feels natural to divide Tolstoy's life into a period of vigorous artistry and experiment (ending with a spiritual crisis in the mid-1870s, during the completion of *Anna Karenina*) and one of moral searching and social action, in which Tolstoy began to cobble his own boots, preach against private property and meat consumption, and argue for the Christian ideals of celibacy, universal brotherhood, and nonviolent resistance. In more basic terms, he moved from artist to thinker. He himself perceived a stark shift, as he explained in *What I Believe* (1885):

> Everything which used to seem good and noble to me—ambition, education, wealth, a complex and sophisticated lifestyle, environment, food, clothes, and formal manners—has become bad and sordid. Everything which seemed bad and sordid—the peasant lifestyle, obscurity, poverty, crudity, simple surroundings, food, clothes, manners—has become good and noble.

But Tolstoy's black-and-white version of his personal history, his beard trembling as he thundered those absolutes, contains a degree of bluster and perhaps of self-deception. In his real life, nothing was so clear-cut. His religious conversion was genuine but protracted—about a ten-year process of rethinking, revelation, backsliding—with roots that extended into childhood. He had always had a solitary, ascetic streak, always sympathized with peasants and the apparent simplicity of their lives and their religious faith. As a student, he had drawn up drastic programs of self-improvement, including a two-year learning plan that would take an ordinary man a lifetime (Number eight: "To attain a degree of perfection in music and painting," and

---

*From a review titled "Leo Tolstoy: Russia's Thunderous Prophet," *Financial Times* (UK), 20 November 2010.

number nine: "To write down rules."). As a soldier, when not gambling or contracting gonorrhea, he had dreamed of founding a new religion, "the religion of Christ, but purged of all dogma and mystery."

Tolstoy's spiritual searching took him several times to Optina Puystin Monastery outside Moscow, a "font of Orthodoxy" and austerity so inspiring to the budding sage that he made Optina the first stop on his nighttime flight from Yasnaya Polyana. He had long since renounced the Orthodox Church, but clearly felt a lingering kinship with the monks.*

Never a joiner, Tolstoy found much to dislike in Orthodoxy: the Trinity, the miracles of the saints, even the divinity of Christ. He scoured the Gospels for evidence of the truth of these tenets. Tradition was not enough. In addition, the political role of the Church (as the established religion of Russia, fundamentally allied with the state and the status quo) sickened him. "Prayers for a long life and the subjugation of one's enemies is blasphemy," he declared after hearing a militaristic sermon. "A Christian should pray for his enemies, not against them." The afterlife was an afterthought for Tolstoy; he wanted to know the best way to live now, on earth. Fastening on a selective but literal reading of the Gospels, he drew from it a determination to live as Christ taught in the Sermon on the Mount, in selflessness, poverty, and chastity, at peace with his fellow men, accepting no master but God.

Here Newton's Third Law kicks in: For every action, there is an equal and opposite reaction. Tolstoy published his religious musings in *A Confession* (1882) and Church censors immediately shut him down. He resolved to live in peace, and plunged his family into chaos

---

*Also, after a scandalous life, his sister had entered a convent attached to Optina. Tolstoy seems to have considered asking permission to retire to a cottage near her. For their part, the elders hoped he had returned to reconcile himself with the Orthodox Church, but he left again before speaking to any of them.

and discord. The Tolstoys could tolerate the peasant shirts, the wood chopping, the moralizing, but giving away his possessions—their possessions!—and the copyrights to his work?

After the bliss of their first months together, Tolstoy and his much younger wife had settled into the kind of relationship described in the story "Family Happiness," a relatively calm accommodation to their many differences and to Tolstoy's unfortunate views on women. Their marriage had been fruitful. Sofya Andreyevna had borne thirteen children and written out and corrected as many as seven versions of *War and Peace* from Tolstoy's near-illegible rough drafts. Though they became deeply unhappy together over time, it was she who pushed for Tolstoy to publish his own books rather than merely release his novels serially in journals. She had made him rich from his writings, not only his ancestral fortune, and her diaries show constant anxiety about his state of mind and his well-being.

With his conversion came titanic domestic clashes. His behavior seemed embarrassing and inconsistent to his family. Sofya Andreyevna mistrusted anyone close to Tolstoy, and grew weary of "the dark ones"—the Tolstoyans of various persuasions who began showing up at Yasnaya Polyana to kneel at the Master's feet, often expecting to be housed and fed, as well. On 31 August 1909, she wrote: "This morning we had a visit from a 30-year-old Romanian who had castrated himself at the age of 18 after reading *The Kreutzer Sonata*. He then took to working on his land—just 19 acres—and was terribly disillusioned today to see that Tolstoy writes one thing but lives in luxury."

At least one disciple, Vladimir Chertkov, knowingly undermined the marriage. In the months before Tolstoy's death, Sofya Andreyevna nearly drove herself insane over fear that, under Chertkov's influence, the old man had written a secret will. (He had.) Eventually, the children took sides—forced, as A. N. Wilson phrased it, to choose "between God and *maman*."

That her husband still visited her bed despite their emotional estrangement, Sofya Andreyevna found both tiring and flattering. He once shocked the playwright Anton Chekhov by asking if he had whored much as a young man. "I was indefatigable!" Tolstoy exclaimed. Always a bit of a prude despite his boisterous appetite, he now lacerated himself in his diary each time he yielded. "Copulation is an abomination which can only be thought of without revulsion under the influence of sexual desire," he confided in his late sixties. "Even in order to have children you wouldn't do this to a woman you love."

And if his family was having difficulty with Tolstoy, still more so his literary friends* and fellow noblemen, and the government officials who had earlier dared to raid his estate just because he had opened a school for peasants. It is hard to overstate how repressive the tsarist government was, working in tandem with the conservative Orthodox Church. Hardly a major writer of the nineteenth century had escaped prison and/or exile: Pushkin, Turgenev, Lermentov, Gogol, to name only a few. In 1849, the novelist Dostoyevsky had been arrested, subjected to a mock execution, and sentenced to four years in Siberia with hard labor merely for having read some essays by the socialist Vissarion Belinsky.

The further Tolstoy went, the thinner the branch beneath him. Some of his writings were censored, such as the late work *The Law of Love and the Law of Violence*, which advocated passive resistance to the government and shaped the thinking, decades later, of the young Martin Luther King Jr. Others were banned outright, like *The Kingdom of God Is Within You*, a profound influence on Mohandas Gandhi. *The Kreutzer Sonata* was also banned—even in America, where Theodore Roosevelt declared Tolstoy a "sexual moral pervert." Censorship was nothing new to Tolstoy, whose earliest published

---

*Turgenev wrote from his deathbed in 1883, begging Tolstoy to return to writing literature.

story, "The Raid" (1852), had come under the censor's pen, but he burned to deliver his religious message. To thwart censors, he eventually resorted to publishing much of his work abroad, where he reached a large, avid readership.

Suspicious of his growing spiritual influence, the secret police watched him carefully. After the assassination of Tsar Alexander II in 1881, Tolstoy wrote to the new emperor, asking that the young man forgive his father's assassins. He was marked as a potential agitator, "a madman, from whom one might expect anything."*

What kept Tolstoy from arrest? Certainly his elite social status—the very hierarchy he now railed against—protected him. Educated Russians were also immensely proud of Tolstoy's artistic achievements and fame; from his earliest writings, but especially in *War and Peace*, his feeling for the Russian land and people endeared him to readers. His views were suspect but his sincerity was appealing, especially after he began to work in famine relief and other humanitarian causes. Dostoyevky declared that Tolstoy was "unquestionably . . . the most beloved of Russian writers among the public of all shades." By 1900 he was the most famous writer in the world.

Mixed feelings toward Tolstoy are evident in the early writings of two revolutionary leaders: Lenin and Leon Trotsky. Tolstoy was no less impressive or irritating regarded from the political left than from the right. In Lenin's 1908 essay "Leo Tolstoy as the Mirror of the Russian Revolution," he acknowledged Tolstoy's desire to break with the past, but ridiculed his religiosity and his contradictions. "On the one hand, we have the great artist, the genius who has drawn incomparable pen pictures of Russian life, and made world-class contributions to world literature," he conceded.

---

*So Tolstoy's second cousin Dimitry Tolstoy, a government minister, wrote in a letter discouraging a literary society from engaging Leo Tolstoy as a speaker.

On the other hand, we have the crazy landlord obsessed with Christ. On the one hand, we have his remarkably powerful, forthright, and sincere protest against social falsehood and hypocrisy. And on the other hand we have the "Tolstoyan," i.e., the jaded, hysterical sniveler called the Russian intellectual.

With less vitriol, Trotsky praised Tolstoy's tract against the death penalty, *I Cannot Be Silent* (1908), and his overall good intentions, even though Tolstoy did not support revolutionary aims: "We shall not condemn him. And we shall always value in him not alone his great genius . . . but also his unbending moral courage which did not permit him tranquilly to remain in the ranks of *their* hypocritical church, *their* society and *their* state but doomed him to remain a solitary among his countless admirers."

By the terms of the secret will, drafted by the perfidious Chertkov, rights to all Tolstoy's literary property—letters, books, diaries, published and unpublished—were bequeathed to his favorite daughter, Alexandra (Sasha), a fervent Tolstoyan, with the understanding that she would transfer ownership to the public without benefit to herself. His papers were to be delivered to Chertkov to edit and publish as he saw fit. This was the germ of what would become the ninety-volume Jubilee Edition of Tolstoy, authorized by Lenin, funded mostly under Joseph Stalin, supplemented with the Marxist critique that rendered Tolstoy palatable to the Soviets. Though Tolstoy had openly opposed socialism, Lenin stipulated that his works should be published in full, with everything restored that had been suppressed by the Imperial government. This was about as likely in Stalin's Russia as the resurrection of Tolstoy from his grave at Yasnaya Polyana. Censorship under Stalin made Imperial censorship seem like a kitten's paw. The editors of the Jubilee Edition scrambled to find inoffensive volumes to issue out of order—some letters here, diaries there—to

avoid publishing his religious writings during the Stalinist purges.*

Still, in Soviet Russia, Tolstoy's words circulated by
the millions. Lidiya Ginzburg's harrowing *Blockade Diary* of the nine-hundred-day Nazi siege of Leningrad
records how those around her reread *War and Peace*,
finding comfort in its depiction of Napoleon's rebuffed
invasion of Russia. Extracts from Tolstoy's stirring early
war writings were broadcast from loudspeakers in Palace
Square, and Stalin distributed hundreds of thousands of
copies of the Battle of Borodin section from *War and
Peace* to shore up patriotism during the Occupation.

Tolstoy's Moscow house was preserved immediately
after his death as a literary shrine. Given a pension by
Tsar Nicholas II, Sofya Andreyevna also worked to maintain Yasnaya Polyana: preserving her husband's study
and bedroom, among other acts of wifely homage. War
and the Revolution interrupted, but in 1921, under the
custodianship of Alexandra Tolstoya, the property opened
as a museum. Yasnaya Polyana was now expected to rep-
resent Soviet values—an uneasy accommodation that
Alexandra kept up until ideological conflicts with the re-
gime forced her to emigrate in 1929.† Tolstoy may have
been lauded in the Stalinist era, but Tolstoyans were per-
secuted, exiled, and shot. The contents of the house were
wisely evacuated before a Nazi occupation in October
1941, and a restoration conducted afterward, since the
Nazis set the house on fire as they left. In the post-Soviet
era, guardianship has returned to a Tolstoy family member.

Russia has long embraced literary tourism (the country
maintains a bewildering number of writers' homes), and
visitors from Moscow can now catch an express "Yasnaya
Polyana" train on the weekends. The day-tripper's rever-

---

*Rosamund Bartlett's *Tolstoy: A Russian Life* (2010) provides a fasci-
nating account of his reputation in the Soviet and post-Soviet eras.
†From her new home in the United States, she helped many other Russian intellectuals, such as Vladimir Nabokov, escape the Bolsheviks.

ence may have assumed a quality different from in Tolstoy's day, though. "Every age finds the Tolstoy it needs," as Kathleen Parthé, founding editor of the *Tolstoy Studies* journal, points out. Although his novels are widely read and adapted in his native country, the fierce, visionary Tolstoy "has retreated into the background as the rich, talented, and worldly Count Lev Nikolaevich Tolstoy emerges. Tolstoy's provincial estate is promoted to the Russian public as an example of good taste in home décor."

The completion of the Jubilee Edition after Stalin's death in 1953 could be seen to mark Russia's acceptance, at last, of the complete Tolstoy: writer, seeker, holy fool. Given the official silence on his death centenary, this is probably overstating the case. As his family maintains, Tolstoy asked questions for which we still lack answers. He leaves us uncomfortable, as he had hoped. "I fear the death of Tolstoy," Chekhov wrote in 1900.

> In the first place, there is no other person whom I love as I love him. Secondly, when literature possesses a Tolstoy, it is easy and pleasant to be a writer. . . . What he does serves to justify all the hopes and aspirations invested in literature. . . . Were it not for him the world of literature would be a flock of sheep without a shepherd. . . .

As much as Tolstoy would have enjoyed hearing these words from his old friend, few tributes could have pleased him more than the telegram sent from Abbot elder Varsonofy of Optina Puystin Monastery to Bishop Benjamin of Kaluga on November 7th (old style calendar) at 7:10 a.m: "Count Tolstoy died today, November 7th at 6 a.m. . . . He died without repentance. I was not invited."

—Regina Marler

THE DEATH OF
IVAN ILYCH
AND OTHER STORIES

Family Happiness

PART ONE

i

WE WERE in mourning for my mother, who had died in the autumn, and I spent all that winter alone in the country with Katya and Sonya.

Katya was an old friend of the family, our governess who had brought us all up, and I had known and loved her since my earliest recollections. Sonya was my younger sister. It was a dark and sad winter which we spent in our old house of Pokrovskoe. The weather was cold and so windy that the snowdrifts came higher than the windows; the panes were almost always dimmed by frost, and we seldom walked or drove anywhere throughout the winter. Our visitors were few, and those who came brought no addition of cheerfulness or happiness to the household. They all wore sad faces and spoke low, as if they were afraid of waking someone; they never laughed, but sighed and often shed tears as they looked at me and especially at little Sonya in her black frock. The feeling of death clung to the house; the air was still filled with the grief and horror of death. My mother's room was kept locked; and whenever I passed it on my way to bed, I felt a strange uncomfortable impulse to look into that cold empty room.

I was then seventeen; and in the very year of her death my mother was intending to move to Petersburg, in order to take me into society. The loss of my mother was a great grief to me; but I must confess to another feeling behind that grief — a feeling that although I was young and pretty (so everybody told me), I was wasting a second winter in the solitude of the country. Before the winter ended, this sense of dejection, solitude, and simple boredom increased to such an extent that I refused to leave my room or open the piano or take up a book. When Katya urged me to find some occupation, I said that I did not feel able for it; but in my heart I said, "What is the good of it? What is the good of doing anything, when the best part of my life is being wasted like this?" And to this question, tears were my only answer.

I was told that I was growing thin and losing my looks; but even this failed to interest me. What did it matter? For whom? I felt that my whole life was bound to go on in the same solitude and helpless dreariness, from which I had myself no strength and even no wish to escape. Towards the end of winter Katya became anxious about me and determined to make an effort to take me abroad. But money was needed for this, and we hardly knew how our affairs stood after my mother's death. Our guardian, who was to come and clear up our position, was expected every day.

In March he arrived.

"Well, thank God!" Katya said to me one day, when I was walking up and down the room like a shadow, without occupation, without a thought, and without a wish.

"Sergey Mikhaylych has arrived; he has sent to inquire about us and means to come here for dinner. You must rouse yourself, dear Mashechka," she added, "or what will he think of you? He was so fond of you all."

Sergey Mikhaylych was our near neighbour, and, though a much younger man, had been a friend of my father's. His coming was likely to change our plans and to make it possible to leave the country; and also I had grown up in the habit of love and regard for him; and when Katya begged me to rouse myself, she guessed rightly that it would give me especial pain to show to disadvantage before him, more than before any other of our friends. Like everyone in the house, from Katya and his goddaughter Sonya down to the helper in the stables, I loved him from old habit; and also he had a special significance for me, owing to a remark which my mother had once made in my presence. "I should like you to marry a man like him," she said. At the time this seemed to me strange and even unpleasant. My ideal husband was quite different: he was to be thin, pale, and sad; and Sergey Mikhaylych was middle-aged, tall, robust, and always, as it seemed to me, in good spirits. But still my mother's words stuck in my head; and even six years before this time, when I was eleven, and he still said "thou" to me, and played with me, and called me by the pet-name of "violet" — even then I sometimes asked myself in a fright, "What *shall* I do, if he suddenly wants to marry me?"

Before our dinner, to which Katya made an addition of sweets and a dish of spinach, Sergey Mikhaylych arrived. From the window I watched him drive up to the house in a small sleigh; but as soon as it turned the corner, I hastened to the drawing-room, meaning to pretend that his visit was a complete surprise. But when I heard his tramp and loud voice and Katya's footsteps in the hall, I lost patience and went to meet him myself. He was holding Katya's hand, talking loud, and smiling. When he saw me, he stopped and looked at me for a time without bowing. I was uncomfortable and felt myself blushing.

"Can this be really you?" he said in his plain decisive way, walking towards me with his arms apart. "Is so great a change possible? How grown-up you are! I used to call you 'violet,' but now you are a rose in full bloom!"

He took my hand in his own large hand and pressed it so hard that it almost hurt. Expecting him to kiss my hand, I bent towards him, but he only pressed it again and looked straight into my eyes with the old firmness and cheerfulness in his face.

It was six years since I had seen him last. He was much changed—older and darker in complexion; and he now wore whiskers which did not become him at all; but much remained the same—his simple manner, the large features of his honest open face, his bright intelligent eyes, his friendly, almost boyish, smile.

Five minutes later he had ceased to be a visitor and had become the friend of us all, even of the servants, whose visible eagerness to wait on him proved their pleasure at his arrival.

He behaved quite unlike the neighbours who had visited us after my mother's death. They had thought it necessary to be silent when they sat with us, and to shed tears. He, on the contrary, was cheerful and talkative, and said not a word about my mother, so that this indifference seemed strange to me at first and even improper on the part of so close a friend. But I understood later that what seemed indifference was sincerity, and I felt grateful for it. In the evening Katya poured out tea, sitting in her old place in the drawing-room, where she used to sit in my mother's lifetime; Sonya and I sat near him; our old butler Grigori had hunted out one of my father's pipes and brought it to him; and he began to walk up and down the room as he used to do in past days.

"How many terrible changes there are in this house, when one thinks of it all!" he said, stopping in his walk.

"Yes," said Katya with a sigh; and then she put the lid on the samovar and looked at him, quite ready to burst out crying.

"I suppose you remember your father?" he said, turning to me.

"Not clearly," I answered.

"How happy you would have been together now!" he added in a low voice, looking thoughtfully at my face above the eyes. "I was very fond of him," he added in a still lower tone, and it seemed to me that his eyes were shining more than usual.

"And now God has taken her too!" said Katya; and at once she laid her napkin on the teapot, took out her handkerchief, and began to cry.

"Yes, the changes in this house are terrible," he repeated, turning away. "Sonya, show me your toys," he added after a little and went off to the parlour. When he had gone, I looked at Katya with eyes full of tears.

"What a splendid friend he is!" she said. And, though he was no relation, I did really feel a kind of warmth and comfort in the sympathy of this good man.

I could hear him moving about in the parlour with Sonya, and the sound of her high childish voice. I sent tea to him there; and I heard him sit down at the piano and strike the keys with Sonya's little hands.

Then his voice came—"Marya Alexandrovna, come here and play something."

I liked his easy behaviour to me and his friendly tone of command; I got up and went to him.

"Play this," he said, opening a book of Beethoven's music at the adagio of the *Moonlight Sonata*. "Let me hear how you play," he added, and went off to a corner of the room, carrying his cup with him.

I somehow felt that with him it was impossible to refuse or to say beforehand that I played badly: I sat down obediently at the piano and began to play as well as I could; yet I was afraid of criticism, because I knew that he understood and enjoyed music. The adagio suited the remembrance of past days evoked by our conversation at tea, and I believe that I played it fairly well. But he would not let me play the scherzo. "No," he said, coming up to me; "you

don't play that right; don't go on; but the first movement
was not bad; you seem to be musical." This moderate
praise pleased me so much that I even reddened. I felt it
pleasant and strange that a friend of my father's, and his
contemporary, should no longer treat me like a child but
speak to me seriously. Katya now went upstairs to put Sonya to bed, and we were left alone in the parlour.

He talked to me about my father, and about the beginning of their friendship and the happy days they had
spent together, while I was still busy with lesson-books
and toys; and his talk put my father before me in quite a
new light, as a man of simple and delightful character.
He asked me too about my tastes, what I read and what
I intended to do, and gave me advice. The man of mirth
and jest who used to tease me and make me toys had
disappeared; here was a serious, simple, and affectionate
friend, for whom I could not help feeling respect and
sympathy. It was easy and pleasant to talk to him; and
yet I felt an involuntary strain also. I was anxious about
each word I spoke: I wished so much to earn for my own
sake the love which had been given me already merely
because I was my father's daughter.

After putting Sonya to bed, Katya joined us and began to complain to him of my apathy, about which I had
said nothing.

"So she never told me the most important thing of
all!" he said, smiling and shaking his head reproachfully
at me.

"Why tell you?" I said. "It is very tiresome to talk
about, and it will pass off." (I really felt now, not only
that my dejection would pass off, but that it had already
passed off, or rather had never existed.)

"It is a bad thing," he said, "not to be able to stand
solitude. Can it be that you are a young lady?"

"Of course, I am a young lady," I answered, laughing.

"Well, I can't praise a young lady who is alive only
when people are admiring her, but as soon as she is left
alone, collapses and finds nothing to her taste—one who
is all for show and has no resources in herself."

"You have a flattering opinion of me!" I said, just for the sake of saying something.

He was silent for a little. Then he said: "Yes; your likeness to your father means something. There is something in you . . ." and his kind attentive look again flattered me and made me feel a pleasant embarrassment.

I noticed now for the first time that his face, which gave one at first the impression of high spirits, had also an expression peculiar to himself—bright at first and then more and more attentive and rather sad.

"You ought not to be bored and you cannot be," he said; "you have music, which you appreciate, books, study; your whole life lies before you, and now or never is the time to prepare for it and save yourself future regrets. A year hence it will be too late."

He spoke to me like a father or an uncle, and I felt that he kept a constant check upon himself, in order to keep on my level. Though I was hurt that he considered me as inferior to himself, I was pleased that for me alone he thought it necessary to try to be different.

For the rest of the evening, he talked about business with Katya.

"Well, good-bye, dear friends," he said. Then he got up, came towards me, and took my hand.

"When shall we see you again?" asked Katya.

"In spring," he answered, still holding my hand. "I shall go now to Danilovka" (this was another property of ours), "look into things there and make what arrangements I can; then I go to Moscow on business of my own; and in summer we shall meet again."

"Must you really be away so long?" I asked, and I felt terribly grieved. I had really hoped to see him every day, and I felt a sudden shock of regret, and a fear that my depression would return. And my face and voice must have made this plain.

"You must find more to do and not get depressed," he said; and I thought his tone too cool and unconcerned. "I shall put you through an examination in spring," he added, letting go my hand and not looking at me.

When we saw him off in the hall, he put on his fur coat in a hurry and still avoided looking at me. "He is taking a deal of trouble for nothing!" I thought. "Does he think me so anxious that he should look at me? He is a good man, a very good man; but that's all."

That evening, however, Katya and I sat up late, talking, not about him but about our plans for the summer, and where we should spend next winter and what we should do then. I had ceased to ask that terrible question—what is the good of it all? Now it seemed quite plain and simple: the proper object of life was happiness, and I promised myself much happiness ahead. It seemed as if our gloomy old house had suddenly become full of light and life.

ii

MEANWHILE spring arrived. My old dejection passed away and gave place to the unrest which spring brings with it, full of dreams and vague hopes and desires. Instead of living as I had done at the beginning of winter, I read and played the piano and gave lessons to Sonya; but also I often went into the garden and wandered for long alone through the avenues, or sat on a bench there; and heaven knows what my thoughts and wishes and hopes were at such times. Sometimes at night, especially if there was a moon, I sat by my bedroom window till dawn; sometimes, when Katya was not watching, I stole out into the garden wearing only a wrapper and ran through the dew as far as the pond; and once I went all the way to the open fields and walked right round the garden alone at night.

I find it difficult now to recall and understand the dreams which then filled my imagination. Even when I *can* recall them, I find it hard to believe that my dreams were just like that: they were so strange and so remote from life.

Sergey Mikhaylych kept his promise: he returned from his travels at the end of May.

His first visit to us was in the evening and was quite unexpected. We were sitting in the veranda, preparing for tea. By this time the garden was all green, and the nightingales had taken up their quarters for the whole of St. Peter's Fast in the leafy borders. The tops of the round lilac bushes had a sprinkling of white and purple—a sign that their flowers were ready to open. The foliage of the birch avenue was all transparent in the light of the setting sun. In the veranda there was shade and freshness. The evening dew was sure to be heavy on the grass. Out of doors beyond the garden the last sounds of day were audible, and the noise of the sheep and cattle, as they were driven home. Nikon, the half-witted boy, was driving his water-cart along the path outside the veranda, and a cold stream of water from the sprinkler made dark circles on the mould round the stems and supports of the dahlias. In our veranda the polished samovar shone and hissed on the white tablecloth; there were cracknels and biscuits and cream on the table. Katya was busy washing the cups with her plump hands. I was too hungry after bathing to wait for tea, and was eating bread with thick fresh cream. I was wearing a gingham blouse with loose sleeves, and my hair, still wet, was covered with a kerchief. Katya saw him first, even before he came in.

"You, Sergey Mikhaylych!" she cried. "Why, we were just talking about you."

I got up, meaning to go and change my dress, but he caught me just by the door.

"Why stand on such ceremony in the country?" he said, looking with a smile at the kerchief on my head. "You don't mind the presence of your butler, and I am really the same to you as Grigori is." But I felt just then that he was looking at me in a way quite unlike Grigori's way, and I was uncomfortable.

"I shall come back at once," I said, as I left them.

"But what is wrong?" he called out after me; "it's just the dress of a young peasant woman."

"How strangely he looked at me!" I said to myself as I was quickly changing upstairs. "Well, I'm glad he has come; things will be more lively." After a look in the glass I ran gaily downstairs and into the veranda; I was out of breath and did not disguise my haste. He was sitting at the table, talking to Katya about our affairs. He glanced at me and smiled; then he went on talking. From what he said it appeared that our affairs were in capital shape: it was now possible for us, after spending the summer in the country, to go either to Petersburg for Sonya's education, or abroad.

"If only you would go abroad with us—" said Katya; "without you we shall be quite lost there."

"Oh, I should like to go round the world with you," he said, half in jest and half in earnest.

"All right," I said; "let us start off and go round the world."

He smiled and shook his head.

"What about my mother? What about my business?" he said. "But that's not the question just now: I want to know how you have been spending your time. Not depressed again, I hope?"

When I told him that I had been busy and not bored during his absence, and when Katya confirmed my report, he praised me as if he had a right to do so, and his words and looks were kind, as they might have been to a child. I felt obliged to tell him in detail and with perfect frankness all my good actions, and to confess, as if I were in church, all that he might disapprove of. The evening was so fine that we stayed in the veranda after tea was cleared away; and the conversation interested me so much that I did not notice how we ceased by degrees to hear any sound of the servants indoors. The scent of flowers grew stronger and came from all sides; the grass was drenched with dew; a nightingale struck up in a lilac bush close by and then stopped on hearing our voices; the starry sky seemed to come down lower over our heads.

It was growing dusk, but I did not notice it till a bat suddenly and silently flew in beneath the veranda awning and began to flutter round my white shawl. I shrank back against the wall and nearly cried out; but the bat as silently and swiftly dived out from under the awning and disappeared in the half-darkness of the garden.

"How fond I am of this place of yours!" he said, changing the conversation; "I wish I could spend all my life here, sitting in this veranda."

"Well, do then!" said Katya.

"That's all very well," he said, "but life won't sit still."

"Why don't you marry?" asked Katya; "you would make an excellent husband."

"Because I like sitting still?" and he laughed. "No, Katerina Karlovna, too late for you and me to marry. People have long ceased to think of me as a marrying man, and I am even surer of it myself; and I declare I have felt quite comfortable since the matter was settled."

It seemed to me that he said this in an unnaturally persuasive way.

"Nonsense!" said Katya; "a man of thirty-six makes out that he is too old!"

"Too old indeed," he went on, "when all one wants is to sit still. For a man who is going to marry that's not enough. Just you ask her," he added, nodding at me; "people of her age should marry, and you and I can rejoice in their happiness."

The sadness and constraint latent in his voice was not lost upon me. He was silent for a little, and neither Katya nor I spoke.

"Well, just fancy," he went on, turning a little on his seat; "suppose that by some mischance I married a girl of seventeen, Masha, if you like—I mean, Marya Alexandrovna. The instance is good; I am glad it turned up; there could not be a better instance."

I laughed; but I could not understand why he was glad, or what it was that had turned up.

"Just tell me honestly, with your hand on your heart," he said, turning as if playfully to me, "would it not be a misfortune for you to unite your life with that of an old worn-out man who only wants to sit still, whereas heaven knows what wishes are fermenting in that heart of yours?"

I felt uncomfortable and was silent, not knowing how to answer him.

"I am not making you a proposal, you know," he said, laughing; "but am I really the kind of husband you dream of when walking alone in the avenue at twilight? It would be a misfortune, would it not?"

"No, not a misfortune," I began.

"But a bad thing," he ended my sentence.

"Perhaps; but I may be mistaken . . ." He interrupted me again.

"There, you see! She is quite right, and I am grateful to her for her frankness, and very glad to have had this conversation. And there is something else to be said—" he added: "for me too it would be a very great misfortune."

"How odd you are! You have not changed in the least," said Katya, and then left the veranda, to order supper to be served.

When she had gone, we were both silent and all was still around us, but for one exception. A nightingale, which had sung last night by fitful snatches, now flooded the garden with a steady stream of song, and was soon answered by another from the dell below, which had not sung till that evening. The nearer bird stopped and seemed to listen for a moment, and then broke out again still louder than before, pouring out his song in piercing long-drawn cadences. There was a regal calm in the birds' voices, as they floated through the realm of night which belongs to those birds and not to man. The gardener walked past to his sleeping-quarters in the greenhouse, and the noise of his heavy boots grew fainter and fainter along the path. Someone whistled twice sharply at the foot of the hill; and then all was still again. The rustling of leaves could just be heard; the veranda awning flapped; a faint perfume, floating in the air, came down on the veranda and filled it. I felt silence awkward after what had been said, but what to say I did not know. I looked at him. His eyes, bright in the half-darkness, turned towards me.

"How good life is!" he said.

I sighed, I don't know why.

"Well?" he asked.

"Life is good," I repeated after him.

Again we were silent, and again I felt uncomfortable. I could not help fancying that I had wounded him by agreeing that he was old; and I wished to comfort him but did not know how.

"Well, I must be saying good-bye," he said, rising; "my mother expects me for supper; I have hardly seen her all day."

"I meant to play you the new sonata," I said.

"That must wait," he replied; and I thought that he spoke coldly.

"Good-bye."

I felt still more certain that I had wounded him, and I was sorry. Katya and I went to the steps to see him off and stood for a while in the open, looking along the road where he had disappeared from view. When we ceased to hear the sound of his horse's hoofs, I walked round the house to the veranda, and again sat looking into the garden; and all I wished to see and hear, I still saw and heard for a long time in the dewy mist filled with the sounds of night.

He came a second time, and a third; and the awkwardness arising from that strange conversation passed away entirely, never to return. During that whole summer he came two or three times a week; and I grew so accustomed to his presence, that, when he failed to come for some time, I missed him and felt angry with him, and thought he was behaving badly in deserting me. He treated me like a boy whose company he liked, asked me questions, invited the most cordial frankness on my part, gave me advice and encouragement, or sometimes scolded and checked me. But in spite of his constant effort to keep on my level, I was aware that behind the part of him which I could understand there remained an entire region of mystery, into which he did not consider it necessary to admit me; and this fact did much to preserve my respect for him and his attraction for me. I knew from Katya and from our neighbours that he had not only to care for his old mother with whom he lived, and to manage his own estate and our affairs, but was also responsible for some public business which was the source of serious worries; but what view he took of all this, what were his convictions, plans, and hopes, I could not in the least find out from him. Whenever I turned the conversation to his affairs, he frowned in a way peculiar to himself and seemed to imply, "Please stop! That is no business of yours"; and then he changed the subject. This hurt me at first; but I soon grew accustomed to confining our talk to my affairs, and felt this to be quite natural.

There was another thing which displeased me at first and then became pleasant to me. This was his complete indifference and even contempt for my personal appearance. Never by word or look did he imply that I was pretty; on the contrary, he frowned and laughed, whenever the word was applied to me in his presence. He even liked to find fault with my looks and tease me about them. On special days Katya liked to dress me out in fine clothes and to arrange my hair effectively; but my finery met only with mockery from him, which pained kindhearted Katya and at first disconcerted me. She had made up her mind that he admired me; and she could not understand how a man could help wishing a woman whom he admired to appear to the utmost advantage. But I soon understood what he wanted. He wished to make sure that I had not a trace of affectation. And when I understood this I was really quite free from affectation in the clothes I wore, or the arrangement of my hair, or my movements; but a very obvious form of affectation took its place—an affectation of simplicity, at a time when I could not yet be really simple. That he loved me, I knew; but I did not yet ask myself whether he loved me as a child or as a woman. I valued his love; I felt that he thought me better than all other young women in the world, and I could not help wishing him to go on being deceived about me. Without wishing to deceive him, I did deceive him, and I became better myself while deceiving him. I felt it a better and worthier course to show him the good points of my head and mind than of my body. My hair, hands, face, ways—all these, whether good or bad, he had appraised at once and knew so well, that I could add nothing to my external appearance except the wish to deceive him. But my mind and heart he did not know, because he loved them, and because they were in the very process of growth and development; and on this point I could and did deceive him. And how easy I felt in his company, once I understood this clearly! My causeless bashfulness and awkward movements completely disappeared. Whether he saw me from in front, or in profile, sitting or standing, with my hair up or my hair down, I felt that he knew me from head to foot, and, I fancied, was satisfied with me as I was. If, contrary to his habit, he had suddenly said to me as other people did, that I had a pretty face, I believe that I should not have liked it at all. But, on the other hand, how light and happy my heart was when, after I had said something, he looked hard at me and said, hiding emotion under a mask of raillery:

"Yes, there *is* something in you! you are a fine girl— that I must tell you."

And for what did I receive such rewards, which filled my heart with pride and joy? Merely for saying that I felt for old Grigóri in his love for his little granddaughter; or because the reading of some poem or novel moved me to tears; or because I liked Mozart better than Schulhof. And I was surprised at my own quickness in guessing what was good and worthy of love, when I certainly did not know then what *was* good and worthy to be loved. Most of my former tastes and habits did not please him; and a mere look of his, or a twitch of his eyebrow, was enough to show that he did not like what I was trying to say; and I felt at once that my own standard was changed. Sometimes, when he was about to give me a piece of advice, I seemed to know beforehand what he would say. When he looked in my face and asked me a question, his

very look would draw out of me the answer he wanted.
All my thoughts and feelings of that time were not really
mine: they were his thoughts and feelings, which had
suddenly become mine and passed into my life and
lighted it up. Quite unconsciously I began to look at everything with different eyes—at Katya and the servants
and Sonya and myself and my occupations. Books, which
I used to read merely to escape boredom, now became
one of the chief pleasures of my life, merely because he
brought me the books and we read and discussed them
together. The lessons I gave to Sonya had been a burdensome obligation which I forced myself to go through
from a sense of duty; but, after he was present at a lesson,
it became a joy to me to watch Sonya's progress. It used
to seem to me an impossibility to learn a whole piece of
music by heart; but now, when I knew that he would hear
it and might praise it, I would play a single movement
forty times over without stopping, till poor Katya stuffed
her ears with cotton-wool, while I was still not weary of
it. The same old sonatas seemed quite different in their
expression, and came out quite changed and much im-
proved. Even Katya, whom I knew and loved like a second self, became different in my eyes. I now understood
for the first time that she was not in the least bound to
be the mother, friend, and slave that she was to us. Now
I appreciated all the self-sacrifice and devotion of this
affectionate creature, and all my obligations to her; and
I began to love her even better. It was he too who taught
me to take quite a new view of our serfs and servants
and maids. It is an absurd confession to make—but I had
spent seventeen years among these people and yet knew
less about them than about strangers whom I had never
seen; it had never once occurred to me that they had
their affections and wishes and sorrows, just as I had.
Our garden and woods and fields, which I had known so
long, became suddenly new and beautiful to me. He was
right in saying that the only certain happiness in life is to
live for others. At the time his words seemed to me
strange, and I did not understand them; but by degrees

this became a conviction with me, without thinking about it. He revealed to me a whole new world of joys in the present, without changing anything in my life, without adding anything except himself to each impression in my mind. All that had surrounded me from childhood without saying anything to me, suddenly came to life. The mere sight of him made everything begin to speak and press for admittance to my heart, filling it with happiness.

Often during that summer, when I went upstairs to my room and lay down on my bed, the old unhappiness of spring with its desires and hopes for the future gave place to a passionate happiness in the present. Unable to sleep, I often got up and sat on Katya's bed, and told her how perfectly happy I was, though I now realize that this was quite unnecessary, as she could see it for herself. But she told me that she was quite content and perfectly happy, and kissed me. I believed her—it seemed to me so necessary and just that everyone should be happy. But Katya could think of sleep too; and sometimes, pretending to be angry, she drove me from her bed and went to sleep, while I turned over and over in my mind all that made me so happy. Sometimes I got up and said my prayers over again, praying in my own words and thanking God for all the happiness he had given me.

All was quiet in the room; there was only the even breathing of Katya in her sleep, and the ticking of the clock by her bed, while I turned from side to side and whispered words of prayer, or crossed myself and kissed the cross round my neck. The door was shut and the windows shuttered; perhaps a fly or gnat hung buzzing in the air. I felt a wish never to leave that room—a wish that dawn might never come, that my present frame of mind might never change. I felt that my dreams and thoughts and prayers were live things, living there in the dark with me, hovering about my bed, and standing over me. And every thought was his thought, and every feeling his feeling. I did not know yet that this was love; I thought that things might go on so forever, and that this feeling involved no consequences.

iii

ONE DAY when the corn was being carried, I went with Katya and Sonya to our favourite seat in the garden, in the shade of the lime-trees and above the dell, beyond which the fields and woods lay open before us. It was three days since Sergey Mikhaylych had been to see us; we were expecting him, all the more because our bailiff reported that he had promised to visit the harvest-field. At two o'clock we saw him ride on to the rye-field. With a smile and a glance at me, Katya ordered peaches and cherries, of which he was very fond, to be brought; then she lay down on the bench and began to doze. I tore off a crooked flat lime-tree branch, which made my hand wet with its juicy leaves and juicy bark. Then I fanned Katya with it and went on with my book, breaking off from time to time, to look at the field-path along which he must come. Sonya was making a dolls' house at the root of an old lime-tree. The day was sultry, windless, and steaming; the clouds were packing and growing blacker; all morning a thunderstorm had been gathering, and I felt restless, as I always did before thunder. But by afternoon the clouds began to part, the sun sailed out into a clear sky, and only in one quarter was there a faint rumbling. A single heavy cloud, louring above the horizon and mingling with the dust from the fields, was rent from time to time by pale zigzags of lightning which ran down to the ground. It was clear that for today the storm would pass off, with us at all events. The road beyond the garden was visible in places, and we could see a procession of high creaking carts slowly moving along it with their load of sheaves, while the empty carts rattled at a faster pace to meet them, with swaying legs and shirts fluttering in them. The thick dust neither blew away nor settled down—it stood still beyond the fence, and we could see it through the transparent foliage of the garden trees. A little farther off, in the stack-yard, the same voices and the same creaking of wheels were audible; and the same yellow sheaves that had moved slowly past the fence were now flying aloft, and I could see the oval stacks gradually rising higher, and their conspicuous pointed tops, and the labourers swarming upon them. On the dusty field in front more carts were moving and more yellow sheaves were visible; and the noise of the carts, with the sound of talking and singing, came to us from a distance. At one side the bare stubble, with strips of fallow covered with wormwood, came more and more into view. Lower down, to the right, the gay dresses of the women were visible, as they bent down and swung their arms to bind the sheaves. Here the bare stubble looked untidy; but the disorder was cleared by degrees, as the pretty sheaves were ranged at close intervals. It seemed as if summer had suddenly turned to autumn before my eyes. The dust and heat were everywhere, except in our favourite nook in the garden; and everywhere, in this heat and dust and under the burning sun, the labourers carried on their heavy task with talk and noise.

Meanwhile Katya slept so sweetly on our shady bench, beneath her white cambric handkerchief, the black juicy cherries glistened so temptingly on the plate, our dresses were so clean and fresh, the water in the jug was so bright with rainbow colours in the sun, and I felt so happy! "How can I help it?" I thought; "am I to blame for being happy? And how can I share my happiness? How and to whom can I surrender all myself and all my happiness?"

By this time the sun had sunk behind the tops of the birch avenue, the dust was settling on the fields, the distance became clearer and brighter in the slanting light. The clouds had dispersed altogether; I could see through the trees the thatch of three new corn-stacks. The labourers came down off the stacks; the carts hurried past, evidently for the last time, with a loud noise of shouting; the women, with rakes over their shoulders and straw-bands in their belts, walked home past us, singing loudly; and still there was no sign of Sergey Mikhaylych, though I had seen him ride down the hill long ago. Suddenly he appeared upon the avenue, coming from a quarter where I was not looking for him. He had walked round by the dell. He came quickly towards me, with his hat off and radiant with high spirits. Seeing that Katya was asleep, he bit his lip, closed his eyes, and advanced on tiptoe; I saw at once that he was in that peculiar mood of cause-less merriment which I always delighted to see in him, and which we called "wild ecstasy." He was just like a schoolboy playing truant; his whole figure, from head to foot, breathed content, happiness, and boyish frolic.

"Well, young violet, how are you? All right?" he said in a whisper, coming up to me and taking my hand. Then, in answer to my question, "Oh, I'm splendid today, I feel like a boy of thirteen—I want to play at horses and climb trees."

"Is it wild ecstasy?" I asked, looking into his laughing eyes, and feeling that the "wild ecstasy" was infecting me.

"Yes," he answered, winking and checking a smile. "But I don't see why you need hit Katerina Karlovna on the nose."

With my eyes on him I had gone on waving the branch, without noticing that I had knocked the hand-kerchief off Katya's face and was now brushing her with the leaves. I laughed.

"She will say she was awake all the time," I whispered, as if not to awake Katya; but that was not my real rea-son—it was only that I liked to whisper to him.

He moved his lips in imitation of me, pretending that my voice was too low for him to hear. Catching sight of the dish of cherries, he pretended to steal it, and carried it off to Sonya under the lime-tree, where he sat down on her dolls. Sonya was angry at first, but he soon made his peace with her by starting a game, to see which of them could eat cherries faster.

"If you like, I will send for more cherries," I said; "or let us go ourselves."

He took the dish and set the dolls on it, and we all three started for the orchard. Sonya ran behind us, laughing and pulling at his coat, to make him surrender the dolls. He gave them up and then turned to me, speaking more seriously.

"You really are a violet," he said, still speaking low, though there was no longer any fear of waking anybody; "when I came to you out of all that dust and heat and toil, I positively smelt violets at once. But not the sweet violet—you know, that early dark violet that smells of melting snow and spring grass."

"Is harvest going on well?" I asked, in order to hide the happy agitation which his words produced in me.

"First-rate! Our people are always splendid. The more you know them, the better you like them."

"Yes," I said; "before you came I was watching them from the garden, and suddenly I felt ashamed to be so comfortable myself while they were hard at work, and so . . ."

He interrupted me, with a kind but grave look: "Don't talk like that, my dear; it is too sacred a matter to talk of lightly. God forbid that you should use fine phrases about that!"

"But it is only to *you* I say this."

"All right, I understand. But what about those cherries?"

The orchard was locked, and no gardener to be seen: he had sent them all off to help with the harvest. Sonya ran to fetch the key. But he would not wait for her: climbing up a corner of the wall, he raised the net and jumped down on the other side.

His voice came over the wall—"If you want some, give me the dish."

"No," I said; "I want to pick for myself. I shall fetch the key; Sonya won't find it."

But suddenly I felt that I must see what he was doing there and what he looked like—that I must watch his movements while he supposed that no one saw him. Besides, I was simply unwilling just then to lose sight of him

for a single minute. Running on tiptoe through the net-
tles to the other side of the orchard where the wall was
lower, I mounted on an empty cask, till the top of the
wall was on a level with my waist, and then leaned over
into the orchard. I looked at the gnarled old trees, with
their broad dented leaves and the ripe black cherries
hanging straight and heavy among the foliage; then I
pushed my head under the net, and from under the knotted bough of an old cherry-tree I caught sight of Sergey
Mikhaylych. He evidently thought that I had gone away
and that no one was watching him. With his hat off and
his eyes shut, he was sitting on the fork of an old tree and
carefully rolling into a ball a lump of cherry-tree gum.
Suddenly he shrugged his shoulders, opened his eyes,
muttered something, and smiled. Both words and smile
were so unlike him that I felt ashamed of myself for
eavesdropping. It seemed to me that he had said, "Masha!" "Impossible," I thought. "Darling Masha!" he said
again, in a lower and more tender tone. There was no
possible doubt about the two words this time. My heart
beat hard, and such a passionate joy—illicit joy, as I
felt—took hold of me, that I clutched at the wall, fearing
to fall and betray myself. Startled by the sound of my
movement, he looked round—he dropped his eyes instantly, and his face turned red, even scarlet, like a child's.
He tried to speak, but in vain; again and again his face
positively flamed up. Still he smiled as he looked at me,
and I smiled too. Then his whole face grew radiant with
happiness. He had ceased to be the old uncle who spoiled
or scolded me; he was a man on my level, who loved and
feared me as I loved and feared him. We looked at one
another without speaking. But suddenly he frowned; the
smile and light in his eyes disappeared, and he resumed
his cold paternal tone, just as if we were doing something
wrong and he was repenting and calling on me to repent.

"You had better get down, or you will hurt yourself,"
he said: "and do put your hair straight; just think what
you look like!"

"What makes him pretend? what makes him want to

give me pain?" I thought in my vexation. And the same
instant brought an irresistible desire to upset his composure again and test my power over him.

"No," I said; "I mean to pick for myself." I caught hold
of the nearest branch and climbed to the top of the wall;
then, before he had time to catch me, I jumped down on
the other side.

"What foolish things you do!" he muttered, flushing
again and trying to hide his confusion under a pretence
of annoyance; "you might really have hurt yourself. But
how do you mean to get out of this?"

He was even more confused than before, but this time
his confusion frightened rather than pleased me. It infected me too and made me blush; avoiding his eye and
not knowing what to say, I began to pick cherries though
I had nothing to put them in. I reproached myself, I re-
pented of what I had done, I was frightened; I felt that I
had lost his good opinion forever by my folly. Both of us
were silent and embarrassed. From this difficult situation
Sonya rescued us by running back with the key in her
hand. For some time we both addressed our conversation to her and said nothing to each other. When we returned to Katya, who assured us that she had never been
asleep and was listening all the time, I calmed down, and
he tried to drop into his fatherly patronizing manner
again, but I was not taken in by it. A discussion which we
had had some days before came back clear before me.

Katya had been saying that it was easier for a man to
be in love and declare his love than for a woman.

"A man may say that he is in love, and a woman can't,"
she said.

"I disagree," said he; "a man has no business to say,
and can't say, that he is in love."

"Why not?" I asked.

"Because it never can be true. What sort of a revelation is that, that a man is in love? A man seems to think
that whenever he says the word, something will go
pop!—that some miracle will be worked, signs and wonders, with all the big guns firing at once! In my opinion,"

he went on, "whoever solemnly brings out the words 'I love you' is either deceiving himself or, which is even worse, deceiving others."

"Then how is a woman to know that a man is in love with her, unless he tells her?" asked Katya.

"That I don't know," he answered; "every man has his own way of telling things. If the feeling exists, it will out somehow. But when I read novels, I always fancy the crestfallen look of Lieutenant Strelsky or Alfred, when he says, 'I love you, Eleanora,' and expects something wonderful to happen at once, and no change at all takes place in either of them—their eyes and their noses and their whole selves remain exactly as they were."

Even then I had felt that this banter covered something serious that had reference to myself. But Katya resented his disrespectful treatment of the heroes in novels.

"You are never serious," she said; "but tell me truthfully, have you never yourself told a woman that you loved her?"

"Never, and never gone down on one knee," he answered, laughing; "and never will."

This conversation I now recalled, and I reflected that there was no need for him to tell me that he loved me. "I know that he loves me," I thought, "and all his endeavours to seem indifferent will not change my opinion."

He said little to me throughout the evening, but in every word he said to Katya and Sonya and in every look and movement of his I saw love and felt no doubt of it. I was only vexed and sorry for him, that he thought it necessary still to hide his feelings and pretend coldness, when it was all so clear, and when it would have been so simple and easy to be boundlessly happy. But my jumping down to him in the orchard weighed on me like a crime. I kept feeling that he would cease to respect me and was angry with me.

After tea I went to the piano, and he followed me.

"Play me something—it is long since I heard you," he said, catching me up in the parlour.

"I was just going to," I said. Then I looked straight in his face and said quickly, "Sergey Mikhaylych, you are not angry with me, are you?"

"What for?" he asked.

"For not obeying you this afternoon," I said, blushing.

He understood me: he shook his head and made a grimace, which implied that I deserved a scolding but that he did not feel able to give it.

"So it's all right, and we are friends again?" I said, sitting down at the piano.

"Of course!" he said.

In the drawing-room, a large lofty room, there were only two lighted candles on the piano, the rest of the room remaining in half-darkness. Outside the open windows the summer night was bright. All was silent, except when the sound of Katya's footsteps in the unlighted parlour was heard occasionally, or when his horse, which was tied up under the window, snorted or stamped his hoof on the burdocks that grew there. He sat behind me, where I could not see him; but everywhere — in the half-darkness of the room, in every sound, in myself — I felt his presence. Every look, every movement of his, though I could not see them, found an echo in my heart. I played a sonata of Mozart's which he had brought me and which I had learnt in his presence and for him. I was not thinking at all of what I was playing, but I believe that I played it well, and I thought that he was pleased. I was conscious of his pleasure, and conscious too, though I never looked at him, of the gaze fixed on me from behind. Still moving my fingers mechanically, I turned round quite involuntarily and looked at him. The night had grown brighter, and his head stood out on a background of darkness. He was sitting with his head propped on his hands, and his eyes shone as they gazed at me. Catching his look, I smiled and stopped playing. He smiled too and shook his head reproachfully at the music, for me to go on. When I stopped, the moon had grown brighter and was riding high in the heavens; and the faint light of the candles was supplemented by a new silvery light which came in through the windows and fell on the floor. Katya called out that it was really too bad—that I had stopped at the best part of the piece, and that I was playing badly. But he declared that I had never played so well; and then he began to walk about the rooms— through the drawing-room to the unlighted parlour and back again to the drawing-room, and each time he looked at me and smiled. I smiled too; I wanted even to laugh with no reason; I was so happy at something that had happened that very day. Katya and I were standing by the piano; and each time that he vanished through the drawing-room door, I started kissing her in my favourite place, the soft part of her neck under the chin; and each time he came back, I made a solemn face and refrained with difficulty from laughing.

"What is the matter with her today?" Katya asked him.

He only smiled at me without answering; he knew what was the matter with me.

"Just look what a night it is!" he called out from the parlour, where he had stopped by the open French window looking into the garden.

We joined him; and it really was such a night as I have never seen since. The full moon shone above the house and behind us, so that we could not see it, and half the shadow, thrown by the roof and pillars of the house and by the veranda awning, lay slanting and foreshortened on the gravel path and the strip of turf beyond. Everything else was bright and saturated with the silver of the dew and the moonlight. The broad garden-path, on one side of which the shadows of the dahlias and their supports lay aslant, all bright and cold, and shining on the inequalities of the gravel, ran on till it vanished in the mist. Through the trees the roof of the greenhouse shone bright, and a growing mist rose from the dell. The lilac bushes, already partly leafless, were all bright to the centre. Each flower was distinguishable apart, and all were drenched with dew. In the avenues light and shade were so mingled that they looked, not like paths and trees but like transparent houses, swaying and moving. To our right, in the shadow of the house, everything was black, indistinguishable, and uncanny. But all the brighter for the surrounding darkness was the top of a poplar, with a fantastic crown of leaves, which for some strange reason remained there close to the house, towering into the bright light, instead of flying away into the dim distance, into the retreating dark-blue of the sky.

"Let us go for a walk," I said.

Katya agreed, but said I must put on galoshes.

"I don't want them, Katya," I said; "Sergey Mikhaylych will give me his arm."

As if that would prevent me from wetting my feet! But to us three this seemed perfectly natural at the time. Though he never used to offer me his arm, I now took it of my own accord, and he saw nothing strange in it. We all went down from the veranda together. That whole world, that sky, that garden, that air, were different from those that I knew.

We were walking along an avenue, and it seemed to me, whenever I looked ahead, that we could go no farther in the same direction, that the world of the possible ended there, and that the whole scene must remain fixed forever in its beauty. But we still moved on, and the magic wall kept parting to let us in; and still we found the familiar garden with trees and paths and withered leaves. And we were really walking along the paths, treading on patches of light and shade; and a withered leaf was really crackling under my foot, and a live twig brushing my face. And that was really he, walking steadily and slowly at my side, and carefully supporting my arm; and that was really Katya walking beside us with her creaking shoes. And that must be the moon in the sky, shining down on us through the motionless branches.

But at each step the magic wall closed up again behind us and in front, and I ceased to believe in the possibility of advancing farther—I ceased to believe in the reality of it all.

"Oh, there's a frog!" cried Katya.

"Who said that? and why?" I thought. But then I realized it was Katya, and that she was afraid of frogs. Then I looked at the ground and saw a little frog which gave a jump and then stood still in front of me, while its tiny shadow was reflected on the shining clay of the path.

"You're not afraid of frogs, are you?" he asked.

I turned and looked at him. Just where we were there was a gap of one tree in the lime avenue, and I could see his face clearly—it was so handsome and so happy!

Though he had spoken of my fear of frogs, I knew that he meant to say, "I love you, my dear one!" "I love you, I love you" was repeated by his look, by his arm; the light, the shadow, and the air all repeated the same words.

We had gone all round the garden. Katya's short steps had kept up with us, but now she was tired and out of breath. She said it was time to go in; and I felt very sorry for her. "Poor thing!" I thought; "why does not she feel as we do? why are we not all young and happy, like this night and like him and me?"

We went in, but it was a long time before he went away, though the cocks had crowed, and everyone in the house was asleep, and his horse, tethered under the window, snorted continually and stamped his hoof on the burdocks. Katya never reminded us of the hour, and we sat on talking of the merest trifles and not thinking of the time, till it was past two. The cocks were crowing for the third time and the dawn was breaking when he rode away. He said good-bye as usual and made no special allusion; but I knew that from that day he was mine, and that I should never lose him now. As soon as I had confessed to myself that I loved him, I took Katya into my confidence. She rejoiced in the news and was touched by my telling her; but she was actually able—poor thing!— to go to bed and sleep! For me, I walked for a long, long time about the veranda; then I went down to the garden, where, recalling each word, each movement, I walked along the same avenues through which I had walked with him. I did not sleep at all that night, and saw sunrise and early dawn for the first time in my life. And never again did I see such a night and such a morning. "Only why does he not tell me plainly that he loves me?" I thought; "what makes him invent obstacles and call himself old, when all is so simple and so splendid? What makes him waste this golden time which may never return? Let him say 'I love you'—say it in plain words; let him take my hand in his and bend over it and say 'I love you.' Let him blush and look down before me; and then I will tell him all. No! not tell him, but throw my arms round him and press close to him and weep." But then a thought came to me—"What if I am mistaken and he does not love me?"

I was startled by this fear—God knows where it might have led me. I recalled his embarrassment and mine, when I jumped down to him in the orchard; and my heart grew very heavy. Tears gushed from my eyes, and I began to pray. A strange thought occurred to me, calming me and bringing hope with it. I resolved to begin fasting on that day, to take the Communion on my birthday, and on that same day to be betrothed to him.

How this result would come to pass I had no idea; but from that moment I believed and felt sure it would be so. The dawn had fully come and the labourers were getting up when I went back to my room.

iv

THE FAST of the Assumption falling in August, no one in the house was surprised by my intention of fasting.

During the whole of week he never once came to see us; but, far from being surprised or vexed or made uneasy by his absence, I was glad of it—I did not expect him until my birthday. Each day during the week I got up early. While the horses were being harnessed, I walked in the garden alone, turning over in my mind the sins of the day before, and considering what I must do today, so as to be satisfied with my day and not spoil it by a single

sin. It seemed so easy to me then to abstain from sin altogether; only a trifling effort seemed necessary. When
the horses came round, I got into the carriage with Katya
or one of the maids, and we drove to the church two
miles away. While entering the church, I always recalled
the prayer for those who "come unto the Temple in the
fear of God," and tried to get just that frame of mind
when mounting the two grass-grown steps up to the
building. At that hour there were not more than a dozen
worshippers—household servants or peasant women
keeping the Fast. They bowed to me, and I returned their
bows with studied humility. Then, with what seemed to
me a great effort of courage, I went myself and got candles from the man who kept them, an old soldier and an
Elder; and I placed the candles before the icons. Through
the central door of the altar-screen I could see the altar-
cloth which my mother had worked; on the screen were
the two angels which had seemed so big to me when I
was little, and the dove with a golden halo which had
fascinated me long ago. Behind the choir stood the old
battered font, where I had been christened myself and
had stood godmother to so many of the servants' children. The old priest came out, wearing a cope made of
the pall that had covered my father's coffin, and began
to read in the same voice that I had heard all my life—at
services held in our house, at Sonya's christening, at memorial services for my father, and at my mother's funeral. The same old quavering voice of the deacon rose
in the choir; and the same old woman, whom I could
remember at every service in that church, crouched by
the wall, fixing her streaming eyes on an icon in the choir,
pressing her folded fingers against her faded kerchief,
and muttering with her toothless gums. And these objects were no longer merely curious to me, merely interesting from old recollections—each had become important
and sacred in my eyes and seemed charged with profound meaning. I listened to each word of the prayers
and tried to suit my feeling to it; and if I failed to understand, I prayed silently that God would enlighten me, or

made up a prayer of my own in place of what I had failed
to catch. When the penitential prayers were repeated, I
recalled my past life, and that innocent childish past
seemed to me so black when compared to the present
brightness of my soul, that I wept and was horrified at
myself; but I felt too that all those sins would be forgiven, and that if my sins had been even greater, my repentance would be all the sweeter. At the end of the
service when the priest said, "The blessing of the Lord be
upon you!" I seemed to feel an immediate sensation of
physical well-being, of a mysterious light and warmth
that instantly filled my heart. The service over, the priest
came and asked me whether he should come to our
house to say Mass, and what hour would suit me; and I
thanked him for the suggestion, intended, as I thought,
to please me, but said that I would come to church instead, walking or driving.

"Is that not too much trouble?" he asked. And I was
at a loss for an answer, fearing to commit a sin of pride.

After the Mass, if Katya was not with me, I always
sent the carriage home and walked back alone, bowing
humbly to all who passed, and trying to find an opportunity of giving help or advice. I was eager to sacrifice myself for someone, to help in lifting a fallen cart, to rock a
child's cradle, to give up the path to others by stepping
into the mud. One evening I heard the bailiff report to
Katya that Simon, one of our serfs, had come to beg
some boards to make a coffin for his daughter, and a
ruble to pay the priest for the funeral; the bailiff had
given what he asked. "Are they as poor as that?" I asked.
"Very poor, Miss," the bailiff answered; "they have no
salt to their food." My heart ached to hear this, and yet I
felt a kind of pleasure too. Pretending to Katya that I
was merely going for a walk, I ran upstairs, got out all my
money (it was very little but it was all I had), crossed
myself, and started off alone, through the veranda and
the garden, on my way to Simon's hut. It stood at the end
of the village, and no one saw me as I went up to the
window, placed the money on the sill, and tapped on the

pane. Someone came out, making the door creak, and
hailed me; but I hurried home, cold and shaking with
fear like a criminal. Katya asked where I had been and
what was the matter with me; but I did not answer, and
did not even understand what she was saying. Everything suddenly seemed to me so petty and insignificant.
I locked myself up in my own room, and walked up and
down alone for a long time, unable to do anything, unable to think, unable to understand my own feelings. I
thought of the joy of the whole family, and of what they
would say of their benefactor; and I felt sorry that I had
not given them the money myself. I thought too of what
Sergey Mikhaylych would say, if he knew what I had
done; and I was glad to think that no one would ever find
out. I was so happy, and I felt myself and everyone else
so bad, and yet was so kindly disposed to myself and to
all the world, that the thought of death came to me as a
dream of happiness. I smiled and prayed and wept, and
felt at that moment a burning passion of love for all the
world, myself included. Between services I used to read
the Gospel; and the book became more and more intelligible to me, and the story of that divine life simpler and
more touching; and the depths of thought and feeling I
found in studying it became more awful and impenetra-
ble. On the other hand, how clear and simple everything
seemed to me when I rose from the study of this book
and looked again on life around me and reflected on it!
It was so difficult, I felt, to lead a bad life, and so simple
to love everyone and be loved. All were so kind and
gentle to me; even Sonya, whose lessons I had not broken off, was quite different—trying to understand and
please me and not to vex me. Everyone treated me as I
treated them. Thinking over my enemies, of whom I
must ask pardon before confession, I could only remember one—one of our neighbours, a girl, whom I had
made fun of in company a year ago, and who had ceased
to visit us. I wrote to her, confessing my fault and asking
her forgiveness. She replied that she forgave me and
wished me to forgive her. I cried for joy over her simple

words, and saw in them, at the time, a deep and touching feeling. My old nurse cried, when I asked her to forgive me. "What makes them all so kind to me? what have I done to deserve their love?" I asked myself. Sergey Mikhaylych would come into my mind, and I thought for long about him. I could not help it, and I did not consider these thoughts sinful. But my thoughts of him were quite different from what they had been on the night when I first realized that I loved him: he seemed to me now like a second self, and became a part of every plan for the future. The inferiority which I had always felt in his presence had vanished entirely: I felt myself his equal, and could understand him thoroughly from the moral elevation I had reached. What had seemed strange in him was now quite clear to me. Now I could see what he meant by saying that to live for others was the only true happiness, and I agreed with him perfectly. I believed that our life together would be endlessly happy and untroubled. I looked forward, not to foreign tours or fashionable society or display, but to a quite different scene—a quiet family life in the country, with constant self-sacrifice, constant mutual love, and constant recognition in all things of the kind hand of Providence.

I carried out my plan of taking the Communion on my birthday. When I came back from church that day, my heart was so swelling with happiness that I was afraid of life, afraid of any feeling that might break in on that happiness. We had hardly left the carriage for the steps in front of the house, when there was a sound of wheels on the bridge, and I saw Sergey Mikhaylych drive up in his well-known trap. He congratulated me,* and we went together to the parlour. Never since I had known him had I been so much at my ease with him and so self-possessed as on that morning. I felt in myself a whole new world, out of his reach and beyond his comprehension. I was not conscious of the slightest embarrassment

*It is the custom in Russia to congratulate anyone on his or her birthday, and also on receiving Communion.

in speaking to him. He must have understood the cause of this feeling; for he was tender and gentle beyond his wont and showed a kind of reverent consideration for me. When I made for the piano, he locked it and put the key in his pocket.

"Don't spoil your present mood," he said; "you have the sweetest of all music in your soul just now."

I was grateful for his words, and yet I was not quite pleased at his understanding too easily and clearly what ought to have been an exclusive secret in my heart. At dinner he said that he had come to congratulate me and also to say good-bye; for he must go to Moscow tomorrow. He looked at Katya as he spoke; but then he stole a glance at me, and I saw that he was afraid he might detect signs of emotion on my face. But I was neither surprised nor agitated; I did not even ask whether he would be long away. I knew he would say this, and I knew that he would not go. How did I know? I cannot explain that to myself now; but on that memorable day it seemed that I knew everything that had been and that would be. It was like a delightful dream, when all that happens seems to have happened already and to be quite familiar, and it will all happen over again, and one knows that it will happen.

He meant to go away immediately after dinner; but, as Katya was tired after church and went to lie down for a little, he had to wait until she woke up in order to say good-bye to her. The sun shone into the drawing-room, and we went out to the veranda. When we were seated, I began at once, quite calmly, the conversation that was bound to fix the fate of my heart. I began to speak, no sooner and no later, but at the very moment when we sat down, before our talk had taken any turn or colour that might have hindered me from saying what I meant to say. I cannot tell myself where it came from—my coolness and determination and preciseness of expression. It was as if something independent of my will was speaking through my lips. He sat opposite me with his elbows resting on the rails of the veranda; he pulled a lilac-branch towards him and stripped the leaves off it. When I began to speak, he let go the branch and leaned his head on one hand. His attitude might have shown either perfect calmness or strong emotion.

"Why are you going?" I asked, significantly, deliberately, and looking straight at him.

He did not answer at once.

"Business!" he muttered at last and dropped his eyes.

I realized how difficult he found it to lie to me, and in reply to such a frank question.

"Listen," I said; "you know what today is to me, how important for many reasons. If I question you, it is not to show an interest in your doings (you know that I have become intimate with you and fond of you)—I ask you this question, because I *must* know the answer. Why are you going?"

"It is very hard for me to tell you the true reason," he said. "During this week I have thought much about you and about myself, and have decided that I must go. You understand why; and if you care for me, you will ask no questions." He put up a hand to rub his forehead and cover his eyes. "I find it very difficult.... But you will understand."

My heart began to beat fast.

"I cannot understand you," I said; "I *cannot*! you must tell me; in God's name and for the sake of this day tell me what you please, and I shall hear it with calmness," I said.

He changed his position, glanced at me, and again drew the lilac twig towards him.

"Well!" he said, after a short silence, in a voice that tried in vain to seem steady, "it is a foolish business and impossible to put into words, and I feel the difficulty, but I will try to explain it to you," he added, frowning as if in bodily pain.

"Well?" I said.

"Just imagine the existence of a man—let us call him A—who has left youth far behind, and of a woman whom we may call B, who is young and happy and has seen nothing as yet of life or of the world. Family circumstances of various kinds brought them together, and he grew to love her as a daughter, and had no fear that his love would change its nature."

He stopped, but I did not interrupt him.

"But he forgot that B was so young, that life was still all a May-game to her," he went on with a sudden swiftness and determination and without looking at me, "and that it was easy to fall in love with her in a different way, and that this would amuse her. He made a mistake and was suddenly aware of another feeling, as heavy as remorse, making its way into his heart, and he was afraid. He was afraid that their old friendly relations would be destroyed, and he made up his mind to go away before that happened." As he said this, he began again to rub his eyes, with a pretence of indifference, and to close them.

"Why was he afraid to love differently?" I asked very low; but I restrained my emotion and spoke in an even voice. He evidently thought that I was not serious; for he answered as if he were hurt.

"You are young, and I am not young. You want amusement, and I want something different. Amuse yourself, if you like, but not with me. If you do, I shall take it seriously; and then I shall be unhappy, and you will repent. That is what A said," he added; "however, this is all nonsense; but you understand why I am going. And don't let us continue this conversation. Please not!"

"No! No!" I said, "we must continue it," and tears began to tremble in my voice. "Did he love her, or not?"

He did not answer.

"If he did not love her, why did he treat her as a child and pretend to her?" I asked.

"Yes, A behaved badly," he interrupted me quickly; "but it all came to an end and they parted friends."

"This is horrible! Is there no other ending?" I said with a great effort, and then felt afraid of what I had said.

"Yes, there is," he said, showing a face full of emotion and looking straight at me. "There are two different endings. But, for God's sake, listen to me quietly and don't interrupt. Some say"—here he stood up and smiled with a smile that was heavy with pain—"some say that A went off his head, fell passionately in love with B, and told her so. But she only laughed. To her it was all a jest, but to him a matter of life and death."

I shuddered and tried to interrupt him—tried to say that he must not dare to speak for me; but he checked me, laying his hand on mine.

"Wait!" he said, and his voice shook. "The other story is that she took pity on him, and fancied, poor child, from her ignorance of the world, that she really could love him, and so consented to be his wife. And he, in his madness, believed it—believed that his whole life could begin anew; but she saw herself that she had deceived him and that he had deceived her. . . . But let us drop the subject finally," he ended, clearly unable to say more; and then he began to walk up and down in silence before me.

Though he had asked that the subject should be dropped, I saw that his whole soul was hanging on my answer. I tried to speak, but the pain at my heart kept me dumb. I glanced at him—he was pale and his lower lip trembled. I felt sorry for him. With a sudden effort I broke the bonds of silence which had held me fast, and began to speak in a low inward voice, which I feared would break every moment.

"There is a third ending to the story," I said, and then paused, but he said nothing; "the third ending is that he did not love her, but hurt her, hurt her, and thought that he was right; and he left her and was actually proud of himself. You have been pretending, not I; I have loved you since the first day we met, loved you," I repeated, and at the word "loved" my low inward voice changed, without intention of mine, to a wild cry which frightened me myself.

He stood pale before me, his lip trembled more and more violently, and two tears came out upon his cheeks.

"It is wrong!" I almost screamed, feeling that I was choking with angry unshed tears. "Why do you do it?" I cried, and got up to leave him.

But he would not let me go. His head was resting on

my knees, his lips were kissing my still trembling hands, and his tears were wetting them. "My God! if I had only known!" he whispered.

"Why? why?" I kept on repeating, but in my heart there was happiness, happiness which had now come back, after so nearly departing forever.

Five minutes later Sonya was rushing upstairs to Katya and proclaiming all over the house that Masha intended to marry Sergey Mikhaylych.

v

THERE were no reasons for putting off our wedding, and neither he nor I wished for delay. Katya, it is true, thought we ought to go to Moscow, to buy and order wedding-clothes; and his mother tried to insist that, before the wedding, he must set up a new carriage, buy new furniture, and repaper the whole house. But we two together carried our point, that all these things, if they were really indispensable, should be done afterwards, and that we should be married within a fortnight after my birthday, quietly, without wedding-clothes, without a party, without best men and supper and champagne, and all the other conventional features of a wedding. He told me how dissatisfied his mother was that there should be no band, no mountain of luggage, no renovation of the whole house—so unlike her own marriage which had cost thirty thousand rubles; and he told of the solemn and secret confabulations which she held in her store-room with her housekeeper, Maryushka, rummaging the chests and discussing carpets, curtains, and salvers as indispensable conditions of our happiness. At our house Katya did just the same with my old nurse, Kuzminichna. It was impossible to treat the matter lightly with Katya. She was firmly convinced that he and I, when discussing our future, were merely talking the sentimental nonsense natural to people in our position; and that our real future happiness depended on the hemming of tablecloths and

napkins and the proper cutting-out and stitching of
under-clothing. Several times a day secret information
passed between the two houses, to communicate what
was going forward in each; and though the external relations between Katya and his mother were most affectionate, yet a slightly hostile though very subtle diplomacy
was already perceptible in their dealings. I now became
more intimate with Tatyana Semënovna, the mother of
Sergey Mikhaylych, an old-fashioned lady, strict and formal in the management of her household. Her son loved
her, and not merely because she was his mother: he
thought her the best, cleverest, kindest, and most affectionate woman in the world. She was always kind to us
and to me especially, and was glad that her son should be
getting married; but when I was with her after our engagement, I always felt that she wished me to understand that, in her opinion, her son might have looked
higher, and that it would be as well for me to keep that
in mind. I understood her meaning perfectly and thought
her quite right.

During that fortnight he and I met every day. He
came to dinner regularly and stayed on till midnight. But
though he said — and I knew he was speaking the truth —
that he had no life apart from me, yet he never spent the
whole day with me, and tried to go on with his ordinary
occupations. Our outward relations remained unchanged
to the very day of our marriage: we went on saying "you",
and not "thou" to each other; he did not even kiss my
hand; he did not seek, but even avoided, opportunities of
being alone with me. It was as if he feared to yield to the
harmful excess of tenderness he felt. I don't know which
of us had changed; but I now felt myself entirely his
equal; I no longer found in him the pretence of simplicity
which had displeased me earlier; and I often delighted to
see in him, not a grown man inspiring respect and awe
but a loving and wildly happy child. "How mistaken I
was about him!" I often thought; "he is just such another
human being as myself!" It seemed to me now that his
whole character was before me and that I thoroughly

understood it. And how simple was every feature of his character, and how congenial to my own! Even his plans for our future life together were just my plans, only more clearly and better expressed in his words.

The weather was bad just then, and we spent most of our time indoors. The corner between the piano and the window was the scene of our best intimate talks. The candlelight was reflected on the blackness of the window near us; from time to time drops struck the glistening pane and rolled down. The rain pattered on the roof; the water splashed in a puddle under the spout; it felt damp near the window; but our corner seemed all the brighter and warmer and happier for that.

"Do you know, there is something I have long wished to say to you," he began one night when we were sitting up late in our corner; "I was thinking of it all the time you were playing."

"Don't say it, I know all about it," I replied.

"All right! mum's the word!"

"No! what is it?" I asked.

"Well, it is this. You remember the story I told you about A and B?"

"I should just think I did! What a stupid story! Lucky that it ended as it did!"

"Yes, I was very near destroying my happiness by my own act. You saved me. But the main thing is that I was always telling lies then, and I'm ashamed of it, and I want to have my say out now."

"Please don't! you really mustn't!"

"Don't be frightened," he said, smiling. "I only want to justify myself. When I began then, I meant to argue."

"It is always a mistake to argue," I said.

"Yes, I argued wrong. After all my disappointments and mistakes in life, I told myself firmly when I came to the country this year that love was no more for me, and that all I had to do was to grow old decently. So for a long time, I was unable to clear up my feeling towards you, or to make out where it might lead me. I hoped, and I didn't hope: at one time I thought you were trifling with me; at another I felt sure of you but could not decide what to do. But after that evening, you remember, when we walked in the garden at night, I got alarmed: the present happiness seemed too great to be real. What if I allowed myself to hope and then failed? But of course I was thinking only of myself, for I am disgustingly selfish."

He stopped and looked at me.

"But it was not all nonsense that I said then. It was possible and right for me to have fears. I take so much from you and can give so little. You are still a child, a bud that has yet to open; you have never been in love before, and I ..."

"Yes, do tell me the truth ..." I began, and then stopped, afraid of his answer. "No, never mind," I added.

"Have I been in love before? Is that it?" he said, guessing my thoughts at once. "That I can tell you. No, never before—nothing at all like what I feel now." But a sudden painful recollection seemed to flash across his mind. "No," he said sadly; "in this too I need your compassion, in order to have the right to love you. Well, was I not bound to think twice before saying that I loved you? What do I give you? Love, no doubt."

"And is that little?" I asked, looking him in the face.

"Yes, my dear, it is little to give *you*," he continued; "you have youth and beauty. I often lie awake at night from happiness, and all the time I think of our future life together. I have lived through much, and now I think I have found what is needed for happiness. A quiet secluded life in the country, with the possibility of being useful to people to whom it is easy to do good, and who are not accustomed to have it done to them; then work which one hopes may be of some use; then rest, nature, books, music, love for one's neighbour—such is my idea of happiness. And then, on the top of all that, you for a mate, and children, perhaps—what more can the heart of man desire?"

"It should be enough," I said.

"Enough for me whose youth is over," he went on,

"but not for you. Life is still before you, and you will perhaps seek happiness, and perhaps find it, in something different. You think now that this is happiness, because you love me."

"You are wrong," I said; "I have always desired just that quiet domestic life and prized it. And you only say just what I have thought."

He smiled.

"So you think, my dear; but that is not enough for you. You have youth and beauty," he repeated thoughtfully.

But I was angry because he disbelieved me and seemed to cast my youth and beauty in my teeth.

"Why do you love me then?" I asked angrily; "for my youth or for myself?"

"I don't know, but I love you," he answered, looking at me with his attentive and attractive gaze.

I did not reply and involuntarily looked into his eyes. Suddenly a strange thing happened to me: first I ceased to see what was around me; then his face seemed to vanish till only the eyes were left, shining over against mine; next the eyes seemed to be in my own head, and then all became confused—I could see nothing and was forced to shut my eyes, in order to break loose from the feeling of pleasure and fear which his gaze was producing in me....

The day before our wedding-day, the weather cleared up towards evening. The rains which had begun in summer gave place to clear weather, and we had our first autumn evening, bright and cold. It was a wet, cold, shining world, and the garden showed for the first time the spaciousness and colour and bareness of autumn. The sky was clear, cold and pale. I went to bed happy in the thought that tomorrow, our wedding-day, would be fine. I awoke with the sun, and the thought that this very day ... seemed alarming and surprising. I went out into the garden. The sun had just risen and shone fitfully through the meagre yellow leaves of the lime avenue. The path was strewn with rustling leaves, clusters of mountain-ash berries hung red and wrinkled on the boughs, with a sprinkling of frostbitten crumpled leaves; the dahlias were black and wrinkled. The first rime lay like silver on the pale green of the grass and on the broken burdock plants round the house. In the clear cold sky there was not, and could not be, a single cloud.

"Can it possibly be today?" I asked myself, incredulous of my own happiness. "Is it possible that I shall wake tomorrow, not here but in that strange house with the pillars? Is it possible that I shall never again wait for his coming and meet him, and sit up late with Katya to talk about him? Shall I never sit with him beside the piano in our drawing-room? never see him off and feel uneasy about him on dark nights?" But I remembered that he promised yesterday to pay a last visit, and that Katya had insisted on my trying on my wedding-dress, and had said "For tomorrow." I believed for a moment that it was all real, and then doubted again. "Can it be that after today I shall be living there with a mother-in-law, without Nadëzha or old Grigori or Katya? Shall I go to bed without kissing my old nurse good night and hearing her say, while she signs me with the cross from old custom, 'Good night, Miss'? Shall I never again teach Sonya and play with her and knock through the wall to her in the morning and hear her hearty laugh? Shall I become from today someone that I myself do not know? And is a new world, that will realize my hopes and desires, opening before me? And will that new world last forever?" Alone with these thoughts I was depressed and impatient for his arrival. He came early, and it required his presence to convince me that I should really be his wife that very day, and the prospect ceased to frighten me.

Before dinner we walked to our church, to attend a memorial service for my father.

"If only he were living now!" I thought as we were returning and I leant silently on the arm of him who had been the dearest friend of the object of my thoughts. During the service, while I pressed my forehead against

the cold stone of the chapel floor, I called up my father
so vividly; I was so convinced that he understood me and
approved my choice, that I felt as if his spirit were still
hovering over us and blessing me. And my recollections
and hopes, my joy and sadness, made up one solemn and
satisfied feeling which was in harmony with the fresh still
air, the silence, the bare fields and pale sky, from which
the bright but powerless rays, trying in vain to burn my
cheek, fell over all the landscape. My companion seemed
to understand and share my feeling. He walked slowly
and silently; and his face, at which I glanced from time to
time, expressed the same serious mood between joy and
sorrow which I shared with nature.

Suddenly he turned to me, and I saw that he intended
to speak. "Suppose he starts some other subject than
that which is in my mind?" I thought. But he began to
speak of my father and did not even name him.

"He once said to me in jest, 'you should marry my
Masha,'" he began.

"He would have been happy now," I answered, pressing closer the arm which held mine.

"You were a child then," he went on, looking into my
eyes; "I loved those eyes then and used to kiss them only
because they were like his, never thinking they would be
so dear to me for their own sake. I used to call you Masha then."

"I want you to say 'thou' to me," I said.

"I was just going to," he answered; "I feel for the first
time that *thou art* entirely mine"; and his calm happy
gaze that drew me to him rested on me.

We went on along the footpath over the beaten and
trampled stubble; our voices and footsteps were the only
sounds. On one side the brownish stubble stretched over
a hollow to a distant leafless wood; across it at some distance a peasant was noiselessly ploughing a black strip
which grew wider and wider. A drove of horses scattered
under the hill seemed close to us. On the other side, as
far as the garden and our house peeping through the
trees, a field of winter corn, thawed by the sun, showed

black with occasional patches of green. The winter sun
shone over everything, and everything was covered with
long gossamer spiders' webs, which floated in the air
round us, lay on the frost-dried stubble, and got into our
eyes and hair and clothes. When we spoke, the sound of
our voices hung in the motionless air above us, as if we
two were alone in the whole world—alone under that
azure vault, in which the beams of the winter sun played
and flashed without scorching.

I too wished to say "thou" to him, but I felt ashamed.
"Why *dost thou* walk so fast?" I said quickly and almost in a whisper; I could not help blushing.

He slackened his pace, and the gaze he turned on me
was even more affectionate, gay, and happy.

At home we found that his mother and the inevitable
guests had arrived already, and I was never alone with
him again till we came out of church to drive to Nikolskoe.

The church was nearly empty; I just caught a glimpse
of his mother standing up straight on a mat by the choir
and of Katya wearing a cap with purple ribbons and with
tears on her cheeks, and of two or three of our servants
looking curiously at me. I did not look at him, but felt his
presence there beside me. I attended to the words of the
prayers and repeated them, but they found no echo in
my heart. Unable to pray, I looked listlessly at the icons,
the candles, the embroidered cross on the priest's cope,
the screen, and the window, and took nothing in. I only
felt that something strange was being done to me. At last
the priest turned to us with the cross in his hand, congratulated us, and said, "I christened you and by God's
mercy have lived to marry you." Katya and his mother
kissed us, and Grigori's voice was heard, calling up the
carriage. But I was only frightened and disappointed: all
was over, but nothing extraordinary, nothing worthy of
the Sacrament I had just received, had taken place in
myself. He and I exchanged kisses, but the kiss seemed
strange and not expressive of our feeling. "Is this all?" I
thought. We went out of church, the sound of wheels re-

verberated under the vaulted roof, the fresh air blew on my face, he put on his hat and handed me into the carriage. Through the window I could see a frosty moon with a halo round it. He sat down beside me and shut the door after him. I felt a sudden pang. The assurance of his proceedings seemed to me insulting. Katya called out that I should put something on my head; the wheels rumbled on the stone and then moved along the soft road, and we were off. Huddling in a corner, I looked out at the distant fields and the road flying past in the cold glitter of the moon. Without looking at him, I felt his presence beside me. "Is this all I have got from the moment of which I expected so much?" I thought; and still it seemed humiliating and insulting to be sitting alone with him, and so close. I turned to him, intending to speak; but the words would not come, as if my love had vanished, giving place to a feeling of mortification and alarm.

"Till this moment I did not believe it was possible," he said in a low voice in answer to my look.

"But I am afraid somehow," I said.

"Afraid of me, my dear?" he said, taking my hand and bending over it.

My hand lay lifeless in his, and the cold at my heart was painful.

"Yes," I whispered.

But at that moment my heart began to beat faster, my hand trembled and pressed his, I grew hot, my eyes sought his in the half-darkness, and all at once I felt that I did not fear him, that this fear was love—a new love still more tender and stronger than the old. I felt that I was wholly his, and that I was happy in his power over me.

PART TWO

i

Days, weeks, two whole months, of seclusion in the country slipped by unnoticed, as we thought then; and yet those two months comprised feelings, emotions, and happiness sufficient for a lifetime. Our plans for the regulation of our life in the country were not carried out at all in the way that we expected; but the reality was not inferior to our ideal. There was none of that hard work, performance of duty, self-sacrifice, and life for others, which I had pictured to myself before our marriage; there was, on the contrary, merely a selfish feeling of love for one another, a wish to be loved, a constant causeless gaiety and entire oblivion of all the world. It is true that my husband sometimes went to his study to work, or drove to town on business, or walked about attending to the management of the estate; but I saw what it cost him to tear himself away from me. He confessed later that every occupation, in my absence, seemed to him mere nonsense in which it was impossible to take any interest. It was just the same with me. If I read, or played the piano, or passed my time with his mother, or taught in the school, I did so only because each of these occupations was connected with him and won his approval; but whenever the thought of him was not associated with any duty, my hands fell by my sides and it seemed to me absurd to think that anything existed apart from him. Perhaps it was a wrong and selfish feeling, but it gave me happiness and lifted me high above all the world. He alone existed on earth for

me, and I considered him the best and most faultless man
in the world; so that I could not live for anything else than
for him, and my one object was to realize his conception
of me. And in his eyes I was the first and most excellent
woman in the world, the possessor of all possible virtues;
and I strove to be that woman in the opinion of the first
and best of men. He came to my room one day while I
was praying. I looked round at him and went on with my
prayers. Not wishing to interrupt me, he sat down at a
table and opened a book. But I thought he was looking
at me and looked round myself. He smiled, I laughed, and
had to stop my prayers.

"Have you prayed already?" I asked.

"Yes. But you go on; I'll go away."

"You do say your prayers, I hope?"

He made no answer and was about to leave the room
when I stopped him.

"Darling, for my sake, please repeat the prayers with
me!" He stood up beside me, dropped his arms awkwardly, and began, with a serious face and some hesitation. Occasionally he turned towards me, seeking signs
of approval and aid in my face.

When he came to an end. I laughed and embraced
him.

"I feel just as if I were ten! And you do it all!" he said,
blushing and kissing my hands.

Our house was one of those old-fashioned country
houses in which several generations have passed their
lives together under one roof, respecting and loving one
another. It was all redolent of good sound family tradi-
tions, which as soon as I entered it seemed to become
mine too. The management of the household was carried
on by Tatyana Semënovna, my mother-in-law, on old-
fashioned lines. Of grace and beauty there was not much;
but, from the servants down to the furniture and food,
there was abundance of everything, and a general clean-
liness, solidity, and order, which inspired respect. The
drawing-room furniture was arranged symmetrically;
there were portraits on the walls, and the floor was cov-

ered with home-made carpets and mats. In the morning-room there was an old piano, with chiffoniers of two different patterns, sofas, and little carved tables with bronze ornaments. My sitting-room, specially arranged by Tatyana Semënovna, contained the best furniture in the house, of many styles and periods, including an old pier-glass, which I was frightened to look into at first, but came to value as an old friend. Though Tatyana Semënovna's voice was never heard, the whole household went like a clock. The number of servants was far too large (they all wore soft boots with no heels, because Tatyana Semënovna had an intense dislike for stamping heels and creaking soles); but they all seemed proud of their calling, trembled before their old mistress, treated my husband and me with an affectionate air of patronage, and performed their duties, to all appearance, with extreme satisfaction. Every Saturday the floors were scoured and the carpets beaten without fail; on the first of every month there was a religious service in the house and holy water was sprinkled; on Tatyana Semënovna's name-day and on her son's (and on mine too, beginning from that autumn) an entertainment was regularly provided for the whole neighbourhood. And all this had gone on without a break ever since the beginning of Tatyana Semënovna's life.

My husband took no part in the household management; he attended only to the farmwork and the labourers, and gave much time to this. Even in winter he got up so early that I often woke to find him gone. He generally came back for early tea, which we drank alone together; and at that time, when the worries and vexations of the farm were over, he was almost always in that state of high spirits which we called "wild ecstasy." I often made him tell me what he had been doing in the morning, and he gave such absurd accounts that we both laughed till we cried. Sometimes I insisted on a serious account, and he gave it, restraining a smile. I watched his eyes and moving lips and took nothing in: the sight of him and the sound of his voice was pleasure enough.

"Well, what have I been saying? repeat it," he would sometimes say. But I could repeat nothing. It seemed so absurd that *he* should talk to *me* of any other subject than ourselves. As if it mattered in the least what went on in the world outside! It was at a much later time that I began to some extent to understand and take an interest in his occupations. Tatyana Semënovna never appeared before dinner: she breakfasted alone and said good-morning to us by deputy. In our exclusive little world of frantic happiness a voice from the staid orderly region in which she dwelt was quite startling: I often lost self-control and could only laugh without speaking, when the maid stood before me with folded hands and made her formal report: "The mistress bade me inquire how you slept after your walk yesterday evening; and about her I was to report that she had pain in her side all night, and a stupid dog barked in the village and kept her awake: and also I was to ask how you liked the bread this morning, and to tell you that it was not Taras who baked today, but Nikolashka, who was trying his hand for the first time; and she says his baking is not at all bad, especially the cracknels: but the tea-rusks were overbaked." Before dinner we saw little of each other: he wrote or went out again while I played the piano or read; but at four o'clock we all met in the drawing-room before dinner. Tatyana Semënovna sailed out of her own room, and certain poor and pious maiden ladies, of whom there were always two or three living in the house, made their appearance also. Every day without fail my husband by old habit offered his arm to his mother, to take her in to dinner; but she insisted that I should take the other, so that every day, without fail, we stuck in the doors and got in each other's way. She also presided at dinner, where the conversation, if rather solemn, was polite and sensible. The commonplace talk between my husband and me was a pleasant interruption to the formality of those entertainments. Sometimes there were squabbles between mother and son and they bantered one another; and I especially enjoyed those scenes, because they were the best proof of the strong and tender love which united the two. After dinner Tatyana Semënovna went to the parlour, where she sat in an armchair and ground her snuff or cut the leaves of new books, while we read aloud or went off to the piano in the morning-room. We read much together at this time, but music was our favourite and best enjoyment, always evoking fresh chords in our hearts and as it were revealing each afresh to the other. While I played his favourite pieces, he sat on a distant sofa where I could hardly see him. He was ashamed to betray the impression produced on him by the music; but often, when he was not expecting it, I rose from the piano, went up to him, and tried to detect on his face signs of emotion—the unnatural brightness and moistness of the eyes, which he tried in vain to conceal. Tatyana Semënovna, though she often wanted to take a look at us there, was also anxious to put no constraint upon us. So she always passed through the room with an air of indifference and a pretence of being busy; but I knew that she had no real reason for going to her room and returning so soon. In the evening I poured out tea in the large drawing-room, and all the household met again. This solemn ceremony of distributing cups and glasses before the solemnly shining samovar made me nervous for a long time. I felt myself still unworthy of such a distinction, too young and frivolous to turn the tap of such a big samovar, to put glasses on Nikita's salver, saying "For Peter Ivanovich," "For Marya Minichna," to ask "Is it sweet enough?" and to leave out lumps of sugar for Nurse and other deserving persons. "Capital! Capital! Just like a grown-up person!" was a frequent comment from my husband, which only increased my confusion.

After tea Tatyana Semënovna played patience or listened to Marya Minichna telling fortunes by the cards. Then she kissed us both and signed us with the cross, and we went off to our own rooms. But we generally sat up together till midnight, and that was our best and pleasantest time. He told me stories of his past life; we made plans and sometimes even talked philosophy; but we tried always to speak low, for fear we should be heard upstairs and reported to Tatyana Semënovna, who insisted on our going to bed early. Sometimes we grew hungry; and then we stole off to the pantry, secured a cold supper by the good offices of Nikita, and ate it in my sitting-room by the light of one candle. He and I lived like strangers in that big old house, where the uncompromising spirit of the past and of Tatyana Semënovna ruled supreme. Not she only, but the servants, the old ladies, the furniture, even the pictures, inspired me with respect and a little alarm, and made me feel that he and I were a little out of place in that house and must always be very careful and cautious in our doings. Thinking it over now, I see that many things—the pressure of that unvarying routine, and that crowd of idle and inquisitive servants—were uncomfortable and oppressive; but at the time that very constraint made our love for one another still keener. Not I only, but he also, never grumbled openly at anything; on the contrary he shut his eyes to what was amiss. Dmitri Sidorov, one of the footmen, was a great smoker; and regularly every day, when we two were in the morning-room after dinner, he went to my husband's study to take tobacco from the jar; and it was a sight to see Sergey Mikhaylych creeping on tiptoe to me with a face between delight and terror, and a wink and a warning forefinger, while he pointed at Dmitri Sidorov, who was quite unconscious of being watched. Then, when Dmitri Sidorov had gone away without having seen us, in his joy that all had passed off successfully, he declared (as he did on every other occasion) that I was a darling, and kissed me. At times his calm connivance and apparent indifference to everything annoyed me, and I took it for weakness, never noticing that I acted in the same way myself. "It's like a child who dares not show his will," I thought.

"My dear! my dear!" he said once when I told him that his weakness surprised me; "how can a man, as happy as I am, be dissatisfied with anything? Better to give way myself than to put compulsion on others; of that I have long been convinced. There is no condition in which one cannot be happy; but our life is such bliss! I simply cannot be angry; to me now nothing seems bad, but only pitiful and amusing. Above all—*le mieux est l'ennemi du bien.** Will you believe it, when I hear a ring at the bell, or receive a letter, or even wake up in the morning, I'm frightened. Life must go on, something may change; and nothing can be better than the present."

I believed him but did not understand him. I was happy; but I took that as a matter of course, the invariable experience of people in our position, and believed that there was somewhere, I knew not where, a different happiness, not greater but different.

So two months went by and winter came with its cold and snow; and, in spite of his company, I began to feel lonely, that life was repeating itself, that there was nothing new either in him or myself, and that we were merely going back to what had been before. He began to give more time to business which kept him away from me, and my old feeling returned, that there was a special department of his mind into which he was unwilling to admit me. His unbroken calmness provoked me. I loved him as much as ever and was as happy as ever in his love; but my love, instead of increasing, stood still; and another new and disquieting sensation began to creep into my heart. To love him was not enough for me after the happiness I had felt in falling in love. I wanted movement and not a calm course of existence. I wanted excitement and danger and the chance to sacrifice myself for my love. I felt in myself a superabundance of energy which found no outlet in our quiet life. I had fits of depression which I was ashamed of and tried to conceal from him, and fits of excessive tenderness and high spirits which alarmed him. He realized my state of mind before I did, and proposed a visit to Petersburg; but I begged him to give this up and not to change our manner of life or spoil our happiness. Happy indeed I was; but I

*The better is the enemy of the good.

was tormented by the thought that this happiness cost me no effort and no sacrifice, though I was even painfully conscious of my power to face both. I loved him and saw that I was all in all to him; but I wanted everyone to see our love; I wanted to love him in spite of obstacles. My mind, and even my senses, were fully occupied; but there was another feeling of youth and craving for movement, which found no satisfaction in our quiet life. What made him say that, whenever I liked, we could go to town? Had he not said so I might have realized that my uncomfortable feelings were my own fault and dangerous nonsense, and that the sacrifice I desired was there before me, in the task of overcoming these feelings. I was haunted by the thought that I could escape from depression by a mere change from the country; and at the same time I felt ashamed and sorry to tear him away, out of selfish motives, from all he cared for. So time went on, the snow grew deeper, and there we remained together, all alone and just the same as before, while outside I knew there was noise and glitter and excitement, and hosts of people suffering or rejoicing without one thought of us and our remote existence. I suffered most from the feeling that custom was daily petrifying our lives into one fixed shape, that our minds were losing their freedom and becoming enslaved to the steady passionless course of time. The morning always found us cheerful; we were polite at dinner, and affectionate in the evening. "It is all right," I thought, "to do good to others and lead upright lives, as he says; but there is time for that later; and there are other things, for which the time is now or never." I wanted, not what I had got, but a life of struggle; I wanted feeling to be the guide of life, and not life to guide feeling. If only I could go with him to the edge of a precipice and say, "One step, and I shall fall over—one movement, and I shall be lost!" then, pale with fear, he would catch me in his strong arms and hold me over the edge till my blood froze, and then carry me off whither he pleased.

This state of feeling even affected my health, and I

began to suffer from nerves. One morning I was worse
than usual. He had come back from the estate office out
of sorts, which was a rare thing with him. I noticed it at
once and asked what was the matter. He would not tell
me and said it was of no importance. I found out afterwards that the police inspector, out of spite against my
husband, was summoning our peasants, making illegal
demands on them, and using threats to them. My husband could not swallow this at once; he could not feel it
merely "pitiful and amusing." He was provoked, and
therefore unwilling to speak of it to me. But it seemed to
me that he did not wish to speak to me about it because
he considered me a mere child, incapable of understanding his concerns. I turned from him and said no more. I
then told the servant to ask Marya Minichna, who was
staying in the house, to join us at breakfast. I ate my
breakfast very fast and took her to the morning-room,
where I began to talk loudly to her about some trifle
which did not interest me in the least. He walked about
the room, glancing at us from time to time. This made me
more and more inclined to talk and even to laugh; all
that I said myself, and all that Marya Minichna said,
seemed to me laughable. Without a word to me he went
off to his study and shut the door behind him. When I
ceased to hear him, all my high spirits vanished at once:
indeed Marya Minichna was surprised and asked what
was the matter. I sat down on a sofa without answering,
and felt ready to cry. "What has he got on his mind?" I
wondered; "some trifle which he thinks important; but, if
he tried to tell it me, I should soon show him it was mere
nonsense. But he must needs think that I won't understand, must humiliate me by his majestic composure, and
always be in the right as against me. But I too am in the
right when I find things tiresome and trivial," I reflected;
"and I do well to want an active life rather than to stag-
nate in one spot and feel life flowing past me. I want to
move forward, to have some new experience every day
and every hour, whereas he wants to stand still and to
keep me standing beside him. And how easy it would be

for him to gratify me! He need not take me to town; he need only be like me and not put compulsion on himself and regulate his feelings, but live simply. That is the advice he gives me, but he is not simple himself. That is what is the matter."

I felt the tears rising and knew that I was irritated with him. My irritation frightened me, and I went to his study. He was sitting at the table, writing. Hearing my step, he looked up for a moment and then went on writing; he seemed calm and unconcerned. His look vexed me: instead of going up to him, I stood beside his writing-table, opened a book, and began to look at it. He broke off his writing again and looked at me.

"Masha, are you out of sorts?" he asked.

I replied with a cold look, as much as to say, "You are very polite, but what is the use of asking?" He shook his head and smiled with a tender timid air; but his smile, for the first time, drew no answering smile from me.

"What happened to you today?" I asked; "why did you not tell me?"

"Nothing much—a trifling nuisance," he said. "But I might tell you now. Two of our serfs went off to the town. . . ."

But I would not let him go on.

"Why would you not tell me, when I asked you at breakfast?"

"I was angry then and should have said something foolish."

"I wished to know then."

"Why?"

"Why do you suppose that I can never help you in anything?"

"Not help me!" he said, dropping his pen. "Why, I believe that without you I could not live. You not only help me in everything I do, but you do it yourself. You are very wide of the mark," he said, and laughed. "My life depends on you. I am pleased with things, only because you are there, because I need you. . . ."

"Yes, I know; I am a delightful child who must be humoured and kept quiet," I said in a voice that astonished him, so that he looked up as if this was a new experience; "but I don't want to be quiet and calm; that is more in your line, and too much in your line," I added.

"Well," he began quickly, interrupting me and evidently afraid to let me continue, "when I tell you the facts, I should like to know your opinion."

"I don't want to hear them now," I answered. I did want to hear the story, but I found it so pleasant to break down his composure. "I don't want to play at life," I said, "but to live, as you do yourself."

His face, which reflected every feeling so quickly and so vividly, now expressed pain and intense attention.

"I want to share your life, to ..." but I could not go on—his face showed such deep distress. He was silent for a moment.

"But what part of my life do you not share?" he asked; "is it because I, and not you, have to bother with the inspector and with tipsy labourers?"

"That's not the only thing," I said.

"For God's sake try to understand me, my dear!" he cried. "I know that excitement is always painful; I have learnt that from the experience of life. I love you, and I can't but wish to save you from excitement. My life consists of my love for you; so you should not make life impossible for me."

"You are always in the right," I said without looking at him.

I was vexed again by his calmness and coolness while I was conscious of annoyance and some feeling akin to penitence.

"Masha, what is the matter?" he asked. "The question is not, which of us is in the right—not at all; but rather, what grievance have you against me? Take time before you answer, and tell me all that is in your mind. You are dissatisfied with me: and you are, no doubt, right; but let me understand what I have done wrong."

But how could I put my feeling into words? That he understood me at once, that I again stood before him

like a child, that I could do nothing without his understanding and foreseeing it—all this only increased my
agitation.

"I have no complaint to make of you," I said; "I am
merely bored and want not to be bored. But you say that
it can't be helped, and, as always, you are right."

I looked at him as I spoke. I had gained my object: his
calmness had disappeared, and I read fear and pain in
his face.

"Masha," he began in a low troubled voice, "this is no
mere trifle: the happiness of our lives is at stake. Please
hear me out without answering. Why do you wish to torment me?"

But I interrupted him.

"Oh, I know you will turn out to be right. Words are
useless; of course you are right." I spoke coldly, as if
some evil spirit were speaking with my voice.

"If you only knew what you are doing!" he said, and
his voice shook.

I burst out crying and felt relieved. He sat down beside me and said nothing. I felt sorry for him, ashamed
of myself, and annoyed at what I had done. I avoided
looking at him. I felt that any look from him at that moment must express severity or perplexity. At last I looked
up and saw his eyes: they were fixed on me with a tender
gentle expression that seemed to ask for pardon. I caught
his hand and said,

"Forgive me! I don't know myself what I have been
saying."

"But I do; and you spoke the truth."

"What do you mean?" I asked.

"That we must go to Petersburg," he said; "there is
nothing for us to do here just now."

"As you please," I said.

He took me in his arms and kissed me.

"You must forgive me," he said; "for I am to blame."

That evening I played to him for a long time, while he
walked about the room. He had a habit of muttering to
himself; and when I asked him what he was muttering, he

always thought for a moment and then told me exactly what it was. It was generally verse, and sometimes mere nonsense, but I could always judge of his mood by it. When I asked him now, he stood still, thought an instant, and then repeated two lines from Lermontov:

> *He in his madness prays for storms,*
> *And dreams that storms will bring him peace.*

"He is really more than human," I thought; "he knows everything. How can one help loving him?"

I got up, took his arm, and began to walk up and down with him, trying to keep step.

"Well?" he asked, smiling and looking at me.

"All right," I whispered. And then a sudden fit of merriment came over us both: our eyes laughed, we took longer and longer steps, and rose higher and higher on tiptoe. Prancing in this manner, to the profound dissatisfaction of the butler and astonishment of my mother-in-law, who was playing patience in the parlour, we proceeded through the house till we reached the dining-room; there we stopped, looked at one another, and burst out laughing.

A fortnight later, before Christmas, we were in Petersburg.

ii

THE JOURNEY to Petersburg, a week in Moscow, visits to my own relations and my husband's, settling down in our new quarters, travel, new towns and new faces—all this passed before me like a dream. It was all so new, various, and delightful, so warmly and brightly lighted up by his presence and his love, that our quiet life in the country seemed to me something very remote and unimportant. I had expected to find people in society proud and cold; but to my great surprise, I was received everywhere with unfeigned cordiality and pleasure, not only by relations, but also by strangers. I seemed to be the one object of their thoughts, and my arrival the one thing they wanted, to complete their happiness. I was surprised too to discover in what seemed to me the very best society a number of people acquainted with my husband, though he had never spoken of them to me; and I often felt it odd and disagreeable to hear him now speak disapprovingly of some of these people who seemed to me so kind. I could not understand his coolness towards them or his endeavours to avoid many acquaintances that seemed to me flattering. Surely, the more kind people one knows, the better; and here everyone was kind.

"This is how we must manage, you see," he said to me before we left the country; "here we are little Croesuses, but in town we shall not be at all rich. So we must not stay after Easter, or go into society, or we shall get into difficulties. For your sake too I should not wish it."

"Why should we go into society?" I asked; "we shall have a look at the theatres, see our relations, go to the opera, hear some good music, and be ready to come home before Easter."

But these plans were forgotten the moment we got to Petersburg. I found myself at once in such a new and delightful world, surrounded by so many pleasures and confronted by such novel interests, that I instantly, though unconsciously, turned my back on my past life and its plans. "All that was preparatory, a mere playing at life; but here is the real thing! And there is the future too!" Such were my thoughts. The restlessness and symptoms of depression which had troubled me at home vanished at once and entirely, as if by magic. My love for my husband grew calmer, and I ceased to wonder whether he loved me less. Indeed I could not doubt his love: every thought of mine was understood at once, every feeling shared, and every wish gratified by him. His composure, if it still existed, no longer provoked me. I also began to realize that he not only loved me but was proud of me. If we paid a call, or made some new acquaintance, or gave an evening party, at which I, trembling inwardly from fear of disgracing myself, acted as hostess, he often said when it was over: "Bravo, young woman! capital! you needn't be frightened; a real success!" And his praise gave me great pleasure. Soon after our arrival he wrote to his mother and asked me to add a postscript, but refused to let me see his letter; of course I insisted on reading it; and he had said: "You would not know Masha again, I don't myself. Where does she get that charming graceful self-confidence and ease, such social gifts with such simplicity and charm and kindliness? Everybody is delighted with her. I can't admire her enough myself, and should be more in love with her than ever, if that were possible."

"Now I know what I am like," I thought. In my joy and pride I felt that I loved him more than before. My success with all our new acquaintances was a complete surprise to me. I heard on all sides, how this uncle had taken a special fancy for me, and that aunt was raving about me; I was told by one admirer that I had no rival among the Petersburg ladies, and assured by another, a lady, that I might, if I cared, lead the fashion in society. A cousin of my husband's, in particular, a Princess D., middle-aged and very much at home in society, fell in love with me at first sight and paid me compliments which turned my head. The first time that she invited me to a ball and spoke to my husband about it, he turned to me and asked if I wished to go; I could just detect a sly smile on his face. I nodded assent and felt that I was blushing.

"She looks like a criminal when confessing what she wishes," he said with a good-natured laugh.

"But you said that we must not go into society, and you don't care for it yourself," I answered, smiling and looking imploringly at him.

"Let us go, if you want to very much," he said.

"Really, we had better not."

"Do you want to? very badly?" he asked again.

I said nothing.

"Society in itself is no great harm," he went on; "but unsatisfied social aspirations are a bad and ugly business. We must certainly accept, and we will."

"To tell you the truth," I said, "I never in my life longed for anything as much as I do for this ball."

So we went, and my delight exceeded all my expectations. It seemed to me, more than ever, that I was the centre round which everything revolved, that for my sake alone this great room was lighted up and the band played, and that this crowd of people had assembled to admire me. From the hairdresser and the lady's maid to my partners and the old gentlemen promenading the ball-room, all alike seemed to make it plain that they were in love with me. The general verdict formed at the ball about me and reported by my cousin, came to this: I was quite unlike the other women and had a rural simplicity and charm of my own. I was so flattered by my success that I frankly told my husband I should like to attend two or three more balls during the season, and "so get thoroughly sick of them," I added; but I did not mean what I said.

He agreed readily; and he went with me at first with obvious satisfaction. He took pleasure in my success, and seemed to have quite forgotten his former warning or to have changed his opinion.

But a time came when he was evidently bored and wearied by the life we were leading. I was too busy, however, to think about that. Even if I sometimes noticed his eyes fixed questioningly on me with a serious attentive gaze, I did not realize its meaning. I was utterly blinded by this sudden affection which I seemed to evoke in all our new acquaintances, and confused by the unfamiliar atmosphere of luxury, refinement, and novelty. It pleased me so much to find myself in these surroundings not merely his equal but his superior, and yet to love him better and more independently than before, that I could not understand what he could object to for me in society life. I had a new sense of pride and self-satisfaction when my entry at a ball attracted all eyes, while he, as if ashamed to confess his ownership of me in public, made haste to leave my side and efface himself in the crowd of black coats. "Wait a little!" I often said in my heart, when

I identified his obscure and sometimes woebegone figure at the end of the room—"Wait till we get home! Then you will see and understand for whose sake I try to be beautiful and brilliant, and what it is I love in all that surrounds me this evening!" I really believed that my success pleased me only because it enabled me to give it up for his sake. One danger I recognized as possible— that I might be carried away by a fancy for some new acquaintance, and that my husband might grow jealous. But he trusted me so absolutely, and seemed so undisturbed and indifferent, and all the young men were so inferior to him, that I was not alarmed by this one danger. Yet the attention of so many people in society gave me satisfaction, flattered my vanity, and made me think that there was some merit in my love for my husband. Thus I became more offhand and self-confident in my behaviour to him.

"Oh, I saw you this evening carrying on a most animated conversation with Mme. N.," I said one night on returning from a ball, shaking my finger at him. He had really been talking to this lady, who was a well-known figure in Petersburg society. He was more silent and depressed than usual, and I said this to rouse him up.

"What is the good of talking like that, for *you* especially, Masha?" he said with half-closed teeth and frowning as if in pain. "Leave that to others; it does not suit you and me. Pretence of that sort may spoil the true relation between us, which I still hope may come back."

I was ashamed and said nothing.

"Will it ever come back, Masha, do you think?" he asked.

"It never was spoilt and never will be," I said; and I really believed this then.

"God grant that you are right!" he said; "if not, we ought to be going home."

But he only spoke like this once—in general he seemed as satisfied as I was, and I was so gay and so happy! I comforted myself too by thinking, "If he is bored sometimes, I endured the same thing for his sake in the country. If the relation between us has become a little different, everything will be the same again in summer, when we shall be alone in our house at Nikolskoe with Tatyana Seménovna."

So the winter slipped by, and we stayed on, in spite of our plans, over Easter in Petersburg. A week later we were preparing to start; our packing was all done; my husband, who had bought things—plants for the garden and presents for people at Nikolskoe—was in a specially cheerful and affectionate mood. Just then Princess D. came and begged us to stay till the Saturday, in order to be present at a reception to be given by Countess R. The Countess was very anxious to secure me, because a foreign prince, who was visiting Petersburg and had seen me already at a ball, wished to make my acquaintance; indeed this was his motive for attending the reception, and he declared that I was the most beautiful woman in Russia. All the world was to be there; and, in a word, it would really be too bad, if I did not go too.

My husband was talking to someone at the other end of the drawing-room.

"So you will go, won't you, Mary?" said the Princess.

"We meant to start for the country the day after to-morrow," I answered undecidedly, glancing at my husband. Our eyes met, and he turned away at once.

"I must persuade him to stay," she said, "and then we can go on Saturday and turn all heads. All right?"

"It would upset our plans; and we have packed," I answered, beginning to give way.

"She had better go this evening and make her curtsey to the Prince," my husband called out from the other end of the room; and he spoke in a tone of suppressed irritation which I had never heard from him before.

"I declare he's jealous, for the first time in his life," said the lady, laughing. "But it's not for the sake of the Prince I urge it, Sergey Mikhaylych, but for all our sakes. The Countess was so anxious to have her."

"It rests with her entirely," my husband said coldly, and then left the room.

I saw that he was much disturbed, and this pained me. I gave no positive promise. As soon as our visitor left, I went to my husband. He was walking up and down his room, thinking, and neither saw nor heard me when I came in on tiptoe.

Looking at him I said to myself: "He is dreaming already of his dear Nikolskoe, our morning coffee in the bright drawing-room, the land and the labourers, our evenings in the music-room, and our secret midnight suppers." Then I decided in my own heart: "Not for all the balls and all the flattering princes in the world will I give up his glad confusion and tender cares." I was just about to say that I did not wish to go to the ball and would refuse, when he looked round, saw me, and frowned. His face, which had been gentle and thoughtful, changed at once to its old expression of sagacity, penetration, and patronizing composure. He would not show himself to me as a mere man, but had to be a demigod on a pedestal.

"Well, my dear?" he asked, turning towards me with an unconcerned air.

I said nothing. I was provoked, because he was hiding his real self from me, and would not continue to be the man I loved.

"Do you want to go to this reception on Saturday?" he asked.

"I did, but you disapprove. Besides, our things are all packed," I said.

Never before had I heard such coldness in his tone to me, and never before seen such coldness in his eye.

"I shall order the things to be unpacked," he said, "and I shall stay till Tuesday. So you can go to the party, if you like. I hope you will; but I shall not go."

Without looking at me, he began to walk about the room jerkily, as his habit was when perturbed.

"I simply can't understand you," I said, following him with my eyes from where I stood. "You say that you never lose self-control" (he had never really said so); "then why do you talk to me so strangely? I am ready on your account to sacrifice this pleasure, and then you, in a sarcastic tone which is new from you to me, insist that I should go."

"So you make a *sacrifice*!" He threw special emphasis on the last word. "Well, so do I. What could be better? We compete in generosity—what an example of family happiness!"

Such harsh and contemptuous language I had never heard from his lips before. I was not abashed, but mortified by his contempt; and his harshness did not frighten me but made me harsh too. How could *he* speak thus, he who was always so frank and simple and dreaded insincerity in our speech to one another? And what had I done that he should speak so? I really intended to sacrifice for his sake a pleasure in which I could see no harm; and a moment ago I loved him and understood his feelings as well as ever. We had changed parts: now he avoided direct and plain words, and I desired them.

"You are much changed," I said, with a sigh. "How am I guilty before you? It is not this party—you have something else, some old count against me. Why this insincerity? You used to be so afraid of it yourself. Tell me plainly what you complain of." "What will he say?" thought I, and reflected with some complacency that I had done nothing all winter which he could find fault with.

I went into the middle of the room, so that he had to pass close to me, and looked at him. I thought, "He will come and clasp me in his arms, and there will be an end of it." I was even sorry that I should not have the chance of proving him wrong. But he stopped at the far end of the room and looked at me.

"Do you not understand yet?" he asked.

"No, I don't."

"Then I must explain. What I feel, and cannot help feeling, positively sickens me for the first time in my life." He stopped, evidently startled by the harsh sound of his own voice.

"What do you mean?" I asked, with tears of indignation in my eyes.

"It sickens me that the Prince admired you, and you

therefore run to meet him, forgetting your husband and yourself and womanly dignity; and you wilfully misunderstand what your want of self-respect makes your husband feel for you: you actually come to your husband and speak of the 'sacrifice' you are making, by which you mean — 'To show myself to His Highness is a great pleasure to me, but I "sacrifice" it.'"

The longer he spoke, the more he was excited by the sound of his own voice, which was hard and rough and cruel. I had never seen him, had never thought of seeing him, like that. The blood rushed to my heart and I was frightened; but I felt that I had nothing to be ashamed of, and the excitement of wounded vanity made me eager to punish him.

"I have long been expecting this," I said. "Go on. Go on!"

"What you expected, I don't know," he went on; "but I might well expect the worst, when I saw you day after day sharing the dirtiness and idleness and luxury of this foolish society, and it has come at last. Never have I felt such shame and pain as now—pain for myself, when your friend thrusts her unclean fingers into my heart and speaks of my jealousy!—jealousy of a man whom neither you nor I know; and you refuse to understand me and offer to make a sacrifice for me—and what sacrifice? I am ashamed for you, for your degradation! . . . Sacrifice!" he repeated again.

"Ah, so this is a husband's power," thought I: "to insult and humiliate a perfectly innocent woman. Such may be a husband's rights, but I will not submit to them." I felt the blood leave my face and a strange distension of my nostrils, as I said, "No! I make no sacrifice on your account. I shall go to the party on Saturday without fail."

"And I hope you may enjoy it. But all is over between us two!" he cried out in a fit of unrestrained fury. "But you shall not torture me any longer! I was a fool, when I . . ." but his lips quivered, and he refrained with a visible effort from ending the sentence.

I feared and hated him at that moment. I wished to

say a great deal to him and punish him for all his insults; but if I had opened my mouth, I should have lost my dignity by bursting into tears. I said nothing and left the room. But as soon as I ceased to hear his footsteps, I was horrified at what we had done. I feared that the tie which had made all my happiness might really be snapped forever; and I thought of going back. But then I wondered: "Is he calm enough now to understand me, if I mutely stretch out my hand and look at him? Will he realize my generosity? What if he calls my grief a mere pretence? Or he may feel sure that he is right and accept my repentance and forgive me with unruffled pride. And why, oh why, did he whom I loved so well insult me so cruelly?"

I went not to him but to my own room, where I sat for a long time and cried. I recalled with horror each word of our conversation, and substituted different words, kind words, for those that we had spoken, and added others; and then again I remembered the reality with horror and a feeling of injury. In the evening I went down for tea and met my husband in the presence of a friend who was staying with us; and it seemed to me that a wide gulf had opened between us from that day. Our friend asked me when we were to start; and before I could speak, my husband answered:

"On Tuesday," he said; "we have to stay for Countess R.'s reception." He turned to me: "I believe you intend to go?" he asked.

His matter-of-fact tone frightened me, and I looked at him timidly. His eyes were directed straight at me with an unkind and scornful expression; his voice was cold and even.

"Yes," I answered.

When we were alone that evening, he came up to me and held out his hand.

"Please forget what I said to you today," he began.

As I took his hand, a smile quivered on my lips and the tears were ready to flow; but he took his hand away and sat down on an armchair at some distance, as if fearing a sentimental scene. "Is it possible that he still thinks himself in the right?" I wondered; and, though I was quite ready to explain and to beg that we might not go to the party, the words died on my lips.

"I must write to my mother that we have put off our departure," he said; "otherwise she will be uneasy."

"When do you think of going?" I asked.

"On Tuesday, after the reception," he replied.

"I hope it is not on my account," I said, looking into his eyes; but those eyes merely looked—they said nothing, and a veil seemed to cover them from me. His face seemed to me to have grown suddenly old and disagreeable.

We went to the reception, and good friendly relations between us seemed to have been restored, but these relations were quite different from what they had been.

At the party I was sitting with other ladies when the Prince came up to me, so that I had to stand up in order to speak to him. As I rose, my eyes involuntarily sought my husband. He was looking at me from the other end of the room, and now turned away. I was seized by a sudden sense of shame and pain; in my confusion I blushed all over my face and neck under the Prince's eye. But I was forced to stand and listen, while he spoke, eyeing me from his superior height. Our conversation was soon over: there was no room for him beside me, and he, no doubt, felt that I was uncomfortable with him. We talked of the last ball, of where I should spend the summer, and so on. As he left me, he expressed a wish to make the acquaintance of my husband, and I saw them meet and begin a conversation at the far end of the room. The Prince evidently said something about me; for he smiled in the middle of their talk and looked in my direction.

My husband suddenly flushed up. He made a low bow and turned away from the Prince without being dismissed. I blushed too: I was ashamed of the impression which I and, still more, my husband must have made on the Prince. Everyone, I thought, must have noticed my awkward shyness when I was presented, and my husband's eccentric behaviour. "Heaven knows how they will interpret such conduct. Perhaps they know already about my scene with my husband!"

Princess D. drove me home, and on the way I spoke to her about my husband. My patience was at an end, and I told her the whole story of what had taken place between us owing to this unlucky party. To calm me, she said that such differences were very common and quite unimportant, and that our quarrel would leave no trace behind. She explained to me her view of my husband's character—that he had become very stiff and unsociable. I agreed, and believed that I had learned to judge him myself more calmly and more truly.

But when I was alone with my husband later, the thought that I had sat in judgement upon him weighed like a crime upon my conscience; and I felt that the gulf which divided us had grown still greater.

iii

FROM THAT day there was a complete change in our life and our relations to each other. We were no longer as happy when we were alone together as before. To certain subjects we gave a wide berth, and conversation flowed more easily in the presence of a third person. When the talk turned on life in the country, or on a ball, we were uneasy and shrank from looking at one another. Both of us knew where the gulf between us lay, and seemed afraid to approach it. I was convinced that he was proud and irascible, and that I must be careful not to touch him on his weak point. He was equally sure that I disliked the country and was dying for social distraction, and that he must put up with this unfortunate taste of mine. We both avoided frank conversation on these topics, and each misjudged the other. We had long ceased to think each other the most perfect people in the world; each now judged the other in secret, and measured the offender by the standard of other people. I fell ill before we left Petersburg, and we went from there to a house near town,

from which my husband went on alone, to join his
mother at Nikolskoe. By that time I was well enough to
have gone with him, but he urged me to stay on the pretext of my health. I knew, however, that he was really
afraid we should be uncomfortable together in the country; so I did not insist much, and he went off alone. I felt
it dull and solitary in his absence; but when he came
back, I saw that he did not add to my life what he had
added formerly. In the old days every thought and experience weighed on me like a crime till I had imparted it
to him; every action and word of his seemed to me a
model of perfection; we often laughed for joy at the mere
sight of each other. But these relations had changed, so
imperceptibly that we had not even noticed their disap-
pearance. Separate interests and cares, which we no longer tried to share, made their appearance, and even the
fact of our estrangement ceased to trouble us. The idea
became familiar, and, before a year had passed, each
could look at the other without confusion. His fits of
boyish merriment with me had quite vanished; his mood
of calm indulgence to all that passed, which used to provoke me, had disappeared; there was an end of those
penetrating looks which used to confuse and delight me,
an end of the ecstasies and prayers which we once shared
in common. We did not even meet often: he was continually absent, with no fears or regrets for leaving me alone;
and I was constantly in society, where I did not need him.

There were no further scenes or quarrels between us.
I tried to satisfy him, he carried out all my wishes, and we
seemed to love each other.

When we were by ourselves, which we seldom were, I
felt neither joy nor excitement nor embarrassment in his
company: it seemed like being alone. I realized that he
was my husband and no mere stranger, a good man, and
as familiar to me as my own self. I was convinced that I
knew just what he would say and do, and how he would
look; and if anything he did surprised me, I concluded
that he had made a mistake. I expected nothing from
him. In a word, he was my husband—and that was all. It

seemed to me that things must be so, as a matter of course, and that no other relations between us had ever existed. When he left home, especially at first, I was lonely and frightened and felt keenly my need of support; when he came back, I ran to his arms with joy, though two hours later my joy was quite forgotten, and I found nothing to say to him. Only at moments which sometimes occurred between us of quiet and undemonstrative affection, I felt something wrong and some pain at my heart, and I seemed to read the same story in his eyes. I was conscious of a limit to tenderness, which he seemingly would not, and I could not, overstep. This saddened me sometimes; but I had no leisure to reflect on anything, and my regret for a change which I vaguely realized I tried to drown in the distractions which were always within my reach. Fashionable life, which had dazzled me at first by its glitter and flattery of my self-love, now took entire command of my nature, became a habit, laid its fetters upon me, and monopolized my capacity for feeling. I could not bear solitude, and was afraid to reflect on my position. My whole day, from late in the morning till late at night, was taken up by the claims of society; even if I stayed at home, my time was not my own. This no longer seemed to me either gay or dull, but it seemed that so, and not otherwise, it always had to be.

So three years passed, during which our relations to one another remained unchanged and seemed to have taken a fixed shape which could not become either better or worse. Though two events of importance in our family life took place during that time, neither of them changed my own life. These were the birth of my first child and the death of Tatyana Semënovna. At first the feeling of motherhood did take hold of me with such power, and produce in me such a passion of unanticipated joy, that I believed this would prove the beginning of a new life for me. But, in the course of two months, when I began to go out again, my feeling grew weaker and weaker, till it passed into mere habit and the lifeless performance of a duty. My husband, on the contrary, from the birth of our first boy, became his old self again—gentle, composed, and home-loving, and transferred to the child his old tenderness and gaiety. Many a night when I went, dressed for a ball, to the nursery, to sign the child with the cross before he slept, I found my husband there and felt his eyes fixed on me with something of reproof in their serious gaze. Then I was ashamed and even shocked by my own callousness, and asked myself if I was worse than other women. "But it can't be helped," I said to myself; "I love my child, but to sit beside him all day long would bore me; and nothing will make me pretend what I do not really feel."

His mother's death was a great sorrow to my husband; he said that he found it painful to go on living at Nikolskoe. For myself, although I mourned for her and sympathized with my husband's sorrow, yet I found life in that house easier and pleasanter after her death. Most of those three years we spent in town: I went only once to Nikolskoe for two months; and the third year we went abroad and spent the summer at Baden.

I was then twenty-one; our financial position was, I believed, satisfactory; my domestic life gave me all that I asked of it; everyone I knew, it seemed to me, loved me; my health was good; I was the best-dressed woman in Baden; I knew that I was good-looking; the weather was fine; I enjoyed the atmosphere of beauty and refinement; and, in short, I was in excellent spirits. They had once been even higher at Nikolskoe, when my happiness was in myself and came from the feeling that I deserved to be happy, and from the anticipation of still greater happiness to come. That was a different state of things; but I did very well this summer also. I had no special wishes or hopes or fears; it seemed to me that my life was full and my conscience easy. Among all the visitors at Baden that season there was no one man whom I preferred to the rest, or even to our old ambassador, Prince K., who was assiduous in his attentions to me. One was young, and another old; one was English and fair, another French and wore a beard—to me they were all alike, but all in-

dispensable. Indistinguishable as they were, they together made up the atmosphere which I found so
pleasant. But there was one, an Italian marquis, who
stood out from the rest by reason of the boldness with
which he expressed his admiration. He seized every opportunity of being with me—danced with me, rode with
me, and met me at the casino; and everywhere he spoke
to me of my charms. Several times I saw him from my
windows loitering round our hotel, and the fixed gaze of
his bright eyes often troubled me, and made me blush
and turn away. He was young, handsome, and well-
mannered; and, above all, by his smile and the expression of his brow, he resembled my husband, though much
handsomer than he. He struck me by this likeness,
though in general, in his lips, eyes, and long chin, there
was something coarse and animal which contrasted with
my husband's charming expression of kindness and no-
ble serenity. I supposed him to be passionately in love
with me, and thought of him sometimes with proud com-
miseration. When I tried at times to soothe him and
change his tone to one of easy, half-friendly confidence,
he resented the suggestion with vehemence, and continued to disquiet me by a smouldering passion which was
ready at any moment to burst forth. Though I would not
own it even to myself, I feared him and often thought of
him against my will. My husband knew him, and treated
him—even more than other acquaintances of ours who
regarded him only as my husband—with coldness and
disdain.

Towards the end of the season I fell ill and stayed indoors for a fortnight. The first evening that I went out
again to hear the band, I learnt that Lady S., an English-
woman famous for her beauty, who had long been expected, had arrived in my absence. My return was
welcomed, and a group gathered round me; but a more
distinguished group attended the beautiful stranger. She
and her beauty were the one subject of conversation
around me. When I saw her, she was really beautiful, but
her self-satisfied expression struck me as disagreeable,

and I said so. That day everything that had formerly seemed amusing, seemed dull. Lady S. arranged an expedition to the ruined castle for the next day; but I declined to be of the party. Almost everyone else went; and my opinion of Baden underwent a complete change. Everything and everybody seemed to me stupid and tiresome; I wanted to cry, to break off my cure, to return to Russia. There was some evil feeling in my soul, but I did not yet acknowledge it to myself. Pretending that I was not strong, I ceased to appear at crowded parties; if I went out, it was only in the morning by myself, to drink the waters; and my only companion was Mme. M., a Russian lady, with whom I sometimes took drives in the surrounding country. My husband was absent: he had gone to Heidelberg for a time, intending to return to Russia when my cure was over, and only paid me occasional visits at Baden.

One day when Lady S. had carried off all the company on a hunting expedition, Mme. M. and I drove in the afternoon to the castle. While our carriage moved slowly along the winding road, bordered by ancient chestnut-trees and commanding a vista of the pretty and pleasant country round Baden, with the setting sun lighting it up, our conversation took a more serious turn than had ever happened to us before. I had known my companion for a long time; but she appeared to me now in a new light, as a well-principled and intelligent woman, to whom it was possible to speak without reserve, and whose friendship was worth having. We spoke of our private concerns, of our children, of the emptiness of life at Baden, till we felt a longing for Russia and the Russian countryside. When we entered the castle we were still under the impression of this serious feeling. Within the walls there was shade and coolness; the sunlight played from above upon the ruins. Steps and voices were audible. The landscape, charming enough but cold to a Russian eye, lay before us in the frame made by a doorway. We sat down to rest and watched the sunset in silence. The voices now sounded louder, and I thought I heard my own name. I listened and could not help overhearing every word. I recognized the voices: the speakers were the Italian marquis and a French friend of his whom I knew also. They were talking of me and of Lady S., and the Frenchman was comparing us as rival beauties. Though he said nothing insulting, his words made my pulse quicken. He explained in detail the good points of us both. I was already a mother, while Lady S. was only nineteen; though I had the advantage in hair, my rival had a better figure. "Besides," he added, "Lady S. is a real *grande dame,* and the other is nothing in particular, only one of those obscure Russian princesses who turn up here nowadays in such numbers." He ended by saying that I was wise in not attempting to compete with Lady S., and that I was completely buried as far as Baden was concerned.

"I am sorry for her—unless indeed she takes a fancy to console herself with you," he added with a hard ringing laugh.

"If she goes away, I follow her"—the words were blurted out in an Italian accent.

"Happy man! he is still capable of a passion!" laughed the Frenchman.

"Passion!" said the other voice and then was still for a moment. "It is a necessity to me: I cannot live without it. To make life a romance is the one thing worth doing. And with me romance never breaks off in the middle, and this affair I shall carry through to the end."

"Bonne chance, mon ami!" said the Frenchman.

They now turned a corner, and the voices stopped. Then we heard them coming down the steps, and a few minutes later they came out upon us by a side-door. They were much surprised to see us. I blushed when the marquis approached me, and felt afraid when we left the castle and he offered me his arm. I could not refuse, and we set off for the carriage, walking behind Mme. M. and his friend. I was mortified by what the Frenchman had said of me, though I secretly admitted that he had only put in words what I felt myself; but the plain speaking of the Italian had surprised and upset me by its coarseness.

I was tormented by the thought that, though I had over-
heard him, he showed no fear of me. It was hateful to
have him so close to me; and I walked fast after the other
couple, not looking at him or answering him and trying
to hold his arm in such a way as not to hear him. He
spoke of the fine view, of the unexpected pleasure of our
meeting, and so on; but I was not listening. My thoughts
were with my husband, my child, my country; I felt
ashamed, distressed, anxious; I was in a hurry to get back
to my solitary room in the Hôtel de Bade, there to think
at leisure of the storm of feeling that had just risen in my
heart. But Mme. M. walked slowly, it was still a long way
to the carriage, and my escort seemed to loiter on purpose as if he wished to detain me. "None of that!" I
thought, and resolutely quickened my pace. But it soon
became unmistakable that he was detaining me and
even pressing my arm. Mme. M. turned a corner, and we
were quite alone. I was afraid.

"Excuse me," I said coldly and tried to free my arm;
but the lace of my sleeve caught on a button of his coat.
Bending towards me, he began to unfasten it, and his
ungloved fingers touched my arm. A feeling new to me,
half horror and half pleasure, sent an icy shiver down my
back. I looked at him, intending by my coldness to con-
vey all the contempt I felt for him; but my look expressed
nothing but fear and excitement. His liquid blazing eyes,
right up against my face, stared strangely at me, at my
neck and breast; both his hands fingered my arm above
the wrist; his parted lips were saying that he loved me,
and that I was all the world to him; and those lips were
coming nearer and nearer, and those hands were squeez-
ing mine harder and harder and burning me. A fever ran
through my veins, my sight grew dim, I trembled, and the
words intended to check him died in my throat. Suddenly I felt a kiss on my cheek. Trembling all over and
turning cold, I stood still and stared at him. Unable to
speak or move, I stood there, horrified, expectant, even
desirous. It was over in a moment, but the moment was
horrible! In that short time I saw him exactly as he was—

the low straight forehead (that forehead so like my husband's!) under the straw hat; the handsome regular nose
and dilated nostrils; the long waxed moustache and short
beard; the close-shaved cheeks and sunburnt neck. I
hated and feared him; he was utterly repugnant and
alien to me. And yet the excitement and passion of this
hateful strange man raised a powerful echo in my own
heart; I felt an irresistible longing to surrender myself to
the kisses of that coarse handsome mouth, and to the
pressure of those white hands with their delicate veins
and jewelled fingers; I was tempted to throw myself
headlong into the abyss of forbidden delights that had
suddenly opened up before me.

"I am so unhappy already," I thought; "let more and
more storms of unhappiness burst over my head!"

He put one arm round me and bent towards my face.
"Better so!" I thought: "let sin and shame cover me ever
deeper and deeper!"

"Je vous aime!" he whispered in the voice which was
so like my husband's. At once I thought of my husband
and child, as creatures once precious to me who had now
passed altogether out of my life. At that moment I heard
Mme. M.'s voice; she called to me from round the corner.
I came to myself, tore my hand away without looking at
him, and almost ran after her: I only looked at him after
she and I were already seated in the carriage. Then I saw
him raise his hat and ask some commonplace question
with a smile. He little knew the inexpressible aversion I
felt for him at that moment.

My life seemed so wretched, the future so hopeless,
the past so black! When Mme. M. spoke, her words
meant nothing to me. I thought that she talked only out
of pity, and to hide the contempt I aroused in her. In
every word and every look I seemed to detect this contempt and insulting pity. The shame of that kiss burnt my
cheek, and the thought of my husband and child was
more than I could bear. When I was alone in my own
room, I tried to think over my position; but I was afraid
to be alone. Without drinking the tea which was brought

me, and uncertain of my own motives, I got ready with feverish haste to catch the evening train and join my husband at Heidelberg.

I found seats for myself and my maid in an empty carriage. When the train started and the fresh air blew through the window on my face, I grew more composed and pictured my past and future to myself more clearly. The course of our married life from the time of our first visit to Petersburg now presented itself to me in a new light, and lay like a reproach on my conscience. For the first time I clearly recalled our start at Nikolskoe and our plans for the future; and for the first time I asked myself what happiness had my husband had since then. I felt that I had behaved badly to him. "But why," I asked myself, "did he not stop me? Why did he make pretences? Why did he always avoid explanations? Why did he insult me? Why did he not use the power of his love to influence me? Or did he not love me?" But whether he was to blame or not, I still felt the kiss of that strange man upon my cheek. The nearer we got to Heidelberg, the clearer grew my picture of my husband, and the more I dreaded our meeting. "I shall tell him all," I thought, "and wipe out everything with tears of repentance; and he will forgive me." But I did not know myself what I meant by "everything"; and I did not believe in my heart that he would forgive me.

As soon as I entered my husband's room and saw his calm though surprised expression, I felt at once that I had nothing to tell him, no confession to make, and nothing to ask forgiveness for. I had to suppress my unspoken grief and penitence.

"What put this into your head?" he asked. "I meant to go to Baden tomorrow." Then he looked more closely at me and seemed to take alarm. "What's the matter with you? What has happened?" he said.

"Nothing at all," I replied, almost breaking down. "I am not going back. Let us go home, tomorrow if you like, to Russia."

For some time he said nothing but looked at me at-

tentively. Then he said, "But do tell me what has happened to you."

I blushed involuntarily and looked down. There came
into his eyes a flash of anger and displeasure. Afraid of
what he might imagine, I said with a power of pretence
that surprised myself:

"Nothing at all has happened. It was merely that I
grew weary and sad by myself; and I have been thinking
a great deal of our way of life and of you. I have long
been to blame towards you. Why do you take me abroad,
when you can't bear it yourself? I have long been to
blame. Let us go back to Nikolskoe and settle there forever."

"Spare us these sentimental scenes, my dear," he said
coldly. "To go back to Nikolskoe is a good idea, for our
money is running short; but the notion of stopping there
'forever' is fanciful. I know you would not settle down.
Have some tea, and you will feel better," and he rose to
ring for the waiter.

I imagined all he might be thinking about me; and I
was offended by the horrible thoughts which I ascribed
to him when I encountered the dubious and shame-faced
look he directed at me. "He will not and cannot understand me." I said I would go and look at the child, and I
left the room. I wished to be alone, and to cry and cry
and cry. . . .

iv

THE HOUSE at Nikolskoe, so long unheated and uninhab-
ited, came to life again; but much of the past was dead
beyond recall. Tatyana Seménovna was no more, and we
were now alone together. But far from desiring such
close companionship, we even found it irksome. To me
that winter was the more trying because I was in bad
health, from which I only recovered after the birth of my
second son. My husband and I were still on the same
terms as during our life in Petersburg: we were coldly

friendly to each other; but in the country each room and wall and sofa recalled what he had once been to me, and what I had lost. It was as if some unforgiven grievance held us apart, as if he were punishing me and pretending not to be aware of it. But there was nothing to ask pardon for, no penalty to deprecate; my punishment was merely this, that he did not give his whole heart and mind to me as he used to do; but he did not give it to anyone or to anything; as though he had no longer a heart to give. Sometimes it occurred to me that he was only pretending to be like that, in order to hurt me, and that the old feeling was still alive in his breast; and I tried to call it forth. But I always failed: he always seemed to avoid frankness, evidently suspecting me of insincerity, and dreading the folly of any emotional display. I could read in his face and the tone of his voice, "What is the good of talking? I know all the facts already, and I know what is on the tip of your tongue, and I know that you will say one thing and do another." At first I was mortified by his dread of frankness, but I came later to think that it was rather the absence, on his part, of any need of frankness. It would never have occurred to me now, to tell him of a sudden that I loved him, or to ask him to repeat the prayers with me or listen while I played the piano. Our intercourse came to be regulated by a fixed code of good manners. We lived our separate lives: he had his own occupations in which I was not needed, and which I no longer wished to share, while I continued my idle life which no longer vexed or grieved him. The children were still too young to form a bond between us.

But spring came round and brought Katya and Sonya to spend the summer with us in the country. As the house at Nikolskoe was under repair, we went to live at my old home at Pokrovskoe. The old house was unchanged—the veranda, the folding table and the piano in the sunny drawing-room, and my old bedroom with its white curtains and the dreams of my girlhood which I seemed to have left behind me there. In that room there were two beds: one had been mine, and in it now my plump little

Kokosha lay sprawling, when I went at night to sign him with the cross; the other was a crib, in which the little face of my baby, Vanya, peeped out from his swaddling-clothes. Often, when I had made the sign over them and remained standing in the middle of the quiet room, suddenly there rose up from all the corners, from the walls and curtains, old forgotten visions of youth. Old voices began to sing the songs of my girlhood. Where were those visions now? where were those dear old sweet songs? All that I had hardly dared to hope for had come to pass. My vague confused dreams had become a reality, and the reality had become an oppressive, difficult, and joyless life. All remained the same—the garden visible through the window, the grass, the path, the very same bench over there above the dell, the same song of the nightingale by the pond, the same lilacs in full bloom, the same moon shining above the house; and yet, in everything such a terrible inconceivable change! Such coldness in all that might have been near and dear! Just as in old times, Katya and I sit quietly alone together in the parlour and talk, and talk of him. But Katya has grown wrinkled and pale; and her eyes no longer shine with joy and hope, but express only sympathy, sorrow, and regret. We do not go into raptures as we used to, we judge him coolly; we do not wonder what we have done to deserve such happiness, or long to proclaim our thoughts to all the world. No! we whisper together like conspirators and ask each other for the hundredth time why all has changed so sadly. Yet he was still the same man, save for the deeper furrow between his eyebrows and the whiter hair on his temples; but his serious attentive look was constantly veiled from me by a cloud. And I am the same woman, but without love or desire for love, with no longing for work and no content with myself. My religious ecstasies, my love for my husband, the fullness of my former life— all these now seem utterly remote and visionary. Once it seemed so plain and right that to live for others was happiness; but now it has become unintelligible. Why live for others, when life had no attraction even for oneself?

I had given up my music altogether since the time of our first visit to Petersburg; but now the old piano and the old music tempted me to begin again.

One day I was not well and stayed indoors alone. My husband had taken Katya and Sonya to see the new buildings at Nikolskoe. Tea was laid; I went downstairs and while waiting for them sat down at the piano. I opened the *Moonlight Sonata* and began to play. There was no one within sight or sound, the windows were open over the garden, and the familiar sounds floated through the room with a solemn sadness. At the end of the first movement I looked round instinctively to the corner where he used once to sit and listen to my playing. He was not there; his chair, long unmoved, was still in its place; through the window I could see a lilac bush against the light of the setting sun; the freshness of evening streamed in through the open windows. I rested my elbows on the piano and covered my face with both hands; and so I sat for a long time, thinking. I recalled with pain the irrevocable past, and timidly imagined the future. But for me there seemed to be no future, no desires at all and no hopes. "Can life be over for me?" I thought with horror; then I looked up, and, trying to forget and not to think, I began playing the same movement over again. "O God!" I prayed, "forgive me if I have sinned, or restore to me all that once blossomed in my heart, or teach me what to do and how to live now." There was a sound of wheels on the grass and before the steps of the house; then I heard cautious and familiar footsteps pass along the veranda and cease; but my heart no longer replied to the sound. When I stopped playing the footsteps were behind me and a hand was laid on my shoulder.

"How clever of you to think of playing that!" he said.

I said nothing.

"Have you had tea?" he asked.

I shook my head without looking at him—I was unwilling to let him see the signs of emotion on my face.

"They'll be here immediately," he said; "the horse gave trouble, and they got out on the high road to walk home."

"Let us wait for them," I said, and went out to the
veranda, hoping that he would follow; but he asked
about the children and went upstairs to see them. Once
more his presence and simple kindly voice made me
doubt if I had really lost anything. What more could I
wish? "He is kind and gentle, a good husband, a good
father; I don't know myself what more I want." I sat
down under the veranda awning on the very bench on
which I had sat when we became engaged. The sun had
set, it was growing dark, and a little spring raincloud
hung over the house and garden, and only behind the
trees the horizon was clear, with the fading glow of twilight, in which one star had just begun to twinkle. The
landscape, covered by the shadow of the cloud, seemed
waiting for the light spring shower. There was not a
breath of wind; not a single leaf or blade of grass stirred;
the scent of lilac and bird-cherry was so strong in the
garden and veranda that it seemed as if all the air was in
flower; it came in wafts, now stronger and now weaker,
till one longed to shut both eyes and ears and drink in
that fragrance only. The dahlias and rosebushes, not yet
in flower, stood motionless on the black mould of the
border, looking as if they were growing slowly upwards
on their white-shaved props; beyond the dell, the frogs
were making the most of their time before the rain drove
them to the pond, croaking busily and loudly. Only the
high continuous note of water falling at some distance
rose above their croaking. From time to time the nightingales called to one another, and I could hear them flitting restlessly from bush to bush. Again this spring a
nightingale had tried to build in a bush under the window, and I heard her fly off across the avenue when I
went into the veranda. From there she whistled once and
then stopped; she too was expecting the rain.

I tried in vain to calm my feelings: I had a sense of
anticipation and regret.

He came downstairs again and sat down beside me.

"I am afraid they will get wet," he said.

"Yes," I answered; and we sat for long without speaking.

The cloud came down lower and lower with no wind. The air grew stiller and more fragrant. Suddenly a drop fell on the canvas awning and seemed to rebound from it; then another broke on the gravel path; soon there was a splash on the burdock leaves, and a fresh shower of big drops came down faster and faster. Nightingales and frogs were both dumb; only the high note of the falling water, though the rain made it seem more distant, still went on; and a bird, which must have sheltered among the dry leaves near the veranda, steadily repeated its two unvarying notes. My husband got up to go in.

"Where are you going?" I asked, trying to keep him; "it is so pleasant here."

"We must send them an umbrella and galoshes," he replied.

"Don't trouble—it will soon be over."

He thought I was right, and we remained together in the veranda. I rested one hand upon the wet slippery rail and put my head out. The fresh rain wetted my hair and neck in places. The cloud, growing lighter and thinner, was passing overhead; the steady patter of the rain gave place to occasional drops that fell from the sky or dripped from the trees. The frogs began to croak again in the dell; the nightingales woke up and began to call from the dripping bushes from one side and then from another. The whole prospect before us grew clear.

"How delightful!" he said, seating himself on the veranda rail and passing a hand over my wet hair.

This simple caress had on me the effect of a reproach: I felt inclined to cry.

"What more can a man need?" he said; "I am so content now that I want nothing; I am perfectly happy!"

He told me a different story once, I thought. He had said that, however great his happiness might be, he always wanted more and more. Now he is calm and contented, while my heart is full of unspoken repentance and unshed tears.

"I think it delightful too," I said; "but I am sad just because of the beauty of it all. All is so fair and lovely

outside me, while my own heart is confused and baffled
and full of vague unsatisfied longing. Is it possible that
there is no element of pain, no yearning for the past, in
your enjoyment of nature?"

He took his hand off my head and was silent for a
little.

"I used to feel that too," he said, as though recalling
it, "especially in spring. I used to sit up all night too, with
my hopes and fears for company, and good company
they were! But life was all before me then. Now it is all
behind me, and I am content with what I have. I find life
capital," he added with such careless confidence that I
believed, whatever pain it gave me to hear it, that it was
the truth.

"But is there nothing you wish for?" I asked.

"I don't ask for impossibilities," he said, guessing my
thoughts. "You go and get your head wet," he added,
stroking my head like a child's and again passing his
hand over the wet hair; "you envy the leaves and the
grass their wetting from the rain, and you would like
yourself to be the grass and the leaves and the rain. But
I am content to enjoy them and everything else that is
good and young and happy."

"And do you regret nothing of the past?" I asked,
while my heart grew heavier and heavier.

Again he thought for a time before replying. I saw
that he wished to reply with perfect frankness.

"Nothing," he said shortly.

"Not true! not true!" I said, turning towards him and
looking into his eyes. "Do you really not regret the
past?"

"No!" he repeated; "I am grateful for it, but I don't
regret it."

"But would you not like to have it back?" I asked.

He turned away and looked out over the garden.

"No; I might as well wish to have wings. It is impossible."

"And would you not alter the past? do you not reproach yourself or me?"

"No, never! It was all for the best."

"Listen to me!" I said, touching his arm to make him look round. "Why did you never tell me that you wished me to live as you really wished me to? Why did you give me a freedom for which I was unfit? Why did you stop teaching me? If you had wished it, if you had guided me differently, none of all this would have happened!" said I in a voice that increasingly expressed cold displeasure and reproach, in place of the love of former days.

"What would not have happened?" he asked, turning to me in surprise. "As it is, there is nothing wrong. Things are all right, quite all right," he added with a smile.

"Does he really not understand?" I thought; "or, still worse, does he not wish to understand?"

Then I suddenly broke out, "Had you acted differently, I should not now be punished, for no fault at all, by your indifference and even contempt, and you would not have taken from me unjustly all that I valued in life!"

"What do you mean, my dear one?" he asked—he seemed not to understand me.

"No! don't interrupt me! You have taken from me your confidence, your love, even your respect; for I cannot believe, when I think of the past, that you still love me. No! don't speak! I must once for all say out what has long been torturing me. Is it my fault that I knew nothing of life, and that you left me to learn experience for myself? Is it my fault that now, when I have gained the knowledge and have been struggling for nearly a year to come back to you, you push me away and pretend not to understand what I want? And you always do it so that it is impossible to reproach you, while I am guilty and unhappy. Yes, you wish to drive me out again to that life which might rob us both of happiness."

"How did I show that?" he asked in evident alarm and surprise.

"No later than yesterday you said, and you constantly say, that I can never settle down here, and that we must spend this winter too at Petersburg; and I hate Petersburg!" I went on. "Instead of supporting me, you avoid

all plain speaking; you never say a single frank affectionate word to me. And then, when I fall utterly, you will
reproach me and rejoice in my fall."

"Stop!" he said with cold severity. "You have no right
to say that. It only proves that you are ill-disposed towards me, that you don't . . ."

"That I don't love you? Don't hesitate to say it!" I
cried, and the tears began to flow. I sat down on the
bench and covered my face with my handkerchief.

"So that is how he understood me!" I thought, trying
to restrain the sobs which choked me. "Gone, gone is our
former love!" said a voice at my heart. He did not come
close or try to comfort me. He was hurt by what I had
said. When he spoke, his tone was cool and dry.

"I don't know what you reproach me with," he began.
"If you mean that I don't love you as I once did . . ."

"Did love!" I said, with my face buried in the handkerchief, while the bitter tears fell still more abundantly.

"If so, time is to blame for that, and we ourselves.
Each time of life has its own kind of love." He was silent
for a moment. "Shall I tell you the whole truth, if you
really wish for frankness? In that summer when I first
knew you, I used to lie awake all night, thinking about
you, and I made that love myself, and it grew and grew
in my heart. So again, in Petersburg and abroad, in the
course of horrible sleepless nights, I strove to shatter and
destroy that love, which had come to torture me. I did
not destroy it, but I destroyed that part of it which gave
me pain. Then I grew calm; and I feel love still, but it is a
different kind of love."

"You call it love, but I call it torture!" I said. "Why did
you allow me to go into society, if you thought so badly
of it that you ceased to love me on that account?"

"No, it was not society, my dear," he said.

"Why did you not exercise your authority?" I went on;
"why did you not lock me up or kill me? That would have
been better than the loss of all that formed my happiness.
I should have been happy, instead of being ashamed."

I began to sob again, and hid my face.

Just then Katya and Sonya, wet and cheerful, came out to the veranda, laughing and talking loudly. They were silent as soon as they saw us, and went in again immediately.

We remained silent for a long time. I had had my cry out and felt relieved. I glanced at him. He was sitting with his head resting on his hand; he intended to make some reply to my glance, but only sighed deeply and resumed his former position.

I went up to him and removed his hand. His eyes turned thoughtfully to my face.

"Yes," he began, as if continuing his thoughts aloud, "all of us, and especially you women, must have personal experience of all the nonsense of life, in order to get back to life itself; the evidence of other people is no good. At that time you had not got near the end of that charming nonsense which I admired in you. So I let you go through it alone, feeling that I had no right to put pressure on you, though my own time for that sort of thing was long past."

"If you loved me," I said, "how could you stand beside me and suffer me to go through it?"

"Because it was impossible for you to take my word for it, though you would have tried to. Personal experience was necessary, and now you have had it."

"There was much calculation in all that," I said, "but little love."

Again we were silent.

"What you said just now is severe, but it is true," he began, rising suddenly and beginning to walk about the veranda. "Yes, it is true. I was to blame," he added, stopping opposite me; "I ought either to have kept myself from loving you at all, or to have loved you in a simpler way."

"Let us forget it all," I said timidly.

"No," he said; "the past can never come back, never," and his voice softened as he spoke.

"It is restored already," I said, laying a hand on his shoulder.

He took my hand away and pressed it.

"I was wrong when I said that I did not regret the past. I do regret it; I weep for that past love which can never return. Who is to blame, I do not know. Love remains, but not the old love; its place remains, but it is all wasted away and has lost all strength and substance; recollections are still left, and gratitude; but . . ."

"Do not say that!" I broke in. "Let all be as it was before! Surely that is possible?" I asked, looking into his eyes; but their gaze was clear and calm, and did not look deeply into mine.

Even while I spoke, I knew that my wishes and my petition were impossible. He smiled calmly and gently; and I thought it the smile of an old man.

"How young you are still!" he said, "and I am so old. What you seek in me is no longer there. Why deceive ourselves?" he added, still smiling.

I stood silent opposite to him, and my heart grew calmer.

"Don't let us try to repeat life," he went on. "Don't let us make pretences to ourselves. Let us be thankful that there is an end of the old emotions and excitements. The excitement of searching is over for us; our quest is done, and happiness enough has fallen to our lot. Now we must stand aside and make room—for him, if you like," he said, pointing to the nurse who was carrying Vanya out and had stopped at the veranda door. "That's the truth, my dear one," he said, drawing down my head and kissing it, not a lover any longer but an old friend.

The fragrant freshness of the night rose ever stronger and sweeter from the garden; the sounds and the silence grew more solemn; star after star began to twinkle overhead. I looked at him, and suddenly my heart grew light; it seemed that the cause of my suffering had been removed like an aching nerve. Suddenly I realized clearly and calmly that the past feeling, like the past time itself, was gone beyond recall, and that it would be not only impossible but painful and uncomfortable to bring it back. And after all, was that time so good which seemed to me so happy? And it was all so long, long ago!

"Time for tea!" he said, and we went together to the parlour. At the door we met the nurse with the baby. I took him in my arms, covered his bare little red legs, pressed him to me, and kissed him with the lightest touch of my lips. Half asleep, he moved the parted fingers of one creased little hand and opened dim little eyes, as if he was looking for something or recalling something. All at once his eyes rested on me, a spark of consciousness shone in them, the little pouting lips, parted before, now met and opened in a smile. "Mine, mine, mine!" I thought, pressing him to my breast with such an impulse of joy in every limb that I found it hard to restrain myself from hurting him. I fell to kissing the cold little feet, his stomach and hand and head with its thin covering of down. My husband came up to me, and I quickly covered the child's face and uncovered it again.

"Ivan Sergeich!" said my husband, tickling him under the chin. But I made haste to cover Ivan Sergeich up again. None but I had any business to look long at him. I glanced at my husband. His eyes smiled as he looked at me; and I looked into them with an ease and happiness which I had not felt for a long time.

That day ended the romance of our marriage; the old feeling became a precious irrecoverable remembrance; but a new feeling of love for my children and the father of my children laid the foundation of a new life and a quite different happiness; and that life and happiness have lasted to the present time.

The Death of Ivan Ilych

———✦———

i

DURING an interval in the Melvinski trial in the large building of the law courts, the members and public prosecutor met in Ivan Egorovich Shebek's private room, where the conversation turned on the celebrated Krasovski case. Fëdor Vasilievich warmly maintained that it was not subject to their jurisdiction, Ivan Egorovich maintained the contrary, while Peter Ivanovich, not having entered into the discussion at the start, took no part in it but looked through the *Gazette* which had just been handed in.

"Gentlemen," he said, "Ivan Ilych has died!"

"You don't say so!"

"Here, read it yourself," replied Peter Ivanovich, handing Fëdor Vasilievich the paper still damp from the press. Surrounded by a black border were the words: "Praskovya Fëdorovna Golovina, with profound sorrow, informs relatives and friends of the demise of her beloved husband Ivan Ilych Golovin, Member of the Court of Justice, which occurred on February the 4th of this year 1882. The funeral will take place on Friday at one o'clock in the afternoon."

Ivan Ilych had been a colleague of the gentlemen present and was liked by them all. He had been ill for some weeks with an illness said to be incurable. His post had been kept open for him, but there had been conjectures that in case of his death Alexeev might receive his appointment, and that either Vinnikov or Shtabel would succeed Alexeev. So on receiving the news of Ivan Ilych's death the first thought of each of the gentlemen in that private room was of the changes and promotions it might occasion among themselves or their acquaintances.

"I shall be sure to get Shtabel's place or Vinnikov's," thought Fëdor Vasilievich. "I was promised that long ago, and the promotion means an extra eight hundred rubles a year for me besides the allowance."

"Now I must apply for my brother-in-law's transfer from Kaluga," thought Peter Ivanovich. "My wife will be very glad, and then she won't be able to say that I never do anything for her relations."

"I thought he would never leave his bed again," said Peter Ivanovich aloud. "It's very sad."

"But what really was the matter with him?"

"The doctors couldn't say—at least they could, but each of them said something different. When last I saw him I thought he was getting better."

"And I haven't been to see him since the holidays. I always meant to go."

"Had he any property?"

"I think his wife had a little—but something quite trifling."

"We shall have to go to see her, but they live so terribly far away."

"Far away from you, you mean. Everything's far away from your place."

"You see, he never can forgive my living on the other

side of the river," said Peter Ivanovich, smiling at She-bek. Then, still talking of the distances between different parts of the city, they returned to the court.

Besides considerations as to the possible transfers and promotions likely to result from Ivan Ilych's death, the mere fact of the death of a near acquaintance aroused, as usual, in all who heard of it the complacent feeling that "it is he who is dead and not I."

Each one thought or felt, "Well, he's dead but I'm alive!" But the more intimate of Ivan Ilych's acquaintances, his so-called friends, could not help thinking also that they would now have to fulfil the very tiresome demands of propriety by attending the funeral service and paying a visit of condolence to the widow.

Fëdor Vasilievich and Peter Ivanovich had been his nearest acquaintances. Peter Ivanovich had studied law with Ivan Ilych and had considered himself to be under obligations to him.

Having told his wife at dinner-time of Ivan Ilych's death and of his conjecture that it might be possible to get her brother transferred to their circuit, Peter Ivanovich sacrificed his usual nap, put on his evening clothes, and drove to Ivan Ilych's house.

At the entrance stood a carriage and two cabs. Leaning against the wall in the hall downstairs near the cloak-stand was a coffin-lid covered with cloth of gold, ornamented with gold cord and tassels, that had been polished up with metal powder. Two ladies in black were taking off their fur cloaks. Peter Ivanovich recognized one of them as Ivan Ilych's sister, but the other was a stranger to him. His colleague Schwartz was just coming downstairs, but on seeing Peter Ivanovich enter he stopped and winked at him, as if to say: "Ivan Ilych has made a mess of things—not like you and me."

Schwartz's face, with his Piccadilly whiskers and his slim figure in evening dress, had as usual an air of elegant solemnity which contrasted with the playfulness of his character and had a special piquancy here, or so it seemed to Peter Ivanovich.

Peter Ivanovich allowed the ladies to precede him and slowly followed them upstairs. Schwartz did not come down but remained where he was, and Peter Ivanovich understood that he wanted to arrange where they should play bridge that evening. The ladies went upstairs to the widow's room, and Schwartz with seriously compressed lips but a playful look in his eyes, indicated by a twist of his eyebrows the room to the right where the body lay.

Peter Ivanovich, like everyone else on such occasions, entered feeling uncertain what he would have to do. All he knew was that at such times it is always safe to cross oneself. But he was not quite sure whether one should make obeisances while doing so. He therefore adopted a middle course. On entering the room he began crossing himself and made a slight movement resembling a bow. At the same time, as far as the motion of his head and arm allowed, he surveyed the room. Two young men— apparently nephews, one of whom was a high school pupil—were leaving the room, crossing themselves as they did so. An old woman was standing motionless, and a lady with strangely arched eyebrows was saying something to her in a whisper. A vigorous, resolute Church Reader, in a frock-coat, was reading something in a loud voice with an expression that precluded any contradiction. The butler's assistant, Gerasim, stepping lightly in front of Peter Ivanovich, was strewing something on the floor. Noticing this, Peter Ivanovich was immediately aware of a faint odour of a decomposing body.

The last time he had called on Ivan Ilych, Peter Ivanovich had seen Gerasim in the study. Ivan Ilych had been particularly fond of him and he was performing the duty of a sick nurse.

Peter Ivanovich continued to make the sign of the cross, slightly inclining his head in an intermediate direction between the coffin, the Reader, and the icons on the table in a corner of the room. Afterwards, when it seemed to him that this movement of his arm in crossing himself had gone on too long, he stopped and began to look at the corpse.

The dead man lay, as dead men always lie, in a specially heavy way, his rigid limbs sunk in the soft cushions of the coffin, with the head forever bowed on the pillow. His yellow waxen brow with bald patches over his sunken temples was thrust up in the way peculiar to the dead, the protruding nose seeming to press on the upper lip. He was much changed and had grown even thinner since Peter Ivanovich had last seen him, but, as is always the case with the dead, his face was handsomer and above all more dignified than when he was alive. The expression on the face said that what was necessary had been accomplished, and accomplished rightly. Besides this there was in that expression a reproach and a warning to the living. This warning seemed to Peter Ivanovich out of place, or at least not applicable to him. He felt a certain discomfort and so he hurriedly crossed himself once more and turned and went out of the door—too hurriedly and too regardless of propriety, as he himself was aware.

Schwartz was waiting for him in the adjoining room with legs spread wide apart and both hands toying with his top-hat behind his back. The mere sight of that playful, well-groomed, and elegant figure refreshed Peter Ivanovich. He felt that Schwartz was above all these happenings and would not surrender to any depressing influences. His very look said that this incident of a church service for Ivan Ilych could not be a sufficient reason for infringing the order of the session—in other words, that it would certainly not prevent his unwrapping a new pack of cards and shuffling them that evening while a footman placed four fresh candles on the table: in fact, that there was no reason for supposing that this incident would hinder their spending the evening agreeably. Indeed he said this in a whisper as Peter Ivanovich passed him, proposing that they should meet for a game at Fëdor Vasilievich's. But apparently Peter Ivanovich was not destined to play bridge that evening. Praskovya Fëdorovna (a short, fat woman who despite all efforts to the contrary had continued to broaden steadily from her shoulders downwards and who had the same extraordinarily arched eyebrows as the lady who had been standing by the coffin), dressed all in black, her head covered with lace, came out of her own room with some other ladies, conducted them to the room where the dead body lay, and said: "The service will begin immediately. Please go in."

Schwartz, making an indefinite bow, stood still, evidently neither accepting nor declining this invitation. Praskovya Fëdorovna, recognizing Peter Ivanovich, sighed, went close up to him, took his hand, and said: "I know you were a true friend to Ivan Ilych . . ." and looked at him awaiting some suitable response. And Peter Ivanovich knew that, just as it had been the right thing to cross himself in that room, so what he had to do here was to press her hand, sigh, and say, "Believe me. . . ." So he did all this and as he did it felt that the desired result had been achieved: that both he and she were touched.

"Come with me. I want to speak to you before it begins," said the widow. "Give me your arm."

Peter Ivanovich gave her his arm and they went to the inner rooms, passing Schwartz, who winked at Peter Ivanovich compassionately.

"That does for our bridge! Don't object if we find another player. Perhaps you can cut in when you do escape," said his playful look.

Peter Ivanovich sighed still more deeply and despondently, and Praskovya Fëdorovna pressed his arm gratefully. When they reached the drawing-room, upholstered in pink cretonne and lighted by a dim lamp, they sat down at the table—she on a sofa and Peter Ivanovich on a low pouffe, the springs of which yielded spasmodically under his weight. Praskovya Fëdorovna had been on the point of warning him to take another seat, but felt that such a warning was out of keeping with her present condition and so changed her mind. As he sat down on the pouffe Peter Ivanovich recalled how Ivan Ilych had arranged this room and had consulted him regarding this pink cretonne, with green leaves. The whole room was full of furniture and knick-knacks, and on her way to the sofa the lace of the widow's black shawl caught on the carved edge of the table. Peter Ivanovich rose to detach it, and the springs of the pouffe, relieved of his weight, rose also and gave him a push. The widow began detaching her shawl herself, and Peter Ivanovich again sat down, suppressing the rebellious springs of the pouffe under him. But the widow had not quite freed herself and Peter Ivanovich got up again, and again the pouffe rebelled and even creaked. When this was all over she took out a clean cambric handkerchief and began to weep. The episode with the shawl and the struggle with the pouffe had cooled Peter Ivanovich's emotions and he sat there with a sullen look on his face. This awkward situation was interrupted by Sokolov, Ivan Ilych's butler, who came to report that the plot in the cemetery that Praskovya Fëdorovna had chosen would cost two hundred rubles. She stopped weeping and, looking at Peter Ivanovich with the air of a victim, remarked in French that it was very hard for her. Peter Ivanovich made a silent gesture signifying his full conviction that it must indeed be so.

"Please smoke," she said in a magnanimous yet crushed voice, and turned to discuss with Sokolov the price of the plot for the grave.

Peter Ivanovich while lighting his cigarette heard her inquiring very circumstantially into the prices of different plots in the cemetery and finally decide which she would take. When that was done she gave instructions about engaging the choir. Sokolov then left the room.

"I look after everything myself," she told Peter Ivanovich, shifting the albums that lay on the table; and noticing that the table was endangered by his cigarette-ash, she immediately passed him an ash-tray, saying as she did so: "I consider it an affectation to say that my grief prevents my attending to practical affairs. On the contrary, if anything can—I won't say console me, but—distract me, it is seeing to everything concerning him."

She again took out her handkerchief as if preparing to cry, but suddenly, as if mastering her feeling, she shook herself and began to speak calmly. "But there is something I want to talk to you about."

Peter Ivanovich bowed, keeping control of the springs of the pouffe, which immediately began quivering under him.

"He suffered terribly the last few days."

"Did he?" said Peter Ivanovich.

"Oh, terribly! He screamed unceasingly, not for minutes but for hours. For the last three days he screamed incessantly. It was unendurable. I cannot understand how I bore it; you could hear him three rooms off. Oh, what I have suffered!"

"Is it possible that he was conscious all that time?" asked Peter Ivanovich.

"Yes," she whispered. "To the last moment. He took leave of us a quarter of an hour before he died, and asked us to take Volodya away."

The thought of the sufferings of this man he had known so intimately, first as a merry little boy, then as a schoolmate, and later as a grown-up colleague, suddenly struck Peter Ivanovich with horror, despite an unpleasant consciousness of his own and this woman's dissimulation. He again saw that brow, and that nose pressing down on the lip, and felt afraid for himself.

"Three days of frightful suffering and then death! Why, that might suddenly, at any time, happen to me," he thought, and for a moment felt terrified. But—he did not himself know how—the customary reflection at once occurred to him that this had happened to Ivan Ilych and not to him, and that it should not and could not happen to him, and that to think that it could would be yielding to depression which he ought not to do, as Schwartz's expression plainly showed. After which reflection Peter Ivanovich felt reassured, and began to ask with interest about the details of Ivan Ilych's death, as though death was an accident natural to Ivan Ilych but certainly not to himself.

After many details of the really dreadful physical sufferings Ivan Ilych had endured (which details he learnt
only from the effect those sufferings had produced on
Praskovya Fëdorovna's nerves), the widow apparently
found it necessary to get to business.

"Oh, Peter Ivanovich, how hard it is! How terribly,
terribly hard!" and she again began to weep.

Peter Ivanovich sighed and waited for her to finish
blowing her nose. When she had done so he said, "Believe me . . ." and she again began talking and brought
out what was evidently her chief concern with him—
namely, to question him as to how she could obtain a
grant of money from the government on the occasion of
her husband's death. She made it appear that she was
asking Peter Ivanovich's advice about her pension, but
he soon saw that she already knew about that to the mi-
nutest detail, more even than he did himself. She knew
how much could be got out of the government in consequence of her husband's death, but wanted to find out
whether she could not possibly extract something more.
Peter Ivanovich tried to think of some means of doing so,
but after reflecting for a while and, out of propriety, con-
demning the government for its niggardliness, he said he
thought that nothing more could be got. Then she sighed
and evidently began to devise means of getting rid of her
visitor. Noticing this, he put out his cigarette, rose,
pressed her hand, and went out into the anteroom.

In the dining-room where the clock stood that Ivan
Ilych had liked so much and had bought at an antique
shop, Peter Ivanovich met a priest and a few acquaintances who had come to attend the service, and he recognized Ivan Ilych's daughter, a handsome young
woman. She was in black and her slim figure appeared
slimmer than ever. She had a gloomy, determined, almost angry expression, and bowed to Peter Ivanovich as
though he were in some way to blame. Behind her, with
the same offended look, stood a wealthy young man, an
examining magistrate, whom Peter Ivanovich also knew
and who was her fiancé, as he had heard. He bowed

mournfully to them and was about to pass into the death-chamber, when from under the stairs appeared the figure of Ivan Ilych's schoolboy son, who was extremely like his father. He seemed a little Ivan Ilych, such as Peter Ivanovich remembered when they studied law together. His tearstained eyes had in them the look that is seen in the eyes of boys of thirteen or fourteen who are not pure-minded. When he saw Peter Ivanovich he scowled morosely and shamefacedly. Peter Ivanovich nodded to him and entered the death-chamber. The service began: candles, groans, incense, tears, and sobs. Peter Ivanovich stood looking gloomily down at his feet. He did not look once at the dead man, did not yield to any depressing influence, and was one of the first to leave the room. There was no one in the anteroom, but Gerasim darted out of the dead man's room, rummaged with his strong hands among the fur coats to find Peter Ivanovich's and helped him on with it.

"Well, friend Gerasim," said Peter Ivanovich, so as to say something. "It's a sad affair, isn't it?"

"It's God's will. We shall all come to it some day," said Gerasim, displaying his teeth—the even, white teeth of a healthy peasant—and, like a man in the thick of urgent work, he briskly opened the front door, called the coachman, helped Peter Ivanovich into the sledge, and sprang back to the porch as if in readiness for what he had to do next.

Peter Ivanovich found the fresh air particularly pleasant after the smell of incense, the dead body, and carbolic acid.

"Where to, sir?" asked the coachman.

"It's not too late even now. . . . I'll call round on Fëdor Vasilievich."

He accordingly drove there and found them just finishing the first rubber, so that it was quite convenient for him to cut in.

ii

IVAN ILYCH'S life had been most simple and most ordinary and therefore most terrible.

He had been a member of the Court of Justice, and died at the age of forty-five. His father had been an official who after serving in various ministries and departments in Petersburg had made the sort of career which brings men to positions from which by reason of their long service they cannot be dismissed, though they are obviously unfit to hold any responsible position, and for whom therefore posts are specially created, which though fictitious carry salaries of from six to ten thousand rubles that are not fictitious, and in receipt of which they live on to a great age.

Such was the Privy Councillor and superfluous member of various superfluous institutions, Ilya Epimovich Golovin.

He had three sons, of whom Ivan Ilych was the second. The eldest son was following in his father's footsteps only in another department, and was already approaching that stage in the service at which a similar sinecure would be reached. The third son was a failure. He had ruined his prospects in a number of positions and was now serving in the railway department. His father and brothers, and still more their wives, not merely disliked meeting him, but avoided remembering his existence unless compelled to do so. His sister had married Baron Greff, a Petersburg official of her father's type. Ivan Ilych was *le phénix de la famille* as people said. He was neither as cold and formal as his elder brother nor as wild as the younger, but was a happy mean between them—an intelligent, polished, lively and agreeable man. He had studied with his younger brother at the School of Law, but the latter had failed to complete the course and was expelled when he was in the fifth class. Ivan Ilych finished the course well. Even when he was at the School of Law he was just what he remained for the rest of his life: a capable, cheerful, good-natured, and sociable man, though strict in the fulfilment of what he considered to be his duty: and he considered his duty to be what was so considered by those in authority. Neither as a boy nor as a man was he a toady, but from early youth was by nature attracted to people of high station as a fly is drawn to the light, assimilating their ways and views of life and establishing friendly relations with them. All the enthusiasms of childhood and youth passed without leaving much trace on him; he succumbed to sensuality, to vanity, and latterly among the highest classes to liberalism, but always within limits which his instinct unfailingly indicated to him as correct.

At school he had done things which had formerly seemed to him very horrid and made him feel disgusted with himself when he did them; but when later on he saw that such actions were done by people of good position and that they did not regard them as wrong, he was able not exactly to regard them as right, but to forget about them entirely or not be at all troubled at remembering them.

Having graduated from the School of Law and qualified for the tenth rank of the civil service, and having received money from his father for his equipment, Ivan Ilych ordered himself clothes at Scharmer's, the fashionable tailor, hung a medallion inscribed *respice finem* on his watch-chain, took leave of his professor and the prince who was patron of the school, had a farewell dinner with his comrades at Donon's first-class restaurant, and with his new and fashionable portmanteau, linen, clothes, shaving and other toilet appliances, and a travelling rug, all purchased at the best shops, he set off for one of the provinces where, through his father's influence, he had been attached to the governor as an official for special service.

In the province Ivan Ilych soon arranged as easy and agreeable a position for himself as he had had at the School of Law. He performed his official tasks, made his career, and at the same time amused himself pleasantly and decorously. Occasionally he paid official visits to country districts, where he behaved with dignity both to his superiors and inferiors, and performed the duties entrusted to him, which related chiefly to the sectarians, with an exactness and incorruptible honesty of which he could not but feel proud.

In official matters, despite his youth and taste for frivolous gaiety, he was exceedingly reserved, punctilious, and even severe; but in society he was often amusing and witty, and always good-natured, correct in his manner, and *bon enfant,* as the governor and his wife—with whom he was like one of the family—used to say of him.

In the province he had an affair with a lady who made advances to the elegant young lawyer, and there was also a milliner; and there were carousals with aides-de-camp who visited the district, and after-supper visits to a certain outlying street of doubtful reputation; and there was too some obsequiousness to his chief and even to his chief's wife, but all this was done with such a tone of good breeding that no hard names could be applied to it. It all came under the heading of the French saying: *"Il faut que jeunesse se passe."** It was all done with clean hands, in clean linen, with French phrases, and above all among people of the best society and consequently with the approval of people of rank.

So Ivan Ilych served for five years and then came a change in his official life. The new and reformed judicial institutions were introduced, and new men were needed. Ivan Ilych became such a new man. He was offered the post of examining magistrate, and he accepted it though the post was in another province and obliged him to give up the connexions he had formed and to make new ones. His friends met to give him a send-off; they had a group photograph taken and presented him with a silver cigarette-case, and he set off to his new post.

As examining magistrate Ivan Ilych was just as *comme il faut* and decorous a man, inspiring general respect and capable of separating his official duties from his private

*Youth must have its fling.

life, as he had been when acting as an official on special service. His duties now as examining magistrate were far more interesting and attractive than before. In his former position it had been pleasant to wear an undress uniform made by Scharmer, and to pass through the crowd of petitioners and officials who were timorously awaiting an audience with the governor, and who envied him as with free and easy gait he went straight into his chief's private room to have a cup of tea and a cigarette with him. But not many people had then been directly dependent on him—only police officials and the sectarians when he went on special missions—and he liked to treat them politely, almost as comrades, as if he were letting them feel that he who had the power to crush them was treating them in this simple, friendly way. There were then but few such people. But now, as an examining magistrate, Ivan Ilych felt that everyone without exception, even the most important and self-satisfied, was in his power, and that he need only write a few words on a sheet of paper with a certain heading, and this or that important, self-satisfied person would be brought before him in the role of an accused person or a witness, and if he did not choose to allow him to sit down, would have to stand before him and answer his questions. Ivan Ilych never abused his power; he tried on the contrary to soften its expression, but the consciousness of it and of the possibility of softening its effect supplied the chief interest and attraction of his office. In his work itself, especially in his examinations, he very soon acquired a method of eliminating all considerations irrelevant to the legal aspect of the case, and reducing even the most complicated case to a form in which it would be presented on paper only in its externals, completely excluding his personal opinion of the matter, while above all observing every prescribed formality. The work was new and Ivan Ilych was one of the first men to apply the new Code of 1864.*

---

*The emancipation of the serfs in 1861 was followed by a thorough all-round reform of judicial proceedings. A.M.

On taking up the post of examining magistrate in a new town, he made new acquaintances and connexions, placed himself on a new footing, and assumed a somewhat different tone. He took up an attitude of rather dignified aloofness towards the provincial authorities, but picked out the best circle of legal gentlemen and wealthy gentry living in the town and assumed a tone of slight dissatisfaction with the government, of moderate liberalism, and of enlightened citizenship. At the same time, without at all altering the elegance of his toilet, he ceased shaving his chin and allowed his beard to grow as it pleased.

Ivan Ilych settled down very pleasantly in this new town. The society there, which inclined towards opposition to the governor, was friendly, his salary was larger, and he began to play *vint* [a form of bridge], which he found added not a little to the pleasure of life, for he had a capacity for cards, played good-humouredly, and calculated rapidly and astutely, so that he usually won.

After living there for two years he met his future wife, Praskovya Fëdorovna Mikhel, who was the most attractive, clever, and brilliant girl of the set in which he moved, and among other amusements and relaxations from his labours as examining magistrate, Ivan Ilych established light and playful relations with her.

While he had been an official on special service he had been accustomed to dance, but now as an examining magistrate it was exceptional for him to do so. If he danced now, he did it as if to show that though he served under the reformed order of things, and had reached the fifth official rank, yet when it came to dancing he could do it better than most people. So at the end of an evening he sometimes danced with Praskovya Fëdorovna, and it was chiefly during these dances that he captivated her. She fell in love with him. Ivan Ilych had at first no definite intention of marrying, but when the girl fell in love with him he said to himself: "Really, why shouldn't I marry?"

Praskovya Fëdorovna came of a good family, was not

bad looking, and had some little property. Ivan Ilych might have aspired to a more brilliant match, but even this was good. He had his salary, and she, he hoped, would have an equal income. She was well connected, and was a sweet, pretty, and thoroughly correct young woman. To say that Ivan Ilych married because he fell in love with Praskovya Fëdorovna and found that she sympathized with his views of life would be as incorrect as to say that he married because his social circle approved of the match. He was swayed by both these considerations: the marriage gave him personal satisfaction, and at the same time it was considered the right thing by the most highly placed of his associates.

So Ivan Ilych got married.

The preparations for marriage and the beginning of married life, with its conjugal caresses, the new furniture, new crockery, and new linen, were very pleasant until his wife became pregnant—so that Ivan Ilych had begun to think that marriage would not impair the easy, agreeable, gay and always decorous character of his life, approved of by society and regarded by himself as natural, but would even improve it. But from the first months of his wife's pregnancy, something new, unpleasant, depressing, and unseemly, and from which there was no way of escape, unexpectedly showed itself.

His wife, without any reason—*de gaieté de cœur* as Ivan Ilych expressed it to himself—began to disturb the pleasure and propriety of their life. She began to be jealous without any cause, expected him to devote his whole attention to her, found fault with everything, and made coarse and ill-mannered scenes.

At first Ivan Ilych hoped to escape from the unpleasantness of this state of affairs by the same easy and decorous relation to life that had served him heretofore: he tried to ignore his wife's disagreeable moods, continued to live in his usual easy and pleasant way, invited friends to his house for a game of cards, and also tried going out to his club or spending his evenings with friends. But one day his wife began upbraiding him so vigorously, using such coarse words, and continued to abuse him every time he did not fulfil her demands, so resolutely and with such evident determination not to give way till he submitted—that is, till he stayed at home and was bored just as she was—that he became alarmed. He now realized that matrimony—at any rate with Praskovya Fëdorovna—was not always conducive to the pleasures and amenities of life, but on the contrary often infringed both comfort and propriety, and that he must therefore entrench himself against such infringement. And Ivan Ilych began to seek for means of doing so. His official duties were the one thing that imposed upon Praskovya Fëdorovna, and by means of his official work and the duties attached to it he began struggling with his wife to secure his own independence.

With the birth of their child, the attempts to feed it and the various failures in doing so, and with the real and imaginary illnesses of mother and child, in which Ivan Ilych's sympathy was demanded but about which he understood nothing, the need of securing for himself an existence outside his family life became still more imperative.

As his wife grew more irritable and exacting and Ivan Ilych transferred the centre of gravity of his life more and more to his official work, so did he grow to like his work better and became more ambitious than before.

Very soon, within a year of his wedding, Ivan Ilych had realized that marriage, though it may add some comforts to life, is in fact a very intricate and difficult affair towards which in order to perform one's duty, that is, to lead a decorous life approved of by society, one must adopt a definite attitude just as towards one's official duties.

And Ivan Ilych evolved such an attitude towards married life. He only required of it those conveniences—dinner at home, housewife, and bed—which it could give him, and above all that propriety of external forms required by public opinion. For the rest he looked for light-hearted pleasure and propriety, and was very thankful when he found them, but if he met with antagonism and querulousness he at once retired into his separate fenced-off world of official duties, where he found satisfaction.

Ivan Ilych was esteemed a good official, and after three years was made Assistant Public Prosecutor. His new duties, their importance, the possibility of indicting and imprisoning anyone he chose, the publicity his speeches received, and the success he had in all these things, made his work still more attractive.

More children came. His wife became more and more querulous and ill-tempered, but the attitude Ivan Ilych had adopted towards his home life rendered him almost impervious to her grumbling.

After seven years' service in that town he was transferred to another province as Public Prosecutor. They moved, but were short of money and his wife did not like the place they moved to. Though the salary was higher the cost of living was greater, besides which two of their children died and family life became still more unpleasant for him.

Praskovya Fëdorovna blamed her husband for every inconvenience they encountered in their new home. Most of the conversations between husband and wife, especially as to the children's education, led to topics which recalled former disputes, and those disputes were apt to flare up again at any moment. There remained only those rare periods of amorousness which still came to them at times but did not last long. These were islets at which they anchored for a while and then again set out upon that ocean of veiled hostility which showed itself in their aloofness from one another. This aloofness might have grieved Ivan Ilych had he considered that it ought not to exist, but he now regarded the position as normal, and even made it the goal at which he aimed in family life. His aim was to free himself more and more from those unpleasantnesses and to give them a semblance of harmlessness and propriety. He attained this by spending less and less time with his family, and when obliged to be at home he tried to safeguard his position by the presence of outsiders. The chief thing, however, was that he had his official duties. The whole interest of his life now centred in the official world and that interest absorbed him. The consciousness of his power, being able to ruin anybody he wished to ruin, the importance, even the external dignity of his entry into court, or meetings with his subordinates, his success with superiors and inferiors, and above all his masterly handling of cases, of which he was conscious—all this gave him pleasure and filled his life, together with chats with his colleagues, dinners, and bridge. So that on the whole Ivan Ilych's life continued to flow as he considered it should do—pleasantly and properly.

So things continued for another seven years. His eldest daughter was already sixteen, another child had died, and only one son was left, a schoolboy and a subject of dissension. Ivan Ilych wanted to put him in the School of Law, but to spite him Praskovya Fëdorovna entered him at the high school. The daughter had been educated at home and had turned out well: the boy did not learn badly either.

iii

So Ivan Ilych lived for seventeen years after his marriage. He was already a Public Prosecutor of long standing, and had declined several proposed transfers while awaiting a more desirable post, when an unanticipated and unpleasant occurrence quite upset the peaceful course of his life. He was expecting to be offered the post of presiding judge in a University town, but Happe somehow came to the front and obtained the appointment instead. Ivan Ilych became irritable, reproached Happe, and quarrelled both with him and with his immediate superiors—who became colder to him and again passed him over when other appointments were made.

This was in 1880, the hardest year of Ivan Ilych's life. It was then that it became evident on the one hand that his salary was insufficient for them to live on, and on the other that he had been forgotten, and not only this, but that what was for him the greatest and most cruel injustice appeared to others a quite ordinary occurrence. Even his father did not consider it his duty to help him. Ivan Ilych felt himself abandoned by everyone, and that they regarded his position with a salary of three thousand five hundred rubles as quite normal and even fortunate. He alone knew that with the consciousness of the injustices done him, with his wife's incessant nagging, and with the debts he had contracted by living beyond his means, his position was far from normal.

In order to save money that summer he obtained leave of absence and went with his wife to live in the country at her brother's place.

In the country, without his work, he experienced *ennui* for the first time in his life, and not only *ennui* but intolerable depression, and he decided that it was impossible to go on living like that, and that it was necessary to take energetic measures.

Having passed a sleepless night pacing up and down the veranda, he decided to go to Petersburg and bestir himself, in order to punish those who had failed to appreciate him and to get transferred to another ministry.

Next day, despite many protests from his wife and her brother, he started for Petersburg with the sole object of obtaining a post with a salary of five thousand rubles a year. He was no longer bent on any particular department, or tendency, or kind of activity. All he now wanted was an appointment to another post with a salary of five thousand rubles, either in the administration, in the banks, with the railways, in one of the Empress Marya's Institutions, or even in the customs — but it had to carry with it a salary of five thousand rubles and be in a ministry other than that in which they had failed to appreciate him.

And this quest of Ivan Ilych's was crowned with remarkable and unexpected success. At Kursk an acquaintance of his, F. I. Ilyin, got into the first-class carriage, sat down beside Ivan Ilych, and told him of a telegram just received by the Governor of Kursk announcing that a change was about to take place in the ministry: Peter Ivanovich was to be superseded by Ivan Semënovich.

The proposed change, apart from its significance for Russia, had a special significance for Ivan Ilych, because by bringing forward a new man, Peter Petrovich, and consequently his friend Zachar Ivanovich, it was highly favourable for Ivan Ilych, since Zachar Ivanovich was a friend and colleague of his.

In Moscow this news was confirmed, and on reaching Petersburg Ivan Ilych found Zachar Ivanovich and received a definite promise of an appointment in his former department of Justice.

A week later he telegraphed to his wife: "Zachar in Miller's place. I shall receive appointment on presentation of report."

Thanks to this change of personnel, Ivan Ilych had unexpectedly obtained an appointment in his former ministry which placed him two stages above his former colleagues besides giving him five thousand rubles salary and three thousand five hundred rubles for expenses connected with his removal. All his ill humour towards his former enemies and the whole department vanished, and Ivan Ilych was completely happy.

He returned to the country more cheerful and contented than he had been for a long time. Praskovya Fëdorovna also cheered up and a truce was arranged between them. Ivan Ilych told of how he had been fêted by everybody in Petersburg, how all those who had been his enemies were put to shame and now fawned on him, how envious they were of his appointment, and how much everybody in Petersburg had liked him.

Praskovya Fëdorovna listened to all this and appeared to believe it. She did not contradict anything, but only made plans for their life in the town to which they were going. Ivan Ilych saw with delight that these plans were his plans, that he and his wife agreed, and that, after a stumble, his life was regaining its due and natural character of pleasant lightheartedness and decorum.

Ivan Ilych had come back for a short time only, for he had to take up his new duties on the 10th of September. Moreover, he needed time to settle into the new place, to move all his belongings from the province, and to buy and order many additional things: in a word, to make such arrangements as he had resolved on, which were almost exactly what Praskovya Fëdorovna too had decided on.

Now that everything had happened so fortunately, and that he and his wife were at one in their aims and moreover saw so little of one another, they got on together better than they had done since the first years of marriage. Ivan Ilych had thought of taking his family away with him at once, but the insistence of his wife's brother and her sister-in-law, who had suddenly become particularly amiable and friendly to him and his family, induced him to depart alone.

So he departed, and the cheerful state of mind induced by his success and by the harmony between his wife and himself, the one intensifying the other, did not leave him. He found a delightful house, just the thing both he and his wife had dreamt of. Spacious, lofty reception rooms in the old style, a convenient and dignified study, rooms for his wife and daughter, a study for his son—it might have been specially built for them. Ivan Ilych himself superintended the arrangements, chose the wallpapers, supplemented the furniture (preferably with antiques which he considered particularly *comme il faut*), and supervised the upholstering. Everything progressed and progressed and approached the ideal he had set himself: even when things were only half completed they exceeded his expectations. He saw what a refined and elegant character, free from vulgarity, it would all have when it was ready. On falling asleep he pictured to himself how the reception-room would look. Looking at the yet unfinished drawing-room he could see the fire-

place, the screen, the what-not, the little chairs dotted
here and there, the dishes and plates on the walls, and
the bronzes, as they would be when everything was in
place. He was pleased by the thought of how his wife and
daughter, who shared his taste in this matter, would be
impressed by it. They were certainly not expecting as
much. He had been particularly successful in finding, and
buying cheaply, antiques which gave a particularly aristocratic character to the whole place. But in his letters he
intentionally understated everything in order to be able
to surprise them. All this so absorbed him that his new
duties—though he liked his official work—interested
him less than he had expected. Sometimes he even had
moments of absent-mindedness during the court sessions, and would consider whether he should have
straight or curved cornices for his curtains. He was so
interested in it all that he often did things himself, rear-
ranging the furniture, or rehanging the curtains. Once
when mounting a stepladder to show the upholsterer,
who did not understand, how he wanted the hangings
draped, he made a false step and slipped, but being a
strong and agile man he clung on and only knocked his
side against the knob of the window frame. The bruised
place was painful but the pain soon passed, and he felt
particularly bright and well just then. He wrote: "I feel
fifteen years younger." He thought he would have everything ready by September, but it dragged on till mid-
October. But the result was charming not only in his
eyes but to everyone who saw it.

In reality it was just what is usually seen in the houses
of people of moderate means who want to appear rich,
and therefore succeed only in resembling others like
themselves: there were damasks, dark wood, plants, rugs,
and dull and polished bronzes—all the things people of
a certain class have in order to resemble other people of
that class. His house was so like the others that it would
never have been noticed, but to him it all seemed to be
quite exceptional. He was very happy when he met his
family at the station and brought them to the newly fur-

nished house all lit up, where a footman in a white tie opened the door into the hall decorated with plants, and when they went on into the drawing-room and the study, uttering exclamations of delight. He conducted them everywhere, drank in their praises eagerly, and beamed with pleasure. At tea that evening, when Praskovya Fëdorovna among other things asked him about his fall, he laughed and showed them how he had gone flying and had frightened the upholsterer.

"It's a good thing I'm a bit of an athlete. Another man might have been killed, but I merely knocked myself, just here; it hurts when it's touched, but it's passing off already—it's only a bruise."

So they began living in their new home—in which, as always happens, when they got thoroughly settled in they found they were just one room short—and with the increased income, which as always was just a little (some five hundred rubles) too little, but it was all very nice.

Things went particularly well at first, before everything was finally arranged and while something had still to be done: this thing bought, that thing ordered, another thing moved, and something else adjusted. Though there were some disputes between husband and wife, they were both so well satisfied and had so much to do that it all passed off without any serious quarrels. When nothing was left to arrange it became rather dull and something seemed to be lacking, but they were then making acquaintances, forming habits, and life was growing fuller.

Ivan Ilych spent his mornings at the law court and came home to dinner, and at first he was generally in a good humour, though he occasionally became irritable just on account of his house. (Every spot on the table-cloth or the upholstery, and every broken window-blind string, irritated him. He had devoted so much trouble to arranging it all that every disturbance of it distressed him.) But on the whole his life ran its course as he believed life should do: easily, pleasantly, and decorously.

He got up at nine, drank his coffee, read the paper,

and then put on his undress uniform and went to the law courts. There the harness in which he worked had already been stretched to fit him and he donned it without a hitch: petitioners, inquiries at the chancery, the chancery itself, and the sittings public and administrative. In all this the thing was to exclude everything fresh and vital, which always disturbs the regular course of official business, and to admit only official relations with people, and then only on official grounds. A man would come, for instance, wanting some information. Ivan Ilych, as one in whose sphere the matter did not lie, would have nothing to do with him: but if the man had some business with him in his official capacity, something that could be expressed on officially stamped paper, he would do everything, positively everything he could within the limits of such relations, and in doing so would maintain the semblance of friendly human relations, that is, would observe the courtesies of life. As soon as the official relations ended, so did everything else. Ivan Ilych possessed this capacity to separate his real life from the official side of affairs and not mix the two, in the highest degree, and by long practise and natural aptitude had brought it to such a pitch that sometimes, in the manner of a virtuoso, he would even allow himself to let the human and official relations mingle. He let himself do this just because he felt that he could at any time he chose resume the strictly official attitude again and drop the human relation. And he did it all easily, pleasantly, correctly, and even artistically. In the intervals between the sessions he smoked, drank tea, chatted a little about politics, a little about general topics, a little about cards, but most of all about official appointments. Tired, but with the feelings of a virtuoso—one of the first violins who has played his part in an orchestra with precision—he would return home to find that his wife and daughter had been out paying calls, or had a visitor, and that his son had been to school, had done his homework with his tutor, and was duly learning what is taught at high schools. Everything was as it should be. After dinner, if they had no visitors,

Ivan Ilych sometimes read a book that was being much discussed at the time, and in the evening settled down to work, that is, read official papers, compared the depositions of witnesses, and noted paragraphs of the Code applying to them. This was neither dull nor amusing. It was dull when he might have been playing bridge, but if no bridge was available it was at any rate better than doing nothing or sitting with his wife. Ivan Ilych's chief pleasure was giving little dinners to which he invited men and women of good social position, and just as his drawing-room resembled all other drawing-rooms so did his enjoyable little parties resemble all other such parties.

Once they even gave a dance. Ivan Ilych enjoyed it and everything went off well, except that it led to a violent quarrel with his wife about the cakes and sweets. Praskovya Fëdorovna had made her own plans, but Ivan Ilych insisted on getting everything from an expensive confectioner and ordered too many cakes, and the quarrel occurred because some of those cakes were left over and the confectioner's bill came to forty-five rubles. It was a great and disagreeable quarrel. Praskovya Fëdorovna called him "a fool and an imbecile," and he clutched at his head and made angry allusions to divorce.

But the dance itself had been enjoyable. The best people were there, and Ivan Ilych had danced with Princess Trufonova, a sister of the distinguished founder of the Society "Bear my Burden."

The pleasures connected with his work were pleasures of ambition; his social pleasures were those of vanity; but Ivan Ilych's greatest pleasure was playing bridge. He acknowledged that whatever disagreeable incident happened in his life, the pleasure that beamed like a ray of light above everything else was to sit down to bridge with good players, not noisy partners, and of course to four-handed bridge (with five players it was annoying to have to stand out, though one pretended not to mind), to play a clever and serious game (when the cards allowed it), and then to have supper and drink a glass of wine. After a game of bridge, especially if he had won a little (to win a large sum was unpleasant), Ivan Ilych went to bed in specially good humour.

So they lived. They formed a circle of acquaintances among the best people and were visited by people of importance and by young folk. In their views as to their acquaintances, husband, wife and daughter were entirely agreed, and tacitly and unanimously kept at arm's length and shook off the various shabby friends and relations who, with much show of affection, gushed into the drawing-room with its Japanese plates on the walls. Soon these shabby friends ceased to obtrude themselves and only the best people remained in the Golovins' set.

Young men made up to Lisa, and Petrishchev, an examining magistrate and Dmitri Ivanovich Petrishchev's son and sole heir, began to be so attentive to her that Ivan Ilych had already spoken to Praskovya Fëdorovna about it, and considered whether they should not arrange a party for them, or get up some private theatricals.

So they lived, and all went well, without change, and life flowed pleasantly.

iv

THEY WERE all in good health. It could not be called ill health if Ivan Ilych sometimes said that he had a queer taste in his mouth and felt some discomfort in his left side.

But this discomfort increased and, though not exactly painful, grew into a sense of pressure in his side accompanied by ill humour. And his irritability became worse and worse and began to mar the agreeable, easy, and correct life that had established itself in the Golovin family. Quarrels between husband and wife became more and more frequent, and soon the ease and amenity disappeared and even the decorum was barely maintained. Scenes again became frequent, and very few of those islets remained on which husband and wife could meet without an explosion. Praskovya Fëdorovna now had good reason to say that her husband's temper was trying. With characteristic exaggeration she said he had always had a dreadful temper, and that it had needed all her good nature to put up with it for twenty years. It was true that now the quarrels were started by him. His bursts of temper always came just before dinner, often just as he began to eat his soup. Sometimes he noticed that a plate or dish was chipped, or the food was not right, or his son put his elbow on the table, or his daughter's hair was not done as he liked it, and for all this he blamed Praskovya Fëdorovna. At first she retorted and said disagreeable things to him, but once or twice he fell into such a rage at the beginning of dinner that she realized it was due to some physical derangement brought on by taking food, and so she restrained herself and did not answer, but only hurried to get the dinner over. She regarded this self-restraint as highly praiseworthy. Having come to the conclusion that her husband had a dreadful temper and made her life miserable, she began to feel sorry for herself, and the more she pitied herself the more she hated her husband. She began to wish he would die; yet she did not want him to die because then his salary would cease. And this irritated her against him still more. She considered herself dreadfully unhappy just because not even his death could save her, and though she concealed her exasperation, that hidden exasperation of hers increased his irritation also.

After one scene in which Ivan Ilych had been particularly unfair and after which he had said in explanation that he certainly was irritable but that it was due to his not being well, she said that if he was ill it should be attended to, and insisted on his going to see a celebrated doctor.

He went. Everything took place as he had expected and as it always does. There was the usual waiting and the important air assumed by the doctor, with which he was so familiar (resembling that which he himself assumed in court), and the sounding and listening, and the

questions which called for answers that were foregone
conclusions and were evidently unnecessary, and the
look of importance which implied that "if only you put
yourself in our hands we will arrange everything—we
know indubitably how it has to be done, always in the
same way for everybody alike." It was all just as it was in
the law courts. The doctor put on just the same air
towards him as he himself put on towards an accused
person.

   The doctor said that so-and-so indicated that there
was so-and-so inside the patient, but if the investigation
of so-and-so did not confirm this, then he must assume
that and that. If he assumed that and that, then ... and so
on. To Ivan Ilych only one question was important: was
his case serious or not? But the doctor ignored that inappropriate question. From his point of view it was not the
one under consideration; the real question was to decide
between a floating kidney, chronic catarrh, or appendicitis. It was not a question of Ivan Ilych's life or death, but
one between a floating kidney and appendicitis. And
that question the doctor solved brilliantly, as it seemed
to Ivan Ilych, in favour of the appendix, with the reserva-
tion that should an examination of the urine give fresh
indications the matter would be reconsidered. All this
was just what Ivan Ilych had himself brilliantly accomplished a thousand times in dealing with men on trial.
The doctor summed up just as brilliantly, looking over
his spectacles triumphantly and even gaily at the accused. From the doctor's summing up Ivan Ilych concluded that things were bad, but that for the doctor, and
perhaps for everybody else, it was a matter of indifference, though for him it was bad. And this conclusion
struck him painfully, arousing in him a great feeling of
pity for himself and of bitterness towards the doctor's
indifference to a matter of such importance.

   He said nothing of this, but rose, placed the doctor's fee
on the table, and remarked with a sigh: "We sick people
probably often put inappropriate questions. But tell me,
in general, is this complaint dangerous, or not? ..."

The doctor looked at him sternly over his spectacles with one eye, as if to say: "Prisoner, if you will not keep to the questions put to you, I shall be obliged to have you removed from the court."

"I have already told you what I consider necessary and proper. The analysis may show something more." And the doctor bowed.

Ivan Ilych went out slowly, seated himself disconsolately in his sledge, and drove home. All the way home he was going over what the doctor had said, trying to translate those complicated, obscure, scientific phrases into plain language and find in them an answer to the question: "Is my condition bad? Is it very bad? Or is there as yet nothing much wrong?" And it seemed to him that the meaning of what the doctor had said was that it was very bad. Everything in the streets seemed depressing. The cabmen, the houses, the passers-by, and the shops were dismal. His ache, this dull gnawing ache that never ceased for a moment, seemed to have acquired a new and more serious significance from the doctor's dubious remarks. Ivan Ilych now watched it with a new and oppressive feeling.

He reached home and began to tell his wife about it. She listened, but in the middle of his account his daughter came in with her hat on, ready to go out with her mother. She sat down reluctantly to listen to this tedious story, but could not stand it long, and her mother too did not hear him to the end.

"Well, I am very glad," she said. "Mind now to take your medicine regularly. Give me the prescription and I'll send Gerasim to the chemist's." And she went to get ready to go out.

While she was in the room Ivan Ilych had hardly taken time to breathe, but he sighed deeply when she left it.

"Well," he thought, "perhaps it isn't so bad after all."

He began taking his medicine and following the doctor's directions, which had been altered after the examination of the urine. But then it happened that there was a contradiction between the indications drawn from the examination of the urine and the symptoms that showed themselves. It turned out that what was happening differed from what the doctor had told him, and that he had either forgotten, or blundered, or hidden something from him. He could not, however, be blamed for that, and Ivan Ilych still obeyed his orders implicitly and at first derived some comfort from doing so.

From the time of his visit to the doctor, Ivan Ilych's chief occupation was the exact fulfilment of the doctor's instructions regarding hygiene and the taking of medicine, and the observation of his pain and his excretions. His chief interests came to be people's ailments and people's health. When sickness, deaths, or recoveries were mentioned in his presence, especially when the illness resembled his own, he listened with agitation which he tried to hide, asked questions, and applied what he heard to his own case.

The pain did not grow less, but Ivan Ilych made efforts to force himself to think that he was better. And he could do this so long as nothing agitated him. But as soon as he had any unpleasantness with his wife, any lack of success in his official work, or held bad cards at bridge, he was at once acutely sensible of his disease. He had formerly borne such mischances, hoping soon to adjust what was wrong, to master it and attain success, or make a grand slam. But now every mischance upset him and plunged him into despair. He would say to himself: "There now, just as I was beginning to get better and the medicine had begun to take effect, comes this accursed misfortune, or unpleasantness. . . ." And he was furious with the mishap, or with the people who were causing the unpleasantness and killing him, for he felt that this fury was killing him but could not restrain it. One would have thought that it should have been clear to him that this exasperation with circumstances and people aggravated his illness, and that he ought therefore to ignore unpleasant occurrences. But he drew the very opposite conclusion: he said that he needed peace, and he watched for everything that might disturb it and became irritable at the slightest infringement of it. His condition was rendered worse by the fact that he read medical books and consulted doctors. The progress of his disease was so gradual that he could deceive himself when comparing one day with another—the difference was so slight. But when he consulted the doctors it seemed to him that he was getting worse, and even very rapidly. Yet despite this he was continually consulting them.

That month he went to see another celebrity, who told him almost the same as the first had done but put his questions rather differently, and the interview with this celebrity only increased Ivan Ilych's doubts and fears. A friend of a friend of his, a very good doctor, diagnosed his illness again quite differently from the others, and though he predicted recovery, his questions and suppositions bewildered Ivan Ilych still more and increased his doubts. A homoeopathist diagnosed the disease in yet another way, and prescribed medicine which Ivan Ilych took secretly for a week. But after a week, not feeling any improvement and having lost confidence both in the former doctor's treatment and in this one's, he became still more despondent. One day a lady acquaintance mentioned a cure effected by a wonder-working icon. Ivan Ilych caught himself listening attentively and beginning to believe that it had occurred. This incident alarmed him. "Has my mind really weakened to such an extent?" he asked himself. "Nonsense! It's all rubbish. I mustn't give way to nervous fears but having chosen a doctor must keep strictly to his treatment. That is what I will do. Now it's all settled. I won't think about it, but will follow the treatment seriously till summer, and then we shall see. From now there must be no more of this wavering!" This was easy to say but impossible to carry out. The pain in his side oppressed him and seemed to grow worse and more incessant, while the taste in his mouth grew stranger and stranger. It seemed to him that his breath had a disgusting smell, and he was conscious of a loss of appetite and strength. There was no deceiving himself: something terrible, new, and more important than anything before in his life was taking place within him of which he alone was aware. Those about him did not understand or would not understand it, but thought everything in the world was going on as usual. That tormented Ivan Ilych more than anything. He saw that his household, especially his wife and daughter who were in a perfect whirl of visiting, did not understand anything of it and were annoyed that he was so depressed and so exacting, as if he were to blame for it. Though they tried to disguise it he saw that he was an obstacle in their path, and that his wife had adopted a definite line in regard to his illness and kept to it regardless of anything he said or did. Her attitude was this: "You know," she would say to her friends, "Ivan Ilych can't do as other people do, and keep to the treatment prescribed for him. One day he'll take his drops and keep strictly to his diet and go to bed in good time, but the next day unless I watch him he'll suddenly forget his medicine, eat sturgeon—which is forbidden—and sit up playing cards till one o'clock in the morning."

"Oh, come, when was that?" Ivan Ilych would ask in vexation. "Only once at Peter Ivanovich's."

"And yesterday with Shebek."

"Well, even if I hadn't stayed up, this pain would have kept me awake."

"Be that as it may, you'll never get well like that, but will always make us wretched."

Praskovya Fëdorovna's attitude to Ivan Ilych's illness, as she expressed it both to others and to him, was that it was his own fault and was another of the annoyances he caused her. Ivan Ilych felt that this opinion escaped her involuntarily—but that did not make it easier for him.

At the law courts too, Ivan Ilych noticed, or thought he noticed, a strange attitude towards himself. It sometimes seemed to him that people were watching him inquisitively as a man whose place might soon be vacant. Then again, his friends would suddenly begin to chaff him in a friendly way about his low spirits, as if the awful, horrible, and unheard-of thing that was going on within him, incessantly gnawing at him and irresistibly drawing him away, was a very agreeable subject for jests. Schwartz in particular irritated him by his jocularity, vivacity, and *savoir-faire,* which reminded him of what he himself had been ten years ago.

Friends came to make up a set and they sat down to cards. They dealt, bending the new cards to soften them, and he sorted the diamonds in his hand and found he had seven. His partner said "No trumps" and supported him with two diamonds. What more could be wished for? It ought to be jolly and lively. They would make a grand slam. But suddenly Ivan Ilych was conscious of that gnawing pain, that taste in his mouth, and it seemed ridiculous that in such circumstances he should be pleased to make a grand slam.

He looked at his partner, Mikhail Mikhaylovich, who rapped the table with his strong hand and instead of snatching up the tricks pushed the cards courteously and indulgently towards Ivan Ilych that he might have the pleasure of gathering them up without the trouble of stretching out his hand for them. "Does he think I am too weak to stretch out my arm?" thought Ivan Ilych, and forgetting what he was doing he over-trumped his partner, missing the grand slam by three tricks. And what was most awful of all was that he saw how upset Mikhail Mikhaylovich was about it but did not himself care. And it was dreadful to realize why he did not care.

They all saw that he was suffering, and said: "We can stop if you are tired. Take a rest." Lie down? No, he was not at all tired, and he finished the rubber. All were gloomy and silent. Ivan Ilych felt that he had diffused this gloom over them and could not dispel it. They had supper and went away, and Ivan Ilych was left alone with the consciousness that his life was poisoned and was poisoning the lives of others, and that this poison did not weaken but penetrated more and more deeply into his whole being.

With this consciousness, and with physical pain besides the terror, he must go to bed, often to lie awake the greater part of the night. Next morning he had to get up again, dress, go to the law courts, speak, and write; or if he did not go out, spend at home those twenty-four hours a day each of which was a torture. And he had to live thus all alone on the brink of an abyss, with no one who understood or pitied him.

v

So ONE month passed and then another. Just before the New Year his brother-in-law came to town and stayed at their house. Ivan Ilych was at the law courts and Praskovya Fëdorovna had gone shopping. When Ivan Ilych came home and entered his study he found his brother-in-law there — a healthy, florid man — unpacking his portmanteau himself. He raised his head on hearing Ivan Ilych's footsteps and looked up at him for a moment without a word. That stare told Ivan Ilych everything. His brother-in-law opened his mouth to utter an exclamation of surprise but checked himself, and that action confirmed it all.

"I have changed, eh?"

"Yes, there is a change."

And after that, try as he would to get his brother-in-law to return to the subject of his looks, the latter would say nothing about it. Praskovya Fëdorovna came home and her brother went out to her. Ivan Ilych locked the door and began to examine himself in the glass, first full face, then in profile. He took up a portrait of himself taken with his wife, and compared it with what he saw in the glass. The change in him was immense. Then he bared his arms to the elbow, looked at them, drew the sleeves down again, sat down on an ottoman, and grew blacker than night.

"No, no, this won't do!" he said to himself, and jumped up, went to the table, took up some law papers and began to read them, but could not continue. He unlocked the door and went into the reception-room. The door leading to the drawing-room was shut. He approached it on tiptoe and listened.

"No, you are exaggerating!" Praskovya Fëdorovna was saying.

"Exaggerating! Don't you see it? Why, he's a dead man! Look at his eyes—there's no light in them. But what is it that is wrong with him?"

"No one knows. Nikolaevich [that was another doctor] said something, but I don't know what. And Leshchetitsky [this was the celebrated specialist] said quite the contrary . . ."

Ivan Ilych walked away, went to his own room, lay down, and began musing: "The kidney, a floating kidney." He recalled all the doctors had told him of how it detached itself and swayed about. And by an effort of imagination he tried to catch that kidney and arrest it and support it. So little was needed for this, it seemed to him. "No, I'll go to see Peter Ivanovich again." [That was the friend whose friend was a doctor.] He rang, ordered the carriage, and got ready to go.

"Where are you going, Jean?" asked his wife, with a specially sad and exceptionally kind look.

This exceptionally kind look irritated him. He looked morosely at her.

"I must go to see Peter Ivanovich."

He went to see Peter Ivanovich, and together they went to see his friend, the doctor. He was in, and Ivan Ilych had a long talk with him.

Reviewing the anatomical and physiological details of what in the doctor's opinion was going on inside him, he understood it all.

There was something, a small thing, in the vermiform appendix. It might all come right. Only stimulate the energy of one organ and check the activity of another, then absorption would take place and everything would come right. He got home rather late for dinner, ate his dinner, and conversed cheerfully, but could not for a long time bring himself to go back to work in his room. At last, however, he went to his study and did what was neces-

sary, but the consciousness that he had put something
aside—an important, intimate matter which he would
revert to when his work was done—never left him. When
he had finished his work he remembered that this intimate matter was the thought of his vermiform appendix.
But he did not give himself up to it, and went to the
drawing-room for tea. There were callers there, including
the examining magistrate who was a desirable match for
his daughter, and they were conversing, playing the piano, and singing. Ivan Ilych, as Praskovya Fëdorovna
remarked, spent that evening more cheerfully than usual,
but he never for a moment forgot that he had postponed
the important matter of the appendix. At eleven o'clock
he said good night and went to his bedroom. Since his
illness he had slept alone in a small room next to his study.
He undressed and took up a novel by Zola, but instead
of reading it he fell into thought, and in his imagination
that desired improvement in the vermiform appendix
occurred. There was the absorption and evacuation and
the reestablishment of normal activity. "Yes, that's it!" he
said to himself. "One need only assist nature, that's all."
He remembered his medicine, rose, took it, and lay down
on his back watching for the beneficent action of the
medicine and for it to lessen the pain. "I need only take
it regularly and avoid all injurious influences. I am already feeling better, much better." He began touching
his side: it was not painful to the touch. "There, I really
don't feel it. It's much better already." He put out the
light and turned on his side.... "The appendix is getting
better, absorption is occurring." Suddenly he felt the old,
familiar, dull, gnawing pain, stubborn and serious. There
was the same familiar loathsome taste in his mouth. His
heart sank and he felt dazed. "My God! My God!" he
muttered. "Again, again! and it will never cease." And
suddenly the matter presented itself in a quite different
aspect. "Vermiform appendix! Kidney!" he said to himself. "It's not a question of appendix or kidney, but of life
and ... death. Yes, life was there and now it is going, going and I cannot stop it. Yes. Why deceive myself? Isn't it

obvious to everyone but me that I'm dying, and that it's only a question of weeks, days . . . it may happen this moment. There was light and now there is darkness. I was here and now I'm going there! Where?" A chill came over him, his breathing ceased, and he felt only the throbbing of his heart.

"When I am not, what will there be? There will be nothing. Then where shall I be when I am no more? Can this be dying? No, I don't want to!" He jumped up and tried to light the candle, felt for it with trembling hands, dropped candle and candlestick on the floor, and fell back on his pillow.

"What's the use? It makes no difference," he said to himself, staring with wide-open eyes into the darkness. "Death. Yes, death. And none of them know or wish to know it, and they have no pity for me. Now they are playing." (He heard through the door the distant sound of a song and its accompaniment.) "It's all the same to them, but they will die too! Fools! I first, and they later, but it will be the same for them. And now they are merry . . . the beasts!"

Anger choked him and he was agonizingly, unbearably miserable. "It is impossible that all men have been doomed to suffer this awful horror!" He raised himself.

"Something must be wrong. I must calm myself— must think it all over from the beginning." And he again began thinking. "Yes, the beginning of my illness: I knocked my side, but I was still quite well that day and the next. It hurt a little, then rather more. I saw the doctors, then followed despondency and anguish, more doctors, and I drew nearer to the abyss. My strength grew less and I kept coming nearer and nearer, and now I have wasted away and there is no light in my eyes. I think of the appendix—but this is death! I think of mending the appendix, and all the while here is death! Can it really be death?" Again terror seized him and he gasped for breath. He leant down and began feeling for the matches, pressing with his elbow on the stand beside the bed. It was in his way and hurt him; he grew furious with it, pressed on it still harder, and upset it. Breathless and in despair he fell on his back, expecting death to come immediately.

Meanwhile the visitors were leaving. Praskovya Fëdorovna was seeing them off. She heard something fall and came in.

"What has happened?"

"Nothing. I knocked it over accidentally."

She went out and returned with a candle. He lay there panting heavily, like a man who has run a thousand yards, and stared upwards at her with a fixed look.

"What is it, Jean?"

"No . . . o . . . thing. I upset it." ("Why speak of it? She won't understand," he thought.)

And in truth she did not understand. She picked up the stand, lit his candle, and hurried away to see another visitor off. When she came back he still lay on his back, looking upwards.

"What is it? Do you feel worse?"

"Yes."

She shook her head and sat down.

"Do you know, Jean, I think we must ask Leshchetitsky to come and see you here."

This meant calling in the famous specialist, regardless of expense. He smiled malignantly and said "No." She remained a little longer and then went up to him and kissed his forehead.

While she was kissing him he hated her from the bottom of his soul and with difficulty refrained from pushing her away.

"Good night. Please God you'll sleep."

"Yes."

vi

IVAN ILYCH saw that he was dying, and he was in continual despair.

In the depth of his heart he knew he was dying, but

not only was he not accustomed to the thought, he simply did not and could not grasp it.

The syllogism he had learnt from Kiezewetter's Logic: "Caius is a man, men are mortal, therefore Caius is mortal," had always seemed to him correct as applied to Caius, but certainly not as applied to himself. That Caius—man in the abstract—was mortal, was perfectly correct, but he was not Caius, not an abstract man, but a creature quite, quite separate from all others. He had been little Vanya, with a mamma and a papa, with Mitya and Volodya, with the toys, a coachman and a nurse, afterwards with Katenka and with all the joys, griefs, and delights of childhood, boyhood, and youth. What did Caius know of the smell of that striped leather ball Vanya had been so fond of? Had Caius kissed his mother's hand like that, and did the silk of her dress rustle so for Caius? Had he rioted like that at school when the pastry was bad? Had Caius been in love like that? Could Caius preside at a session as he did? "Caius really was mortal, and it was right for him to die; but for me, little Vanya, Ivan Ilych, with all my thoughts and emotions, it's altogether a different matter. It cannot be that I ought to die. That would be too terrible."

Such was his feeling.

"If I had to die like Caius I should have known it was so. An inner voice would have told me so, but there was nothing of the sort in me and I and all my friends felt that our case was quite different from that of Caius. And now here it is!" he said to himself. "It can't be. It's impossible! But here it is. How is this? How is one to understand it?"

He could not understand it, and tried to drive this false, incorrect, morbid thought away and to replace it by other proper and healthy thoughts. But that thought, and not the thought only but the reality itself, seemed to come and confront him.

And to replace that thought he called up a succession of others, hoping to find in them some support. He tried to get back into the former current of thoughts that had

once screened the thought of death from him. But
strange to say, all that had formerly shut off, hidden, and
destroyed his consciousness of death, no longer had that
effect. Ivan Ilych now spent most of his time in attempting to reestablish that old current. He would say to himself: "I will take up my duties again—after all I used to
live by them." And banishing all doubts he would go to
the law courts, enter into conversation with his colleagues, and sit carelessly as was his wont, scanning the
crowd with a thoughtful look and leaning both his emaciated arms on the arms of his oak chair; bending over as
usual to a colleague and drawing his papers nearer he
would interchange whispers with him, and then suddenly
raising his eyes and sitting erect would pronounce certain words and open the proceedings. But suddenly in
the midst of those proceedings the pain in his side, regardless of the stage the proceedings had reached, would
begin its own gnawing work. Ivan Ilych would turn his
attention to it and try to drive the thought of it away, but
without success. *It* would come and stand before him and
look at him, and he would be petrified and the light
would die out of his eyes, and he would again begin asking himself whether *It* alone was true. And his colleagues
and subordinates would see with surprise and distress
that he, the brilliant and subtle judge, was becoming confused and making mistakes. He would shake himself, try
to pull himself together, manage somehow to bring the
sitting to a close, and return home with the sorrowful
consciousness that his judicial labours could not as formerly hide from him what he wanted them to hide, and
could not deliver him from *It*. And what was worst of all
was that *It* drew his attention to itself not in order to
make him take some action but only that he should look
at *It*, look it straight in the face: look at it and without
doing anything, suffer inexpressibly.

And to save himself from this condition Ivan Ilych
looked for consolations—new screens—and new screens
were found and for a while seemed to save him, but
then they immediately fell to pieces or rather became

transparent, as if *It* penetrated them and nothing could veil *It*.

In these latter days he would go into the drawing-room he had arranged—that drawing-room where he had fallen and for the sake of which (how bitterly ridiculous it seemed) he had sacrificed his life—for he knew that his illness originated with that knock. He would enter and see that something had scratched the polished table. He would look for the cause of this and find that it was the bronze ornamentation of an album, that had got bent. He would take up the expensive album which he had lovingly arranged, and feel vexed with his daughter and her friends for their untidiness—for the album was torn here and there and some of the photographs turned upside down. He would put it carefully in order and bend the ornamentation back into position. Then it would occur to him to place all those things in another corner of the room, near the plants. He could call the footman, but his daughter or wife would come to help him. They would not agree, and his wife would contradict him, and he would dispute and grow angry. But that was all right, for then he did not think about *It. It* was invisible.

But then, when he was moving something himself, his wife would say: "Let the servants do it. You will hurt yourself again." And suddenly *It* would flash through the screen and he would see it. It was just a flash, and he hoped it would disappear, but he would involuntarily pay attention to his side. "It sits there as before, gnawing just the same!" And he could no longer forget *It,* but could distinctly see it looking at him from behind the flowers. "What is it all for?"

"It really is so! I lost my life over that curtain as I might have done when storming a fort. Is that possible? How terrible and how stupid. It can't be true! It can't, but it is."

He would go to his study, lie down, and again be alone with *It*: face to face with *It*. And nothing could be done with *It* except to look at it and shudder.

vii

How IT happened it is impossible to say because it came about step by step, unnoticed, but in the third month of Ivan Ilych's illness, his wife, his daughter, his son, his acquaintances, the doctors, the servants, and above all he himself, were aware that the whole interest he had for other people was whether he would soon vacate his place, and at last release the living from the discomfort caused by his presence and be himself released from his sufferings.

He slept less and less. He was given opium and hypodermic injections of morphine, but this did not relieve him. The dull depression he experienced in a somnolent condition at first gave him a little relief, but only as something new; afterwards it became as distressing as the pain itself or even more so.

Special foods were prepared for him by the doctors' orders, but all those foods became increasingly distasteful and disgusting to him.

For his excretions also special arrangements had to be made, and this was a torment to him every time — a torment from the uncleanliness, the unseemliness, and the smell, and from knowing that another person had to take part in it.

But just through this most unpleasant matter, Ivan Ilych obtained comfort. Gerasim, the butler's young assistant, always came in to carry the things out. Gerasim was a clean, fresh peasant lad, grown stout on town food and always cheerful and bright. At first the sight of him, in his clean Russian peasant costume, engaged in that disgusting task embarrassed Ivan Ilych.

Once when he got up from the commode too weak to draw up his trousers, he dropped into a soft armchair and looked with horror at his bare, enfeebled thighs with the muscles so sharply marked on them.

Gerasim with a firm light tread, his heavy boots emitting a pleasant smell of tar and fresh winter air, came in wearing a clean Hessian apron, the sleeves of his print shirt tucked up over his strong bare young arms; and refraining from looking at his sick master out of consideration for his feelings, and restraining the joy of life that beamed from his face, he went up to the commode.

"Gerasim!" said Ivan Ilych in a weak voice.

Gerasim started, evidently afraid he might have committed some blunder, and with a rapid movement turned his fresh, kind, simple young face which just showed the first downy signs of a beard.

"Yes, sir?"

"That must be very unpleasant for you. You must forgive me. I am helpless."

"Oh, why, sir," and Gerasim's eyes beamed and he showed his glistening white teeth, "what's a little trouble? It's a case of illness with you, sir."

And his deft strong hands did their accustomed task, and he went out of the room stepping lightly. Five minutes later he as lightly returned.

Ivan Ilych was still sitting in the same position in the armchair.

"Gerasim," he said when the latter had replaced the freshly-washed utensil. "Please come here and help me." Gerasim went up to him. "Lift me up. It is hard for me to get up, and I have sent Dmitri away."

Gerasim went up to him, grasped his master with his strong arms deftly but gently, in the same way that he stepped—lifted him, supported him with one hand, and with the other drew up his trousers and would have set him down again, but Ivan Ilych asked to be led to the sofa. Gerasim, without an effort and without apparent pressure, led him, almost lifting him, to the sofa and placed him on it.

"Thank you. How easily and well you do it all!"

Gerasim smiled again and turned to leave the room. But Ivan Ilych felt his presence such a comfort that he did not want to let him go.

"One thing more, please move up that chair. No, the other one—under my feet. It is easier for me when my feet are raised."

Gerasim brought the chair, set it down gently in place, and raised Ivan Ilych's legs on to it. It seemed to Ivan Ilych that he felt better while Gerasim was holding up his legs.

"It's better when my legs are higher," he said. "Place that cushion under them."

Gerasim did so. He again lifted the legs and placed them, and again Ivan Ilych felt better while Gerasim held his legs. When he set them down Ivan Ilych fancied he felt worse.

"Gerasim," he said. "Are you busy now?"

"Not at all, sir," said Gerasim, who had learnt from the townsfolk how to speak to gentlefolk.

"What have you still to do?"

"What have I to do? I've done everything except chopping the logs for tomorrow."

"Then hold my legs up a bit higher, can you?"

"Of course I can. Why not?" And Gerasim raised his master's legs higher and Ivan Ilych thought that in that position he did not feel any pain at all.

"And how about the logs?"

"Don't trouble about that, sir. There's plenty of time."

Ivan Ilych told Gerasim to sit down and hold his legs, and began to talk to him. And strange to say it seemed to him that he felt better while Gerasim held his legs up.

After that Ivan Ilych would sometimes call Gerasim and get him to hold his legs on his shoulders, and he liked talking to him. Gerasim did it all easily, willingly, simply, and with a good nature that touched Ivan Ilych. Health, strength, and vitality in other people were offensive to him, but Gerasim's strength and vitality did not mortify but soothed him.

What tormented Ivan Ilych most was the deception, the lie, which for some reason they all accepted, that he was not dying but was simply ill, and that he only need keep quiet and undergo a treatment and then something very good would result. He however knew that do what they would nothing would come of it, only still more agonizing suffering and death. This deception tortured

him—their not wishing to admit what they all knew and
what he knew, but wanting to lie to him concerning his
terrible condition, and wishing and forcing him to participate in that lie. Those lies—lies enacted over him on
the eve of his death and destined to degrade this awful,
solemn act to the level of their visitings. their curtains,
their sturgeon for dinner—were a terrible agony for Ivan
Ilych. And strangely enough, many times when they
were going through their antics over him he had been
within a hairbreadth of calling out to them: "Stop lying!
You know and I know that I am dying. Then at least stop
lying about it!" But he had never had the spirit to do it.
The awful, terrible act of his dying was, he could see, reduced by those about him to the level of a casual, unpleasant, and almost indecorous incident (as if someone
entered a drawing-room diffusing an unpleasant odour)
and this was done by that very decorum which he had
served all his life long. He saw that no one felt for him,
because no one even wished to grasp his position. Only
Gerasim recognized it and pitied him. And so Ivan Ilych
felt at ease only with him. He felt comforted when Gerasim supported his legs (sometimes all night long) and
refused to go to bed, saying: "Don't you worry, Ivan
Ilych. I'll get sleep enough later on," or when he suddenly became familiar and exclaimed: "If you weren't
sick it would be another matter, but as it is, why should I
grudge a little trouble?" Gerasim alone did not lie;
everything showed that he alone understood the facts of
the case and did not consider it necessary to disguise
them, but simply felt sorry for his emaciated and enfeebled master. Once when Ivan Ilych was sending him
away he even said straight out: "We shall all of us die, so
why should I grudge a little trouble?"—expressing the
fact that he did not think his work burdensome, because
he was doing it for a dying man and hoped someone
would do the same for him when his time came.

Apart from this lying, or because of it, what most tormented Ivan Ilych was that no one pitied him as he
wished to be pitied. At certain moments after prolonged

suffering he wished most of all (though he would have been ashamed to confess it) for someone to pity him as a sick child is pitied. He longed to be petted and comforted. He knew he was an important functionary, that he had a beard turning grey, and that therefore what he longed for was impossible, but still he longed for it. And in Gerasim's attitude towards him there was something akin to what he wished for, and so that attitude comforted him. Ivan Ilych wanted to weep, wanted to be petted and cried over, and then his colleague Shebek would come, and instead of weeping and being petted, Ivan Ilych would assume a serious, severe, and profound air, and by force of habit would express his opinion on a decision of the Court of Cassation and would stubbornly insist on that view. This falsity around him and within him did more than anything else to poison his last days.

viii

IT WAS morning. He knew it was morning because Gerasim had gone, and Peter the footman had come and put out the candles, drawn back one of the curtains, and begun quietly to tidy up. Whether it was morning or evening, Friday or Sunday, made no difference, it was all just the same: the gnawing, unmitigated, agonizing pain, never ceasing for an instant, the consciousness of life inexorably waning but not yet extinguished, the approach of that ever dreaded and hateful Death which was the only reality, and always the same falsity. What were days, weeks, hours, in such a case?

"Will you have some tea, sir?"

"He wants things to be regular, and wishes the gentlefolk to drink tea in the morning," thought Ivan Ilych, and only said "No."

"Wouldn't you like to move onto the sofa, sir?"

"He wants to tidy up the room, and I'm in the way. I am uncleanliness and disorder," he thought, and said only:

"No, leave me alone."

The man went on bustling about. Ivan Ilych stretched out his hand. Peter came up, ready to help.

"What is it, sir?"

"My watch."

Peter took the watch which was close at hand and gave it to his master.

"Half-past eight. Are they up?"

"No, sir, except Vladimir Ivanich" (the son) "who has gone to school. Praskovya Fëdorovna ordered me to wake her if you asked for her. Shall I do so?"

"No, there's no need to." "Perhaps I'd better have some tea," he thought, and added aloud: "Yes, bring me some tea."

Peter went to the door, but Ivan Ilych dreaded being left alone. "How can I keep him here? Oh yes, my medicine." "Peter, give me my medicine." "Why not? Perhaps it may still do me some good." He took a spoonful and swallowed it. "No, it won't help. It's all tomfoolery, all deception," he decided as soon as he became aware of the familiar, sickly, hopeless taste. "No, I can't believe in it any longer. But the pain, why this pain? If it would only cease just for a moment!" And he moaned. Peter turned towards him. "It's all right. Go and fetch me some tea."

Peter went out. Left alone Ivan Ilych groaned not so much with pain, terrible though that was, as from mental anguish. Always and forever the same, always these endless days and nights. If only it would come quicker! If only *what* would come quicker? Death, darkness? ... No, no! Anything rather than death!

When Peter returned with the tea on a tray, Ivan Ilych stared at him for a time in perplexity, not realizing who and what he was. Peter was disconcerted by that look and his embarrassment brought Ivan Ilych to himself.

"Oh, tea! All right, put it down. Only help me to wash and put on a clean shirt."

And Ivan Ilych began to wash. With pauses for rest, he washed his hands and then his face, cleaned his teeth, brushed his hair, and looked in the glass. He was terrified by what he saw, especially by the limp way in which his hair clung to his pallid forehead.

While his shirt was being changed he knew that he would be still more frightened at the sight of his body, so he avoided looking at it. Finally he was ready. He drew on a dressing-gown, wrapped himself in a plaid, and sat down in the armchair to take his tea. For a moment he felt refreshed, but as soon as he began to drink the tea he was again aware of the same taste, and the pain also returned. He finished it with an effort, and then lay down stretching out his legs, and dismissed Peter.

Always the same. Now a spark of hope flashes up, then a sea of despair rages, and always pain; always pain, always despair, and always the same. When alone he had a dreadful and distressing desire to call someone, but he knew beforehand that with others present it would be still worse. "Another dose of morphine—to lose consciousness. I will tell him, the doctor, that he must think of something else. It's impossible, impossible, to go on like this."

An hour and another pass like that. But now there is a ring at the door bell. Perhaps it's the doctor? It is. He comes in fresh, hearty, plump, and cheerful, with that look on his face that seems to say: "There now, you're in a panic about something, but we'll arrange it all for you directly!" The doctor knows this expression is out of place here, but he has put it on once for all and can't take it off—like a man who has put on a frock-coat in the morning to pay a round of calls.

The doctor rubs his hands vigorously and reassuringly.

"Brr! How cold it is! There's such a sharp frost; just let me warm myself!" he says, as if it were only a matter of waiting till he was warm, and then he would put everything right.

"Well now, how are you?"

Ivan Ilych feels that the doctor would like to say: "Well, how are our affairs?" but that even he feels that this would not do, and says instead: "What sort of a night have you had?"

Ivan Ilych looks at him as much as to say: "Are you really never ashamed of lying?" But the doctor does not wish to understand this question, and Ivan Ilych says: "Just as terrible as ever. The pain never leaves me and never subsides. If only something ..."

"Yes, you sick people are always like that.... There, now I think I am warm enough. Even Praskovya Fëdorovna, who is so particular, could find no fault with my temperature. Well, now I can say good morning," and the doctor presses his patient's hand.

Then, dropping his former playfulness, he begins with a most serious face to examine the patient, feeling his pulse and taking his temperature, and then begins the sounding and auscultation.

Ivan Ilych knows quite well and definitely that all this is nonsense and pure deception, but when the doctor, getting down on his knee, leans over him, putting his ear first higher then lower, and performs various gymnastic movements over him with a significant expression on his face, Ivan Ilych submits to it all as he used to submit to the speeches of the lawyers, though he knew very well that they were all lying and why they were lying.

The doctor, kneeling on the sofa, is still sounding him when Praskovya Fëdorovna's silk dress rustles at the door and she is heard scolding Peter for not having let her know of the doctor's arrival.

She comes in, kisses her husband, and at once proceeds to prove that she has been up a long time already, and only owing to a misunderstanding failed to be there when the doctor arrived.

Ivan Ilych looks at her, scans her all over, sets against her the whiteness and plumpness and cleanness of her hands and neck, the gloss of her hair, and the sparkle of her vivacious eyes. He hates her with his whole soul. And the thrill of hatred he feels for her makes him suffer from her touch.

Her attitude towards him and his disease is still the

same. Just as the doctor had adopted a certain relation to his patient which he could not abandon, so had she formed one towards him—that he was not doing something he ought to do and was himself to blame, and that she reproached him lovingly for this—and she could not now change that attitude.

"You see he doesn't listen to me and doesn't take his medicine at the proper time. And above all he lies in a position that is no doubt bad for him—with his legs up."

She described how he made Gerasim hold his legs up.

The doctor smiled with a contemptuous affability that said: "What's to be done? These sick people do have foolish fancies of that kind, but we must forgive them."

When the examination was over the doctor looked at his watch, and then Praskovya Fëdorovna announced to Ivan Ilych that it was of course as he pleased, but she had sent today for a celebrated specialist who would examine him and have a consultation with Michael Danilovich (their regular doctor).

"Please don't raise any objections. I am doing this for my own sake," she said ironically, letting it be felt that she was doing it all for his sake and only said this to leave him no right to refuse. He remained silent, knitting his brows. He felt that he was so surrounded and involved in a mesh of falsity that it was hard to unravel anything.

Everything she did for him was entirely for her own sake, and she told him she was doing for herself what she actually was doing for herself, as if that was so incredible that he must understand the opposite.

At half-past eleven the celebrated specialist arrived. Again the sounding began and the significant conversations in his presence and in another room, about the kidneys and the appendix, and the questions and answers, with such an air of importance that again, instead of the real question of life and death which now alone confronted him, the question arose of the kidney and appendix which were not behaving as they ought to and would now be attacked by Michael Danilovich and the specialist and forced to amend their ways.

The celebrated specialist took leave of him with a serious though not hopeless look, and in reply to the timid question Ivan Ilych, with eyes glistening with fear and hope, put to him as to whether there was a chance of recovery, said that he could not vouch for it but there was a possibility. The look of hope with which Ivan Ilych watched the doctor out was so pathetic that Praskovya Fëdorovna, seeing it, even wept as she left the room to hand the doctor his fee.

The gleam of hope kindled by the doctor's encouragement did not last long. The same room, the same pictures, curtains, wallpaper, medicine bottles, were all there, and the same aching suffering body, and Ivan Ilych began to moan. They gave him a subcutaneous injection and he sank into oblivion.

It was twilight when he came to. They brought him his dinner and he swallowed some beef tea with difficulty, and then everything was the same again and night was coming on.

After dinner, at seven o'clock, Praskovya Fëdorovna came into the room in evening dress, her full bosom pushed up by her corset, and with traces of powder on her face. She had reminded him in the morning that they were going to the theatre. Sarah Bernhardt was visiting the town and they had a box, which he had insisted on their taking. Now he had forgotten about it and her toilet offended him, but he concealed his vexation when he remembered that he had himself insisted on their securing a box and going because it would be an instructive and aesthetic pleasure for the children.

Praskovya Fëdorovna came in, self-satisfied but yet with a rather guilty air. She sat down and asked how he was, but, as he saw, only for the sake of asking and not in order to learn about it, knowing that there was nothing to learn—and then went on to what she really wanted to say: that she would not on any account have gone but that the box had been taken and Helen and their daughter were going, as well as Petrishchev (the examining magistrate, their daughter's fiancé) and that it was out of the question to let them go alone; but that she would have much preferred to sit with him for a while; and he must be sure to follow the doctor's orders while she was away.

"Oh, and Fëdor Petrovich" (the fiancé) "would like to come in. May he? And Lisa?"

"All right."

Their daughter came in in full evening dress, her fresh young flesh exposed (making a show of that very flesh which in his own case caused so much suffering), strong, healthy, evidently in love, and impatient with illness, suffering, and death, because they interfered with her happiness.

Fëdor Petrovich came in too, in evening dress, his hair curled *à la Capoul,* a tight stiff collar round his long sinewy neck, an enormous white shirt-front and narrow black trousers tightly stretched over his strong thighs. He had one white glove tightly drawn on, and was holding his opera hat in his hand.

Following him the schoolboy crept in unnoticed, in a new uniform, poor little fellow, and wearing gloves. Terribly dark shadows showed under his eyes, the meaning of which Ivan Ilych knew well.

His son had always seemed pathetic to him, and now it was dreadful to see the boy's frightened look of pity. It seemed to Ivan Ilych that Vasya was the only one besides Gerasim who understood and pitied him.

They all sat down and again asked how he was. A silence followed. Lisa asked her mother about the opera-glasses, and there was an altercation between mother and daughter as to who had taken them and where they had been put. This occasioned some unpleasantness.

Fëdor Petrovich inquired of Ivan Ilych whether he had ever seen Sarah Bernhardt. Ivan Ilych did not at first catch the question, but then replied: "No, have you seen her before?"

"Yes, in *Adrienne Lecouvreur.*"

Praskovya Fëdorovna mentioned some rôles in which Sarah Bernhardt was particularly good. Her daughter disagreed. Conversation sprang up as to the elegance and realism of her acting—the sort of conversation that is always repeated and is always the same.

In the midst of the conversation Fëdor Petrovich glanced at Ivan Ilych and became silent. The others also looked at him and grew silent. Ivan Ilych was staring with glittering eyes straight before him, evidently indignant with them. This had to be rectified, but it was impossible to do so. The silence had to be broken, but for a time no one dared to break it and they all became afraid that the conventional deception would suddenly become obvious and the truth become plain to all. Lisa was the first to pluck up courage and break that silence, but by trying to hide what everybody was feeling, she betrayed it.

"Well, if we are going it's time to start," she said, looking at her watch, a present from her father, and with a faint and significant smile at Fëdor Petrovich relating to something known only to them. She got up with a rustle of her dress.

They all rose, said good night, and went away.

When they had gone it seemed to Ivan Ilych that he felt better; the falsity had gone with them. But the pain remained—that same pain and that same fear that made everything monotonously alike, nothing harder and nothing easier. Everything was worse.

Again minute followed minute and hour followed hour. Everything remained the same and there was no cessation. And the inevitable end of it all became more and more terrible.

"Yes, send Gerasim here," he replied to a question Peter asked.

ix

HIS WIFE returned late at night. She came in on tiptoe, but he heard her, opened his eyes, and made haste to close them again. She wished to send Gerasim away and

to sit with him herself, but he opened his eyes and said:
"No, go away."

"Are you in great pain?"

"Always the same."

"Take some opium."

He agreed and took some. She went away.

Till about three in the morning he was in a state of
stupefied misery. It seemed to him that he and his pain
were being thrust into a narrow, deep black sack, but
though they were pushed further and further in they
could not be pushed to the bottom. And this, terrible
enough in itself, was accompanied by suffering. He was
frightened yet wanted to fall through the sack, he struggled
but yet co-operated. And suddenly he broke through, fell,
and regained consciousness. Gerasim was sitting at the
foot of the bed dozing quietly and patiently, while he
himself lay with his emaciated stockinged legs resting on
Gerasim's shoulders; the same shaded candle was there
and the same unceasing pain.

"Go away, Gerasim," he whispered.

"It's all right, sir. I'll stay a while."

"No. Go away."

He removed his legs from Gerasim's shoulders, turned
sideways onto his arm, and felt sorry for himself. He only
waited till Gerasim had gone into the next room and
then restrained himself no longer but wept like a child.
He wept on account of his helplessness, his terrible loneliness, the cruelty of man, the cruelty of God, and the
absence of God.

"Why hast Thou done all this? Why hast Thou brought
me here? Why, why dost Thou torment me so terribly?"

He did not expect an answer and yet wept because
there was no answer and could be none. The pain again
grew more acute, but he did not stir and did not call. He
said to himself: "Go on! Strike me! But what is it for?
What have I done to Thee? What is it for?"

Then he grew quiet and not only ceased weeping but
even held his breath and became all attention. It was as
though he were listening not to an audible voice but to

the voice of his soul, to the current of thoughts arising within him.

"What is it you want?" was the first clear conception capable of expression in words, that he heard.

"What do you want? What do you want?" he repeated to himself.

"What do I want? To live and not to suffer," he answered.

And again he listened with such concentrated attention that even his pain did not distract him.

"To live? How?" asked his inner voice.

"Why, to live as I used to—well and pleasantly."

"As you lived before, well and pleasantly?" the voice repeated.

And in imagination he began to recall the best moments of his pleasant life. But strange to say none of those best moments of his pleasant life now seemed at all what they had then seemed—none of them except the first recollections of childhood. There, in childhood, there had been something really pleasant with which it would be possible to live if it could return. But the child who had experienced that happiness existed no longer; it was like a reminiscence of somebody else.

As soon as the period began which had produced the present Ivan Ilych, all that had then seemed joys now melted before his sight and turned into something trivial and often nasty.

And the further he departed from childhood and the nearer he came to the present the more worthless and doubtful were the joys. This began with the School of Law. A little that was really good was still found there—there was lightheartedness, friendship, and hope. But in the upper classes there had already been fewer of such good moments. Then during the first years of his official career, when he was in the service of the governor, some pleasant moments again occurred: they were the memories of love for a woman. Then all became confused and there was still less of what was good; later on again there was still less that was good, and the further he went the less there was. His marriage, a mere accident, then the disenchantment that followed it, his wife's bad breath and the sensuality and hypocrisy: then that deadly official life and those preoccupations about money, a year of it, and two, and ten, and twenty, and always the same thing. And the longer it lasted the more deadly it became. "It is as if I had been going downhill while I imagined I was going up. And that is really what it was. I was going up in public opinion, but to the same extent life was ebbing away from me. And now it is all done and there is only death."

"Then what does it mean? Why? It can't be that life is so senseless and horrible. But if it really has been so horrible and senseless, why must I die and die in agony? There is something wrong!"

"Maybe I did not live as I ought to have done," it suddenly occurred to him. "But how could that be, when I did everything properly?" he replied, and immediately dismissed from his mind this, the sole solution of all the riddles of life and death, as something quite impossible.

"Then what do you want now? To live? Live how? Live as you lived in the law courts when the usher proclaimed 'The judge is coming!' The judge is coming, the judge!" he repeated to himself. "Here he is, the judge. But I am not guilty!" he exclaimed angrily. "What is it for?" And he ceased crying, but turning his face to the wall continued to ponder on the same question: why, and for what purpose, is there all this horror? But however much he pondered he found no answer. And whenever the thought occurred to him, as it often did, that it all resulted from his not having lived as he ought to have done, he at once recalled the correctness of his whole life and dismissed so strange an idea.

X

ANOTHER fortnight passed. Ivan Ilych now no longer left his sofa. He would not lie in bed but lay on the sofa, facing the wall nearly all the time. He suffered ever the

same unceasing agonies and in his loneliness pondered
always on the same insoluble question: "What is this?
Can it be that it is Death?" And the inner voice answered: "Yes, it is Death."

"Why these sufferings?" And the voice answered,
"For no reason—they just are so." Beyond and besides
this there was nothing.

From the very beginning of his illness, ever since he
had first been to see the doctor, Ivan Ilych's life had been
divided between two contrary and alternating moods:
now it was despair and the expectation of this uncom-
prehended and terrible death, and now hope and an intently interested observation of the functioning of his
organs. Now before his eyes there was only a kidney or
an intestine that temporarily evaded its duty, and now
only that incomprehensible and dreadful death from
which it was impossible to escape.

These two states of mind had alternated from the
very beginning of his illness, but the further it progressed
the more doubtful and fantastic became the conception
of the kidney, and the more real the sense of impending
death.

He had but to call to mind what he had been three
months before and what he was now, to call to mind with
what regularity he had been going downhill, for every
possibility of hope to be shattered.

Latterly during that loneliness in which he found himself as he lay facing the back of the sofa, a loneliness in
the midst of a populous town and surrounded by numerous acquaintances and relations but that yet could not
have been more complete anywhere—either at the bottom of the sea or under the earth—during that terrible
loneliness Ivan Ilych had lived only in memories of the
past. Pictures of his past rose before him one after another. They always began with what was nearest in time
and then went back to what was most remote—to his
childhood—and rested there. If he thought of the stewed
prunes that had been offered him that day, his mind went
back to the raw shrivelled French plums of his child-

hood, their peculiar flavour and the flow of saliva when he sucked their stones, and along with the memory of that taste came a whole series of memories of those days: his nurse, his brother, and their toys. "No, I mustn't think of that. . . . It is too painful," Ivan Ilych said to himself, and brought himself back to the present—to the button on the back of the sofa and the creases in its morocco. "Morocco is expensive, but it does not wear well: there had been a quarrel about it. It was a different kind of quarrel and a different kind of morocco that time when we tore Father's portfolio and were punished, and Mamma brought us some tarts. . . ." And again his thoughts dwelt on his childhood, and again it was painful and he tried to banish them and fix his mind on something else.

Then again together with that chain of memories another series passed through his mind—of how his illness had progressed and grown worse. There also the further back he looked the more life there had been. There had been more of what was good in life and more of life itself. The two merged together. "Just as the pain went on getting worse and worse, so my life grew worse and worse," he thought. "There is one bright spot there at the back, at the beginning of life, and afterwards all becomes blacker and blacker and proceeds more and more rapidly—in inverse ratio to the square of the distance from death," thought Ivan Ilych. And the example of a stone falling downwards with increasing velocity entered his mind. Life, a series of increasing sufferings, flies further and further towards its end—the most terrible suffering. "I am flying. . . ." He shuddered, shifted himself, and tried to resist, but was already aware that resistance was impossible, and again with eyes weary of gazing but unable to cease seeing what was before them, he stared at the back of the sofa and waited—awaiting that dreadful fall and shock and destruction.

"Resistance is impossible!" he said to himself. "If I could only understand what it is all for! But that too is impossible. An explanation would be possible if it could be said that I have not lived as I ought to. But it is impossible to say that," and he remembered all the legality, correctitude, and propriety of his life. "That at any rate can certainly not be admitted," he thought, and his lips smiled ironically as if someone could see that smile and be taken in by it. "There is no explanation! Agony, death ... What for?"

xi

ANOTHER two weeks went by in this way and during that fortnight an event occurred that Ivan Ilych and his wife had desired. Petrishchev formally proposed. It happened in the evening. The next day Praskovya Fëdorovna came into her husband's room considering how best to inform him of it, but that very night there had been a fresh change for the worse in his condition. She found him still lying on the sofa but in a different position. He lay on his back, groaning and staring fixedly straight in front of him.

She began to remind him of his medicines, but he turned his eyes towards her with such a look that she did not finish what she was saying; so great an animosity, to her in particular, did that look express.

"For Christ's sake let me die in peace!" he said.

She would have gone away, but just then their daughter came in and went up to say good morning. He looked at her as he had done at his wife, and in reply to her inquiry about his health said dryly that he would soon free them all of himself. They were both silent and after sitting with him for a while went away.

"Is it our fault?" Lisa said to her mother. "It's as if we were to blame! I am sorry for Papa, but why should we be tortured?"

The doctor came at his usual time. Ivan Ilych answered "Yes" and "No," never taking his angry eyes from him, and at last said: "You know you can do nothing for me, so leave me alone."

"We can ease your sufferings."

"You can't even do that. Let me be."

The doctor went into the drawing-room and told Praskovya Fëdorovna that the case was very serious and that the only resource left was opium to allay her husband's sufferings, which must be terrible.

It was true, as the doctor said, that Ivan Ilych's physical sufferings were terrible, but worse than the physical sufferings were his mental sufferings, which were his chief torture.

His mental sufferings were due to the fact that that night, as he looked at Gerasim's sleepy, good-natured face with its prominent cheekbones, the question suddenly occurred to him: "What if my whole life has really been wrong?"

It occurred to him that what had appeared perfectly impossible before, namely that he had not spent his life as he should have done, might after all be true. It occurred to him that his scarcely perceptible attempts to struggle against what was considered good by the most highly placed people, those scarcely noticeable impulses which he had immediately suppressed, might have been the real thing, and all the rest false. And his professional duties and the whole arrangement of his life and of his family, and all his social and official interests, might all have been false. He tried to defend all those things to himself and suddenly felt the weakness of what he was defending. There was nothing to defend.

"But if that is so," he said to himself, "and I am leaving this life with the consciousness that I have lost all that was given me and it is impossible to rectify it—what then?"

He lay on his back and began to pass his life in review in quite a new way. In the morning when he saw first his footman, then his wife, then his daughter, and then the doctor, their every word and movement confirmed to him the awful truth that had been revealed to him during the night. In them he saw himself—all that for which he had lived—and saw clearly that it was not real at all, but a terrible and huge deception which had hidden both life and death. This consciousness intensified his physical suffering tenfold. He groaned and tossed about, and pulled at his clothing which choked and stifled him. And he hated them on that account.

He was given a large dose of opium and became unconscious, but at noon his sufferings began again. He drove everybody away and tossed from side to side.

His wife came to him and said:

"Jean, my dear, do this for me. It can't do any harm and often helps. Healthy people often do it."

He opened his eyes wide.

"What? Take Communion? Why? It's unnecessary! However . . ."

She began to cry.

"Yes, do, my dear. I'll send for our priest. He is such a nice man."

"All right. Very well," he muttered.

When the priest came and heard his confession, Ivan Ilych was softened and seemed to feel a relief from his doubts and consequently from his sufferings, and for a moment there came a ray of hope. He again began to think of the vermiform appendix and the possibility of correcting it. He received the sacrament with tears in his eyes.

When they laid him down again afterwards he felt a moment's ease, and the hope that he might live awoke in him again. He began to think of the operation that had been suggested to him. "To live! I want to live!" he said to himself.

His wife came in to congratulate him after his Communion, and when uttering the usual conventional words she added:

"You feel better, don't you?"

Without looking at her he said "Yes."

Her dress, her figure, the expression of her face, the tone of her voice, all revealed the same thing. "This is wrong, it is not as it should be. All you have lived for and still live for is falsehood and deception, hiding life and death from you." And as soon as he admitted that thought, his hatred and his agonizing physical suffering again sprang up, and with that suffering a consciousness of the unavoidable, approaching end. And to this was added a new sensation of grinding shooting pain and a feeling of suffocation.

The expression of his face when he uttered that "yes" was dreadful. Having uttered it, he looked her straight in the eyes, turned on his face with a rapidity extraordinary in his weak state and shouted:

"Go away! Go away and leave me alone!"

xii

FROM THAT moment the screaming began that continued for three days, and was so terrible that one could not hear it through two closed doors without horror. At the moment he answered his wife he realized that he was lost, that there was no return, that the end had come, the very end, and his doubts were still unsolved and remained doubts.

"Oh! Oh! Oh!" he cried in various intonations. He had begun by screaming "I won't!" and continued screaming on the letter *O*.

For three whole days, during which time did not exist for him, he struggled in that black sack into which he was being thrust by an invisible, resistless force. He struggled as a man condemned to death struggles in the hands of the executioner, knowing that he cannot save himself. And every moment he felt that despite all his efforts he was drawing nearer and nearer to what terrified him. He felt that his agony was due to his being thrust into that black hole and still more to his not being able to get right into it. He was hindered from getting into it by his conviction that his life had been a good one. That very justification of his life held him fast and prevented his moving forward, and it caused him most torment of all.

Suddenly some force struck him in the chest and side, making it still harder to breathe, and he fell through the hole and there at the bottom was a light. What had happened to him was like the sensation one sometimes experiences in a railway carriage when one thinks one is going backwards while one is really going forwards and suddenly becomes aware of the real direction.

"Yes, it was all not the right thing," he said to himself, "but that's no matter. It can be done. But what *is* the right thing?" he asked himself, and suddenly grew quiet.

This occurred at the end of the third day, two hours before his death. Just then his schoolboy son had crept softly in and gone up to the bedside. The dying man was still screaming desperately and waving his arms. His hand fell on the boy's head, and the boy caught it, pressed it to his lips, and began to cry.

At that very moment Ivan Ilych fell through and caught sight of the light, and it was revealed to him that though his life had not been what it should have been, this could still be rectified. He asked himself, "What *is* the right thing?" and grew still, listening. Then he felt that someone was kissing his hand. He opened his eyes, looked at his son, and felt sorry for him. His wife came up to him and he glanced at her. She was gazing at him openmouthed, with undried tears on her nose and cheek and a despairing look on her face. He felt sorry for her too.

"Yes, I am making them wretched," he thought. "They are sorry, but it will be better for them when I die." He wished to say this but had not the strength to utter it. "Besides, why speak? I must act," he thought. With a look at his wife he indicated his son and said: "Take him away ... sorry for him ... sorry for you too. ..." He tried to add, "forgive me," but said "forgo" and waved his hand, knowing that He whose understanding mattered would understand.

And suddenly it grew clear to him that what had been oppressing him and would not leave him was all dropping away at once from two sides, from ten sides, and from all sides. He was sorry for them, he must act so as not to hurt them: release them and free himself from these sufferings. "How good and how simple!" he thought. "And the pain?" he asked himself. "What has become of it? Where are you, pain?"

He turned his attention to it.

"Yes, here it is. Well, what of it? Let the pain be."

"And death ... where is it?"

He sought his former accustomed fear of death and did not find it. "Where is it? What death?" There was no fear because there was no death.

In place of death there was light.

"So that's what it is!" he suddenly exclaimed aloud. "What joy!"

To him all this happened in a single instant, and the meaning of that instant did not change. For those present his agony continued for another two hours. Something rattled in his throat, his emaciated body twitched, then the gasping and rattle became less and less frequent.

"It is finished!" said someone near him.

He heard these words and repeated them in his soul.

"Death is finished," he said to himself. "It is no more!"

He drew in a breath, stopped in the midst of a sigh, stretched out, and died.

The Kreutzer Sonata

————~~~————

> But I say unto you, that every one that looketh on
> a woman to lust after her hath committed adultery
> with her already in his heart. Matt. 5:28
>
> The disciples say unto him, If the case of the man
> is so with his wife, it is not expedient to marry. But
> he said unto them, All men cannot receive this say-
> ing, but they to whom it is given. Ibid. 19:10–11

i

IT WAS early spring, and the second day of our journey.
Passengers going short distances entered and left our
carriage, but three others, like myself, had come all the
way with the train. One was a lady, plain and no longer
young, who smoked, had a harassed look, and wore a
mannish coat and cap; another was an acquaintance of
hers, a talkative man of about forty, whose things looked

neat and new; the third was a rather short man who kept himself apart. He was not old, but his curly hair had gone prematurely grey. His movements were abrupt and his unusually glittering eyes moved rapidly from one object to another. He wore an old overcoat, evidently from a first-rate tailor, with an astrakhan collar, and a tall astrakhan cap. When he unbuttoned his overcoat a sleeveless Russian coat and embroidered shirt showed beneath it. A peculiarity of this man was a strange sound he emitted, something like a clearing of his throat, or a laugh begun and sharply broken off.

All the way this man had carefully avoided making acquaintance or having any intercourse with his fellow passengers. When spoken to by those near him he gave short and abrupt answers, and at other times read, looked out of the window, smoked, or drank tea and ate something he took out of an old bag.

It seemed to me that his loneliness depressed him, and I made several attempts to converse with him, but whenever our eyes met, which happened often as he sat nearly opposite me, he turned away and took up his book or looked out of the window.

Towards the second evening, when our train stopped at a large station, this nervous man fetched himself some boiling water and made tea. The man with the neat new things—a lawyer as I found out later—and his neighbour, the smoking lady with the mannish coat, went to the refreshment-room to drink tea.

During their absence several new passengers entered the carriage, among them a tall, shaven, wrinkled old man, evidently a tradesman, in a coat lined with skunk fur, and a cloth cap with an enormous peak. The tradesman sat down opposite the seats of the lady and the lawyer, and immediately started a conversation with a young man who had also entered at that station and, judging by his appearance, was a tradesman's clerk.

I was sitting the other side of the gangway and as the train was standing still I could hear snatches of their conversation when nobody was passing between us. The tradesman began by saying that he was going to his estate which was only one station farther on; then as usual the conversation turned to prices and trade, and they spoke of the state of business in Moscow and then of the Nizhni-Novgorod Fair. The clerk began to relate how a wealthy merchant, known to both of them, had gone on a spree at the fair, but the old man interrupted him by telling of the orgies he had been at in former times at Kunavin Fair. He evidently prided himself on the part he had played in them, and recounted with pleasure how he and some acquaintances, together with the merchant they had been speaking of, had once got drunk at Kunavin and played such a trick that he had to tell of it in a whisper. The clerk's roar of laughter filled the whole carriage; the old man laughed also, exposing two yellow teeth.

Not expecting to hear anything interesting, I got up to stroll about the platform till the train should start. At the carriage door I met the lawyer and the lady who were talking with animation as they approached.

"You won't have time," said the sociable lawyer, "the second bell will ring in a moment."*

And the bell did ring before I had gone the length of the train. When I returned, the animated conversation between the lady and the lawyer was proceeding. The old tradesman sat silent opposite to them, looking sternly before him, and occasionally mumbled disapprovingly as if chewing something.

"Then she plainly informed her husband," the lawyer was smilingly saying as I passed him, "that she was not able, and did not wish, to live with him since . . ."

He went on to say something I could not hear. Several other passengers came in after me. The guard passed, a porter hurried in, and for some time the noise made their voices inaudible. When all was quiet again the con-

---

*It was customary in Russia for a first, second, and third bell to ring before a train left a station. A.M.

versation had evidently turned from the particular case
to general considerations.

The lawyer was saying that public opinion in Europe
was occupied with the question of divorce, and that cases
of "that kind" were occurring more and more often in
Russia. Noticing that his was the only voice audible, he
stopped his discourse and turned to the old man.

"Those things did not happen in the old days, did
they?" he said, smiling pleasantly.

The old man was about to reply, but the train moved
and he took off his cap, crossed himself, and whispered a
prayer. The lawyer turned away his eyes and waited politely. Having finished his prayer and crossed himself
three times, the old man set his cap straight, pulled it well
down over his forehead, changed his position, and began
to speak.

"They used to happen even then, sir, but less often,"
he said. "As times are now they can't help happening.
People have got too educated."

The train moved faster and faster and jolted over the
joints of the rails, making it difficult to hear, but being
interested I moved nearer. The nervous man with the
glittering eyes opposite me, evidently also interested, listened without changing his place.

"What is wrong with education?" said the lady, with a
scarcely perceptible smile. "Surely it can't be better to
marry as they used to in the old days when the bride and
bridegroom did not even see one another before the
wedding," she continued, answering not what her inter-
locutor had said but what she thought he would say, in
the way many ladies have. "Without knowing whether
they loved, or whether they could love, they married just
anybody, and were wretched all their lives. And you
think that was better?" she said, evidently addressing me
and the lawyer chiefly and least of all the old man with
whom she was talking.

"They've got so very educated," the tradesman reiter-
ated, looking contemptuously at the lady and leaving her
question unanswered.

"It would be interesting to know how you explain the connexion between education and matrimonial discord," said the lawyer, with a scarcely perceptible smile.

The tradesman was about to speak, but the lady interrupted him.

"No," she said, "those times have passed." But the lawyer stopped her.

"Yes, but allow the gentleman to express his views."

"Foolishness comes from education," the old man said categorically.

"They make people who don't love one another marry, and then wonder that they live in discord," the lady hastened to say, turning to look at the lawyer, at me, and even at the clerk, who had got up and, leaning on the back of the seat, was smilingly listening to the conversation. "It's only animals, you know, that can be paired off as their master likes; but human beings have their own inclinations and attachments," said the lady, with an evident desire to annoy the tradesman.

"You should not talk like that, madam," said the old man; "animals are cattle, but human beings have a law given them."

"Yes, but how is one to live with a man when there is no love?" the lady again hastened to express her argument, which probably seemed very new to her.

"They used not to go into that," said the old man in an impressive tone; "it is only now that all this has sprung up. The least thing makes them say: 'I will leave you!' The fashion has spread even to the peasants. 'Here you are!' she says. 'Here, take your shirts and trousers and I will go with Vanka; his head is curlier than yours.' What can you say? The first thing that should be required of a woman is fear!"

The clerk glanced at the lawyer, at the lady, and at me, apparently suppressing a smile and prepared to ridicule or to approve of the tradesman's words according to the reception they met with.

"Fear of what?" asked the lady.

"Why, this: let her fear her husband! That fear!"

"Oh, the time for that, sir, has passed," said the lady with a certain viciousness.

"No, madam, that time cannot pass. As she, Eve, was made from the rib of a man, so it will remain to the end of time," said the old man, jerking his head with such sternness and such a victorious look that the clerk at once concluded that victory was on his side, and laughed loudly.

"Ah yes, that's the way you men argue," said the lady unyieldingly, and turned to us. "You have given yourselves freedom but want to shut women up in a tower.* You no doubt permit yourselves everything."

"No one is permitting anything, but a man does not bring offspring into the home; while a woman—a wife— is a leaky vessel," the tradesman continued insistently. His tone was so impressive that it evidently vanquished his hearers, and even the lady felt crushed but still did not give in.

"Yes, but I think you will agree that a woman is a human being and has feelings as a man has. What is she to do then, if she does not love her husband?"

"Does not love!" said the tradesman severely, moving his brows and lips. "She'll love, no fear!" This unexpected argument particularly pleased the clerk, and he emitted a sound of approval.

"Oh, no, she won't!" the lady began, "and when there is no love you can't enforce it."

"Well, and supposing the wife is unfaithful, what then?" asked the lawyer.

"That is not admissible," said the old man. "One has to see to that."

"But if it happens, what then? You know it does occur."

"It happens among some, but not among us," said the old man.

*Literally "in the *terem*," the *terem* being the woman's quarter where in olden times the women of a Russian family used to be secluded in Oriental fashion. A.M.

All were silent. The clerk moved, came still nearer, and, evidently unwilling to be behindhand, began with a smile.

"Yes, a young fellow of ours had a scandal. It was a difficult case to deal with. It too was a case of a woman who was a bad lot. She began to play the devil, and the young fellow is respectable and cultured. At first it was with one of the office clerks. The husband tried to persuade her with kindness. She would not stop, but played all sorts of dirty tricks. Then she began to steal his money. He beat her, but she only grew worse. Carried on intrigues, if I may mention it, with an unchristened Jew. What was he to do? He turned her out altogether and lives as a bachelor, while she gads about."

"Because he is a fool," said the old man. "If he'd pulled her up properly from the first and not let her have her way, she'd be living with him, no fear! It's giving way at first that counts. Don't trust your horse in the field, or your wife in the house."

At that moment the guard entered to collect the tickets for the next station. The old man gave up his.

"Yes, the female sex must be curbed in time or else all is lost!"

"Yes, but you yourself just now were speaking about the way married men amuse themselves at the Kunavin Fair," I could not help saying.

"That's a different matter," said the old man and relapsed into silence.

When the whistle sounded the tradesman rose, got out his bag from under the seat, buttoned up his coat, and slightly lifting his cap went out of the carriage.

ii

As soon as the old man had gone several voices were raised.

"A daddy of the old style!" remarked the clerk.

"A living *Domostroy*!"* said the lady. "What barbarous views of women and marriage!"

"Yes, we are far from the European understanding of marriage," said the lawyer.†

"The chief thing such people do not understand," continued the lady, "is that marriage without love is not marriage; that love alone sanctifies marriage, and that real marriage is only such as is sanctified by love."

The clerk listened smilingly, trying to store up for future use all he could of the clever conversation.

In the midst of the lady's remarks we heard, behind me, a sound like that of a broken laugh or sob; and on turning round we saw my neighbour, the lonely grey-haired man with the glittering eyes, who had approached unnoticed during our conversation, which evidently interested him. He stood with his arms on the back of the seat, evidently much excited; his face was red and a muscle twitched in his cheek.

"What kind of love . . . love . . . is it that sanctifies marriage?" he asked hesitatingly.

Noticing the speaker's agitation, the lady tried to answer him as gently and fully as possible.

"True love . . . When such love exists between a man and a woman, then marriage is possible," she said.

"Yes, but how is one to understand what is meant by 'true love'?" said the gentleman with the glittering eyes timidly and with an awkward smile.

"Everybody knows what love is," replied the lady,

The Housebuilder, a sixteenth-century manual, by the monk Silvester, on religion and household management. A.M.

†One Russian edition adds: "First woman's rights, then civil marriage, and then divorce, come as unsettled questions." A.M.

evidently wishing to break off her conversation with him.

"But I don't," said the man. "You must define what you understand. . . ."

"Why? It's very simple," she said, but stopped to consider. "Love? Love is an exclusive preference for one above everybody else," said the lady.

"Preference for how long? A month, two days, or half an hour?" said the grey-haired man and began to laugh.

"Excuse me, we are evidently not speaking of the same thing."

"Oh, yes! Exactly the same."

"She means," interposed the lawyer, pointing to the lady, "that in the first place marriage must be the outcome of attachment—or love, if you please—and only where that exists is marriage sacred, so to speak. Secondly, that marriage when not based on natural attachment—love, if you prefer the word—lacks the element that makes it morally binding. Do I understand you rightly?" he added, addressing the lady.

The lady indicated her approval of his explanation by a nod of her head.

"It follows . . ." the lawyer continued—but the nervous man whose eyes now glowed as if aflame and who had evidently restrained himself with difficulty, began without letting the lawyer finish:

"Yes, I mean exactly the same thing, a preference for one person over everybody else, and I am only asking: a preference for how long?"

"For how long? For a long time; for life sometimes," replied the lady, shrugging her shoulders.

"Oh, but that happens only in novels and never in real life. In real life this preference for one may last for years (that happens very rarely), more often for months, or perhaps for weeks, days, or hours," he said, evidently aware that he was astonishing everybody by his views and pleased that it was so.

"Oh, what are you saying?" "But no . . ." "No, allow

me ..." we all three began at once. Even the clerk uttered an indefinite sound of disapproval.

"Yes, I know," the grey-haired man shouted above our voices, "you are talking about what is supposed to be, but I am speaking of what is. Every man experiences what you call love for every pretty woman."

"Oh, what you say is awful! But the feeling that is called love does exist among people, and is given not for months or years, but for a lifetime!"

"No, it does not! Even if we should grant that a man might prefer a certain woman all his life, the woman in all probability would prefer someone else; and so it always has been and still is in the world," he said, and taking out his cigarette-case he began to smoke.

"But the feeling may be reciprocal," said the lawyer.

"No, sir, it can't!" rejoined the other. "Just as it cannot be that in a cartload of peas, two marked peas will lie side by side. Besides, it is not merely this impossibility, but the inevitable satiety. To love one person for a whole lifetime is like saying that one candle will burn a whole life," he said, greedily inhaling the smoke.

"But you are talking all the time about physical love. Don't you acknowledge love based on identity of ideals, on spiritual affinity?" asked the lady.

"Spiritual affinity! Identity of ideals!" he repeated, emitting his peculiar sound. "But in that case why go to bed together? (Excuse my coarseness!) Or do people go to bed together because of the identity of their ideals?" he said, bursting into a nervous laugh.

"But permit me," said the lawyer. "Facts contradict you. We do see that matrimony exists, that all mankind, or the greater part of it, lives in wedlock, and many people honourably live long married lives."

The grey-haired man again laughed.

"First you say that marriage is based on love, and when I express a doubt as to the existence of a love other than sensual, you prove the existence of love by the fact that marriages exist. But marriages in our days are mere deception!"

"No, allow me!" said the lawyer. "I only say that marriages have existed and do exist."

"They do! But why? They have existed and do exist among people who in marriage something sacramental, a mystery binding them in the sight of God. Among them marriages do exist. Among us, people marry regarding marriage as nothing but copulation, and the result is either deception or coercion. When it is deception it is easier to bear. The husband and wife merely deceive people by pretending to be monogamists, while living polygamously. That is bad, but still bearable. But when, as most frequently happens, the husband and wife have undertaken the external duty of living together all their lives, and begin to hate each other after a month, and wish to part but still continue to live together, it leads to that terrible hell which makes people take to drink, shoot themselves, and kill or poison themselves or one another," he went on, speaking more and more rapidly, not allowing anyone to put in a word and becoming more and more excited. We all felt embarrassed.

"Yes, undoubtedly there are critical episodes in married life," said the lawyer, wishing to end this disturbingly heated conversation.

"I see you have found out who I am!" said the grey-haired man softly, and with apparent calm.

"No, I have not that pleasure."

"It is no great pleasure. I am that Pozdnyshev in whose life that critical episode occurred to which you alluded; the episode when he killed his wife," he said, rapidly glancing at each of us.

No one knew what to say and all remained silent.

"Well, never mind," he said with that peculiar sound of his. "However, pardon me. Ah! . . . I won't intrude on you."

"Oh, no, if you please . . ." said the lawyer, himself not knowing "if you please" what.

But Pozdnyshev, without listening to him, rapidly turned away and went back to his seat. The lawyer and the lady whispered together. I sat down beside Pozdnyshev in silence, unable to think of anything to say. It was too dark to read, so I shut my eyes pretending that I wished to go to sleep. So we travelled in silence to the next station.

At that station the lawyer and the lady moved into another car, having some time previously consulted the guard about it. The clerk lay down on the seat and fell asleep. Pozdnyshev kept smoking and drinking tea which he had made at the last station.

When I opened my eyes and looked at him he suddenly addressed me resolutely and irritably:

"Perhaps it is unpleasant for you to sit with me, knowing who I am? In that case I will go away."

"Oh no, not at all."

"Well, then, won't you have some? Only it's very strong." He poured out some tea for me.

"They talk ... and they always lie ..." he remarked.

"What are you speaking about?" I asked.

"Always about the same thing. About that love of theirs and what it is! Don't you want to sleep?"

"Not at all."

"Then would you like me to tell you how that love led to what happened to me?"

"Yes, if it will not be painful for you."

"No, it is painful for me to be silent. Drink the tea ... or is it too strong?"

The tea was really like beer, but I drank a glass of it.* Just then the guard entered. Pozdnyshev followed him with angry eyes, and only began to speak after he had left.

iii

"WELL, THEN, I'll tell you. But do you really want to hear it?"

I repeated that I wished it very much. He paused, rubbed his face with his hands, and began:

---

*Tëa in Russia is usually drunk out of tumblers. A.M.

"If I am to tell it, I must tell everything from the beginning: I must tell how and why I married, and the kind of man I was before my marriage.

"Till my marriage I lived as everybody does, that is, everybody in our class. I am a landowner and a graduate of the university, and was a marshal of the gentry. Before my marriage I lived as everyone does, that is, dissolutely; and while living dissolutely I was convinced, like everybody in our class, that I was living as one has to. I thought I was a charming fellow and quite a moral man. I was not a seducer, had no unnatural tastes, did not make that the chief purpose of my life as many of my associates did, but I practised debauchery in a steady, decent way for health's sake. I avoided women who might tie my hands by having a child or by attachment for me. However, there may have been children and attachments, but I acted as if there were not. And this I not only considered moral, but I was even proud of it."

He paused and gave vent to his peculiar sound, as he evidently did whenever a new idea occurred to him.

"And you know, that is the chief abomination!" he exclaimed. "Dissoluteness does not lie in anything physical—no kind of physical misconduct is debauchery; real debauchery lies precisely in freeing oneself from moral relations with a woman with whom you have physical intimacy. And such emancipation I regarded as a merit. I remember how I once worried because I had not had an opportunity to pay a woman who gave herself to me (having probably taken a fancy to me) and how I only became tranquil after having sent her some money—thereby intimating that I did not consider myself in any way morally bound to her . . . Don't nod as if you agree with me," he suddenly shouted at me. "Don't I know these things? We all, and you too unless you are a rare exception, hold those same views, just as I used to. Never mind, I beg your pardon, but the fact is that it's terrible, terrible, terrible!"

"What is terrible?" I asked.

"That abyss of error in which we live regarding

women and our relations with them. No, I can't speak calmly about it, not because of that 'episode' as he called it, in my life, but because since that 'episode' occurred my eyes have been opened and I have seen everything in quite a different light. Everything reversed, everything reversed!"

He lit a cigarette and began to speak, leaning his elbows on his knees.

It was too dark to see his face, but, above the jolting of the train, I could hear his impressive and pleasant voice.

iv

"YES, ONLY after such torments as I have endured, only by their means, have I understood where the root of the matter lies—understood what ought to be, and therefore seen all the horror of what is.

"So you will see how and when that which led up to my 'episode' began. It began when I was not quite sixteen. It happened when I still went to the grammar school and my elder brother was a first-year student at the university. I had not yet known any woman, but, like all the unfortunate children of our class, I was no longer an innocent boy. I had been depraved two years before that by other boys. Already woman, not some particular woman but woman as something to be desired, woman, every woman, woman's nudity, tormented me. My solitude was not pure. I was tormented, as ninety-nine per cent of our boys are. I was horrified, I suffered, I prayed, and I fell. I was already depraved in imagination and in fact, but I had not yet taken the last step. I was perishing, but I had not yet laid hands on another human being. But one day a comrade of my brother's, a jolly student, a so-called good fellow, that is, the worst kind of good-for-nothing, who had taught us to drink and to play cards, persuaded us after a carousal to go *there*. We went. My brother was also still innocent, and he fell that same night. And I, a fifteen-year-old boy, defiled myself and took part in defiling a woman, without at all understanding what I was doing. I had never heard from any of my elders that what I was doing was wrong, you know. And indeed no one hears it now. It is true it is in the Commandments, but then the Commandments are only needed to answer the priest at Scripture examination, and even then they are not very necessary, not nearly as necessary as the commandment about the use of *ut* in conditional sentences in Latin.

"And so I never heard those older persons whose opinions I respected say that it was an evil. On the contrary, I heard people I respected say it was good. I had heard that my struggles and sufferings would be eased after that. I heard this and read it, and heard my elders say it would be good for my health, while from my comrades I heard that it was rather a fine, spirited thing to do. So in general I expected nothing but good from it. The risk of disease? But that too had been foreseen. A paternal government saw to that. It sees to the correct working of the brothels,* and makes profligacy safe for schoolboys. Doctors too deal with it for a consideration. That is proper. They assert that debauchery is good for the health, and they organize proper well-regulated debauchery. I know some mothers who attend to their sons' health in that sense. And science sends them to the brothels."

"Why do you say 'science'?" I asked.

"Why, who are the doctors? The priests of science. Who deprave youths by maintaining that this is necessary for their health? They do.

"Yet if a one-hundredth part of the efforts devoted to the cure of syphilis were devoted to the eradication of debauchery, there would long ago not have been a trace

---

*In Russia, as in other continental countries and formerly in England, the *maisons de tolérance* were under the supervision of the government; doctors were employed to examine the women, and, as far as possible, see they did not continue their trade when diseased. A.M.

of syphilis left. But as it is, efforts are made not to eradicate debauchery but to encourage it and to make debauchery safe. This is not the point, however. The point is that with me—and with nine-tenths, if not more, not of our class only but of all classes, even the peasants—this terrible thing happens that happened to me; I fell not because I succumbed to the natural temptation of a particular woman's charm—no, I was not seduced by a woman—but I fell because, in the set around me, what was really a fall was regarded by some as a most legitimate function good for one's health, and by others as a very natural and not only excusable but even innocent amusement for a young man. I did not understand that it was a fall, but simply indulged in that half-pleasure, half-need, which, as was suggested to me, was natural at a certain age. I began to indulge in debauchery as I began to drink and smoke. Yet in that first fall there was something special and pathetic. I remember that at once, on the spot before I left the room, I felt sad, so sad that I wanted to cry—to cry for the loss of my innocence and for my relationship with women, now sullied forever. Yes, my natural, simple relationship with women was spoilt forever. From that time I have not had, and could not have, pure relations with women. I had become what is called a libertine. To be a libertine is a physical condition like that of a morphinist, a drunkard, or a smoker. As a morphinist, a drunkard, or a smoker is no longer normal, so too a man who has known several women for his pleasure is not normal but is a man perverted forever, a libertine. As a drunkard or a morphinist can be recognized at once by his face and manner, so it is with a libertine. A libertine may restrain himself, may struggle, but he will never have those pure, simple, clear, brotherly relations with a woman. By the way he looks at a young woman and examines her, a libertine can always be recognized. And I had become and I remained a libertine, and it was this that brought me to ruin."

v

"AH, YES! After that things went from bad to worse, and there were all sorts of deviations. Oh, God! When I recall the abominations I committed in this respect I am seized with horror! And that is true of me, whom my companions, I remember, ridiculed for my so-called innocence. And when one hears of the 'gilded youths,' of officers, of the Parisians . . . ! And when all these gentlemen, and I—who have on our souls hundreds of the most varied and horrible crimes against women—when we thirty-year-old profligates, very carefully washed, shaved, perfumed, in clean linen and in evening dress or uniform, enter a drawing-room or ballroom, we are emblems of purity, charming!

"Only think of what ought to be, and of what is! When in society such a gentleman comes up to my sister or daughter, I, knowing his life, ought to go up to him, take him aside, and say quietly, 'My dear fellow, I know the life you lead, and how and with whom you pass your nights. This is no place for you. There are pure, innocent girls here. Be off!' That is what ought to be; but what happens is that when such a gentleman comes and dances, embracing our sister or daughter, we are jubilant, if he is rich and well-connected. Maybe after Rigulboche* he will honour my daughter! Even if traces of disease remain, no matter! They are clever at curing that nowadays. Oh, yes, I know several girls in the best society whom their parents enthusiastically gave in marriage to men suffering from a certain disease. Oh, oh . . . the abomination of it! But a time will come when this abomination and falsehood will be exposed!"

He made his strange noise several times and again drank tea. It was fearfully strong and there was no water with which to dilute it. I felt that I was much excited by

*A notorious Parisian *cancanière.* A.M.

the two glasses I had drunk. Probably the tea affected him too, for he became more and more excited. His voice grew increasingly mellow and expressive. He continually changed his position, now taking off his cap and now putting it on again, and his face changed strangely in the semi-darkness in which we were sitting.

"Well, so I lived till I was thirty, not abandoning for a moment the intention of marrying and arranging for myself a most elevated and pure family life. With that purpose I observed the girls suitable for that end," he continued. "I weltered in a mire of debauchery and at the same time was on the lookout for a girl pure enough to be worthy of me.

"I rejected many just because they were not pure enough to suit me, but at last I found one whom I considered worthy. She was one of two daughters of a once-wealthy Penza landowner who had been ruined.

"One evening after we had been out in a boat and had returned by moonlight, and I was sitting beside her admiring her curls and her shapely figure in a tight-fitting jersey, I suddenly decided that it was she! It seemed to me that evening that she understood all that I felt and thought, and that what I felt and thought was very lofty. In reality it was only that the jersey and the curls were particularly becoming to her and that after a day spent near her I wanted to be still closer.

"It is amazing how complete is the delusion that beauty is goodness. A handsome woman talks nonsense, you listen and hear not nonsense but cleverness. She says and does horrid things, and you see only charm. And if a handsome woman does not say stupid or horrid things, you at once persuade yourself that she is wonderfully clever and moral.

"I returned home in rapture, decided that she was the acme of moral perfection, and that therefore she was worthy to be my wife, and I proposed to her next day.

"What a muddle it is! Out of a thousand men who marry (not only among us but unfortunately also among the masses) there is hardly one who has not already been married ten, a hundred, or even, like Don Juan, a thousand times, before his wedding.

"It is true as I have heard and have myself observed that there are nowadays some chaste young men who feel and know that this thing is not a joke but an important matter.

"God help them! But in my time there was not one such in ten thousand. And everybody knows this and pretends not to know it. In all the novels they describe in detail the heroes' feelings and the ponds and bushes beside which they walk, but when their great love for some maiden is described, nothing is said about what has happened to those interesting heroes before: not a word about their frequenting certain houses, or about the servant-girls, cooks, and other people's wives! If there are such improper novels they are not put into the hands of those who most need this information—the unmarried girls.

"We first pretend to these girls that the profligacy which fills half the life of our towns, and even of the villages, does not exist at all.

"Then we get so accustomed to this pretence that at last, like the English, we ourselves really begin to believe that we are all moral people and live in a moral world. The girls, poor things, believe this quite seriously. So too did my unfortunate wife. I remember how, when we were engaged, I showed her my diary, from which she could learn something, if but a little, of my past, especially about my last liaison, of which she might hear from others, and about which I therefore felt it necessary to inform her. I remember her horror, despair, and confusion, when she learnt of it and understood it. I saw that she then wanted to give me up. And why did she not do so? ..."

He again made that sound, swallowed another mouthful of tea, and remained silent for a while.

vi

"No, AFTER all, it is better, better so!" he exclaimed. "It serves me right! But that's not to the point—I meant to say that it is only the unfortunate girls who are deceived.

"The mothers know it, especially mothers educated by their own husbands—they know it very well. While pretending to believe in the purity of men, they act quite differently. They know with what sort of bait to catch men for themselves and for their daughters.

"You see it is only we men who don't know (because we don't wish to know) what women know very well, that the most exalted poetic love, as we call it, depends not on moral qualities but on physical nearness and on the coiffure, and the colour and cut of the dress. Ask an expert coquette who has set herself the task of captivating a man, which she would prefer to risk: to be convicted in his presence of lying, of cruelty, or even of dissoluteness, or to appear before him in an ugly and badly made dress—she will always prefer the first. She knows that we are continually lying about high sentiments, but really only want her body and will therefore forgive any abomination except an ugly tasteless costume that is in bad style.

"A coquette knows that consciously, and every innocent girl knows it unconsciously just as animals do.

"That is why there are those detestable jerseys, bustles, and naked shoulders, arms, almost breasts. A woman, especially if she has passed the male school, knows very well that all the talk about elevated subjects is just talk, but that what a man wants is her body and all that presents it in the most deceptive but alluring light; and she acts accordingly. If we only throw aside our familiarity with this indecency, which has become a second nature to us, and look at the life of our upper classes as it is, in all its shamelessness—why, it is simply a brothel ... You don't agree? Allow me, I'll prove it," he said, interrupting me. "You say that the women of our society have other interests in life than prostitutes have, but I say no, and will prove it. If people differ in the aims of their lives, by the inner content of their lives, this difference will necessarily be reflected in externals and their externals will be different. But look at those unfortunate despised women and at the highest society ladies: the same costumes, the same fashions, the same perfumes, the same exposure of arms, shoulders, and breasts, the same tight skirts over prominent bustles, the same passion for little stones, for costly, glittering objects, the same amusements, dances, music, and singing. As the former employ all means to allure, so do these others."

vii

"WELL, so these jerseys and curls and bustles caught me!

"It was very easy to catch me for I was brought up in the conditions in which amorous young people are forced like cucumbers in a hot-bed. You see our stimulating superabundance of food, together with complete physical idleness, is nothing but a systematic excitement of desire. Whether this astonishes you or not, it is so. Why, till quite recently I did not see anything of this myself, but now I have seen it. That is why it torments me that nobody knows this, and people talk such nonsense as that lady did.

"Yes, last spring some peasants were working in our neighbourhood on a railway embankment. The usual food of a young peasant is rye-bread, kvas, and onions; he keeps alive and is vigorous and healthy; his work is light agricultural work. When he goes to railway-work his rations are buckwheat porridge and a pound of meat a day. But he works off that pound of meat during his sixteen hours' work wheeling barrow-loads of half-a-ton weight, so it is just enough for him. But we who every day consume two pounds of meat, and game, and fish and all sorts of heating foods and drinks—where does that go to? Into excesses of sensuality. And if it goes

there and the safety-valve is open, all is well; but try and
close the safety-valve, as I closed it temporarily, and at
once a stimulus arises which, passing through the prism
of our artificial life, expresses itself in utter infatuation,
sometimes even platonic. And I fell in love as they all do.

"Everything was there to hand: raptures, tenderness,
and poetry. In reality that love of mine was the result, on
the one hand of her mamma's and the dressmakers' activity, and on the other of the superabundance of food
consumed by me while living an idle life. If on the one
hand there had been no boating, no dressmaker with her
waists and so forth, and had my wife been sitting at home
in a shapeless dressing-gown, and had I on the other
hand been in circumstances normal to man—consuming
just enough food to suffice for the work I did, and had
the safety-valve been open—it happened to be closed at
the time—I should not have fallen in love and nothing of
all this would have happened."

viii

"WELL, and now it so chanced that everything combined—
my condition, her becoming dress, and the satisfactory
boating. It had failed twenty times but now it succeeded.
Just like a trap! I am not joking. You see nowadays marriages are arranged that way—like traps. What is the
natural way? The lass is ripe, she must be given in marriage. It seems very simple if the girl is not a fright and
there are men wanting to marry. That is how it was done
in olden times. The lass was grown up and her parents arranged the marriage. So it was done, and is done, among
all mankind—Chinese, Hindus, Mohammedans, and
among our own working classes; so it is done among at
least ninety-nine per cent of the human race. Only
among one per cent or less, among us libertines, has it
been discovered that that is not right, and something
new has been invented. And what is this novelty? It is
that the maidens sit round and the men walk about, as at

a bazaar, choosing. And the maidens wait and think, but dare not say: 'Me, please!' 'No, me!' 'Not her, but me!' 'Look what shoulders and other things I have!' And we men stroll around and look, and are very pleased. 'Yes, I know! I won't be caught!' They stroll about and look, and are very pleased that everything is arranged like that for them. And then in an unguarded moment—snap! He is caught!"

"Then how ought it to be done?" I asked. "Should the woman propose?"

"Oh, I don't know how; only if there's to be equality, let it be equality. If they have discovered that prearranged matches are degrading, why, this is a thousand times worse! Then the rights and chances were equal, but here the woman is a slave in a bazaar or the bait in a trap. Tell any mother, or the girl herself, the truth, that she is only occupied in catching a husband . . . oh dear! what an insult! Yet they all do it and have nothing else to do. What is so terrible is to see sometimes quite innocent poor young girls engaged on it. And again, if it were but done openly—but it is always done deceitfully. 'Ah, the origin of species, how interesting!' 'Oh, Lily takes such an interest in painting! And will you be going to the exhibition? How instructive!' And the troyka-drives, and shows, and symphonies! 'Oh, how remarkable! My Lily is mad on music.' 'And why don't you share these convictions?' And boating . . . But their one thought is: 'Take me, take me!' 'Take my Lily!' 'Or try—at least!' Oh, what an abomination! What falsehood!" he concluded, finishing his tea and beginning to put away the tea-things.

ix

"You know," he began while packing the tea and sugar into his bag, "the domination of women from which the world suffers all arises from this."

"What 'domination of women'?" I asked. "The rights, the legal privileges, are on the man's side."

"Yes, yes! That's just it," he interrupted me. "That's just what I want to say. It explains the extraordinary phenomenon that on the one hand woman is reduced to the lowest stage of humiliation, while on the other she dominates. Just like the Jews: as they pay us back for their oppression by a financial domination, so it is with women. 'Ah, you want us to be traders only—all right, as traders we will dominate you!' say the Jews. 'Ah, you want us to be merely objects of sensuality—all right, as objects of sensuality we will enslave you,' say the women. Woman's lack of rights arises not from the fact that she must not vote or be a judge—to be occupied with such affairs is no privilege—but from the fact that she is not man's equal in sexual intercourse and has not the right to use a man or abstain from him as she likes—is not allowed to choose a man at her pleasure instead of being chosen by him. You say that is monstrous. Very well! Then a man must not have those rights either. As it is at present, a woman is deprived of that right while a man has it. And to make up for that right she acts on man's sensuality, and through his sensuality subdues him so that he only chooses formally, while in reality it is she who chooses. And once she has obtained these means she abuses them and acquires a terrible power over people."

"But where is this special power?" I inquired.

"Where is it? Why, everywhere, in everything! Go round the shops in any big town. There are goods worth millions and you cannot estimate the human labour expended on them, and look whether in nine-tenths of these shops there is anything for the use of men. All the luxuries of life are demanded and maintained by women.

"Count all the factories. An enormous proportion of them produce useless ornaments, carriages, furniture, and trinkets for women. Millions of people, generations of slaves, perish at hard labour in factories merely to satisfy woman's caprice. Women, like queens, keep nine-tenths of mankind in bondage to heavy labour. And all because they have been abased and deprived of equal rights with men. And they revenge themselves by acting on our sensuality and catch us in their nets. Yes, it all comes of that.

"Women have made of themselves such an instrument for acting upon our sensuality that a man cannot quietly consort with a woman. As soon as a man approaches a woman he succumbs to her stupefying influence and becomes intoxicated and crazy. I used formerly to feel uncomfortable and uneasy when I saw a lady dressed up for a ball, but now I am simply frightened and plainly see her as something dangerous and illicit. I want to call a policeman and ask for protection from the peril, and demand that the dangerous object be removed and put away.

"Ah, you are laughing!" he shouted at me, "but it is not at all a joke. I am sure a time will come, and perhaps very soon, when people will understand this and will wonder how a society could exist in which actions were permitted which so disturb social tranquillity as those adornments of the body directly evoking sensuality, which we tolerate for women in our society. Why, it's like setting all sorts of traps along the paths and promenades—it is even worse! Why is gambling forbidden while women in costumes which evoke sensuality are not forbidden? They are a thousand times more dangerous!"

x

"WELL, you see, I was caught that way. I was what is called in love. I not only imagined her to be the height of perfection, but during the time of our engagement I regarded myself also as the height of perfection. You know there is no rascal who cannot, if he tries, find rascals in some respects worse than himself, and who consequently cannot find reasons for pride and self-satisfaction. So it was with me: I was not marrying for money—covetousness had nothing to do with it—unlike the majority of my acquaintances who married for money or connexions— I was rich, she was poor. That was one thing. Another thing I prided myself on was that while others married intending to continue in future the same polygamous life they had lived before marriage, I was firmly resolved to be monogamous after marriage, and there was no limit to my pride on that score. Yes, I was a dreadful pig and imagined myself to be an angel.

"Our engagement did not last long. I cannot now think of that time without shame! What nastiness! Love is supposed to be spiritual and not sensual. Well, if the love is spiritual, a spiritual communion, then that spiritual communion should find expression in words, in conversations, in discourse. There was nothing of the kind. It used to be dreadfully difficult to talk when we were left alone. It was the labour of Sisyphus. As soon as we thought of something to say and said it, we had again to be silent, devising something else. There was nothing to talk about. All that could be said about the life that awaited us, our arrangements and plans, had been said, and what was there more? Now if we had been animals we should have known that speech was unnecessary; but here on the contrary it was necessary to speak, and there was nothing to say, because we were not occupied with what finds vent in speech. And moreover there was that ridiculous custom of giving sweets, of coarse gormandizing on sweets, and all those abominable preparations for the wedding: remarks about the house, the bedroom, beds, wraps, dressing-gowns, underclothing, costumes. You must remember that if one married according to the injunctions of *Domostroy,* as that old fellow was saying, then the featherbeds, the trousseau, and the bedstead— are all but details appropriate to the sacrament. But among us, when of ten who marry there are certainly nine who not only do not believe in the sacrament, but do not even believe that what they are doing entails certain obligations—where scarcely one man out of a hundred has not been married before, and of fifty scarcely one is not preparing in advance to be unfaithful to his wife at every convenient opportunity—when the majority regard the going to church as only a special condition for obtaining possession of a certain woman—think what a dreadful significance all these details acquire. They show that the whole business is only that; they show that it is a kind of sale. An innocent girl is sold to a profligate, and the sale is accompanied by certain formalities."

xi

"THAT IS how everybody marries and that is how I married, and the much vaunted honeymoon began. Why, its very name is vile!" he hissed viciously. "In Paris I once went to see the sights, and noticing a bearded woman and a water-dog on a sign-board, I entered the show. It turned out to be nothing but a man in a woman's low-necked dress, and a dog done up in walrus skin and swimming in a bath. It was very far from being interesting; but as I was leaving, the showman politely saw me out and, addressing the public at the entrance, pointed to me and said, 'Ask the gentleman whether it is not worth seeing! Come in, come in, one franc apiece!' I felt ashamed to say it was not worth seeing, and the showman had probably counted on that. It must be the same with those who have experienced the abomination of a honeymoon and who do not disillusion others. Neither did I disillusion anyone, but I do not now see why I should not tell the truth. Indeed, I think it needful to tell the truth about it. One felt awkward, ashamed, repelled, sorry, and above all dull, intolerably dull! It was something like what I felt when I learnt to smoke—when I felt sick and the saliva gathered in my mouth and I swallowed it and pretended that it was very pleasant. Pleasure from smoking, just as from that, if it comes at all, comes later. The husband must cultivate that vice in his wife in order to derive pleasure from it."

"Why vice?" I said. "You are speaking of the most natural human functions."

"Natural?" he said. "Natural? No, I may tell you that

I have come to the conclusion that it is, on the contrary, *un*natural. Yes, quite *un*natural. Ask a child, ask an un-perverted girl.

"Natural, you say!

"It is natural to eat. And to eat is, from the very be-ginning, enjoyable, easy, pleasant, and not shameful; but this is horrid, shameful, and painful. No, it is unnatural! And an unspoilt girl, as I have convinced myself, always hates it."

"But how," I asked, "would the human race con-tinue?"

"Yes, would not the human race perish?" he said, irri-tably and ironically, as if he had expected this familiar and insincere objection. "Teach abstention from child-bearing so that English lords may always gorge themselves—that is all right. Preach it for the sake of greater pleasure—that is all right; but just hint at abstention from child-bearing in the name of morality—and, my goodness, what a rum-pus . . . ! Isn't there a danger that the human race may die out because they want to cease to be swine? But forgive me! This light is unpleasant, may I shade it?" he said, pointing to the lamp. I said I did not mind; and with the haste with which he did everything, he got up on the seat and drew the woollen shade over the lamp.

"All the same," I said, "if everyone thought this the right thing to do, the human race would cease to exist."

He did not reply at once.

"You ask how the human race will continue to exist," he said, having again sat down in front of me, and spread-ing his legs far apart he leant his elbows on his knees. "Why should it continue?"

"Why? If not, we should not exist."

"And why should we exist?"

"Why? In order to live, of course."

"But why live? If life has no aim, if life is given us for life's sake, there is no reason for living. And if it is so, then the Schopenhauers, the Hartmanns, and all the Buddhists as well are quite right. But if life has an aim, it is clear that it ought to come to an end when that aim is reached. And so it turns out," he said with noticeable agitation, evidently prizing his thought very highly. "So it turns out. Just think: if the aim of humanity is goodness, righteousness, love—call it what you will—if it is what the prophets have said, that all mankind should be united together in love, that the spears should be beaten into pruning-hooks and so forth, what is it that hinders the attainment of this aim? The passions hinder it. Of all the passions the strongest, cruellest, and most stubborn is the sex-passion, physical love; and therefore if the passions are destroyed, including the strongest of them— physical love—the prophecies will be fulfilled, mankind will be brought into a unity, the aim of human existence will be attained, and there will be nothing further to live for. As long as mankind exists the ideal is before it, and of course not the rabbits' and pigs' ideal of breeding as fast as possible, nor that of monkeys or Parisians—to enjoy sex-passion in the most refined manner, but the ideal of goodness attained by continence and purity. Towards that people have always striven and still strive. You see what follows.

"It follows that physical love is a safety-valve. If the present generation has not attained its aim, it has not done so because of its passions, of which the sex-passion is the strongest. And if the sex-passion endures there will be a new generation and consequently the possibility of attaining the aim in the next generation. If the next one does not attain it, then the next after that may, and so on, till the aim is attained, the prophecies fulfilled, and mankind attains unity. If not, what would result? If one admits that God created men for the attainment of a certain aim, and created them mortal but sexless, or created them immortal, what would be the result? Why, if they were mortal but without the sex-passion, and died without attaining the aim, God would have had to create new people to attain his aim. If they were immortal, let us grant that (though it would be more difficult for the same people to correct their mistakes and approach perfection than for those of another generation) they might attain that aim after many thousands of years, but then what use would they be afterwards? What could be done with them? It is best as it is. . . . But perhaps you don't like that way of putting it? Perhaps you are an evolutionist? It comes to the same thing. The highest race of animals, the human race, in order to maintain itself in the struggle with other animals, ought to unite into one whole like a swarm of bees, and not breed continually; it should bring up sexless members as the bees do; that is, again, it should strive towards continence and not towards inflaming desire—to which the whole system of our life is now directed." He paused. "The human race will cease? But can anyone doubt it, whatever his outlook on life may be? Why, it is as certain as death. According to all the teaching of the Church the end of the world will come, and according to all the teaching of science the same result is inevitable."

xii

"IN OUR world it is just the reverse: even if a man does think of continence while he is a bachelor, once married he is sure to think continence no longer necessary. You know those wedding tours—the seclusion into which, with their parents' consent, the young couple go—are nothing but licensed debauchery. But a moral law avenges itself when it is violated. Hard as I tried to make a success of my honeymoon, nothing came of it. It was horrid, shameful, and dull, the whole time. And very soon I began also to experience a painful, oppressive feeling. That began very quickly. I think it was on the third or fourth day that I found my wife depressed. I began asking her the reason and embracing her, which in my view was all she could want, but she removed my arm and began to cry. What about? She could not say. But she felt sad and distressed. Probably her exhausted nerves suggested to her the truth as to the vileness of our relation but she did not know how to express it. I began to question her, and she said something about feeling sad without her mother. It seemed to me that this was untrue, and I began comforting her without alluding to her mother. I did not understand that she was simply depressed and her mother was merely an excuse. But she immediately took offence because I had not mentioned her mother, as though I did not believe her. She told me she saw that I did not love her. I reproached her with being capricious, and suddenly her face changed entirely and instead of sadness it expressed irritation, and with the most venomous words she began accusing me of selfishness and cruelty. I gazed at her. Her whole face showed complete coldness and hostility, almost hatred. I remember how horror-struck I was when I saw this. 'How? What?' I thought. 'Love is a union of souls—and instead of that there is this! Impossible, this is not she!' I tried to soften her, but encountered such an insuperable wall of cold virulent hostility that before I had time to turn round I too was seized with irritation and we said a great many unpleasant things to one another. The impression of that first quarrel was dreadful. I call it a quarrel, but it was not a quarrel but only the disclosure of the abyss that really existed between us. Amorousness was exhausted by the satisfaction of sensuality and we were left confronting one another in our true relation: that is, as two egotists quite alien to each other who wished to get as much pleasure as possible each from the other. I call what took place between us a quarrel, but it was not a quarrel, only the consequence of the cessation of sensuality—revealing our real relations to one another. I did not understand that this cold and hostile relation was our normal state, I did not understand it because at first this hostile attitude was very soon concealed from us by a renewal of redistilled sensuality, that is by love-making.

"I thought we had quarrelled and made it up again, and that it would not recur. But during that same first month of honeymoon a period of satiety soon returned, we again ceased to need one another, and another quar-

rel supervened. This second quarrel struck me even
more painfully than the first. 'So the first one was not an
accident but was bound to happen and will happen
again,' I thought. I was all the more staggered by that
second quarrel because it arose from such an impossible
pretext. It had something to do with money, which I
never grudged and could certainly not have grudged to
my wife. I only remember that she gave the matter such
a twist that some remark of mine appeared to be an expression of a desire on my part to dominate over her by
means of money, to which I was supposed to assert an
exclusive right—it was something impossibly stupid,
mean, and not natural either to me or to her. I became
exasperated, and upbraided her with lack of consideration for me. She accused me of the same thing, and it all
began again. In her words and in the expression of her
face and eyes I again noticed the cruel cold hostility that
had so staggered me before. I had formerly quarrelled
with my brother, my friends, and my father, but there
had never, I remember, been the special venomous mal-
ice which there was here. But after a while this mutual
hatred was screened by amorousness, that is, sensuality,
and I still consoled myself with the thought that these
two quarrels had been mistakes and could be remedied.
But then a third and a fourth quarrel followed and I realized that it was not accidental, but that it was bound to
happen and would happen so, and I was horrified at the
prospect before me. At the same time I was tormented
by the terrible thought that I alone lived on such bad
terms with my wife, so unlike what I had expected,
whereas this did not happen between other married
couples. I did not know then that it is our common fate,
but that everybody imagines, just as I did, that it is their
peculiar misfortune, and everyone conceals this exceptional and shameful misfortune not only from others but
even from himself and does not acknowledge it to himself.

"It began during the first days and continued all the
time, ever increasing and growing more obdurate. In the

depths of my soul I felt from the first weeks that I was
lost, that things had not turned out as I expected, that
marriage was not only no happiness but a very heavy
burden; but like everybody else I did not wish to acknowledge this to myself (I should not have acknowledged it even now but for the end that followed) and I
concealed it not only from others but from myself too.
Now I am astonished that I failed to see my real position.
It might have been seen from the fact that the quarrels
began on pretexts it was impossible to remember when
they were over. Our reason was not quick enough to
devise sufficient excuses for the animosity that always
existed between us. But more striking still was the insuf-
ficiency of the excuses for our reconciliations. Sometimes there were words, explanations, even tears, but
sometimes . . . oh! it is disgusting even now to think of
it—after the most cruel words to one another, came sudden silent glances, smiles, kisses, embraces. . . . Faugh,
how horrid! How is it I did not then see all the vileness
of it?"

xiii

Two FRESH passengers entered and settled down on the
farthest seats. He was silent while they were seating
themselves but as soon as they had settled down continued, evidently not for a moment losing the thread of his
idea.

"You know, what is vilest about it," he began, "is that
in theory love is something ideal and exalted, but in
practice it is something abominable, swinish, which it is
horrid and shameful to mention or remember. It is not
for nothing that nature has made it disgusting and
shameful. And if it is disgusting and shameful one must
understand that it is so. But here, on the contrary, people
pretend that what is disgusting and shameful is beautiful
and lofty. What were the first symptoms of my love? Why,
that I gave way to animal excesses, not without shame

but being somehow even proud of the possibility of these physical excesses, and without in the least considering either her spiritual or even her physical life. I wondered what embittered us against one another, yet it was perfectly simple: that animosity was nothing but the protest of our human nature against the animal nature that overpowered it.

"I was surprised at our enmity to one another; yet it could not have been otherwise. That hatred was nothing but the mutual hatred of accomplices in a crime—both for the incitement to the crime and for the part taken in it. What was it but a crime when she, poor thing, became pregnant in the first month and our *swinish* connexion continued? You think I am straying from my subject? Not at all! I am telling you *how* I killed my wife. They asked me at the trial with what and how I killed her. Fools! They thought I killed her with a knife, on the 5th of October. It was not then I killed her, but much earlier. Just as they are all now killing, all, all . . ."

"But with what?" I asked.

"That is just what is so surprising, that nobody wants to see what is so clear and evident, what doctors ought to know and preach, but are silent about. Yet the matter is very simple. Men and women are created like the animals so that physical love is followed by pregnancy and then by suckling—conditions under which physical love is bad for the woman and for her child. There are an equal number of men and women. What follows from this? It seems clear, and no great wisdom is needed to draw the conclusion that animals do, namely, the need of continence. But no. Science has been able to discover some kind of leucocytes that run about in the blood, and all sorts of useless nonsense, but cannot understand that. At least one does not hear of science teaching it!

"And so a woman has only two ways out: one is to make a monster of herself, to destroy and go on destroying within herself to such degree as may be necessary the capacity of being a woman, that is, a mother, in order that a man may quietly and continuously get his enjoy-

ment; the other way out—and it is not even a way out
but a simple, coarse, and direct violation of the laws of
nature—practised in all so-called decent families—is
that, contrary to her nature, the woman must be her husband's mistress even while she is pregnant or nursing—
must be what not even an animal descends to, and for
which her strength is insufficient. That is what causes
nerve troubles and hysteria in our class, and among the
peasants causes what they call being 'possessed by the
devil'—epilepsy. You will notice that no pure maidens
are ever 'possessed,' but only married women living with
their husbands. That is so here, and it is just the same in
Europe. All the hospitals for hysterical women are full of
those who have violated nature's law. The epileptics and
Charcot's patients are complete wrecks, you know, but
the world is full of half-crippled women. Just think of it,
what a great work goes on within a woman when she
conceives or when she is nursing an infant. That is growing which will continue us and replace us. And this sacred work is violated—by what? It is terrible to think of
it! And they prate about the freedom and the rights of
women! It is as if cannibals fattened their captives to be
eaten, and at the same time declared that they were concerned about their prisoners' rights and freedom."

All this was new to me and startled me.

"What is one to do? If that is so," I said, "it means that
one may love one's wife once in two years, yet men . . ."

"Men must!" he interrupted me. "It is again those precious priests of science who have persuaded everybody
of that. Imbue a man with the idea that he requires
vodka, tobacco, or opium, and all these things will be
indispensable to him. It seems that God did not understand what was necessary and therefore, omitting to consult those wizards, arranged things badly. You see matters
do not tally. They have decided that it is essential for a
man to satisfy his desires, and the bearing and nursing of
children comes and interferes with it and hinders the satisfaction of that need. What is one to do then? Consult
the wizards! They will arrange it. And they have devised

something. Oh! When will those wizards with their de-
ceptions be dethroned? It is high time! It has come to
such a point that people go mad and shoot themselves
and all because of this. How could it be otherwise? The
animals seem to know that their progeny continue their
race, and they keep to a certain law in this matter. Man
alone neither knows it nor wishes to know, but is concerned only to get all the pleasure he can. And who is
doing that? The lord of nature—man! Animals, you see,
only come together at times when they are capable of
producing progeny, but the filthy lord of nature is at it
any time if only it pleases him! And as if that were not
sufficient, he exalts this apish occupation into the most
precious pearl of creation, into love. In the name of this
love, that is, this filth, he destroys—what? Why, half the
human race! All the women who might help the progress
of mankind towards truth and goodness he converts, for
the sake of his pleasure, into enemies instead of help-
mates. See what it is that everywhere impedes the forward movement of mankind. Women! And why are they
what they are? Only because of that. Yes, yes . . ." he repeated several times, and began to move about, and to
get out his cigarettes and to smoke, evidently trying to
calm himself.

xiv

"I too lived like a pig of that sort," he continued in his
former tone. "The worst thing about it was that while
living that horrid life I imagined that, because I did not
go after other women, I was living an honest family life,
that I was a moral man and in no way blame-worthy; and
if quarrels occurred it was her fault and resulted from
her character.

"Of course the fault was not hers. She was like everybody else—like the majority of women. She had been
brought up as the position of women in our society requires, and as therefore all women of the leisured classes

without exception are brought up and cannot help being brought up. People talk about some new kind of education for women. It is all empty words: their education is exactly what it has to be in view of our unfeigned, real, general opinion about women.

"The education of women will always correspond to men's opinion about them. Don't we know how men regard women: *Wein, Weib, und Gesang,* and what the poets say in their verses? Take all poetry, all pictures and sculpture, beginning with love poems and the nude Venuses and Phrynes, and you will see that woman is an instrument of enjoyment; she is so on the Truba and the Grachevka,* and also at the Court† balls. And note the devil's cunning: if they are here for enjoyment and pleasure, let it be known that it is pleasure and that woman is a sweet morsel. But no, first the knights-errant declare that they worship women (worship her, and yet regard her as an instrument of enjoyment), and now people assure us that they respect women. Some give up their places to her, pick up her handkerchief; others acknowledge her right to occupy all positions and to take part in the government, and so on. They do all that, but their outlook on her remains the same. She is a means of enjoyment. Her body is a means of enjoyment. And she knows this. It is just as it is with slavery. Slavery, you know, is nothing else than the exploitation by some of the unwilling labour of many. Therefore to get rid of slavery it is necessary that people should not wish to profit by the forced labour of others and should consider it a sin and a shame. But they go and abolish the external form of slavery and arrange so that one can no longer buy and sell slaves, and they imagine and assure themselves that slavery no longer exists, and do not see or wish to see that it does, because people still want and consider it good and right to exploit the labour of others.

*Streets in Moscow in which brothels were numerous. A.M.
†In the printed and censored Russian edition the word "Court" was changed to "most refined." A.M.

And as long as they consider that good, there will always be people stronger or more cunning than others who will succeed in doing it. So it is with the emancipation of woman: the enslavement of woman lies simply in the fact that people desire, and think it good, to avail themselves of her as a tool of enjoyment. Well, and they liberate woman, give her all sorts of rights equal to man, but continue to regard her as an instrument of enjoyment, and so educate her in childhood and afterwards by public opinion. And there she is, still the same humiliated and depraved slave, and the man still a depraved slave-owner.

"They emancipate women in universities and in law courts, but continue to regard her as an object of enjoyment. Teach her, as she is taught among us, to regard herself as such, and she will always remain an inferior being. Either with the help of those scoundrels the doctors she will prevent the conception of offspring—that is, will be a complete prostitute, lowering herself not to the level of an animal but to the level of a thing—or she will be what the majority of women are, mentally diseased, hysterical, unhappy, and lacking capacity for spiritual development. High schools and universities cannot alter that. It can only be changed by a change in men's outlook on women and women's way of regarding themselves. It will change only when woman regards virginity as the highest state, and does not, as at present, consider the highest state of a human being a shame and a disgrace. While that is not so, the ideal of every girl, whatever her education may be, will continue to be to attract as many men as possible, as many males as possible, so as to have the possibility of choosing.

"But the fact that one of them knows more mathematics, and another can play the harp, makes no difference. A woman is happy and attains all she can desire when she has bewitched a man. Therefore the chief aim of a woman is to be able to bewitch him. So it has been and will be. So it is in her maiden life in our society, and so it continues to be in her married life. For a maiden this is necessary in order to have a choice, for the married woman in order to have power over her husband.

"The one thing that stops this, or at any rate suppresses it for a time, is children, and then only if the mother is not a monster, that is, if she nurses them herself. But here the doctors again come in.

"My wife, who wanted to nurse, and did nurse the four later children herself, happened to be unwell after the birth of her first child. And those doctors, who cynically undressed her and felt her all over—for which I had to thank them and pay them money—those dear doctors considered that she must not nurse the child; and that first time she was deprived of the only means which might have kept her from coquetry. We engaged a wet nurse, that is, we took advantage of the poverty, the need, and the ignorance of a woman, tempted her away from her own baby to ours, and in return gave her a fine head-dress with gold lace.* But that is not the point. The point is that during that time when my wife was free from pregnancy and from suckling, the feminine coquetry which had lain dormant within her manifested itself with particular force. And coinciding with this the torments of jealousy rose up in me with special force. They tortured me all my married life, as they cannot but torture all husbands who live with their wives as I did with mine, that is, immorally."

XV

"DURING THE whole of my married life I never ceased to be tormented by jealousy, but there were periods when I specially suffered from it. One of these periods was when, after the birth of our first child, the doctors forbade my wife to nurse it. I was particularly jealous at that time, in the first place because my wife was experi-

---

*In Russia wet nurses were usually provided with an elaborate national costume by their employers. A.M.

encing that unrest natural to a mother which is sure to
be aroused when the natural course of life is needlessly
violated; and secondly, because seeing how easily she
abandoned her moral obligations as a mother, I rightly
though unconsciously concluded that it would be equally
easy for her to disregard her duty as a wife, especially as
she was quite well and in spite of the precious doctors'
prohibition was able to nurse her later children admira-
bly."

"I see you don't like doctors," I said, noticing a pecu-
liarly malevolent tone in his voice whenever he alluded
to them.

"It is not a case of liking or disliking. They have ruined my life as they have ruined and are ruining the lives
of thousands and hundreds of thousands of human beings, and I cannot help connecting the effect with the
cause. I understand that they want to earn money like
lawyers and others, and I would willingly give them half
my income, and all who realize what they are doing
would willingly give them half of their possessions, if
only they would not interfere with our family life and
would never come near us. I have not collected evidence,
but I know dozens of cases (there are any number of
them!) where they have killed a child in its mother's
womb asserting that she could not give it birth, though
she has had children quite safely later on; or they have
killed the mother on the pretext of performing some operation. No one reckons these murders any more than
they reckoned the murders of the Inquisition, because it
is supposed that it is done for the good of mankind. It is
impossible to number all the crimes they commit. But all
those crimes are as nothing compared to the moral cor-
ruption of materialism they introduce into the world,
especially through women.

"I don't lay stress on the fact that if one is to follow
their instructions, then on account of the infection which
exists everywhere and in everything, people would not
progress towards greater unity but towards separation;
for according to their teaching we ought all to sit apart

and not remove the carbolic atomizer from our mouths (though now they have discovered that even that is of no avail). But that does not matter either. The principal poison lies in the demoralization of the world, especially of women.

"Today one can no longer say: 'You are not living rightly, live better.' One can't say that, either to oneself or to anyone else. If you live a bad life it is caused by the abnormal functioning of your nerves, &c. So you must go to them, and they will prescribe eight penn'orth of medicine from a chemist, which you must take!

"You get still worse: then more medicine and the doctor again. An excellent trick!

"That, however, is not the point. All I wish to say is that she nursed her babies perfectly well and that only her pregnancy and the nursing of her babies saved me from the torments of jealousy. Had it not been for that it would all have happened sooner. The children saved me and her. In eight years she had five children and nursed all except the first herself."

"And where are your children now?" I asked.

"The children?" he repeated in a frightened voice.

"Forgive me, perhaps it is painful for you to be reminded of them."

"No, it does not matter. My wife's sister and brother have taken them. They would not let me have them. I gave them my estate, but they did not give them up to me. You know I am a sort of lunatic. I have left them now and am going away. I have seen them, but they won't let me have them because I might bring them up so that they would not be like their parents, and they have to be just like them. Oh well, what is to be done? Of course they won't let me have them and won't trust me. Besides, I do not know whether I should be able to bring them up. I think not. I am a ruin, a cripple. Still I have one thing in me. I know! Yes, that is true, I know what others are far from knowing.

"Yes, my children are living and growing up just such savages as everybody around them. I saw them, saw them three times. I can do nothing for them, nothing. I am now going to my place in the south. I have a little house and a small garden there.

"Yes, it will be a long time before people learn what I know. How much of iron and other metal there is in the sun and the stars is easy to find out, but anything that exposes our swinishness is difficult, terribly difficult!

"You at least listen to me, and I am grateful for that."

xvi

"You mentioned my children. There again, what terrible lies are told about children! Children a blessing from God, a joy! That is all a lie. It was so once upon a time, but now it is not so at all. Children are a torment and nothing else. Most mothers feel this quite plainly, and sometimes inadvertently say so. Ask most mothers of our propertied classes and they will tell you that they do not want to have children for fear of their falling ill and dying. They don't want to nurse* them if they do have them, for fear of becoming too much attached to them and having to suffer. The pleasure a baby gives them by its loveliness, its little hands and feet, and its whole body, is not as great as the suffering caused by the very fear of its possibly falling ill and dying, not to speak of its actual illness or death. After weighing the advantages and disadvantages it seems disadvantageous, and therefore undesirable, to have children. They say this quite frankly and boldly, imagining that these feelings of theirs arise from their love of children, a good and laudable feeling of which they are proud. They do not notice that by this reflection they plainly repudiate love, and only affirm their own selfishness. They get less pleasure from a baby's loveliness than suffering from fear on its account, and there-

---

*The practice of employing wet nurses was very much more general in Russia than in the English-speaking countries. A.M.

fore the baby they would love is not wanted. They do not
sacrifice themselves for a beloved being, but sacrifice a
being whom they might love, for their own sakes.

"It is clear that this is not love but selfishness. But one
has not the heart to blame them—the mothers in well-
to-do families—for that selfishness, when one remembers how dreadfully they suffer on account of their
children's health, again thanks to the influence of those
same doctors among our well-to-do classes. Even now,
when I do but remember my wife's life and the condition
she was in during the first years when we had three or
four children and she was absorbed in them, I am seized
with horror! We led no life at all, but were in a state of
constant danger, of escape from it, recurring danger, again
followed by a desperate struggle and another escape—
always as if we were on a sinking ship. Sometimes it
seemed to me that this was done on purpose and that she
pretended to be anxious about the children in order to
subdue me. It solved all questions in her favour with
such tempting simplicity. It sometimes seemed as if all
she did and said on these occasions was pretence. But
no! She herself suffered terribly, and continually tormented herself about the children and their health and
illnesses. It was torture for her and for me too; and it was
impossible for her not to suffer. After all, the attachment
to her children, the animal need of feeding, caressing,
and protecting them, was there as with most women, but
there was not the lack of imagination and reason that
there is in animals. A hen is not afraid of what may happen to her chick, does not know all the diseases that may
befall it, and does not know all those remedies with
which people imagine that they can save from illness and
death. And for a hen her young are not a source of torment. She does for them what it is natural and pleasur-
able for her to do; her young ones are a pleasure to her.
When a chick falls ill her duties are quite definite: she
warms and feeds it. And doing this she knows that she is
doing all that is necessary. If her chick dies she does not
ask herself why it died, or where it has gone to; she cack-

les for a while, and then leaves off and goes on living as before. But for our unfortunate women, my wife among them, it was not so. Not to mention illnesses and how to cure them, she was always hearing and reading from all sides endless rules for the rearing and educating of children, which were continually being superseded by others. This is the way to feed a child: feed it in this way, on such a thing; no, not on such a thing, but in this way; clothes, drinks, baths, putting to bed, walking, fresh air — for all these things we, especially she, heard of new rules every week, just as if children had only begun to be born into the world since yesterday. And if a child that had not been fed or bathed in the right way or at the right time fell ill, it appeared that we were to blame for not having done what we ought.

"That was so while they were well. It was a torment even then. But if one of them happened to fall ill, it was all up: a regular hell! It is supposed that illness can be cured and that there is science about it, and people — doctors — who know about it. Ah, but not all of them know — only the very best. When a child is ill one must get hold of the very best one, the one who saves, and then the child is saved; but if you don't get that doctor, or if you don't live in the place where that doctor lives, the child is lost. This was not a creed peculiar to her, it is the creed of all the women of our class, and she heard nothing else from all sides. Catherine Semënovna lost two children because Ivan Zakharych was not called in in time, but Ivan Zakharych saved Mary Ivanovna's eldest girl, and the Petrovs moved in time to various hotels by the doctor's advice, and the children remained alive; but if they had not been segregated the children would have died. Another who had a delicate child moved south by the doctor's advice and saved the child. How can she help being tortured and agitated all the time, when the lives of the children for whom she has an animal attachment depend on her finding out in time what Ivan Zakharych will say! But what Ivan Zakharych will say nobody knows, and he himself least of all, for he is well aware that he knows nothing and therefore cannot be of any use, but just shuffles about at random so that people should not cease to believe that he knows something or other. You see, had she been wholly an animal she would not have suffered so, and if she had been quite a human being she would have had faith in God and would have said and thought, as a believer does: 'The Lord gave and the Lord hath taken away. One can't escape from God.'

"Our whole life with the children, for my wife and consequently for me, was not a joy but a torment. How could she help torturing herself? She tortured herself incessantly. Sometimes when we had just made peace after some scene of jealousy, or simply after a quarrel, and thought we should be able to live, to read, and to think a little, we had no sooner settled down to some occupation than the news came that Vasya was being sick, or Masha showed symptoms of dysentery, or Andrusha had a rash, and there was an end to peace, it was not life any more. Where was one to drive to? For what doctor? How isolate the child? And then it's a case of enemas, temperatures, medicines, and doctors. Hardly is that over before something else begins. We had no regular settled family life but only, as I have already said, continual escapes from imaginary and real dangers. It is like that in most families nowadays, you know, but in my family it was especially acute. My wife was a child-loving and a credulous woman.

"So the presence of children not only failed to improve our life but poisoned it. Besides, the children were a new cause of dissension. As soon as we had children they became the means and the object of our discord, and more often the older they grew. They were not only the object of discord but the weapons of our strife. We used our children, as it were, to fight one another with. Each of us had a favourite weapon among them for our strife. I used to fight her chiefly through Vasya, the eldest

boy, and she me through Lisa. Besides that, as they grew
older and their characters became defined, it came about
that they grew into allies whom each of us tried to draw
to his or her side. They, poor things, suffered terribly
from this, but we, with our incessant warfare, had no time
to think of that. The girl was my ally, and the eldest boy,
who resembled his mother and was her favourite, was
often hateful to me."

xvii

"WELL, and so we lived. Our relations to one another
grew more and more hostile and at last reached a state
where it was not disagreement that caused hostility but
hostility that caused disagreement. Whatever she might
say I disagreed with beforehand, and it was just the same
for her.

"In the fourth year we both, it seemed, came to the
conclusion that we could not understand one another or
agree with one another. We no longer tried to bring any
dispute to a conclusion. We invariably kept to our own
opinions even about the most trivial questions, but especially about the children. As I now recall them, the views
I maintained were not at all so dear to me that I could
not have given them up; but she was of the opposite
opinion and to yield meant yielding to her, and that I
could not do. It was quite the same with her. She probably considered herself quite in the right towards me,
and as for me I always thought myself a saint towards
her. When we were alone together we were doomed almost to silence, or to conversations such as I am convinced animals can carry on with one another: 'What is
the time? Time to go to bed. What is today's dinner?
Where shall we go? What is there in the papers? Send
for the doctor; Masha has a sore throat.' We only needed
to go a hairbreadth beyond this impossibly limited circle
of conversation for irritation to flare up. We had colli-
sions and acrimonious words about the coffee, a table-

cloth, a trap, a lead at bridge,* all of them things that
could not be of any importance to either of us. In me at
any rate there often raged a terrible hatred of her. Sometimes I watched her pouring out tea, swinging her leg,
lifting a spoon to her mouth, smacking her lips and drawing in some liquid, and I hated her for these things as
though they were the worst possible actions. I did not
then notice that the periods of anger corresponded quite
regularly and exactly to the periods of what we called
love. A period of love—then a period of animosity; an
energetic period of love, then a long period of animosity;
a weaker manifestation of love, and a shorter period of
animosity. We did not then understand that this love and
animosity were one and the same animal feeling only at
opposite poles. To live like that would have been awful
had we understood our position; but we neither understood nor saw it. Both salvation and punishment for man
lie in the fact that if he lives wrongly he can befog himself so as not to see the misery of his position. And this
we did. She tried to forget herself in intense and always
hurried occupation with household affairs, busying herself with the arrangements of the house, her own and the
children's clothes, their lessons, and their health; while I
had my own occupations: wine, my office duties, shooting, and cards. We were both continually occupied, and
we both felt that the busier we were the nastier we might
be to each other. 'It's all very well for you to grimace,' I
thought, 'but you have harassed me all night with your
scenes, and I have a meeting on.' 'It's all very well for
you,' she not only thought but said, 'but I have been
awake all night with the baby.' Those new theories of
hypnotism, psychic diseases, and hysterics are not a simple folly, but a dangerous and repulsive one. Charcot
would certainly have said that my wife was hysterical,
and that I was abnormal, and he would no doubt have
tried to cure me. But there was nothing to cure.

*The card game named in the original, and then much played in Russia,
was *vint*, which resembles bridge. A.M.

"Thus we lived in a perpetual fog, not seeing the condition we were in. And if what did happen had not happened, I should have gone on living so to old age and should have thought, when dying, that I had led a good life. I should not have realized the abyss of misery and the horrible falsehood in which I wallowed.

"We were like two convicts hating each other and chained together, poisoning one another's lives and trying not to see it. I did not then know that ninety-nine per cent of married people live in a similar hell to the one I was in and that it cannot be otherwise. I did not then know this either about others or about myself.

"It is strange what coincidences there are in regular, or even in irregular, lives! Just when the parents find life together unendurable, it becomes necessary to move to town for the children's education."

He stopped, and once or twice gave vent to his strange sounds, which were now quite like suppressed sobs. We were approaching a station.

"What is the time?" he asked.

I looked at my watch. It was two o'clock.

"You are not tired?" he asked.

"No, but you are?"

"I am suffocating. Excuse me, I will walk up and down and drink some water."

He went unsteadily through the carriage. I remained alone thinking over what he had said, and I was so engrossed in thought that I did not notice when he re-entered by the door at the other end of the carriage.

xviii

"Yes, I keep diverging," he began. "I have thought much over it. I now see many things differently and I want to express it.

"Well, so we lived in town. In town a man can live for a hundred years without noticing that he has long been dead and has rotted away. He has no time to take account of himself, he is always occupied. Business affairs, social intercourse, health, art, the children's health and their education. Now one has to receive so-and-so and so-and-so, go to see so-and-so and so-and-so; now one has to go and look at this, and hear this man or that woman. In town, you know, there are at any given moment one or two, or even three, celebrities whom one must on no account miss seeing. Then one has to undergo a treatment oneself or get someone else attended to, then there are teachers, tutors, and governesses, but one's own life is quite empty. Well, so we lived and felt less the painfulness of living together. Besides at first we had splendid occupations, arranging things in a new place, in new quarters; and we were also occupied in going from the town to the country and back to town again.

"We lived so through one winter, and the next there occurred, unnoticed by anyone, an apparently unimportant thing, but the cause of all that happened later.

"She was not well and the doctors told her not to have children, and taught her how to avoid it. To me it was disgusting. I struggled against it, but she with frivolous obstinacy insisted on having her own way and I submitted. The last excuse for our swinish life — children — was then taken away, and life became viler than ever.

"To a peasant, a labouring man, children are necessary; though it is hard for him to feed them, still he needs them, and therefore his marital relations have a justification. But to us who have children, more children are unnecessary; they are an additional care and expense, a further division of property, and a burden. So our swinish life has no justification. We either artificially deprive ourselves of children or regard them as a misfortune, the consequences of carelessness, and that is still worse.

"We have no justification. But we have fallen morally so low that we do not even feel the need of any justification.

"The majority of the present educated world devote themselves to this kind of debauchery without the least qualm of conscience.

"There is indeed nothing that can feel qualms, for conscience in our society is non-existent, unless one can call public opinion and the criminal law a 'conscience.' In this case neither the one nor the other is infringed: there is no reason to be ashamed of public opinion for everybody acts in the same way—Mary Pavlona, Ivan Zakharych, and the rest. Why breed paupers or deprive oneself of the possibility of social life? There is no need to fear or be ashamed in face of the criminal law either. Those shameless hussies, or soldiers' wives, throw their babies into ponds or wells, and they of course must be put in prison, but we do it all at the proper time and in a clean way.

"We lived like that for another two years. The means employed by those scoundrel-doctors evidently began to bear fruit; she became physically stouter and handsomer, like the late beauty of summer's end. She felt this and paid attention to her appearance. She developed a provocative kind of beauty which made people restless. She was in the full vigour of a well-fed and excited woman of thirty who is not bearing children. Her appearance disturbed people. When she passed men she attracted their notice. She was like a fresh, well-fed, harnessed horse, whose bridle has been removed. There was no bridle, as is the case with ninety-nine hundredths of our women. And I felt this—and was frightened."

xix

He suddenly rose and sat down close to the window.

"Pardon me," he muttered and, with his eyes fixed on the window, he remained silent for about three minutes. Then he sighed deeply and moved back to the seat opposite mine. His face was quite changed, his eyes looked pathetic, and his lips puckered strangely, almost as if he were smiling. "I am rather tired but I will go on with it. We have still plenty of time, it is not dawn yet. Ah, yes," he began after lighting a cigarette, "she grew plumper after she stopped having babies, and her malady—that everlasting worry about the children—began to pass ... at least not actually to pass, but she as it were woke up from an intoxication, came to herself, and saw that there was a whole divine world with its joys which she had forgotten, but a divine world she did not know how to live in and did not at all understand. 'I must not miss it! Time is passing and won't come back!' So, I imagine, she thought, or rather felt, nor could she have thought or felt differently: she had been brought up in the belief that there was only one thing in the world worthy of attention—love. She had married and received something of that love, but not nearly what had been promised and was expected. Even that had been accompanied by many disappointments and sufferings, and then this unexpected torment: so many children! The torments exhausted her. And then, thanks to the obliging doctors, she learnt that it is possible to avoid having children. She was very glad, tried it, and became alive again for the one thing she knew—for love. But love with a husband, befouled by jealousy and all kinds of anger, was no longer the thing she wanted. She had visions of some other, clean, new love; at least I thought she had. And she began to look about her as if expecting something. I saw this and could not help feeling anxious. It happened again and again that while talking to me, as usual through other people—that is, telling a third person what she meant for me—she boldly, without remembering that she had expressed the opposite opinion an hour before, declared, though half-jokingly, that a mother's cares are a fraud, and that it is not worth while to devote one's life to children when one is young and can enjoy life. She gave less attention to the children and less frenziedly than before, but gave more and more attention to herself, to her appearance (though she tried to conceal this), and to her pleasures, even to her accomplishments. She again enthusiastically took to the piano which she had quite abandoned, and it all began from that."

He turned his weary eyes to the window again but,

evidently making an effort, immediately continued once more.

"Yes, that man made his appearance. . . ." He became confused and once or twice made that peculiar sound with his nose.

I could see that it was painful for him to name that man, to recall him, or speak about him. But he made an effort and, as if he had broken the obstacle that hindered him, continued resolutely.

"He was a worthless man in my opinion and according to my estimate. And not because of the significance he acquired in my life but because he really was so. However, the fact that he was a poor sort of fellow only served to show how irresponsible she was. If it had not been he then it would have been another. It had to be!"

Again he paused. "Yes, he was a musician, a violinist; not a professional, but a semi-professional semi-society man.

"His father, a landowner, was a neighbour of my father's. He had been ruined, and his children—there were three boys—had obtained settled positions; only this one, the youngest, had been handed over to his godmother in Paris. There he was sent to the *Conservatoire* because he had a talent for music, and he came out as a violinist and played at concerts. He was a man . . ." Having evidently intended to say something bad about him, Pozdnyshev restrained himself and rapidly said: "Well, I don't really know how he lived, I only know that he returned to Russia that year and appeared in my house.

"With moist almond-shaped eyes, red smiling lips, a small waxed moustache, hair done in the latest fashion, and an insipidly pretty face, he was what women call 'not bad looking.' His figure was weak though not misshapen, and he had a specially developed posterior, like a woman's, or such as Hottentots are said to have. They too are reported to be musical. Pushing himself as far as possible into familiarity, but sensitive and always ready to yield at the slightest resistance, he maintained his dignity in externals, wore buttoned boots of a special Parisian fashion, bright-coloured ties, and other things foreigners acquire in Paris, which by their noticeable novelty always attract women. There was an affected external gaiety in his manner. That manner, you know, of speaking about everything in allusions and unfinished sentences, as if you knew it all, remembered it, and could complete it yourself.

"It was he with his music who was the cause of it all. You know at the trial the case was put as if it was all caused by jealousy. No such thing: that is, I don't mean 'no such thing,' it was and yet it was not. At the trial it was decided that I was a wronged husband and that I had killed her while defending my outraged honour (that is the phrase they employ, you know). That is why I was acquitted. I tried to explain matters at the trial but they took it that I was trying to rehabilitate my wife's honour.

"What my wife's relations with that musician may have been has no meaning for me, or for her either. What has a meaning is what I have told you about—my swinishness. The whole thing was an outcome of the terrible abyss between us of which I have told you—that dreadful tension of mutual hatred which made the first excuse sufficient to produce a crisis. The quarrels between us had for some time past become frightful, and were all the more startling because they alternated with similarly intense animal passion.

"If he had not appeared there would have been someone else. If the occasion had not been jealousy it would have been something else. I maintain that all husbands who live as I did, must either live dissolutely, separate, or kill themselves or their wives as I have done. If there is anybody who has not done so, he is a rare exception. Before I ended as I did, I had several times been on the verge of suicide, and she too had repeatedly tried to poison herself."

XX

"WELL, that is how things were going not long before it happened. We seemed to be living in a state of truce and had no reason to infringe it. Then we chanced to speak about a dog which I said had been awarded a medal at an exhibition. She remarked, 'Not a medal, but an honourable mention.' A dispute ensues. We jump from one subject to another, reproach one another. 'Oh, that's nothing new, it's always been like that.' 'You said . . .' 'No, I didn't say so.' 'Then I am telling lies! . . .' You feel that at any moment that dreadful quarrelling which makes you wish to kill yourself or her will begin. You know it will begin immediately, and fear it like fire and therefore wish to restrain yourself, but your whole being is seized with fury. She being in the same or even a worse condition purposely misinterprets every word you say, giving it a wrong meaning. Her every word is venomous; where she alone knows that I am most sensitive, she stabs. It gets worse and worse. I shout: 'Be quiet!' or something of that kind.

"She rushes out of the room and into the nursery. I try to hold her back in order to finish what I was saying, to prove my point, and I seize her by the arm. She pretends that I have hurt her and screams: 'Children, your father is striking me!' I shout: 'Don't lie!' 'But it's not the first time!' she screams, or something like that. The children rush to her. She calms them down. I say, 'Don't sham!' She says, 'Everything is sham in your eyes, you would kill any one and say they were shamming. Now I have understood you. That's just what you want!' 'Oh, I wish you were dead as a dog!' I shout. I remember how those dreadful words horrified me. I never thought I could utter such dreadful, coarse words, and am surprised that they escaped me. I shout them and rush away into my study and sit down and smoke. I hear her go out into the ⟨hall⟩ preparing to go away. I ask, 'Where are you going ⟨?⟩ ⟨S⟩he does not reply. 'Well, devil take her,' I say to ⟨myself a⟩nd go back to my study and lie down and smoke.

A thousand different plans of how to revenge myself on her and get rid of her, and how to improve matters and go on as if nothing had happened, come into my head. I think all that and go on smoking and smoking. I think of running away from her, hiding myself, going to America. I get as far as dreaming of how I shall get rid of her, how splendid that will be, and how I shall unite with another, an admirable woman—quite different. I shall get rid of her either by her dying or by a divorce, and I plan how it is to be done. I notice that I am getting confused and not thinking of what is necessary, and to prevent myself from perceiving that my thoughts are not to the point I go on smoking.

"Life in the house goes on. The governess comes in and asks: 'Where is madame? When will she be back?' The footman asks whether he is to serve tea. I go to the dining-room. The children, especially Lisa, who already understands, gaze inquiringly and disapprovingly at me. We drink tea in silence. She has still not come back. The evening passes, she has not returned, and two different feelings alternate within me. Anger because she torments me and all the children by her absence which will end by her returning; and fear that she will not return but will do something to herself. I would go to fetch her, but where am I to look for her? At her sister's? But it would be so stupid to go and ask. And it's all the better: if she is bent on tormenting someone, let her torment herself. Besides, that is what she is waiting for; and next time it would be worse still. But suppose she is not with her sister but is doing something to herself, or has already done it! It's past ten, past eleven! I don't go to the bedroom—it would be stupid to lie there alone waiting—but I'll not lie down here either. I wish to occupy my mind, to write a letter or to read, but I can't do anything. I sit alone in my study, tortured, angry, and listening. It's three o'clock, four o'clock, and she is not back. Towards morning I fall asleep. I wake up, she has still not come!

"Everything in the house goes on in the usual way, but all are perplexed and look at me inquiringly and reproachfully, considering me to be the cause of it all. And in me the same struggle still continues: anger that she is torturing me, and anxiety for her.

"At about eleven in the morning her sister arrives as her envoy. And the usual talk begins. 'She is in a terrible state. What does it all mean?' 'After all, nothing has happened.' I speak of her impossible character and say that I have not done anything.

"'But, you know, it can't go on like this,' says her sister.

"'It's all her doing and not mine,' I say. 'I won't take the first step. If it means separation, let it be separation.'

"My sister-in-law goes away having achieved nothing. I had boldly said that I would not take the first step; but after her departure, when I came out of my study and saw the children piteous and frightened, I was prepared to take the first step. I should be glad to do it, but I don't know how. Again I pace up and down and smoke; at lunch I drink vodka and wine and attain what I unconsciously desire—I no longer see the stupidity and humiliation of my position.

"At about three she comes. When she meets me she does not speak. I imagine that she has submitted, and begin to say that I had been provoked by her reproaches. She, with the same stern expression on her terribly harassed face, says that she has not come for explanations but to fetch the children, because we cannot live together. I begin telling her that the fault is not mine and that she provoked me beyond endurance. She looks severely and solemnly at me and says: 'Do not say any more, you will repent it.' I tell her that I cannot stand comedies. Then she cries out something I don't catch, and rushes into her room. The key clicks behind her— she has locked herself in. I try the door, but getting no answer, go away angrily. Half an hour later Lisa runs in crying. 'What is it? Has anything happened?' 'We can't hear Mamma.' We go. I pull at the double doors with all my might. The bolt had not been firmly secured, and the two halves both open. I approach the bed, on which she is lying awkwardly in her petticoats and with a pair of high boots on. An empty opium bottle is on the table. She is brought to herself. Tears follow, and a reconciliation. No, not a reconciliation: in the heart of each there is still the old animosity, with the additional irritation produced by the pain of this quarrel which each attributes to the other. But one must of course finish it all somehow, and life goes on in the old way. And so the same kind of quarrel, and even worse ones, occurred continually: once a week, once a month, or at times every day. It was always the same. Once I had already procured a passport to go abroad—the quarrel had continued for two days. But there was again a partial explanation, a partial reconciliation, and I did not go."

xxi

"So THOSE were our relations when that man appeared. He arrived in Moscow—his name is Trukhachevski—and came to my house. It was in the morning. I received him. We had once been on familiar terms and he tried to maintain a familiar tone by using non-committal expressions, but I definitely adopted a conventional tone and he at once submitted to it. I disliked him from the first glance. But curiously enough a strange and fatal force led me not to repulse him, not to keep him away, but on the contrary to invite him to the house. After all, what could have been simpler than to converse with him coldly, and say good-bye without introducing him to my wife? But no, as if purposely, I began talking about his playing, and said I had been told he had given up the violin. He replied that, on the contrary, he now played more than ever. He referred to the fact that there had been a time when I myself played. I said I had given it up but that my wife played well. It is an astonishing thing that from the first day, from the first hour of my meeting him, my relations with him were such as they might have been only after all that subsequently happened. There

was something strained in them: I noticed every word,
every expression he or I used, and attributed importance
to them.

"I introduced him to my wife. The conversation immediately turned to music, and he offered to be of use to
her by playing with her. My wife was, as usual of late,
very elegant, attractive, and disquietingly beautiful. He
evidently pleased her at first sight. Besides, she was glad
that she would have someone to accompany her on a
violin, which she was so fond of that she used to engage
a violinist from the theatre for the purpose; and her face
reflected her pleasure. But catching sight of me she at
once understood my feeling and changed her expression,
and a game of mutual deception began. I smiled pleasantly to appear as if I liked it. He, looking at my wife as
all immoral men look at pretty women, pretended that
he was only interested in the subject of the conversation—
which no longer interested him at all; while she tried to
seem indifferent, though my false smile of jealousy with
which she was familiar, and his lustful gaze, evidently
excited her. I saw that from their first encounter her eyes
were particularly bright and, probably as a result of my
jealousy, it seemed as if an electric current had been established between them, evoking as it were an identity
of expressions, looks, and smiles. She blushed and he
blushed. She smiled and he smiled. We spoke about music, Paris, and all sorts of trifles. Then he rose to go, and
stood smilingly, holding his hat against his twitching
thigh and looking now at her and now at me, as if in expectation of what we would do. I remember that instant
just because at that moment I might not have invited
him, and then nothing would have happened. But I
glanced at him and at her and said silently to myself,
'Don't suppose that I am jealous,' 'or that I am afraid of
you,' I added, mentally, addressing him, and I invited him
to come some evening and bring his violin to play with
my wife. She glanced at me with surprise, flushed, and as
if frightened began to decline, saying that she did not
play well enough. This refusal irritated me still more, and

I insisted the more on his coming. I remember the curious feeling with which I looked at the back of his head, with the black hair parted in the middle contrasting with the white nape of his neck, as he went out with his peculiar springing gait suggestive of some kind of a bird. I could not conceal from myself that that man's presence tormented me. 'It depends on me,' I reflected, 'to act so as to see nothing more of him. But that would be to admit that I am afraid of him. No, I am not afraid of him; it would be too humiliating,' I said to myself. And there in the anteroom, knowing that my wife heard me, I insisted that he should come that evening with his violin. He promised to do so, and left.

"In the evening he brought his violin and they played. But it took a long time to arrange matters—they had not the music they wanted, and my wife could not without preparation play what they had. I was very fond of music and sympathized with their playing, arranging a music-stand for him and turning over the pages. They played a few things, some songs without words, and a little sonata by Mozart. They played splendidly, and he had an exceptionally fine tone. Besides that, he had a refined and elevated taste not at all in correspondence with his character.

"He was of course a much better player than my wife, and he helped her, while at the same time politely praising her playing. He behaved himself very well. My wife seemed interested only in music and was very simple and natural. But though I pretended to be interested in the music I was tormented by jealousy all the evening.

"From the first moment his eyes met my wife's I saw that the animal in each of them, regardless of all conditions of their position and of society, asked, 'May I?' and answered, 'Oh, yes, certainly.' I saw that he had not at all expected to find my wife, a Moscow lady, so attractive, and that he was very pleased. For he had no doubt whatever that she was *willing*. The only crux was whether that unendurable husband could hinder them. Had I been pure I should not have understood this, but, like the majority of men, I had myself regarded women in that way before I married and therefore could read his mind like a manuscript. I was particularly tormented because I saw without doubt that she had no other feeling towards me than a continual irritation only occasionally interrupted by the habitual sensuality; but that this man—by his external refinement and novelty and still more by his undoubtedly great talent for music, by the nearness that comes of playing together, and by the influence music, especially the violin, exercises on impressionable natures— was sure not only to please but certainly and without the least hesitation to conquer, crush, bind her, twist her round his little finger and do whatever he liked with her. I could not help seeing this and I suffered terribly. But for all that, or perhaps on account of it, some force obliged me against my will to be not merely polite but amiable to him. Whether I did it for my wife or for him, to show that I was not afraid of him, or whether I did it to deceive myself—I don't know, but I know that from the first I could not behave naturally with him. In order not to yield to my wish to kill him there and then, I had to make much of him. I gave him expensive wines at supper, went into raptures over his playing, spoke to him with a particularly amiable smile, and invited him to dine and play with my wife again the next Sunday. I told him I would ask a few friends who were fond of music to hear him. And so it ended."

Greatly agitated, Pozdnyshev changed his position and emitted his peculiar sound.

"It is strange how the presence of that man acted on me," he began again, with an evident effort to keep calm. "I come home from the Exhibition a day or two later, enter the anteroom, and suddenly feel something heavy, as if a stone had fallen on my heart, and I cannot understand what it is. It was that passing through the anteroom I noticed something which reminded me of him. I realized what it was only in my study, and went back to the anteroom to make sure. Yes, I was not mistaken, there was his overcoat. A fashionable coat, you know.

(Though I did not realize it, I observed everything connected with him with extraordinary attention.) I inquire: sure enough he is there. I pass on to the dancing-room, not through the drawing-room but through the school-room. My daughter, Lisa, sits reading a book and the nurse sits with the youngest boy at the table, making a lid of some kind spin round. The door to the dancing-room is shut but I hear the sound of a rhythmic arpeggio and his and her voices. I listen, but cannot make out anything.

"Evidently the sound of the piano is purposely made to drown the sound of their voices, their kisses ... perhaps. My God! What was aroused in me! Even to think of the beast that then lived in me fills me with horror! My heart suddenly contracted, stopped, and then began to beat like a hammer. My chief feeling, as usual whenever I was enraged, was one of self-pity. 'In the presence of the children! of their nurse!' thought I. Probably I looked awful, for Lisa gazed at me with strange eyes. 'What am I to do?' I asked myself. 'Go in? I can't: heaven only knows what I should do. But neither can I go away.' The nurse looked at me as if she understood my position. 'But it is impossible not to go in,' I said to myself, and I quickly opened the door. He was sitting at the piano playing those arpeggios with his large white upturned fingers. She was standing in the curve of the piano, bending over some open music. She was the first to see or hear, and glanced at me. Whether she was frightened and pretended not to be, or whether she was really not frightened, anyway she did not start or move but only blushed, and that not at once.

"'How glad I am that you have come: we have not decided what to play on Sunday,' she said in a tone she would not have used to me had we been alone. This and her using the word 'we' of herself and him, filled me with indignation. I greeted him silently.

"He pressed my hand, and at once, with a smile which I thought distinctly ironic, began to explain that he had brought some music to practise for Sunday, but that they disagreed about what to play: a classical but more difficult piece, namely Beethoven's sonata for the violin, or a few little pieces. It was all so simple and natural that there was nothing one could cavil at, yet I felt certain that it was all untrue and that they had agreed how to deceive me.

"One of the most distressing conditions of life for a jealous man (and everyone is jealous in our world) are certain society conventions which allow a man and woman the greatest and most dangerous proximity. You would become a laughing-stock to others if you tried to prevent such nearness at balls, or the nearness of doctors to their women-patients, or of people occupied with art, sculpture, and especially music. A couple are occupied with the noblest of arts, music; this demands a certain nearness, and there is nothing reprehensible in that and only a stupid jealous husband can see anything undesirable in it. Yet everybody knows that it is by means of those very pursuits, especially of music, that the greater part of the adulteries in our society occur. I evidently confused them by the confusion I betrayed: for a long time I could not speak. I was like a bottle held upside down from which the water does not flow because it is too full. I wanted to abuse him and to turn him out, but again felt that I must treat him courteously and amiably. And I did so. I acted as though I approved of it all, and again because of the strange feeling which made me behave to him the more amiably the more his presence distressed me. I told him that I trusted his taste and advised her to do the same. He stayed as long as was necessary to efface the unpleasant impression caused by my sudden entrance—looking frightened and remaining silent—and then left, pretending that it was now decided what to play next day. I was, however, fully convinced that compared to what interested them the question of what to play was quite indifferent.

"I saw him out to the anteroom with special politeness. (How could one do less than accompany a man who had come to disturb the peace and destroy the happiness of a whole family?) And I pressed his soft white hand with particular warmth."

xxii

"I DID NOT speak to her all that day—I could not. Nearness to her aroused in me such hatred of her that I was afraid of myself. At dinner in the presence of the children she asked me when I was going away. I had to go next week to the District Meetings of the Zemstvo. I told her the date. She asked whether I did not want anything for the journey. I did not answer but sat silent at table and then went in silence to my study. Latterly she used never to come to my room, especially not at that time of day. I lay in my study filled with anger. Suddenly I heard her familiar step, and the terrible, monstrous idea entered my head that she, like Uriah's wife, wished to conceal the sin she had already committed and that that was why she was coming to me at such an unusual time. 'Can she be coming to me?' thought I, listening to her approaching footsteps. 'If she is coming here, then I am right,' and an inexpressible hatred of her took possession of me. Nearer and nearer came the steps. Is it possible that she won't pass on to the dancing-room? No, the door creaks and in the doorway appears her tall handsome figure, on her face and in her eyes a timid ingratiating look which she tries to hide, but which I see and the meaning of which I know. I almost choked, so long did I hold my breath, and still looking at her I grasped my cigarette-case and began to smoke.

"'Now how can you? One comes to sit with you for a bit, and you begin smoking'—and she sat down close to me on the sofa, leaning against me. I moved away so as not to touch her.

"'I see you are dissatisfied at my wanting to play on Sunday,' she said.

"'I am not at all dissatisfied,' I said.

"'As if I don't see!'

"'Well, I congratulate you on seeing. But I only see that you behave like a coquette.... You always find pleasure in all kinds of vileness, but to me it is terrible!'

"'Oh, well, if you are going to scold like a cabman, I'll go away.'

"'Do, but remember that if you don't value the family honour, I value not you (devil take you) but the honour of the family!'

"'But what is the matter? What?'

"'Go away, for God's sake be off!'

"Whether she pretended not to understand what it was about or really did not understand, at any rate she took offence, grew angry, and did not go away but stood in the middle of the room.

"'You have really become impossible,' she began. 'You have a character that even an angel could not put up with.' And as usual trying to sting me as painfully as possible, she reminded me of my conduct to my sister (an incident when, being exasperated, I said rude things to my sister); she knew I was distressed about it and she stung me just on that spot. 'After that, nothing from you will surprise me,' she said.

"'Yes! Insult me, humiliate me, disgrace me, and then put the blame on me,' I said to myself, and suddenly I was seized by such terrible rage as I had never before experienced.

"For the first time I wished to give physical expression to that rage. I jumped up and went towards her; but just as I jumped up I remember becoming conscious of my rage and asking myself: 'Is it right to give way to this feeling?' and at once I answered that it was right, that it would frighten her, and instead of restraining my fury I immediately began inflaming it still further, and was glad it burnt yet more fiercely within me.

"'Be off, or I'll kill you!' I shouted, going up to her and seizing her by the arm. I consciously intensified the anger in my voice as I said this. And I suppose I was terrible, for she was so frightened that she had not even the strength to go away, but only said: 'Vasya, what is it? What is the matter with you?'

"'Go!' I roared louder still. 'No one but you can drive me to fury. I do not answer for myself!'

"Having given reins to my rage, I revelled in it and wished to do something still more unusual to show the extreme degree of my anger. I felt a terrible desire to beat her, to kill her, but knew that this would not do, and so to give vent to my fury I seized a paper-weight from my table, again shouting 'Go!' and hurled it to the floor near her. I aimed it very exactly past her. Then she left the room, but stopped at the doorway, and immediately, while she still saw it (I did it so that she might see), I began snatching things from the table—candlesticks and ink-stand—and hurling them on the floor still shouting 'Go! Get out! I don't answer for myself!' She went away—and I immediately stopped.

"An hour later the nurse came to tell me that my wife was in hysterics. I went to her; she sobbed, laughed, could not speak, and her whole body was convulsed. She was not pretending, but was really ill.

"Towards morning she grew quiet, and we made peace under the influence of the feeling we called love.

"In the morning when, after our reconciliation, I confessed to her that I was jealous of Trukhachevski, she was not at all confused, but laughed most naturally; so strange did the very possibility of an infatuation for such a man seem to her, she said.

"'Could a decent woman have any other feeling for such a man than the pleasure of his music? Why, if you like I am ready never to see him again ... not even on Sunday, though everybody has been invited. Write and tell him that I am ill, and there's an end of it! Only it is unpleasant that anyone, especially he himself, should imagine that he is dangerous. I am too proud to allow anyone to think that of me!'

"And you know, she was not lying, she believed what she was saying; she hoped by those words to evoke in

herself contempt for him and so to defend herself from
him, but she did not succeed in doing so. Everything was
against her, especially that accursed music. So it all
ended, and on the Sunday the guests assembled and they
again played together."

xxiii

"I SUPPOSE it is hardly necessary to say that I was very
vain: if one is not vain there is nothing to live for in our
usual way of life. So on that Sunday I arranged the dinner and the musical evening with much care. I bought
the provisions myself and invited the guests.

"Towards six the visitors assembled. He came in evening dress with diamond studs that showed bad taste. He
behaved in a free and easy manner, answered everything
hurriedly with a smile of agreement and understanding,
you know, with that peculiar expression which seems to
say that all you may do or say is just what he expected.
Everything that was not in good taste about him I noticed with particular pleasure, because it ought all to
have had the effect of tranquillizing me and showing that
he was so far beneath my wife that, as she had said, she
could not lower herself to his level. I did not now allow
myself to be jealous. In the first place I had worried
through that torment and needed rest, and secondly I
wanted to believe my wife's assurances and did believe
them. But though I was not jealous I was nevertheless
not natural with either of them, and at dinner and during
the first half of the evening before the music began I still
followed their movements and looks.

"The dinner was, as dinners are, dull and pretentious.
The music began pretty early. Oh, how I remember every
detail of that evening! I remember how he brought in his
violin, unlocked the case, took off the cover a lady had
embroidered for him, drew out the violin, and began tun-
ing it. I remember how my wife sat down at the piano
with pretended unconcern, under which I saw that she

was trying to conceal great timidity—chiefly as to her own ability—and then the usual A on the piano began, the pizzicato of the violin, and the arrangement of the music. Then I remember how they glanced at one another, turned to look at the audience who were seating themselves, said something to one another, and began. He took the first chords. His face grew serious, stern, and sympathetic, and listening to the sounds he produced, he touched the strings with careful fingers. The piano answered him. The music began. . . ."

Pozdnyshev paused and produced his strange sound several times in succession. He tried to speak, but sniffed, and stopped.

"They played Beethoven's *Kreutzer Sonata,*" he continued. "Do you know the first presto? You do?" he cried. "Ugh! Ugh! It is a terrible thing, that sonata. And especially that part. And in general music is a dreadful thing! What is it? I don't understand it. What is music? What does it do? And why does it do what it does? They say music exalts the soul. Nonsense, it is not true! It has an effect, an awful effect—I am speaking of myself—but not of an exalting kind. It has neither an exalting nor a debasing effect but it produces agitation. How can I put it? Music makes me forget myself, my real position; it transports me to some other position not my own. Under the influence of music it seems to me that I feel what I do not really feel, that I understand what I do not understand, that I can do what I cannot do. I explain it by the fact that music acts like yawning, like laughter: I am not sleepy, but I yawn when I see someone yawning; there is nothing for me to laugh at, but I laugh when I hear people laughing.

"Music carries me immediately and directly into the mental condition in which the man was who composed it. My soul merges with his and together with him I pass from one condition into another, but why this happens I don't know. You see, he who wrote, let us say, the *Kreutzer Sonata*—Beethoven—knew of course why he was in that condition; that condition caused him to do certain actions and therefore that condition had a meaning for him, but for me—none at all. That is why music only agitates and doesn't lead to a conclusion. Well, when a military march is played the soldiers march to the music and the music has achieved its object. A dance is played, I dance and the music has achieved its object. Mass has been sung, I receive Communion, and that music too has reached a conclusion. Otherwise it is only agitating, and what ought to be done in that agitation is lacking. That is why music sometimes acts so dreadfully, so terribly. In China, music is a State affair. And that is as it should be. How can one allow anyone who pleases to hypnotize another, or many others, and do what he likes with them? And especially that this hypnotist should be the first immoral man who turns up?

"It is a terrible instrument in the hands of any chance user! Take that *Kreutzer Sonata* for instance, how can that first presto be played in a drawing-room among ladies in low-necked dresses? To hear that played, to clap a little, and then to eat ices and talk of the latest scandal? Such things should only be played on certain important significant occasions, and then only when certain actions answering to such music are wanted; play it then and do what the music has moved you to. Otherwise an awakening of energy and feeling unsuited both to the time and the place, to which no outlet is given, cannot but act harmfully. At any rate that piece had a terrible effect on me; it was as if quite new feelings, new possibilities, of which I had till then been unaware, had been revealed to me. 'That's how it is: not at all as I used to think and live, but that way,' something seemed to say within me. What this new thing was that had been revealed to me I could not explain to myself, but the consciousness of this new condition was very joyous. All those same people, including my wife and him, appeared in a new light.

"After that allegro they played the beautiful, but common and unoriginal, andante with trite variations, and the very weak finale. Then, at the request of the visitors, they played Ernst's *Elegy* and a few small pieces. They were all good, but they did not produce on me a one-hundredth part of the impression the first piece had. The effect of the first piece formed the background for them all.

"I felt lighthearted and cheerful the whole evening. I had never seen my wife as she was that evening. Those shining eyes, that severe, significant expression while she played, and her melting languor and feeble, pathetic, and blissful smile after they had finished. I saw all that but did not attribute any meaning to it except that she was feeling what I felt, and that to her as to me new feelings, never before experienced, were revealed or, as it were, recalled. The evening ended satisfactorily and the visitors departed.

"Knowing that I had to go away to attend the Zemstvo Meetings two days later, Trukhachevski on leaving said he hoped to repeat the pleasure of that evening when he next came to Moscow. From this I concluded that he did not consider it possible to come to my house during my absence, and this pleased me.

"It turned out that as I should not be back before he left town, we should not see one another again.

"For the first time I pressed his hand with real pleasure, and thanked him for the enjoyment he had given us. In the same way he bade a final farewell to my wife. Their leave-taking seemed to be most natural and proper. Everything was splendid. My wife and I were both very well satisfied with our evening party."

xxiv

"Two DAYS later I left for the Meetings, parting from my wife in the best and most tranquil of moods.

"In the district there was always an enormous amount to do and a quite special life, a special little world of its own. I spent two ten-hour days at the Council. A letter from my wife was brought me on the second day and I read it there and then.

"She wrote about the children, about uncle, about the nurse, about shopping, and among other things she mentioned, as a most natural occurrence, that Trukhachevski had called, brought some music he had promised, and had offered to play again, but that she had refused.

"I did not remember his having promised any music, but thought he had taken leave for good, and I was therefore unpleasantly struck by this. I was, however, so busy that I had no time to think of it, and it was only in the evening when I had returned to my lodgings that I reread her letter.

"Besides the fact that Trukhachevski had called at my house during my absence, the whole tone of the letter seemed to me unnatural. The mad beast of jealousy began to growl in its kennel and wanted to leap out, but I was afraid of that beast and quickly fastened him in. 'What an abominable feeling this jealousy is!' I said to myself. 'What could be more natural than what she writes?'

"I went to bed and began thinking about the affairs awaiting me next day. During those Meetings, sleeping in a new place, I usually slept badly, but now I fell asleep very quickly. And as sometimes happens, you know, you feel a kind of electric shock and wake up. So I awoke thinking of her, of my physical love for her, and of Trukhachevski, and of everything being accomplished between them. Horror and rage compressed my heart. But I began to reason with myself. 'What nonsense!' said I to myself. 'There are no grounds to go on, there is nothing and there has been nothing. How can I so degrade her and myself as to imagine such horrors? He is a sort of hired violinist, known as a worthless fellow, and suddenly an honourable woman, the respected mother of a family, *my* wife . . . What absurdity!' So it seemed to me on the one hand. 'How could it help being so?' it seemed on the other. 'How could that simplest and most intelligible thing help happening—that for the sake of which I married her, for the sake of which I have been living with her, what alone I wanted of her, and which others includ-

ing this musician must therefore also want? He is an unmarried man, healthy (I remember how he crunched the
gristle of a cutlet and how greedily his red lips clung to
the glass of wine), well-fed, plump, and not merely un-
principled but evidently making it a principle to accept
the pleasures that present themselves. And they have
music, that most exquisite voluptuousness of the senses,
as a link between them. What then could make him re-
frain? She? But who is she? She was, and still is, a mystery. I don't know her. I only know her as an animal. And
nothing can or should restrain an animal.'

"Only then did I remember their faces that evening
when, after the *Kreutzer Sonata*, they played some im-
passioned little piece, I don't remember by whom, im-
passioned to the point of obscenity. 'How dared I go
away?' I asked myself, remembering their faces. Was it
not clear that everything had happened between them
that evening? Was it not evident already then that there
was not only no barrier between them, but that they
both, and she chiefly, felt a certain measure of shame
after what had happened? I remember her weak, piteous, and beatific smile as she wiped the perspiration
from her flushed face when I came up to the piano. Already then they avoided looking at one another, and
only at supper when he was pouring out some water for
her, they glanced at each other with the vestige of a
smile. I now recalled with horror the glance and scarcely
perceptible smile I had then caught. 'Yes, it is all over,'
said one voice, and immediately the other voice said
something entirely different. 'Something has come over
you, it can't be that it is so,' said that other voice. It felt
uncanny lying in the dark and I struck a light, and felt a
kind of terror in that little room with its yellow wallpaper. I lit a cigarette and, as always happens when
one's thoughts go round and round in a circle of insoluble contradictions, I smoked, taking one cigarette after
another in order to befog myself so as not to see those
contradictions.

"I did not sleep all night, and at five in the morning,

having decided that I could not continue in such a state
of tension, I rose, woke the caretaker who attended me
and sent him to get horses. I sent a note to the Council
saying that I had been recalled to Moscow on urgent
business and asking that one of the members should
take my place. At eight o'clock I got into my trap and
started."

XXV

THE CONDUCTOR entered and seeing that our candle had
burnt down put it out, without supplying a fresh one. The
day was dawning. Pozdnyshev was silent, but sighed deeply
all the time the conductor was in the carriage. He continued his story only after the conductor had gone out, and
in the semi-darkness of the carriage only the rattle of the
windows of the moving carriage and the rhythmic snoring of the clerk could be heard. In the half-light of dawn
I could not see Pozdnyshev's face at all, but only heard
his voice becoming ever more and more excited and full
of suffering.

"I had to travel twenty-four miles by road and eight
hours by rail. It was splendid driving. It was frosty autumn weather, bright and sunny. The roads were in that
condition when the tires leave their dark imprint on
them, you know. They were smooth, the light brilliant,
and the air invigorating. It was pleasant driving in the
tarantas. When it grew lighter and I had started I felt
easier. Looking at the houses, the fields, and the passers-
by, I forgot where I was going. Sometimes I felt that I
was simply taking a drive, and that nothing of what was
calling me back had taken place. This oblivion was pecu-
liarly enjoyable. When I remembered where I was going
to, I said to myself, 'We shall see when the time comes; I
must not think about it.' When we were half-way an incident occurred which detained me and still further dis-
tracted my thoughts. The tarantas broke down and had
to be repaired. That break-down had a very important

effect, for it caused me to arrive in Moscow at midnight, instead of at seven o'clock as I had expected, and to reach home between twelve and one, as I missed the express and had to travel by an ordinary train. Going to fetch a cart, having the tarantas mended, settling up, tea at the inn, a talk with the innkeeper—all this still further diverted my attention. It was twilight before all was ready and I started again. By night it was even pleasanter driving than during the day. There was a new moon, a slight frost, still good roads, good horses, and a jolly driver, and as I went on I enjoyed it, hardly thinking at all of what lay before me; or perhaps I enjoyed it just because I knew what awaited me and was saying goodbye to the joys of life. But that tranquil mood, that ability to suppress my feelings, ended with my drive. As soon as I entered the train something entirely different began. That eight-hour journey in a railway carriage was something dreadful, which I shall never forget all my life. Whether it was that having taken my seat in the carriage I vividly imagined myself as having already arrived, or that railway travelling has such an exciting effect on people, at any rate from the moment I sat down in the train I could no longer control my imagination, and with extraordinary vividness which inflamed my jealousy it painted incessantly, one after another, pictures of what had gone on in my absence, of how she had been false to me. I burnt with indignation, anger, and a peculiar feeling of intoxication with my own humiliation, as I gazed at those pictures, and I could not tear myself away from them; I could not help looking at them, could not efface them, and could not help evoking them.

"That was not all. The more I gazed at those imaginary pictures the stronger grew my belief in their reality. The vividness with which they presented themselves to me seemed to serve as proof that what I imagined was real. It was as if some devil against my will invented and suggested to me the most terrible reflections. An old conversation I had had with Trukhachevski's brother came to my mind, and in a kind of ecstasy I rent my heart with that conversation, making it refer to Trukhachevski and my wife.

"That had occurred long before, but I recalled it. Trukhachevski's brother, I remember, in reply to a question whether he frequented houses of ill-fame, had said that a decent man would not go to places where there was danger of infection and it was dirty and nasty, since he could always find a decent woman. And now his brother had found my wife! 'True, she is not in her first youth, has lost a side-tooth, and there is a slight puffiness about her; but it can't be helped, one has to take advantage of what one can get,' I imagined him to be thinking. 'Yes, it is condescending of him to take her for his mistress!' I said to myself. 'And she is safe. . . .' 'No, it is impossible!' I thought, horror-struck. 'There is nothing of the kind, nothing! There are not even any grounds for suspecting such things. Didn't she tell me that the very thought that I could be jealous of him was degrading to her? Yes, but she is lying, she is always lying!' I exclaimed, and everything began anew. . . . There were only two other people in the carriage: an older woman and her husband, both very taciturn, and even they got out at one of the stations and I was quite alone. I was like a caged animal: now I jumped up and went to the window, now I began to walk up and down trying to speed the carriage up; but the carriage with all its seats and windows went jolting on in the same way, just as ours does. . . ."

Pozdnyshev jumped up, took a few steps, and sat down again.

"Oh, I am afraid, afraid of railway carriages, I am seized with horror. Yes, it is awful!" he continued. "I said to myself, 'I will think of something else. Suppose I think of the innkeeper where I had tea,' and there in my mind's eye appears the innkeeper with his long beard and his grandson, a boy of the age of my Vasya. 'My Vasya! He will see how the musician kisses his mother. What will happen in his poor soul? But what does she care? She loves'—and again the same thing rose up in me. 'No, no ... I will think about the inspection of the District Hospital. Oh, yes, about the patient who complained of the doctor yesterday. The doctor has a moustache like Trukhachevski's. And how impudent he is ... they both deceived me when he said he was leaving Moscow,' and it began afresh. Everything I thought of had some connexion with them. I suffered dreadfully. The chief cause of the suffering was my ignorance, my doubt, and the contradictions within me: my not knowing whether I ought to love or hate her. My suffering was of a strange kind. I felt a hateful consciousness of my humiliation and of his victory, but a terrible hatred for her. 'It will not do to put an end to myself and leave her; she must at least suffer to some extent, and at least understand that I have suffered,' I said to myself. I got out at every station to divert my mind. At one station I saw some people drinking, and I immediately drank some vodka. Beside me stood a Jew who was also drinking. He began to talk, and to avoid being alone in my carriage I went with him into his dirty third-class carriage reeking with smoke and bespattered with shells of sunflower seeds. There I sat down beside him and he chattered a great deal and told anecdotes. I listened to him, but could not take in what he was saying because I continued to think about my own affairs. He noticed this and demanded my attention. Then I rose and went back to my carriage. 'I must think it over,' I said to myself. 'Is what I suspect true, and is there any reason for me to suffer?' I sat down, wishing to think it over calmly, but immediately, instead of calm reflection, the same thing began again: instead of reflection, pictures and fancies. 'How often I have suffered like this,' I said to myself (recalling former similar attacks of jealousy), 'and afterwards it all ended in nothing. So it will be now perhaps, yes, certainly it will. I shall find her calmly asleep, she will wake up, be pleased to see me, and by her words and looks I shall know that there has been nothing and that this is all nonsense. Oh, how good that would be! But no, that has happened too often and won't happen again now,' some voice seemed to say; and it began again. Yes, that was where the punishment lay! I wouldn't take a young man to a lock-hospital to knock the hankering after women out of him, but into my soul, to see the devils that were rending it! What was terrible, you know, was that I considered myself to have a complete right to her body as if it were my own, and yet at the same time I felt I could not control that body, that it was not mine and she could dispose of it as she pleased, and that she wanted to dispose of it not as I wished her to. And I could do nothing either to her or to him. He, like Vanka the Steward,* could sing a song before the gallows of how he kissed the sugared lips and so forth. And he would triumph. If she has not yet done it but wishes to—and I know that she does wish to—it is still worse; it would be better if she had done it and I knew it, so that there would be an end to this uncertainty. I could not have said what it was I wanted. I wanted her not to desire that which she was bound to desire. It was utter insanity."

xxvi

"AT THE LAST station but one, when the conductor had been to collect the tickets, I gathered my things together and went out onto the brake-platform, and the consciousness that the crisis was at hand still further increased my agitation. I felt cold, and my jaw trembled so that my teeth chattered. I automatically left the terminus with the crowd, took a cab, got in, and drove off. I rode looking at the few passers-by, the night-watchmen, and the shadows of my trap thrown by the street lamps, now in front and now behind me, and did not think of anything. When we had gone about half a mile my feet felt cold, and I remembered that I had taken off my woollen stockings in the train and put them in my satchel. 'Where

---

Vanka the Steward is the subject and name of some old Russian poems. Vanka seduces his master's wife, boasts of having done so, and is hanged. A.M.

is the satchel? Is it here? Yes.' And my wicker trunk? I remembered that I had entirely forgotten about my luggage, but finding that I had the luggage-ticket I decided that it was not worth while going back for it, and so continued my way.

"Try now as I will, I cannot recall my state of mind at the time. What did I think? What did I want? I don't know at all. All I remember is a consciousness that something dreadful and very important in my life was imminent. Whether that important event occurred because I thought it would, or whether I had a presentiment of what was to happen, I don't know. It may even be that after what has happened all the foregoing moments have acquired a certain gloom in my mind. I drove up to the front porch. It was past midnight. Some cabmen were waiting in front of the porch expecting, from the fact that there were lights in the windows, to get fares. (The lights were in our flat, in the dancing-room and drawing-room.) Without considering why it was still light in our windows so late, I went upstairs in the same state of expectation of something dreadful, and rang. Egor, a kind, willing, but very stupid footman, opened the door. The first thing my eyes fell on in the hall was a man's cloak hanging on the stand with other outdoor coats. I ought to have been surprised but was not, for I had expected it. 'That's it!' I said to myself. When I asked Egor who the visitor was and he named Trukhachevski, I inquired whether there was anyone else. He replied, 'Nobody, sir.' I remember that he replied in a tone as if he wanted to cheer me and dissipate my doubts of there being anybody else there. 'So it is, so it is,' I seemed to be saying to myself. 'And the children?' 'All well, heaven be praised. In bed, long ago.'

"I could not breathe, and could not check the trembling of my jaw. 'Yes, so it is not as I thought: I used to expect a misfortune but things used to turn out all right and in the usual way. Now it is not as usual, but is all as I pictured to myself. I thought it was only fancy, but here it is, all real. Here it all is . . . !'

"I almost began to sob, but the devil immediately suggested to me: 'Cry, be sentimental, and they will get away quietly. You will have no proof and will continue to suffer and doubt all your life.' And my self-pity immediately vanished, and a strange sense of joy arose in me, that my torture would now be over, that now I could punish her, could get rid of her, and could vent my anger. And I gave vent to it—I became a beast, a cruel and cunning beast.

"'Don't!' I said to Egor, who was about to go to the drawing-room. 'Here is my luggage-ticket, take a cab as quick as you can and go and get my luggage. Go!' He went down the passage to fetch his overcoat. Afraid that he might alarm them, I went as far as his little room and waited while he put on his overcoat. From the drawing-room, beyond another room, one could hear voices and the clatter of knives and plates. They were eating and had not heard the bell. 'If only they don't come out now,' thought I. Egor put on his overcoat, which had an astra-khan collar, and went out. I locked the door after him and felt creepy when I knew I was alone and must act at once. How, I did not yet know. I only knew that all was now over, that there could be no doubt as to her guilt, and that I should punish her immediately and end my relations with her.

"Previously I had doubted and had thought: 'Perhaps after all it's not true, perhaps I am mistaken.' But now it was so no longer. It was all irrevocably decided. 'Without my knowledge she is alone with him at night! That is a complete disregard of everything! Or worse still: it is intentional boldness and impudence in crime, that the boldness may serve as a sign of innocence. All is clear. There is no doubt.' I only feared one thing—their parting hastily, inventing some fresh lie, and thus depriving me of clear evidence and of the possibility of proving the fact. So as to catch them more quickly I went on tiptoe to the dancing-room where they were, not through the drawing-room but through the passage and nurseries.

"In the first nursery slept the boys. In the second nursery the nurse moved and was about to wake, and I imagined to myself what she would think when she knew all; and such pity for myself seized me at that thought that I could not restrain my tears, and not to wake the children I ran on tiptoe into the passage and on into my study, where I fell sobbing on the sofa.

"'I, an honest man, I, the son of my parents, I, who have all my life dreamt of the happiness of married life; I, a man who was never unfaithful to her ... And now! Five children, and she is embracing a musician because he has red lips!

"'No, she is not a human being. She is a bitch, an abominable bitch! In the next room to her children whom she has all her life pretended to love. And writing to me as she did! Throwing herself so barefacedly on his neck! But what do I know? Perhaps she long ago carried on with the footmen, and so got the children who are considered mine!

"'Tomorrow I should have come back and she would have met me with her fine coiffure, with her elegant waist and her indolent, graceful movements' (I saw all her attractive, hateful face) 'and that beast of jealousy would forever have sat in my heart lacerating it. What will the nurse think? ... And Egor? And poor little Lisa! She already understands something. Ah, that impudence, those lies! And that animal sensuality which I know so well,' I said to myself.

"I tried to get up but could not. My heart was beating so that I could not stand on my feet. 'Yes, I shall die of a stroke. She will kill me. That is just what she wants. What is killing to her? But no, that would be too advantageous for her and I will not give her that pleasure. Yes, here I sit while they eat and laugh and ... Yes, though she was no longer in her first freshness he did not disdain her. For in spite of that she is not bad looking, and above all she is at any rate not dangerous to his precious health. And why did I not throttle her then?' I said to myself, recalling the moment when, the week before, I drove her out of my study and hurled things about. I vividly recalled the state I had then been in; I not only recalled it, but again felt the need to strike and destroy that I had felt then. I remember how I wished to act, and how all considerations except those necessary for action went out of my head. I entered into that condition when an animal or a man, under the influence of physical excitement at a time of danger, acts with precision and deliberation but without losing a moment and always with a single definite aim in view.

"The first thing I did was to take off my boots and, in my socks, approach the sofa, on the wall above which guns and daggers were hung. I took down a curved Damascus dagger that had never been used and was very sharp. I drew it out of its scabbard. I remember the scabbard fell behind the sofa, and I remember thinking, 'I must find it afterwards or it will get lost.' Then I took off my overcoat which I was still wearing, and stepping softly in my socks I went there."

xxvii

"HAVING crept up stealthily to the door, I suddenly opened it. I remember the expression of their faces. I remember that expression because it gave me a painful pleasure—it was an expression of terror. That was just what I wanted. I shall never forget the look of desperate terror that appeared on both their faces the first instant they saw me. He I think was sitting at the table, but on seeing or hearing me he jumped to his feet and stood with his back to the cupboard. His face expressed nothing but quite unmistakable terror. Her face too expressed terror but there was something else besides. If it had expressed only terror, perhaps what happened might not have happened; but on her face there was, or at any rate so it seemed to me at the first moment, also an expression of regret and annoyance that love's raptures and her happiness with him had been disturbed. It was as if she wanted nothing but that her present happiness should not be interfered with. These expressions remained on their faces but an instant. The look of terror on his changed immediately to one of inquiry: might he, or might he not, begin lying? If he might, he must begin at once; if not, something else would happen. But what? ... He looked inquiringly at her face. On her face the look of vexation and regret changed as she looked at him (so it seemed to me) to one of solicitude for him.

"For an instant I stood in the doorway holding the dagger behind my back.

"At that moment he smiled, and in a ridiculously indifferent tone remarked: 'And we have been having some music.'

"'What a surprise!' she began, falling into his tone. But neither of them finished; the same fury I had experienced the week before overcame me. Again I felt that need of destruction, violence, and a transport of rage, and yielded to it. Neither finished what they were saying. That something else began which he had feared and which immediately destroyed all they were saying. I rushed towards her, still hiding the dagger that he might not prevent my striking her in the side under her breast. I selected that spot from the first. Just as I rushed at her he saw it, and—a thing I never expected of him—seized me by the arm and shouted: 'Think what you are doing! ... Help, someone! ...'

"I snatched my arm away and rushed at him in silence. His eyes met mine and he suddenly grew as pale as a sheet to his very lips. His eyes flashed in a peculiar way, and—what again I had not expected—he darted under the piano and out at the door. I was going to rush after him, but a weight hung on my left arm. It was she. I tried to free myself, but she hung on yet more heavily and would not let me go. This unexpected hindrance, the weight, and her touch, which was loathsome to me, inflamed me still more. I felt that I was quite mad and that I must look frightful, and this delighted me. I swung my left arm with all my might, and my elbow hit her straight in the face. She cried out and let go my arm. I wanted to run after him, but remembered that it is ridiculous to run after one's wife's lover in one's socks; and I did not wish to be ridiculous but terrible. In spite of the fearful frenzy I was in, I was all the time aware of the impression I might produce on others, and was even partly guided by that impression. I turned towards her. She fell on the couch, and holding her hand to her bruised eyes, looked at me. Her face showed fear and hatred of me, the enemy, as a rat's does when one lifts the trap in which it has been caught. At any rate I saw nothing in her expression but this fear and hatred of me. It was just the fear and hatred of me which would be evoked by love for another. But still I might perhaps have restrained myself and not done what I did had she remained silent. But she suddenly began to speak and to catch hold of the hand in which I held the dagger.

"'Come to yourself! What are you doing? What is the matter? There has been nothing, nothing, nothing. . . . I swear it!'

"I might still have hesitated, but those last words of hers, from which I concluded just the opposite—that everything had happened—called forth a reply. And the reply had to correspond to the temper to which I had brought myself, which continued to increase and had to go on increasing. Fury too has its laws.

"'Don't lie, you wretch!' I howled, and seized her arm with my left hand, but she wrenched herself away. Then, still without letting go of the dagger, I seized her by the throat with my left hand, threw her backwards, and began throttling her. What a firm neck it was . . . ! She seized my hand with both hers trying to pull it away from her throat, and as if I had only waited for that, I struck her with all my might with the dagger in the side below the ribs.

"When people say they don't remember what they do in a fit of fury, it is rubbish, falsehood. I remembered everything and did not for a moment lose consciousness of what I was doing. The more frenzied I became the more brightly the light of consciousness burnt in me, so that I could not help knowing everything I did. I knew what I was doing every second. I cannot say that I knew beforehand what I was going to do; but I knew what I was doing when I did it, and even I think a little before, as if to make repentance possible and to be able to tell myself that I could stop. I knew I was hitting below the ribs and that the dagger would enter. At the moment I did it I knew I was doing an awful thing such as I had never done before, which would have terrible consequences. But that consciousness passed like a flash of lightning and the deed immediately followed the consciousness. I realized the action with extraordinary clearness. I felt, and remember, the momentary resistance of her corset and of something else, and then the plunging of the dagger into something soft. She seized the dagger with her hands, and cut them, but could not hold it back.

"For a long time afterwards, in prison when the moral change had taken place in me, I thought of that moment, recalled what I could of it, and considered it. I remembered that for an instant, only an instant, before the action I had terrible consciousness that I was killing, had killed, a defenceless woman, my wife! I remember the horror of that consciousness and conclude from that, and even dimly remember, that having plunged the dagger in I pulled it out immediately, trying to remedy what had been done and to stop it. I stood for a second motionless waiting to see what would happen, and whether it could be remedied.

"She jumped to her feet and screamed: 'Nurse! He has killed me.'

"Having heard the noise the nurse was standing by the door. I continued to stand waiting, and not believing the truth. But the blood rushed from under her corset. Only then did I understand that it could not be remedied, and I immediately decided that it was not necessary it should be, that I had done what I wanted and had to do. I waited till she fell down, and the nurse, crying 'Good God!' ran to her, and only then did I throw away the dagger and leave the room.

"'I must not be excited; I must know what I am do-

ing,' I said to myself without looking at her and at the
nurse. The nurse was screaming—calling for the maid. I
went down the passage, sent the maid, and went into my
study. 'What am I to do now?' I asked myself, and immediately realized what it must be. On entering the
study I went straight to the wall, took down a revolver
and examined it—it was loaded—I put it on the table.
Then I picked up the scabbard from behind the sofa and
sat down there.

"I sat thus for a long time. I did not think of anything
or call anything to mind. I heard the sounds of bustling
outside. I heard someone drive up, then someone else.
Then I heard and saw Egor bring into the room my
wicker trunk he had fetched. As if anyone wanted that!

"'Have you heard what has happened?' I asked. 'Tell
the yard-porter to inform the police.' He did not reply,
and went away. I rose, locked the door, got out my cigarettes and matches and began to smoke. I had not finished the cigarette before sleep overpowered me. I must
have slept for a couple of hours. I remember dreaming
that she and I were friendly together, that we had quarrelled but were making it up, there was something rather
in the way, but we were friends. I was awakened by
someone knocking at the door. 'That is the police!' I
thought, waking up. 'I have committed murder, I think.
But perhaps it is *she,* and nothing has happened.' There
was again a knock at the door. I did not answer, but was
trying to solve the question whether it had happened or
not. Yes, it had! I remembered the resistance of the corset and the plunging in of the dagger, and a cold shiver
ran down my back. 'Yes, it has. Yes, and now I must do
away with myself too,' I thought. But I thought this
knowing that I should *not* kill myself. Still I got up and
took the revolver in my hand. But it is strange: I remember how I had many times been near suicide, how even
that day on the railway it had seemed easy, easy just because I thought how it would stagger her—now I was not
only unable to kill myself but even to think of it. 'Why
should I do it?' I asked myself, and there was no reply.

There was more knocking at the door. 'First I must find out who is knocking. There will still be time for this.' I put down the revolver and covered it with a newspaper. I went to the door and unlatched it. It was my wife's sister, a kindly, stupid widow. 'Vasya, what is this?' and her ever ready tears began to flow.

"'What do you want?' I asked rudely. I knew I ought not to be rude to her and had no reason to be, but I could think of no other tone to adopt.

"'Vasya, she is dying! Ivan Zakharych says so.' Ivan Zakharych was her doctor and adviser.

"'Is he here?' I asked, and all my animosity against her surged up again. 'Well, what of it?'

"'Vasya, go to her. Oh, how terrible it is!' said she.

"'Shall I go to her?' I asked myself, and immediately decided that I must go to her. Probably it is always done, when a husband has killed his wife, as I had—he must certainly go to her. 'If that is what is done, then I must go,' I said to myself. 'If necessary I shall always have time,' I reflected, referring to the shooting of myself, and I went to her. 'Now we shall have phrases, grimaces, but I will not yield to them,' I thought. 'Wait,' I said to her sister, 'it is silly without boots, let me at least put on slippers.'"

xxviii

"WONDERFUL to say, when I left my study and went through the familiar rooms, the hope that nothing had happened again awoke in me; but the smell of that doctor's nastiness—iodoform and carbolic—took me aback. 'No, it has happened.' Going down the passage past the nursery I saw little Lisa. She looked at me with frightened eyes. It even seemed to me that all the five children were there and all looked at me. I approached the door, and the maid opened it from the inside for me and passed out. The first thing that caught my eye was her light-grey dress thrown on a chair and all stained black with blood. She was lying on one of the twin beds (on

mine because it was easier to get at), with her knees
raised. She lay in a very sloping position supported by
pillows, with her dressing jacket unfastened. Something
had been put on the wound. There was a heavy smell of
iodoform in the room. What struck me first and most of
all was her swollen and bruised face, blue on part of the
nose and under the eyes. This was the result of the blow
with my elbow when she had tried to hold me back.
There was nothing beautiful about her, but something
repulsive as it seemed to me. I stopped on the threshold.
'Go up to her, do,' said her sister. 'Yes, no doubt she
wants to confess,' I thought. 'Shall I forgive her? Yes, she
is dying and may be forgiven,' I thought, trying to be
magnanimous. I went up close to her. She raised her eyes
to me with difficulty—one of them was black—and with
an effort said falteringly:

"'You've got your way, killed . . .' and through the
look of suffering and even the nearness of death her face
had the old expression of cold animal hatred that I knew
so well. 'I shan't . . . let you have . . . the children, all the
same. . . . She (her sister) will take . . .'

"Of what to me was the most important matter, her
guilt, her faithlessness, she seemed to consider it beneath
her to speak.

"'Yes, look and admire what you have done,' she said
looking towards the door, and she sobbed. In the doorway stood her sister with the children. 'Yes, see what you
have done.'

"I looked at the children and at her bruised disfigured
face, and for the first time I forgot myself, my rights, my
pride, and for the first time saw a human being in her.
And so insignificant did all that had offended me, all my
jealousy, appear, and so important what I had done, that
I wished to fall with my face to her hand, and say: 'Forgive me,' but dared not do so.

"She lay silent with her eyes closed, evidently too
weak to say more. Then her disfigured face trembled and
puckered. She pushed me feebly away.

"'Why did it all happen? Why?'

"'Forgive me,' I said.

"'Forgive! That's all rubbish! . . . Only not to die! . . .' she cried, raising herself, and her glittering eyes were bent on me. 'Yes, you have had your way! . . . I hate you! Ah! Ah!' she cried, evidently already in delirium and frightened at something. 'Shoot! I'm not afraid! . . . Only kill everyone! . . . He has gone! . . . Gone! . . .'

"After that the delirium continued all the time. She did not recognize anyone. She died towards noon that same day. Before that they had taken me to the police station and from there to prison. There, during the eleven months I remained awaiting trial, I examined myself and my past, and understood it. I began to understand it on the third day: on the third day they took me *there* . . ."

He was going on but, unable to repress his sobs, he stopped. When he recovered himself he continued:

"I only began to understand when I saw her in her coffin . . ."

He gave a sob, but immediately continued hurriedly:

"Only when I saw her dead face did I understand all that I had done. I realized that I, I, had killed her; that it was my doing that she, living, moving, warm, had now become motionless, waxen, and cold, and that this could never, anywhere, or by any means, be remedied. He who has not lived through it cannot understand. . . . Ugh! Ugh! Ugh! . . ." he cried several times and then was silent.

We sat in silence a long while. He kept sobbing and trembling as he sat opposite me without speaking. His face had grown narrow and elongated and his mouth seemed to stretch right across it.

"Yes," he suddenly said. "Had I then known what I know now, everything would have been different. Nothing would have induced me to marry her. . . . I should not have married at all."

Again we remained silent for a long time.

"Well, forgive me. . . ."* He turned away from me and

---

*In Russian the word for "forgive me" is very similar to that for "good-bye," and is sometimes used in place of the latter. A.M.

lay down on the seat, covering himself up with his plaid. At the station where I had to get out (it was at eight o'clock in the morning) I went up to him to say good-bye. Whether he was asleep or only pretended to be, at any rate he did not move. I touched him with my hand. He uncovered his face, and I could see he had not been asleep.

"Good-bye," I said, holding out my hand. He gave me his and smiled slightly, but so piteously that I felt ready to weep.

"Yes, forgive me ..." he said, repeating the same words with which he had concluded his story.

Master and Man

i

IT HAPPENED in the seventies in winter, on the day after
St. Nicholas's Day. There was a fête in the parish and
the innkeeper, Vasili Andreevich Brekhunov, a Second
Guild merchant, being a church elder had to go to
church, and had also to entertain his relatives and friends
at home.

But when the last of them had gone he at once began
to prepare to drive over to see a neighbouring proprietor
about a grove which he had been bargaining over for a
long time. He was now in a hurry to start, lest buyers
from the town might forestall him in making a profitable
purchase.

The youthful landowner was asking ten thousand rubles for the grove simply because Vasili Andreevich was
offering seven thousand. Seven thousand was, however,
only a third of its real value. Vasili Andreevich might per-

haps have got it down to his own price, for the woods
were in his district and he had a long-standing agreement
with the other village dealers that no one should run up
the price in another's district, but he had now learnt that
some timber-dealers from town meant to bid for the
Goryachkin grove, and he resolved to go at once and get
the matter settled. So as soon as the feast was over, he
took seven hundred rubles from his strong box, added to
them two thousand three hundred rubles of church
money he had in his keeping, so as to make up the sum to
three thousand; carefully counted the notes, and having
put them into his pocket-book made haste to start.

Nikita, the only one of Vasili Andreevich's labourers
who was not drunk that day, ran to harness the horse.
Nikita, though an habitual drunkard, was not drunk that
day because since the last day before the fast, when he
had drunk his coat and leather boots, he had sworn off
drink and had kept his vow for two months, and was still
keeping it despite the temptation of the vodka that had
been drunk everywhere during the first two days of the
feast.

Nikita was a peasant of about fifty from a neighbouring village, "not a manager" as the peasants said of him,
meaning that he was not the thrifty head of a household
but lived most of his time away from home as a labourer.
He was valued everywhere for his industry, dexterity,
and strength at work, and still more for his kindly and
pleasant temper. But he never settled down anywhere
for long because about twice a year, or even oftener, he
had a drinking bout, and then besides spending all his
clothes on drink he became turbulent and quarrelsome.
Vasili Andreevich himself had turned him away several
times, but had afterwards taken him back again—valuing
his honesty, his kindness to animals, and especially his
cheapness. Vasili Andreevich did not pay Nikita the
eighty rubles a year such a man was worth, but only
about forty, which he gave him haphazard, in small sums,
and even that mostly not in cash but in goods from his
own shop and at high prices.

Nikita's wife, Martha, who had once been a handsome vigorous woman, managed the homestead with the help of her son and two daughters, and did not urge Nikita to live at home: first because she had been living for some twenty years already with a cooper, a peasant from another village who lodged in their house; and secondly because though she managed her husband as she pleased when he was sober, she feared him like fire when he was drunk. Once when he had got drunk at home, Nikita, probably to make up for his submissiveness when sober, broke open her box, took out her best clothes, snatched up an axe, and chopped all her undergarments and dresses to bits. All the wages Nikita earned went to his wife, and he raised no objection to that. So now, two days before the holiday, Martha had been twice to see Vasili Andreevich and had got from him wheat flour, tea, sugar, and a quart of vodka, the lot costing three rubles, and also five rubles in cash, for which she thanked him as for a special favour, though he owed Nikita at least twenty rubles.

"What agreement did we ever draw up with you?" said Vasili Andreevich to Nikita. "If you need anything, take it; you will work it off. I'm not like others to keep you waiting, and making up accounts and reckoning fines. We deal straightforwardly. You serve me and I don't neglect you."

And when saying this Vasili Andreevich was honestly convinced that he was Nikita's benefactor, and he knew how to put it so plausibly that all those who depended on him for their money, beginning with Nikita, confirmed him in the conviction that he was their benefactor and did not overreach them.

"Yes, I understand, Vasili Andreevich. You know that I serve you and take as much pains as I would for my own father. I understand very well!" Nikita would reply. He was quite aware that Vasili Andreevich was cheating him, but at the same time he felt that it was useless to try to clear up his accounts with him or explain his side of the matter, and that as long as he had nowhere else to go he must accept what he could get.

Now, having heard his master's order to harness, he went as usual cheerfully and willingly to the shed, stepping briskly and easily on his rather turned-in feet; took down from a nail the heavy tasselled leather bridle, and jingling the rings of the bit went to the closed stable where the horse he was to harness was standing by himself.

"What, feeling lonely, feeling lonely, little silly?" said Nikita in answer to the low whinny with which he was greeted by the good-tempered, medium-sized bay stallion, with a rather slanting crupper, who stood alone in the shed. "Now then, now then, there's time enough. Let me water you first," he went on, speaking to the horse just as to someone who understood the words he was using, and having whisked the dusty grooved back of the well-fed young stallion with the skirt of his coat, he put a bridle on his handsome head, straightened his ears and forelock, and having taken off his halter led him out to water.

Picking his way out of the dung-strewn stable, Mukhorty frisked, and making play with his hind leg pretended that he meant to kick Nikita, who was running at a trot beside him to the pump.

"Now then, now then, you rascal!" Nikita called out, well knowing how carefully Mukhorty threw out his hind leg just to touch his greasy sheepskin coat but not to strike him—a trick Nikita much appreciated.

After a drink of the cold water the horse sighed, moving his strong wet lips, from the hairs of which transparent drops fell into the trough; then standing still as if in thought, he suddenly gave a loud snort.

"If you don't want any more, you needn't. But don't go asking for any later," said Nikita quite seriously and fully explaining his conduct to Mukhorty. Then he ran back to the shed pulling the playful young horse, who wanted to gambol all over the yard, by the rein.

There was no one else in the yard except a stranger, the cook's husband, who had come for the holiday.

"Go and ask which sledge is to be harnessed—the wide one or the small one—there's a good fellow!"

The cook's husband went into the house, which stood on an iron foundation and was iron-roofed, and soon returned saying that the little one was to be harnessed. By that time Nikita had put the collar and brass-studded belly-band on Mukhorty and, carrying a light, painted shaft-bow in one hand, was leading the horse with the other up to two sledges that stood in the shed.

"All right, let it be the little one!" he said, backing the intelligent horse, which all the time kept pretending to bite him, into the shafts, and with the aid of the cook's husband he proceeded to harness. When everything was nearly ready and only the reins had to be adjusted, Nikita sent the other man to the shed for some straw and to the barn for a drugget.

"There, that's all right! Now, now, don't bristle up!" said Nikita, pressing down into the sledge the freshly threshed oat straw the cook's husband had brought. "And now let's spread the sacking like this, and the drugget over it. There, like that it will be comfortable sitting," he went on, suiting the action to the words and tucking the drugget all round over the straw to make a seat.

"Thank you, dear man. Things always go quicker with two working at it!" he added. And gathering up the leather reins fastened together by a brass ring, Nikita took the driver's seat and started the impatient horse over the frozen manure which lay in the yard, towards the gate.

"Uncle Nikita! I say, Uncle, Uncle!" a high-pitched voice shouted, and a seven-year-old boy in a black sheepskin coat, new white felt boots, and a warm cap, ran hurriedly out of the house into the yard. "Take me with you!" he cried, fastening up his coat as he ran.

"All right, come along, darling!" said Nikita, and stopping the sledge he picked up the master's pale thin little son, radiant with joy, and drove out into the road.

It was past two o'clock and the day was windy, dull, and cold, with more than twenty degrees Fahrenheit of frost. Half the sky was hidden by a lowering dark cloud. In the yard it was quiet, but in the street the wind was

felt more keenly. The snow swept down from a neighbouring shed and whirled about in the corner near the
bath-house.

Hardly had Nikita driven out of the yard and turned
the horse's head to the house, before Vasili Andreevich
emerged from the high porch in front of the house with
a cigarette in his mouth and wearing a cloth-covered
sheepskin coat tightly girdled low at his waist, and
stepped onto the hard-trodden snow which squeaked
under the leather soles of his felt boots, and stopped.
Taking a last whiff of his cigarette he threw it down,
stepped on it, and letting the smoke escape through his
moustache and looking askance at the horse that was
coming up, began to tuck in his sheepskin collar on both
sides of his ruddy face, clean-shaven except for the
moustache, so that his breath should not moisten the collar.

"See now! The young scamp is there already!" he exclaimed when he saw his little son in the sledge. Vasili
Andreevich was excited by the vodka he had drunk with
his visitors, and so he was even more pleased than usual
with everything that was his and all that he did. The sight
of his son, whom he always thought of as his heir, now
gave him great satisfaction. He looked at him, screwing
up his eyes and showing his long teeth.

His wife—pregnant, thin and pale, with her head and
shoulders wrapped in a shawl so that nothing of her face
could be seen but her eyes—stood behind him in the
vestibule to see him off.

"Now really, you ought to take Nikita with you," she
said timidly, stepping out from the doorway.

Vasili Andreevich did not answer. Her words evidently annoyed him and he frowned angrily and spat.

"You have money on you," she continued in the same
plaintive voice. "What if the weather gets worse! Do
take him, for goodness' sake!"

"Why? Don't I know the road that I must needs take
a guide?" exclaimed Vasili Andreevich, uttering every
word very distinctly and compressing his lips unnatu-

rally, as he usually did when speaking to buyers and sellers.

"Really you ought to take him. I beg you in God's name!" his wife repeated, wrapping her shawl more closely round her head.

"There, she sticks to it like a leech! . . . Where am I to take him?"

"I'm quite ready to go with you, Vasili Andreevich," said Nikita cheerfully. "But they must feed the horses while I am away," he added, turning to his master's wife.

"I'll look after them, Nikita dear. I'll tell Simon," replied the mistress.

"Well, Vasili Andreevich, am I to come with you?" said Nikita, awaiting a decision.

"It seems I must humour my old woman. But if you're coming you'd better put on a warmer cloak," said Vasili Andreevich, smiling again as he winked at Nikita's short sheepskin coat, which was torn under the arms and at the back, was greasy and out of shape, frayed to a fringe round the skirt, and had endured many things in its lifetime.

"Hey, dear man, come and hold the horse!" shouted Nikita to the cook's husband, who was still in the yard.

"No, I will myself, I will myself!" shrieked the little boy, pulling his hands, red with cold, out of his pockets, and seizing the cold leather reins.

"Only don't be too long dressing yourself up. Look alive!" shouted Vasili Andreevich, grinning at Nikita.

"Only a moment, Father, Vasili Andreevich!" replied Nikita, and running quickly with his in-turned toes in his felt boots with their soles patched with felt, he hurried across the yard and into the workmen's hut.

"Arinushka! Get my coat down from the stove. I'm going with the master," he said, as he ran into the hut and took down his girdle from the nail on which it hung.

The workmen's cook, who had had a sleep after dinner and was now getting the samovar ready for her husband, turned cheerfully to Nikita, and infected by his hurry began to move as quickly as he did, got down his miserable worn-out cloth coat from the stove where it was drying, and began hurriedly shaking it out and smoothing it down.

"There now, you'll have a chance of a holiday with your goodman," said Nikita, who from kind-hearted politeness always said something to anyone he was alone with.

Then, drawing his worn narrow girdle round him, he drew in his breath, pulling in his lean stomach still more, and girdled himself as tightly as he could over his sheepskin.

"There now," he said, addressing himself no longer to the cook but the girdle, as he tucked the ends in at the waist, "now you won't come undone!" And working his shoulders up and down to free his arms, he put the coat over his sheepskin, arched his back more strongly to ease his arms, poked himself under the armpits, and took down his leather-covered mittens from the shelf. "Now we're all right!"

"You ought to wrap your feet up, Nikita. Your boots are very bad."

Nikita stopped as if he had suddenly realized this.

"Yes, I ought to. . . . But they'll do like this. It isn't far!" and he ran out into the yard.

"Won't you be cold, Nikita?" said the mistress as he came up to the sledge.

"Cold? No, I'm quite warm," answered Nikita as he pushed some straw up to the forepart of the sledge so that it should cover his feet, and stowed away the whip, which the good horse would not need, at the bottom of the sledge.

Vasili Andreevich, who was wearing two fur-lined coats one over the other, was already in the sledge, his broad back filling nearly its whole rounded width, and taking the reins he immediately touched the horse. Nikita jumped in just as the sledge started, and seated himself in front on the left side, with one leg hanging over the edge.

ii

THE GOOD stallion took the sledge along at a brisk pace over the smooth-frozen road through the village, the runners squeaking slightly as they went.

"Look at him hanging on there! Hand me the whip, Nikita!" shouted Vasili Andreevich, evidently enjoying the sight of his "heir," who, standing on the runners, was hanging on at the back of the sledge. "I'll give it you! Be off to Mamma, you dog!"

The boy jumped down. The horse increased his amble and, suddenly changing foot, broke into a fast trot.

The Crosses, the village where Vasili Andreevich lived, consisted of six houses. As soon as they had passed the blacksmith's hut, the last in the village, they realized that the wind was much stronger than they had thought. The road could hardly be seen. The tracks left by the sledge-runners were immediately covered by snow and the road was only distinguished by the fact that it was higher than the rest of the ground. There was a whirl of snow over the fields and the line where sky and earth met could not be seen. The Telyatin forest, usually clearly visible, now only loomed up occasionally and dimly through the driving snowy dust. The wind came from the left, insistently blowing over to one side the mane on Mukhorty's sleek neck and carrying aside even his fluffy tail, which was tied in a simple knot. Nikita's wide coat collar, as he sat on the windy side, pressed close to his cheek and nose.

"This road doesn't give him a chance—it's too snowy," said Vasili Andreevich, who prided himself on his good horse. "I once drove to Pashutino with him in half an hour."

"What?" asked Nikita, who could not hear on account of his collar.

"I say I once went to Pashutino in half an hour," shouted Vasili Andreevich.

"It goes without saying that he's a good horse," replied Nikita.

They were silent for a while. But Vasili Andreevich wished to talk.

"Well, did you tell your wife not to give the cooper any vodka?" he began in the same loud tone, quite convinced that Nikita must feel flattered to be talking with so clever and important a person as himself, and he was so pleased with his jest that it did not enter his head that the remark might be unpleasant to Nikita.

The wind again prevented Nikita's hearing his master's words.

Vasili Andreevich repeated the jest about the cooper in his loud, clear voice.

"That's their business, Vasili Andreevich. I don't pry into their affairs. As long as she doesn't ill-treat our boy—God be with them."

"That's so," said Vasili Andreevich. "Well, and will you be buying a horse in spring?" he went on, changing the subject.

"Yes, I can't avoid it," answered Nikita, turning down his collar and leaning back towards his master.

The conversation now became interesting to him and he did not wish to lose a word.

"The lad's growing up. He must begin to plough for himself, but till now we've always had to hire someone," he said.

"Well, why not have the lean-cruppered one. I won't charge much for it," shouted Vasili Andreevich, feeling animated, and consequently starting on his favourite occupation—that of horse-dealing—which absorbed all his mental powers.

"Or you might let me have fifteen rubles and I'll buy one at the horse-market," said Nikita, who knew that the horse Vasili Andreevich wanted to sell him would be dear at seven rubles, but that if he took it from him it would be charged at twenty-five, and then he would be unable to draw any money for half a year.

"It's a good horse. I think of your interest as of my own—according to conscience. Brekhunov isn't a man to wrong anyone. Let the loss be mine. I'm not like others. Honestly!" he shouted in the voice in which he hypnotized his customers and dealers. "It's a real good horse."

"Quite so!" said Nikita with a sigh, and convinced that there was nothing more to listen to, he again released his collar, which immediately covered his ear and face.

They drove on in silence for about half an hour. The wind blew sharply onto Nikita's side and arm where his sheepskin was torn.

He huddled up and breathed into the collar which covered his mouth, and was not wholly cold.

"What do you think—shall we go through Karamyshevo or by the straight road?" asked Vasili Andreevich.

The road through Karamyshevo was more frequented and was well marked with a double row of high stakes. The straight road was nearer but little used and had no stakes, or only poor ones covered with snow.

Nikita thought awhile.

"Though Karamyshevo is farther, it is better going," he said.

"But by the straight road, when once we get through the hollow by the forest, it's good going—sheltered," said Vasili Andreevich, who wished to go the nearest way.

"Just as you please," said Nikita, and again let go of his collar.

Vasili Andreevich did as he had said, and having gone about half a verst came to a tall oak stake which had a few dry leaves still dangling on it, and there he turned to the left.

On turning they faced directly against the wind, and snow was beginning to fall. Vasili Andreevich, who was driving, inflated his cheeks, blowing the breath out through his moustache. Nikita dozed.

So they went on in silence for about ten minutes. Suddenly Vasili Andreevich began saying something.

"Eh, what?" asked Nikita, opening his eyes.

Vasili Andreevich did not answer, but bent over, look-

ing behind them and then ahead of the horse. The sweat
had curled Mukhorty's coat between his legs and on his
neck. He went at a walk.

"What is it?" Nikita asked again.

"What is it? What is it?" Vasili Andreevich mimicked
him angrily. "There are no stakes to be seen! We must
have got off the road!"

"Well, pull up then, and I'll look for it," said Nikita,
and jumping down lightly from the sledge and taking the
whip from under the straw, he went off to the left from
his own side of the sledge.

The snow was not deep that year, so that it was possible to walk anywhere, but still in places it was knee-
deep and got into Nikita's boots. He went about feeling
the ground with his feet and the whip, but could not find
the road anywhere.

"Well, how is it?" asked Vasili Andreevich when Nikita came back to the sledge.

"There is no road this side. I must go to the other side
and try there," said Nikita.

"There's something there in front. Go and have a
look."

Nikita went to what had appeared dark, but found
that it was earth which the wind had blown from the
bare fields of winter oats and had strewn over the snow,
colouring it. Having searched to the right also, he returned to the sledge, brushed the snow from his coat,
shook it out of his boots, and seated himself once more.

"We must go to the right," he said decidedly. "The
wind was blowing on our left before, but now it is straight
in my face. Drive to the right," he repeated with decision.

Vasili Andreevich took his advice and turned to the
right, but still there was no road. They went on in that
direction for some time. The wind was as fierce as ever
and it was snowing lightly.

"It seems, Vasili Andreevich, that we have gone quite
astray," Nikita suddenly remarked, as if it were a pleasant thing. "What is that?" he added, pointing to some
potato bines that showed up from under the snow.

Vasili Andreevich stopped the perspiring horse, whose deep sides were heaving heavily.

"What is it?"

"Why, we are on the Zakharov lands. See where we've got to!"

"Nonsense!" retorted Vasili Andreevich.

"It's not nonsense, Vasili Andreevich. It's the truth," replied Nikita. "You can feel that the sledge is going over a potato-field, and there are the heaps of bines which have been carted here. It's the Zakharov factory land."

"Dear me, how we have gone astray!" said Vasili Andreevich. "What are we to do now?"

"We must go straight on, that's all. We shall come out somewhere—if not at Zakharova then at the proprietor's farm," said Nikita.

Vasili Andreevich agreed, and drove as Nikita had indicated. So they went on for a considerable time. At times they came onto bare fields and the sledge-runners rattled over frozen lumps of earth. Sometimes they got onto a winter-rye field, or a fallow field on which they could see stalks of wormwood, and straws sticking up through the snow and swaying in the wind; sometimes they came onto deep and even white snow, above which nothing was to be seen.

The snow was falling from above and sometimes rose from below. The horse was evidently exhausted, his hair had all curled up from sweat and was covered with hoar-frost, and he went at a walk. Suddenly he stumbled and sat down in a ditch or water-course. Vasili Andreevich wanted to stop, but Nikita cried to him:

"Why stop? We've got in and must get out. Hey, pet! Hey, darling! Gee up, old fellow!" he shouted in a cheerful tone to the horse, jumping out of the sledge and himself getting stuck in the ditch.

The horse gave a start and quickly climbed out onto the frozen bank. It was evidently a ditch that had been dug there.

"Where are we now?" asked Vasili Andreevich.

"We'll soon find out!" Nikita replied. "Go on, we'll get somewhere."

"Why, this must be the Goryachkin forest!" said Vasili Andreevich, pointing to something dark that appeared amid the snow in front of them.

"We'll see what forest it is when we get there," said Nikita.

He saw that beside the black thing they had noticed, dry, oblong willow-leaves were fluttering, and so he knew it was not a forest but a settlement, but he did not wish to say so. And in fact they had not gone twenty-five yards beyond the ditch before something in front of them, evidently trees, showed up black, and they heard a new and melancholy sound. Nikita had guessed right: it was not a wood, but a row of tall willows with a few leaves still fluttering on them here and there. They had evidently been planted along the ditch round a threshing-floor. Coming up to the willows, which moaned sadly in the wind, the horse suddenly planted his forelegs above the height of the sledge, drew up his hind legs also, pulling the sledge onto higher ground, and turned to the left, no longer sinking up to his knees in snow. They were back on a road.

"Well, here we are, but heaven only knows where!" said Nikita.

The horse kept straight along the road through the drifted snow, and before they had gone another hundred yards the straight line of the dark wattle wall of a barn showed up black before them, its roof heavily covered with snow which poured down from it. After passing the barn the road turned to the wind and they drove into a snowdrift. But ahead of them was a lane with houses on either side, so evidently the snow had been blown across the road and they had to drive through the drift. And so in fact it was. Having driven through the snow they came out into a street. At the end house of the village some frozen clothes hanging on a line—shirts, one red and one white, trousers, leg-bands, and a petticoat—fluttered wildly in the wind. The white shirt in particular struggled desperately, waving its sleeves about.

"There now, either a lazy woman or a dead one has not taken her clothes down before the holiday," remarked Nikita, looking at the fluttering shirts.

iii

AT THE entrance to the street the wind still raged and the road was thickly covered with snow, but well within the village it was calm, warm, and cheerful. At one house a dog was barking, at another a woman, covering her head with her coat, came running from somewhere and entered the door of a hut, stopping on the threshold to have a look at the passing sledge. In the middle of the village girls could be heard singing.

Here in the village there seemed to be less wind and snow, and the frost was less keen.

"Why, this is Grishkino," said Vasili Andreevich.

"So it is," responded Nikita.

It really was Grishkino, which meant that they had gone too far to the left and had travelled some six miles, not quite in the direction they aimed at, but towards their destination for all that.

From Grishkino to Goryachkin was about another four miles.

In the middle of the village they almost ran into a tall man walking down the middle of the street.

"Who are you?" shouted the man, stopping the horse, and recognizing Vasili Andreevich he immediately took hold of the shaft, went along it hand over hand till he reached the sledge, and placed himself on the driver's seat.

He was Isay, a peasant of Vasili Andreevich's acquaintance, and well known as the principal horse thief in the district.

"Ah, Vasili Andreevich! Where are you off to?" said Isay, enveloping Nikita in the odour of the vodka he had drunk.

"We were going to Goryachkin."

"And look where you've got to! You should have gone through Molchanovka."

"Should have, but didn't manage it," said Vasili Andreevich, holding in the horse.

"That's a good horse," said Isay, with a shrewd glance at Mukhorty, and with a practised hand he tightened the loosened knot high in the horse's bushy tail.

"Are you going to stay the night?"

"No, friend. I must get on."

"Your business must be pressing. And who is this? Ah, Nikita Stepanych!"

"Who else?" replied Nikita. "But I say, good friend, how are we to avoid going astray again?"

"Where can you go astray here? Turn back straight down the street and then when you come out keep straight on. Don't take to the left. You will come out onto the high road, and then turn to the right."

"And where do we turn off the high road? As in summer, or the winter way?" asked Nikita.

"The winter way. As soon as you turn off you'll see some bushes, and opposite them there is a way-mark — a large oak one with branches — and that's the way."

Vasili Andreevich turned the horse back and drove through the outskirts of the village.

"Why not stay the night?" Isay shouted after them.

But Vasili Andreevich did not answer and touched up the horse. Four miles of good road, two of which lay through the forest, seemed easy to manage, especially as the wind was apparently quieter and the snow had stopped.

Having driven along the trodden village street, darkened here and there by fresh manure, past the yard where the clothes hung out and where the white shirt had broken loose and was now attached only by one frozen sleeve, they again came within sound of the weird moan of the willows, and again emerged on the open fields. The storm, far from ceasing, seemed to have grown yet stronger. The road was completely covered with drifting snow, and only the stakes showed that they had not lost their way. But even the stakes ahead of them were not easy to see, since the wind blew in their faces.

Vasili Andreevich screwed up his eyes, bent down his head, and looked out for the way-marks, but trusted mainly to the horse's sagacity, letting it take its own way. And the horse really did not lose the road but followed its windings, turning now to the right and now to the left and sensing it under his feet, so that though the snow fell thicker and the wind strengthened they still continued to see way-marks now to the left and now to the right of them.

So they travelled on for about ten minutes, when suddenly, through the slanting screen of wind-driven snow, something black showed up which moved in front of the horse.

This was another sledge with fellow-travellers. Mukhorty overtook them, and struck his hoofs against the back of the sledge in front of him.

"Pass on . . . hey there . . . get in front!" cried voices from the sledge.

Vasili Andreevich swerved aside to pass the other sledge. In it sat three men and a woman, evidently visitors returning from a feast. One peasant was whacking the snow-covered croup of their little horse with a long switch, and the other two sitting in front waved their arms and shouted something. The woman, completely wrapped up and covered with snow, sat drowsing and bumping at the back.

"Who are you?" shouted Vasili Andreevich.

"From A-a-a . . ." was all that could be heard.

"I say, where are you from?"

"From A-a-a-a!" one of the peasants shouted with all his might, but still it was impossible to make out who they were.

"Get along! Keep up!" shouted another, ceaselessly beating his horse with the switch.

"So you're from a feast, it seems?"

"Go on, go on! Faster, Simon! Get in front! Faster!"

The wings of the sledges bumped against one another,

almost got jammed but managed to separate, and the peasants' sledge began to fall behind.

Their shaggy, big-bellied horse, all covered with snow, breathed heavily under the low shaft-bow and, evidently using the last of its strength, vainly endeavoured to escape from the switch, hobbling with its short legs through the deep snow which it threw up under itself.

Its muzzle, young-looking, with the nether lip drawn up like that of a fish, nostrils distended and ears pressed back from fear, kept up for a few seconds near Nikita's shoulder and then began to fall behind.

"Just see what liquor does!" said Nikita. "They've tired that little horse to death. What pagans!"

For a few minutes they heard the panting of the tired little horse and the drunken shouting of the peasants. Then the panting and the shouts died away, and around them nothing could be heard but the whistling of the wind in their ears and now and then the squeak of their sledge-runners over a wind-swept part of the road.

This encounter cheered and enlivened Vasili Andreevich, and he drove on more boldly without examining the way-marks, urging on the horse and trusting to him.

Nikita had nothing to do, and as usual in such circumstances he drowsed, making up for much sleepless time. Suddenly the horse stopped and Nikita nearly fell forward onto his nose.

"You know we're off the track again!" said Vasili Andreevich.

"How's that?"

"Why, there are no way-marks to be seen. We must have got off the road again."

"Well, if we've lost the road we must find it," said Nikita curtly, and getting out and stepping lightly on his pigeon-toed feet he started once more going about on the snow.

He walked about for a long time, now disappearing and now reappearing, and finally he came back.

"There is no road here. There may be farther on," he said, getting into the sledge.

It was already growing dark. The snow-storm had not increased but had also not subsided.

"If we could only hear those peasants!" said Vasili Andreevich.

"Well, they haven't caught us up. We must have gone far astray. Or maybe they have lost their way too."

"Where are we to go then?" asked Vasili Andreevich.

"Why, we must let the horse take its own way," said Nikita. "He will take us right. Let me have the reins."

Vasili Andreevich gave him the reins, the more willingly because his hands were beginning to feel frozen in his thick gloves.

Nikita took the reins, but only held them, trying not to shake them and rejoicing at his favourite's sagacity. And indeed the clever horse, turning first one ear and then the other now to one side and then to the other, began to wheel round.

"The one thing he can't do is to talk," Nikita kept saying. "See what he is doing! Go on, go on! You know best. That's it, that's it!"

The wind was now blowing from behind and it felt warmer.

"Yes, he's clever," Nikita continued, admiring the horse. "A Kirgiz horse is strong but stupid. But this one—just see what he's doing with his ears! He doesn't need any telegraph. He can scent a mile off."

Before another half-hour had passed they saw something dark ahead of them—a wood or a village—and stakes again appeared to the right. They had evidently come out onto the road.

"Why, that's Grishkino again!" Nikita suddenly exclaimed.

And indeed, there on their left was that same barn with the snow flying from it, and farther on the same line with the frozen washing, shirts and trousers, which still fluttered desperately in the wind.

Again they drove into the street and again it grew quiet, warm, and cheerful, and again they could see the manure-stained street and hear voices and songs and the barking of a dog. It was already so dark that there were lights in some of the windows.

Half-way through the village Vasili Andreevich turned the horse towards a large double-fronted brick house and stopped at the porch.

Nikita went to the lighted snow-covered window, in the rays of which flying snow-flakes glittered, and knocked at it with his whip.

"Who is there?" a voice replied to his knock.

"From Kresty, the Brekhunovs, dear fellow," answered Nikita. "Just come out for a minute."

Someone moved from the window, and a minute or two later there was the sound of the passage door as it came unstuck; then the latch of the outside door clicked and a tall white-bearded peasant, with a sheepskin coat thrown over his white holiday shirt, pushed his way out holding the door firmly against the wind, followed by a lad in a red shirt and high leather boots.

"Is that you, Andreevich?" asked the old man.

"Yes, friend, we've gone astray," said Vasili Andreevich. "We wanted to get to Goryachkin but found ourselves here. We went a second time but lost our way again."

"Just see how you have gone astray!" said the old man. "Petrushka, go and open the gate!" he added, turning to the lad in the red shirt.

"All right," said the lad in a cheerful voice, and ran back into the passage.

"But we're not staying the night," said Vasili Andreevich.

"Where will you go in the night? You'd better stay!"

"I'd be glad to, but I must go on. It's business, and it can't be helped."

"Well, warm yourself at least. The samovar is just ready."

"Warm myself? Yes, I'll do that," said Vasili Andreevich. "It won't get darker. The moon will rise and it will be lighter. Let's go in and warm ourselves, Nikita."

"Well, why not? Let us warm ourselves," replied Nikita, who was stiff with cold and anxious to warm his frozen limbs.

Vasili Andreevich went into the room, with the old man, and Nikita drove through the gate opened for him by Petrushka, by whose advice he backed the horse under the penthouse. The ground was covered with manure and the tall bow over the horse's head caught against the beam. The hens and the cock had already settled to roost there, and clucked peevishly, clinging to the beam with their claws. The disturbed sheep shied and rushed aside, trampling the frozen manure with their hoofs. The dog yelped desperately with fright and anger and then burst out barking like a puppy at the stranger.

Nikita talked to them all, excused himself to the fowls and assured them that he would not disturb them again, rebuked the sheep for being frightened without knowing why, and kept soothing the dog, while he tied up the horse.

"Now that will be all right," he said, knocking the snow off his clothes. "Just hear how he barks!" he added, turning to the dog. "Be quiet, stupid! Be quiet. You are only troubling yourself for nothing. We're not thieves, we're friends. . . ."

"And these are, it's said, the three domestic counsellors," remarked the lad, and with his strong arms he pushed under the pent-roof the sledge that had remained outside.

"Why counsellors?" asked Nikita.

"That's what is printed in Paulson. A thief creeps to a house—the dog barks, that means, 'Be on your guard!' The cock crows, that means, 'Get up!' The cat licks herself—that means, 'A welcome guest is coming. Get ready to receive him!'" said the lad with a smile.

Petrushka could read and write and knew Paulson's primer, his only book, almost by heart, and he was fond of quoting sayings from it that he thought suited the occasion, especially when he had had something to drink, as today.

"That's so," said Nikita.

"You must be chilled through and through," said Petrushka.

"Yes, I am rather," said Nikita, and they went across
the yard and the passage into the house.

iv

THE HOUSEHOLD to which Vasili Andreevich had come was
one of the richest in the village. The family had five allot-
ments, besides renting other land. They had six horses,
three cows, two calves, and some twenty sheep. There were
twenty-two members belonging to the homestead: four
married sons, six grandchildren (one of whom, Petrushka,
was married), two great-grandchildren, three orphans, and
four daughters-in-law with their babies. It was one of the
few homesteads that remained still undivided, but even
here the dull internal work of disintegration which would
inevitably lead to separation had already begun, starting as
usual among the women. Two sons were living in Moscow
as water-carriers, and one was in the army. At home now
were the old man and his wife, their second son who managed the homestead, the eldest who had come from Moscow for the holiday, and all the women and children.
Besides these members of the family there was a visitor, a
neighbour who was godfather to one of the children.

Over the table in the room hung a lamp with a shade,
which brightly lit up the tea-things, a bottle of vodka, and
some refreshments, besides illuminating the brick walls,
which in the far corner were hung with icons on both
sides of which were pictures. At the head of the table sat
Vasili Andreevich in a black sheepskin coat, sucking his
frozen moustache and observing the room and the people around him with his prominent hawk-like eyes. With
him sat the old, bald, white-bearded master of the house
in a white homespun shirt, and next to him the son home
from Moscow for the holiday—a man with a sturdy back
and powerful shoulders and clad in a thin print shirt—
then the second son, also broad-shouldered, who acted

as head of the house, and then a lean red-haired peasant—the neighbour.

Having had a drink of vodka and something to eat,
they were about to take tea, and the samovar standing
on the floor beside the brick oven was already humming.
The children could be seen in the top bunks and on the
top of the oven. A woman sat on a lower bunk with a
cradle beside her. The old housewife, her face covered
with wrinkles which wrinkled even her lips, was waiting
on Vasili Andreevich.

As Nikita entered the house she was offering her
guest a small tumbler of thick glass which she had just
filled with vodka.

"Don't refuse, Vasili Andreevich, you mustn't! Wish us
a merry feast. Drink it, dear!" she said.

The sight and smell of vodka, especially now when he
was chilled through and tired out, much disturbed Nikita's mind. He frowned, and having shaken the snow off
his cap and coat, stopped in front of the icons as if not
seeing anyone, crossed himself three times, and bowed to
the icons. Then, turning to the old master of the house
and bowing first to him, then to all those at table, then to
the women who stood by the oven, and muttering: "A
merry holiday!" he began taking off his outer things
without looking at the table.

"Why, you're all covered with hoar-frost, old fellow!"
said the eldest brother, looking at Nikita's snow-covered
face, eyes, and beard.

Nikita took off his coat, shook it again, hung it up
beside the oven, and came up to the table. He too was
offered vodka. He went through a moment of painful
hesitation and nearly took up the glass and emptied the
clear fragrant liquid down his throat, but he glanced at
Vasili Andreevich, remembered his oath and the boots
that he had sold for drink, recalled the cooper, remembered his son for whom he had promised to buy a horse
by spring, sighed, and declined it.

"I don't drink, thank you kindly," he said frowning,
and sat down on a bench near the second window.

"How's that?" asked the eldest brother.

"I just don't drink," replied Nikita without lifting his eyes but looking askance at his scanty beard and moustache and getting the icicles out of them.

"It's not good for him," said Vasili Andreevich, munching a cracknel after emptying his glass.

"Well, then, have some tea," said the kindly old hostess. "You must be chilled through, good soul. Why are you women dawdling so with the samovar?"

"It is ready," said one of the young women, and after flicking with her apron the top of the samovar which was now boiling over, she carried it with an effort to the table, raised it, and set it down with a thud.

Meanwhile Vasili Andreevich was telling how he had lost his way, how they had come back twice to this same village, and how they had gone astray and had met some drunken peasants. Their hosts were surprised, explained where and why they had missed their way, said who the tipsy people they had met were, and told them how they ought to go.

"A little child could find the way to Molchanovka from here. All you have to do is to take the right turning from the high road. There's a bush you can see just there. But you didn't even get that far!" said the neighbour.

"You'd better stay the night. The women will make up beds for you," said the old woman persuasively.

"You could go on in the morning and it would be pleasanter," said the old man, confirming what his wife had said.

"I can't, friend. Business!" said Vasili Andreevich. "Lose an hour and you can't catch it up in a year," he added, remembering the grove and the dealers who might snatch that deal from him. "We shall get there, shan't we?" he said, turning to Nikita.

Nikita did not answer for some time, apparently still intent on thawing out his beard and moustache.

"If only we don't go astray again," he replied gloomily. He was gloomy because he passionately longed for some vodka, and the only thing that could assuage that longing was tea and he had not yet been offered any.

"But we have only to reach the turning and then we shan't go wrong. The road will be through the forest the whole way," said Vasili Andreevich.

"It's just as you please, Vasili Andreevich. If we're to go, let us go," said Nikita, taking the glass of tea he was offered.

"We'll drink our tea and be off."

Nikita said nothing but only shook his head, and carefully pouring some tea into his saucer began warming his hands, the fingers of which were always swollen with hard work, over the steam. Then, biting off a tiny bit of sugar, he bowed to his hosts, said, "Your health!" and drew in the steaming liquid.

"If somebody would see us as far as the turning," said Vasili Andreevich.

"Well, we can do that," said the eldest son. "Petrushka will harness and go that far with you."

"Well, then, put in the horse, lad, and I shall be thankful to you for it."

"Oh, what for, dear man?" said the kindly old woman. "We are heartily glad to do it."

"Petrushka, go and put in the mare," said the eldest brother.

"All right," replied Petrushka with a smile, and promptly snatching his cap down from a nail he ran away to harness.

While the horse was being harnessed the talk returned to the point at which it had stopped when Vasili Andreevich drove up to the window. The old man had been complaining to his neighbour, the village elder, about his third son who had not sent him anything for the holiday though he had sent a French shawl to his wife.

"The young people are getting out of hand," said the old man.

"And how they do!" said the neighbour. "There's no

managing them! They know too much. There's Demochkin now, who broke his father's arm. It's all from being too clever, it seems."

Nikita listened, watched their faces, and evidently would have liked to share in the conversation, but he was too busy drinking his tea and only nodded his head approvingly. He emptied one tumbler after another and grew warmer and warmer and more and more comfortable. The talk continued on the same subject for a long time—the harmfulness of a household dividing up—and it was clearly not an abstract discussion but concerned the question of a separation in that house: a separation demanded by the second son who sat there morosely silent.

It was evidently a sore subject and absorbed them all, but out of propriety they did not discuss their private affairs before strangers. At last, however, the old man could not restrain himself, and with tears in his eyes declared that he would not consent to a break-up of the family during his lifetime, that his house was prospering, thank God, but that if they separated they would all have to go begging.

"Just like the Matveevs," said the neighbour. "They used to have a proper house, but now they've split up none of them has anything."

"And that is what you want to happen to us," said the old man, turning to his son.

The son made no reply and there was an awkward pause. The silence was broken by Petrushka, who having harnessed the horse had returned to the hut a few minutes before this and had been listening all the time with a smile.

"There's a fable about that in Paulson," he said. "A father gave his sons a broom to break. At first they could not break it, but when they took it twig by twig they broke it easily. And it's the same here," and he gave a broad smile. "I'm ready!" he added.

"If you're ready, let's go," said Vasili Andreevich. "And as to separating, don't you allow it, Grandfather.

You got everything together and you're the master. Go
to the Justice of the Peace. He'll say how things should
be done."

"He carries on so, carries on so," the old man continued in a whining tone. "There's no doing anything with
him. It's as if the devil possessed him."

Nikita having meanwhile finished his fifth tumbler of
tea laid it on its side instead of turning it upside down,
hoping to be offered a sixth glass. But there was no more
water in the samovar, so the hostess did not fill it up for
him. Besides, Vasili Andreevich was putting his things on,
so there was nothing for it but for Nikita to get up too,
put back into the sugar-basin the lump of sugar he had
nibbled all round, wipe his perspiring face with the skirt
of his sheepskin, and go to put on his overcoat.

Having put it on he sighed deeply, thanked his hosts,
said good-bye, and went out of the warm bright room
into the cold dark passage, through which the wind was
howling and where snow was blowing through the cracks
of the shaking door, and from there into the yard.

Petrushka stood in his sheepskin in the middle of the
yard by his horse, repeating some lines from Paulson's
primer. He said with a smile:

> *Storms with mist the sky conceal,*
> *Snowy circles wheeling wild.*
> *Now like savage beast 'twill howl,*
> *And now 'tis wailing like a child.*

Nikita nodded approvingly as he arranged the reins.

The old man, seeing Vasili Andreevich off, brought a
lantern into the passage to show him a light, but it was
blown out at once. And even in the yard it was evident
that the snow-storm had become more violent.

"Well, this is weather!" thought Vasili Andreevich.
"Perhaps we may not get there after all. But there is
nothing to be done. Business! Besides, we have got ready,
our host's horse has been harnessed, and we'll get there
with God's help!"

Their aged host also thought they ought not to go, but
he had already tried to persuade them to stay and had
not been listened to.

"It's no use asking them again. Maybe my age makes
me timid. They'll get there all right, and at least we shall
get to bed in good time and without any fuss," he thought.

Petrushka did not think of danger. He knew the road
and the whole district so well, and the lines about "snowy
circles wheeling wild" described what was happening
outside so aptly that it cheered him up. Nikita did not
wish to go at all, but he had been accustomed not to have
his own way and to serve others for so long that there
was no one to hinder the departing travellers.

v

VASILI ANDREEVICH went over to his sledge, found it with
difficulty in the darkness, climbed in and took the reins.

"Go on in front!" he cried.

Petrushka kneeling in his low sledge started his horse.
Mukhorty, who had been neighing for some time past, now
scenting a mare ahead of him started after her, and they
drove out into the street. They drove again through the outskirts of the village and along the same road, past the yard
where the frozen linen had hung (which, however, was no
longer to be seen), past the same barn, which was now
snowed up almost to the roof and from which the snow was
still endlessly pouring, past the same dismally moaning,
whistling, and swaying willows, and again entered into the
sea of blustering snow raging from above and below. The
wind was so strong that when it blew from the side and
the travellers steered against it, it tilted the sledges and
turned the horses to one side. Petrushka drove his good
mare in front at a brisk trot and kept shouting lustily. Mukhorty pressed after her.

After travelling so for about ten minutes, Petrushka
turned round and shouted something. Neither Vasili Andreevich nor Nikita could hear anything because of the

wind, but they guessed that they had arrived at the turning. In fact Petrushka had turned to the right, and now the wind that had blown from the side blew straight in their faces, and through the snow they saw something dark on their right. It was the bush at the turning.

"Well, now, God speed you!"

"Thank you, Petrushka!"

"Storms with mist the sky conceal!" shouted Petrushka as he disappeared.

"There's a poet for you!" muttered Vasili Andreevich, pulling at the reins.

"Yes, a fine lad—a true peasant," said Nikita.

They drove on.

Nikita, wrapping his coat closely about him and pressing his head down so close to his shoulders that his short beard covered his throat, sat silently, trying not to lose the warmth he had obtained while drinking tea in the house. Before him he saw the straight lines of the shafts which constantly deceived him into thinking they were a well-travelled road, and the horse's swaying crupper with his knotted tail blown to one side, and farther ahead the high shaft-bow and the swaying head and neck of the horse with its waving mane. Now and then he caught sight of a way-sign, so that he knew they were still on a road and that there was nothing for him to be concerned about.

Vasili Andreevich drove on, leaving it to the horse to keep to the road. But Mukhorty, though he had had a breathing-space in the village, ran reluctantly, and seemed now and then to get off the road, so that Vasili Andreevich had repeatedly to correct him.

"Here's a stake to the right, and another, and here's a third," Vasili Andreevich counted, "and here in front is the forest," thought he, as he looked at something dark in front of him. But what had seemed to him a forest was only a bush. They passed the bush and drove on for another hundred yards but there was no fourth way-mark nor any forest.

"We must reach the forest soon," thought Vasili Andreevich, and animated by the vodka and the tea he did not stop but shook the reins, and the good obedient horse responded, now ambling, now slowly trotting in the direction in which he was sent, though he knew that he was not going the right way. Ten minutes went by, but there was still no forest.

"There now, we must be astray again," said Vasili Andreevich, pulling up.

Nikita silently got out of the sledge and holding his coat, which the wind now wrapped closely about him and now almost tore off, started to feel about in the snow, going first to one side and then to the other. Three or four times he was completely lost to sight. At last he returned and took the reins from Vasili Andreevich's hand.

"We must go to the right," he said sternly and peremptorily, as he turned the horse.

"Well, if it's to the right, go to the right," said Vasili Andreevich, yielding up the reins to Nikita and thrusting his freezing hands into his sleeves.

Nikita did not reply.

"Now, then, friend, stir yourself!" he shouted to the horse, but in spite of the shake of the reins Mukhorty moved only at a walk.

The snow in places was up to his knees, and the sledge moved by fits and starts with his every movement.

Nikita took the whip that hung over the front of the sledge and struck him once. The good horse, unused to the whip, sprang forward and moved at a trot, but immediately fell back into an amble and then to a walk. So they went on for five minutes. It was dark and the snow whirled from above and rose from below, so that sometimes the shaft-bow could not be seen. At times the sledge seemed to stand still and the field to run backwards. Suddenly the horse stopped abruptly, evidently aware of something close in front of him. Nikita again sprang lightly out, throwing down the reins, and went ahead to see what had brought him to a standstill, but hardly had he made a step in front of the horse before his feet slipped and he went rolling down an incline.

"Whoa, whoa, whoa!" he said to himself as he fell, and he tried to stop his fall but could not, and only stopped when his feet plunged into a thick layer of snow that had drifted to the bottom of the hollow.

The fringe of a drift of snow that hung on the edge of the hollow, disturbed by Nikita's fall, showered down on him and got inside his collar.

"What a thing to do!" said Nikita reproachfully, addressing the drift and the hollow and shaking the snow from under his collar.

"Nikita! Hey, Nikita!" shouted Vasili Andreevich from above.

But Nikita did not reply. He was too occupied in shaking out the snow and searching for the whip he had dropped when rolling down the incline. Having found the whip he tried to climb straight up the bank where he had rolled down, but it was impossible to do so: he kept rolling down again, and so he had to go along at the foot of the hollow to find a way up. About seven yards farther on he managed with difficulty to crawl up the incline on all fours; then he followed the edge of the hollow back to the place where the horse should have been. He could not see either horse or sledge, but as he walked against the wind he heard Vasili Andreevich's shouts and Mukhorty's neighing, calling him.

"I'm coming! I'm coming! What are you cackling for?" he muttered.

Only when he had come up to the sledge could he make out the horse, and Vasili Andreevich standing beside it and looking gigantic.

"Where the devil did you vanish to? We must go back, if only to Grishkino," he began reproaching Nikita.

"I'd be glad to get back, Vasili Andreevich, but which way are we to go? There is such a ravine here that if we once get in it we shan't get out again. I got stuck so fast there myself that I could hardly get out."

"What shall we do, then? We can't stay here! We must go somewhere!" said Vasili Andreevich.

Nikita said nothing. He seated himself in the sledge

with his back to the wind, took off his boots, shook out the snow that had got into them, and taking some straw from the bottom of the sledge, carefully plugged with it a hole in his left boot.

Vasili Andreevich remained silent, as though now leaving everything to Nikita. Having put his boots on again, Nikita drew his feet into the sledge, put on his mittens and took up the reins, and directed the horse along the side of the ravine. But they had not gone a hundred yards before the horse again stopped short. The ravine was in front of him again.

Nikita again climbed out and again trudged about in the snow. He did this for a considerable time and at last appeared from the opposite side to that from which he had started.

"Vasili Andreevich, are you alive?" he called out.

"Here!" replied Vasili Andreevich. "Well, what now?"

"I can't make anything out. It's too dark. There's nothing but ravines. We must drive against the wind again."

They set off once more. Again Nikita went stumbling through the snow, again he fell in, again climbed out and trudged about, and at last quite out of breath he sat down beside the sledge.

"Well, how now?" asked Vasili Andreevich.

"Why, I am quite worn out and the horse won't go."

"Then what's to be done?"

"Why, wait a minute."

Nikita went away again but soon returned.

"Follow me!" he said, going in front of the horse.

Vasili Andreevich no longer gave orders but implicitly did what Nikita told him.

"Here, follow me!" Nikita shouted, stepping quickly to the right, and seizing the rein he led Mukhorty down towards a snowdrift.

At first the horse held back, then jerked forward, hoping to leap the drift, but he had not the strength and sank into it up to his collar.

"Get out!" Nikita called to Vasili Andreevich, who still sat in the sledge, and taking hold of one shaft he moved the sledge closer to the horse. "It's hard, brother!" he said to Mukhorty, "but it can't be helped. Make an effort! Now, now, just a little one!" he shouted.

The horse gave a tug, then another, but failed to clear himself and settled down again as if considering something.

"No, brother, this won't do!" Nikita admonished him. "Now once more!"

Again Nikita tugged at the shaft on his side, and Vasili Andreevich did the same on the other.

Mukhorty lifted his head and then gave a sudden jerk.

"That's it! That's it!" cried Nikita. "Don't be afraid— you won't sink!"

One plunge, another, and a third, and at last Mukhorty was out of the snowdrift, and stood still, breathing heavily and shaking the snow off himself. Nikita wished to lead him farther, but Vasili Andreevich, in his two fur coats, was so out of breath that he could not walk farther and dropped into the sledge.

"Let me get my breath!" he said, unfastening the kerchief with which he had tied the collar of his fur coat at the village.

"It's all right here. You lie there," said Nikita. "I will lead him along." And with Vasili Andreevich in the sledge, he led the horse by the bridle about ten paces down and then up a slight rise, and stopped.

The place were Nikita had stopped was not completely in the hollow where the snow sweeping down from the hillocks might have buried them altogether, but still it was partly sheltered from the wind by the side of the ravine. There were moments when the wind seemed to abate a little, but that did not last long and as if to make up for that respite the storm swept down with tenfold vigour and tore and whirled the more fiercely. Such a gust struck them at the moment when Vasili Andreevich, having recovered his breath, got out of the sledge and went up to Nikita to consult him as to what they should do. They both bent down involuntarily and waited till the violence of the squall should have passed. Mukhorty too laid back his ears and shook his head discontentedly. As soon as the violence of the blast had abated a little, Nikita took off his mittens, stuck them into his belt, breathed on to his hands, and began to undo the straps of the shaft-bow.

"What's that you are doing there?" asked Vasili Andreevich.

"Unharnessing. What else is there to do? I have no strength left," said Nikita as though excusing himself.

"Can't we drive somewhere?"

"No, we can't. We shall only kill the horse. Why, the poor beast is not himself now," said Nikita, pointing to the horse, which was standing submissively waiting for what might come, with his steep wet sides heaving heavily. "We shall have to stay the night here," he said, as if preparing to spend the night at an inn, and he proceeded to unfasten the collar-straps. The buckles came undone.

"But shan't we be frozen?" remarked Vasili Andreevich.

"Well, if we are we can't help it," said Nikita.

vi

ALTHOUGH Vasili Andreevich felt quite warm in his two fur coats, especially after struggling in the snowdrift, a cold shiver ran down his back on realizing that he must really spend the night where they were. To calm himself he sat down in the sledge and got out his cigarettes and matches.

Nikita meanwhile unharnessed Mukhorty. He unstrapped the belly-band and the back-band, took away the reins, loosened the collar-strap, and removed the shaft-bow, talking to him all the time to encourage him.

"Now come out! Come out!" he said, leading him clear of the shafts. "Now we'll tie you up here and I'll put down some straw and take off your bridle. When you've had a bite you'll feel more cheerful."

But Mukhorty was restless and evidently not comforted by Nikita's remarks. He stepped now on one foot and now on another, and pressed close against the sledge, turning his back to the wind and rubbing his head on Nikita's sleeve. Then, as if not to pain Nikita by refusing his offer of the straw he put before him, he hurriedly snatched a wisp out of the sledge, but immediately decided that it was now no time to think of straw and threw it down, and the wind instantly scattered it, carried it away, and covered it with snow.

"Now we will set up a signal," said Nikita, and turning the front of the sledge to the wind he tied the shafts together with a strap and set them up on end in front of the sledge. "There now, when the snow covers us up, good folk will see the shafts and dig us out," he said, slapping his mittens together and putting them on. "That's what the old folk taught us!"

Vasili Andreevich meanwhile had unfastened his coat, and holding its skirts up for shelter, struck one sulphur match after another on the steel box. But his hands trembled, and one match after another either did not kindle or was blown out by the wind just as he was lifting it to the cigarette. At last a match did burn up, and its flame lit up for a moment the fur of his coat, his hand with the gold ring on the bent forefinger, and the snow-sprinkled oat-straw that stuck out from under the drugget. The cigarette lighted, he eagerly took a whiff or two, inhaled the smoke, let it out through his moustache, and would have inhaled again, but the wind tore off the burning tobacco and whirled it away as it had done the straw.

But even these few puffs had cheered him.

"If we must spend the night here, we must!" he said with decision. "Wait a bit, I'll arrange a flag as well," he added, picking up the kerchief which he had thrown down in the sledge after taking it from round his collar, and drawing off his gloves and standing up on the front of the sledge and stretching himself to reach the strap, he tied the handkerchief to it with a tight knot.

The kerchief immediately began to flutter wildly, now clinging round the shaft, now suddenly streaming out, stretching and flapping.

"Just see what a fine flag!" said Vasili Andreevich, admiring his handiwork and letting himself down into the
sledge. "We should be warmer together, but there's not
room enough for two," he added.

"I'll find a place," said Nikita. "But I must cover up
the horse first—he sweated so, poor thing. Let go!" he
added, drawing the drugget from under Vasili Andreevich.

Having got the drugget he folded it in two, and after
taking off the breechband and pad, covered Mukhorty
with it.

"Anyhow it will be warmer, silly!" he said, putting
back the breechband and the pad on the horse over the
drugget. Then having finished that business he returned
to the sledge, and addressing Vasili Andreevich, said:
"You won't need the sackcloth, will you? And let me
have some straw."

And having taken these things from under Vasili Andreevich, Nikita went behind the sledge, dug out a hole
for himself in the snow, put straw into it, wrapped his
coat well round him, covered himself with the sackcloth,
and pulling his cap well down seated himself on the
straw he had spread, and leant against the wooden back
of the sledge to shelter himself from the wind and the
snow.

Vasili Andreevich shook his head disapprovingly at
what Nikita was doing, as in general he disapproved of
the peasants' stupidity and lack of education, and he began to settle himself down for the night.

He smoothed the remaining straw over the bottom of
the sledge, putting more of it under his side; then he
thrust his hands into his sleeves and settled down, shel-
tering his head in the corner of the sledge from the wind
in front.

He did not wish to sleep. He lay and thought: thought
ever of the one thing that constituted the sole aim, meaning, pleasure, and pride of his life—of how much money
he had made and might still make, of how much other
people he knew had made and possessed, and of how

those others had made and were making it, and how he, like them, might still make much more. The purchase of the Goryachkin grove was a matter of immense importance to him. By that one deal he hoped to make perhaps ten thousand rubles. He began mentally to reckon the value of the wood he had inspected in autumn, and on five acres of which he had counted all the trees.

"The oaks will go for sledge-runners. The undergrowth will take care of itself, and there'll still be some thirty sazheens of firewood left on each desyatin," said he to himself. "That means there will be at least two hundred and twenty-five rubles' worth left on each desyatin. Fifty-six desyatins means fifty-six hundreds, and fifty-six hundreds, and fifty-six tens, and another fifty-six tens, and then fifty-six fives. . . ." He saw that it came out to more than twelve thousand rubles, but could not reckon it up exactly without a counting-frame. "But I won't give ten thousand, anyhow. I'll give about eight thousand with a deduction on account of the glades. I'll grease the surveyor's palm—give him a hundred rubles, or a hundred and fifty, and he'll reckon that there are some five desyatins of glade to be deducted. And he'll let it go for eight thousand. Three thousand cash down. That'll move him, no fear!" he thought, and he pressed his pocket-book with his forearm.

"God only knows how we missed the turning. The forest ought to be there, and a watchman's hut, and dogs barking. But the damned things don't bark when they're wanted." He turned his collar down from his ear and listened, but as before only the whistling of the wind could be heard, the flapping and fluttering of the kerchief tied to the shafts, and the pelting of the snow against the woodwork of the sledge. He again covered up his ear.

"If I had known I would have stayed the night. Well, no matter, we'll get there tomorrow. It's only one day lost. And the others won't travel in such weather." Then he remembered that on the 9th he had to receive payment from the butcher for his oxen. "He meant to come himself, but he won't find me, and my wife won't know how to receive the money. She doesn't know the right way of doing things," he thought, recalling how at their party the day before she had not known how to treat the police officer who was their guest. "Of course she's only a woman! Where could she have seen anything? In my father's time what was our house like? Just a rich peasant's house: just an oat-mill and an inn—that was the whole property. But what have I done in these fifteen years? A shop, two taverns, a flour-mill, a grain-store, two farms leased out, and a house with an iron-roofed barn," he thought proudly. "Not as it was in Father's time! Who is talked of in the whole district now? Brekhunov! And why? Because I stick to business. I take trouble, not like others who lie abed or waste their time on foolishness while I don't sleep of nights. Blizzard or no blizzard I start out. So business gets done. They think money-making is a joke. No, take pains and rack your brains! You get overtaken out of doors at night, like this, or keep awake night after night till the thoughts whirling in your head make the pillow turn," he meditated with pride. "They think people get on through luck. After all, the Mironovs are now millionaires. And why? Take pains and God gives. If only He grants me health!"

The thought that he might himself be a millionaire like Mironov, who began with nothing, so excited Vasili Andreevich that he felt the need of talking to somebody. But there was no one to talk to. . . . If only he could have reached Goryachkin he would have talked to the landlord and shown him a thing or two.

"Just see how it blows! It will snow us up so deep that we shan't be able to get out in the morning!" he thought, listening to a gust of wind that blew against the front of the sledge, bending it and lashing the snow against it. He raised himself and looked round. All he could see through the whirling darkness was Mukhorty's dark head, his back covered by the fluttering drugget, and his thick knotted tail; while all round, in front and behind, was the same fluctuating whitey darkness, sometimes seeming to get a little lighter and sometimes growing denser still.

"A pity I listened to Nikita," he thought. "We ought to have driven on. We should have come out somewhere, if only back to Grishkino and stayed the night at Taras's. As it is we must sit here all night. But what was I thinking about? Yes, that God gives to those who take trouble, but not to loafers, lie-abeds, or fools. I must have a smoke!"

He sat down again, got out his cigarette-case, and stretched himself flat on his stomach, screening the matches with the skirt of his coat. But the wind found its way in and put out match after match. At last he got one to burn and lit a cigarette. He was very glad that he had managed to do what he wanted, and though the wind smoked more of the cigarette than he did, he still got two or three puffs and felt more cheerful. He again leant back, wrapped himself up, started reflecting and remembering, and suddenly and quite unexpectedly lost consciousness and fell asleep.

Suddenly something seemed to give him a push and awoke him. Whether it was Mukhorty who had pulled some straw from under him, or whether something within him had startled him, at all events it woke him, and his heart began to beat faster and faster so that the sledge seemed to tremble under him. He opened his eyes. Everything around him was just as before. "It looks lighter," he thought. "I expect it won't be long before dawn." But he at once remembered that it was lighter because the moon had risen. He sat up and looked first at the horse. Mukhorty still stood with his back to the wind, shivering all over. One side of the drugget, which was completely covered with snow, had been blown back, the breeching had slipped down and the snow-covered head with its waving forelock and mane were now more visible. Vasili Andreevich leant over the back of the sledge and looked behind. Nikita still sat in the same position in which he had settled himself. The sacking with which he was covered, and his legs, were thickly covered with snow.

"If only that peasant doesn't freeze to death! His clothes are so wretched. I may be held responsible for him. What shiftless people they are—such a want of education," thought Vasili Andreevich, and he felt like taking the drugget off the horse and putting it over Nikita, but it would be very cold to get out and move about and, moreover, the horse might freeze to death. "Why did I bring him with me? It was all her stupidity!" he thought, recalling his unloved wife, and he rolled over into his old place at the front part of the sledge. "My uncle once spent a whole night like this," he reflected, "and was all right." But another case came at once to his mind. "But when they dug Sebastian out he was dead—stiff like a frozen carcass. If I'd only stopped the night in Grishkino all this would not have happened!"

And wrapping his coat carefully round him so that none of the warmth of the fur should be wasted but should warm him all over, neck, knees, and feet, he shut his eyes and tried to sleep again. But try as he would he could not get drowsy; on the contrary he felt wide awake and animated. Again he began counting his gains and the debts due to him, again he began bragging to himself and feeling pleased with himself and his position, but all this was continually disturbed by a stealthily approaching fear and by the unpleasant regret that he had not remained in Grishkino.

"How different it would be to be lying warm on a bench!" He turned over several times in his attempts to get into a more comfortable position more sheltered from the wind, he wrapped up his legs closer, shut his eyes, and lay still. But either his legs in their strong felt boots began to ache from being bent in one position, or the wind blew in somewhere, and after lying still for a short time he again began to recall the disturbing fact that he might now have been lying quietly in the warm hut at Grishkino. He again sat up, turned about, muffled himself up, and settled down once more.

Once he fancied that he heard a distant cock crow. He felt glad, turned down his coat collar and listened with strained attention, but in spite of all his efforts nothing could be heard but the wind whistling between the shafts, the flapping of the kerchief, and the snow pelting against the frame of the sledge.

Nikita sat just as he had done all the time, not moving and not even answering Vasili Andreevich who had addressed him a couple of times. "He doesn't care a bit — he's probably asleep!" thought Vasili Andreevich, with vexation, looking behind the sledge at Nikita who was covered with a thick layer of snow.

Vasili Andreevich got up and lay down again some twenty times. It seemed to him that the night would never end. "It must be getting near morning," he thought, getting up and looking around. "Let's have a look at my watch. It will be cold to unbutton, but if I only know that it's getting near morning I shall at any rate feel more cheerful. We could begin harnessing."

In the depth of his heart Vasili Andreevich knew that it could not yet be near morning, but he was growing more and more afraid, and wished both to get to know and yet to deceive himself. He carefully undid the fastening of his sheepskin, pushed in his hand, and felt about for a long time before he got to his waistcoat. With great difficulty he managed to draw out his silver watch with its enamelled flower design, and tried to make out the time. He could not see anything without a light. Again he went down on his knees and elbows as he had done when he lighted a cigarette, got out his matches, and proceeded to strike one. This time he went to work more carefully, and feeling with his fingers for a match with the largest head and the greatest amount of phosphorus, lit it at the first try. Bringing the face of the watch under the light he could hardly believe his eyes. . . . It was only ten minutes past twelve. Almost the whole night was still before him.

"Oh, how long the night is!" he thought, feeling a cold shudder run down his back, and having fastened his fur coats again and wrapped himself up, he snuggled into a corner of the sledge intending to wait patiently. Sud-

denly, above the monotonous roar of the wind, he clearly
distinguished another new and living sound. It steadily
strengthened, and having become quite clear diminished
just as gradually. Beyond all doubt it was a wolf, and he
was so near that the movement of his jaws as he changed
his cry was brought down the wind. Vasili Andreevich
turned back the collar of his coat and listened attentively. Mukhorty too strained to listen, moving his ears,
and when the wolf had ceased its howling he shifted
from foot to foot and gave a warning snort. After this
Vasili Andreevich could not fall asleep again or even
calm himself. The more he tried to think of his accounts,
his business, his reputation, his worth and his wealth, the
more and more he was mastered by fear; and regrets that
he had not stayed the night at Grishkino dominated and
mingled in all his thoughts.

   "Devil take the forest! Things were all right without
it, thank God. Ah, if we had only put up for the night!"
he said to himself. "They say it's drunkards that freeze,"
he thought, "and I have had some drink." And observing
his sensations he noticed that he was beginning to shiver,
without knowing whether it was from cold or from fear.
He tried to wrap himself up and lie down as before, but
could no longer do so. He could not stay in one position.
He wanted to get up, to do something to master the gathering fear that was rising in him and against which he felt
himself powerless. He again got out his cigarettes and
matches, but only three matches were left and they were
bad ones. The phosphorus rubbed off them all without
lighting.

   "The devil take you! Damned thing! Curse you!" he
muttered, not knowing whom or what he was cursing, and
he flung away the crushed cigarette. He was about to
throw away the matchbox too, but checked the movement
of his hand and put the box in his pocket instead. He was
seized with such unrest that he could no longer remain in
one spot. He climbed out of the sledge and standing with
his back to the wind began to shift his belt again, fastening
it lower down in the waist and tightening it.

"What's the use of lying and waiting for death? Better mount the horse and get away!" The thought suddenly occurred to him. "The horse will move when he has someone on his back. As for him," he thought of Nikita — "it's all the same to him whether he lives or dies. What is his life worth? He won't grudge his life, but I have something to live for, thank God."

He untied the horse, threw the reins over his neck and tried to mount, but his coats and boots were so heavy that he failed. Then he clambered up in the sledge and tried to mount from there, but the sledge tilted under his weight, and he failed again. At last he drew Mukhorty nearer to the sledge, cautiously balanced on one side of it, and managed to lie on his stomach across the horse's back. After lying like that for a while he shifted forward once and again, threw a leg over, and finally seated himself, supporting his feet on the loose breeching-straps. The shaking of the sledge awoke Nikita. He raised himself, and it seemed to Vasili Andreevich that he said something.

"Listen to such fools as you! Am I to die like this for nothing?" exclaimed Vasili Andreevich. And tucking the loose skirts of his fur coat in under his knees, he turned the horse and rode away from the sledge in the direction in which he thought the forest and the forester's hut must be.

vii

FROM THE TIME he had covered himself with the sackcloth and seated himself behind the sledge, Nikita had not stirred. Like all those who live in touch with nature and have known want, he was patient and could wait for hours, even days, without growing restless or irritable. He heard his master call him, but did not answer because he did not want to move or talk. Though he still felt some warmth from the tea he had drunk and from his energetic struggle when clambering about in the snowdrift, he knew that his warmth would not last long and that he had no strength left to warm himself again by moving about, for he felt as tired as a horse when it stops and refuses to go further in spite of the whip, and its master sees that it must be fed before it can work again. The foot in the boot with a hole in it had already grown numb, and he could no longer feel his big toe. Besides that, his whole body began to feel colder and colder.

The thought that he might, and very probably would, die that night occurred to him, but did not seem particularly unpleasant or dreadful. It did not seem particularly unpleasant, because his whole life had been not a continual holiday, but on the contrary an unceasing round of toil of which he was beginning to feel weary. And it did not seem particularly dreadful, because besides the masters he had served here, like Vasili Andreevich, he always felt himself dependent on the Chief Master, who had sent him into this life, and he knew that when dying he would still be in that Master's power and would not be ill-used by Him. "It seems a pity to give up what one is used to and accustomed to. But there's nothing to be done; I shall get used to the new things."

"Sins?" he thought, and remembered his drunkenness, the money that had gone on drink, how he had offended his wife, his cursing, his neglect of church and of the fasts, and all the things the priest blamed him for at confession. "Of course they are sins. But then, did I take them on of myself? That's evidently how God made me. Well, and the sins? Where am I to escape to?"

So at first he thought of what might happen to him that night, and then did not return to such thoughts but gave himself up to whatever recollections came into his head of themselves. Now he thought of Martha's arrival, of the drunkenness among the workers and his own renunciation of drink, then of their present journey and of Taras's house and the talk about the breaking-up of the family, then of his own lad, and of Mukhorty now sheltered under the drugget, and then of his master who made the sledge creak as he tossed about in it. "I expect you're sorry yourself that you started out, dear man," he thought. "It would seem hard to leave a life such as his! It's not like the likes of us."

Then all these recollections began to grow confused and got mixed in his head, and he fell asleep.

But when Vasili Andreevich, getting on the horse, jerked the sledge against the back of which Nikita was leaning, and it shifted away and hit him in the back with one of its runners, he awoke and had to change his position whether he liked it or not. Straightening his legs with difficulty and shaking the snow off them he got up, and an agonizing cold immediately penetrated his whole body. On making out what was happening he called to Vasili Andreevich to leave him the drugget which the horse no longer needed, so that he might wrap himself in it.

But Vasili Andreevich did not stop, but disappeared amid the powdery snow.

Left alone, Nikita considered for a moment what he should do. He felt that he had not the strength to go off in search of a house. It was no longer possible to sit down in his old place—it was by now all filled with snow. He felt that he could not get warmer in the sledge either, for there was nothing to cover himself with, and his coat and sheepskin no longer warmed him at all. He felt as cold as though he had nothing on but a shirt. He became frightened. "Lord, heavenly Father!" he muttered, and was comforted by the consciousness that he was not alone but that there was One who heard him and would not abandon him. He gave a deep sigh, and keeping the sackcloth over his head he got inside the sledge and lay down in the place where his master had been.

But he could not get warm in the sledge either. At first he shivered all over; then the shivering ceased and little by little he began to lose consciousness. He did not know whether he was dying or falling asleep, but felt equally prepared for the one as for the other.

viii

MEANWHILE Vasili Andreevich, with his feet and the ends of the reins, urged the horse on in the direction in which for some reason he expected the forest and the forester's hut to be. The snow covered his eyes and the wind seemed intent on stopping him, but bending forward and constantly lapping his coat over and pushing it between himself and the cold harness pad which prevented him from sitting properly, he kept urging the horse on. Mukhorty ambled on obediently though with difficulty, in the direction in which he was driven.

Vasili Andreevich rode for about five minutes straight ahead, as he thought, seeing nothing but the horse's head and white waste, and hearing only the whistle of the wind about the horse's ears and his coat-collar.

Suddenly a dark patch showed up in front of him. His heart beat with joy, and he rode towards the object, already seeing in imagination the walls of village houses. But the dark patch was not stationary, it kept moving; and it was not a village but some tall stalks of wormwood sticking up through the snow on the boundary between two fields, and desperately tossing about under the pressure of the wind which beat it all to one side and whistled through it. The sight of that wormwood tormented by the pitiless wind made Vasili Andreevich shudder, he knew not why, and he hurriedly began urging the horse on, not noticing that when riding up to the wormwood he had quite changed his direction and was now heading the opposite way, though still imagining that he was riding towards where the hut should be. But the horse kept making towards the right, and Vasili Andreevich kept guiding it to the left.

Again something dark appeared in front of him. Again he rejoiced, convinced that now it was certainly a village. But once more it was the same boundary line overgrown with wormwood, once more the same wormwood desperately tossed by the wind and carrying unreasoning terror to his heart. But its being the same wormwood was not all, for beside it there was a horse's track partly snowed over. Vasili Andreevich stopped, stooped down and looked carefully. It was a horse-track only partially covered with snow, and could be none but his own horse's hoofprints. He had evidently gone round in a small circle. "I shall perish like that!" he thought, and not to give way to his terror he urged on the horse still more, peering into the snowy darkness in which he saw only flitting and fitful points of light. Once he thought he heard the barking of dogs or the howling of wolves, but the sounds were so faint and indistinct that he did not know whether he heard them or merely imagined them, and he stopped and began to listen intently.

Suddenly some terrible, deafening cry resounded near his ears, and everything shivered and shook under him. He seized Mukhorty's neck, but that too was shaking all over and the terrible cry grew still more frightful. For some seconds Vasili Andreevich could not collect himself or understand what was happening. It was only that Mukhorty, whether to encourage himself or to call for help, had neighed loudly and resonantly. "Ugh, you wretch! How you frightened me, damn you!" thought Vasili Andreevich. But even when he understood the cause of his terror he could not shake it off.

"I must calm myself and think things over," he said to himself, but yet he could not stop, and continued to urge the horse on, without noticing that he was now going with the wind instead of against it. His body, especially between his legs where it touched the pad of the harness and was not covered by his overcoats, was getting painfully cold, especially when the horse walked slowly. His legs and arms trembled and his breathing came fast. He saw himself perishing amid this dreadful snowy waste, and could see no means of escape.

Suddenly the horse under him tumbled into something and, sinking into a snowdrift, began to plunge and fell on his side. Vasili Andreevich jumped off, and in so doing dragged to one side the breechband on which his foot was resting, and twisted round the pad to which he held as he dismounted. As soon as he had jumped off, the horse struggled to his feet, plunged forward, gave one leap and another, neighed again, and dragging the drugget and the breechband after him, disappeared, leaving Vasili Andreevich alone in the snowdrift.

The latter pressed on after the horse, but the snow lay so deep and his coats were so heavy that, sinking above his knees at each step, he stopped breathless after taking not more than twenty steps. "The copse, the oxen, the leasehold, the shop, the tavern, the house with the iron-roofed barn, and my heir," thought he. "How can I leave all that? What does this mean? It cannot be!" These thoughts flashed through his mind. Then he thought of the wormwood tossed by the wind, which he had twice ridden past, and he was seized with such terror that he did not believe in the reality of what was happening to him. "Can this be a dream?" he thought, and tried to wake up but could not. It was real snow that lashed his face and covered him and chilled his right hand from which he had lost the glove, and this was a real desert in which he was now left alone like that wormwood, awaiting an inevitable, speedy, and meaningless death.

"Queen of Heaven! Holy Father Nicholas, teacher of temperance!" he thought, recalling the service of the day before and the holy icon with its black face and gilt frame, and the tapers which he sold to be set before that icon and which were almost immediately brought back to him scarcely burnt at all, and which he put away in the store-chest.* He began to pray to that same Nicholas the Wonder-Worker to save him, promising him a thanksgiving service and some candles. But he clearly and indubitably realized that the icon, its frame, the candles, the priest, and the thanksgiving service, though very impor-

---

*As churchwarden Vasili Andreevich sold the tapers the worshippers bought to set before the icons. These were collected at the end of the service, and could afterwards be resold to the advantage of the church revenue. A.M.

tant and necessary in church, could do nothing for him
here, and that there was and could be no connexion between those candles and services and his present disas-
trous plight. "I must not despair," he thought. "I must
follow the horse's track before it is snowed under. He
will lead me out, or I may even catch him. Only I must
not hurry, or I shall stick fast and be more lost than ever."

But in spite of his resolution to go quietly, he rushed
forward and even ran, continually falling, getting up and
falling again. The horse's track was already hardly visible
in places where the snow did not lie deep. "I am lost!"
thought Vasili Andreevich. "I shall lose the track and not
catch the horse." But at that moment he saw something
black. It was Mukhorty, and not only Mukhorty, but the
sledge with the shafts and the kerchief. Mukhorty, with
the sacking and the breechband twisted round to one
side, was standing not in his former place but nearer to
the shafts, shaking his head which the reins he was stepping on drew downwards. It turned out that Vasili Andreevich had sunk in the same ravine Nikita had
previously fallen into, and that Mukhorty had been
bringing him back to the sledge and he had got off his
back no more than fifty paces from where the sledge was.

ix

HAVING stumbled back to the sledge, Vasili Andreevich
caught hold of it and for a long time stood motionless,
trying to calm himself and recover his breath. Nikita was
not in his former place, but something, already covered
with snow, was lying in the sledge and Vasili Andreevich
concluded that this was Nikita. His terror had now quite
left him, and if he felt any fear it was lest the dreadful
terror should return that he had experienced when on
the horse and especially when he was left alone in the
snowdrift. At any cost he had to avoid that terror, and to
keep it away he must do something—occupy himself
with something. And the first thing he did was to turn his

back to the wind and open his fur coat. Then, as soon as he recovered his breath a little, he shook the snow out of his boots and out of his left-hand glove (the right-hand glove was hopelessly lost and by this time probably lying somewhere under a dozen inches of snow), then as was his custom when going out of his shop to buy grain from the peasants, he pulled his girdle low down and tightened it and prepared for action. The first thing that occurred to him was to free Mukhorty's leg from the rein. Having done that, and tethered him to the iron cramp at the front of the sledge where he had been before, he was going round the horse's quarters to put the breechband and pad straight and cover him with the cloth, but at that moment he noticed that something was moving in the sledge and Nikita's head rose up out of the snow that covered it. Nikita, who was half frozen, rose with great difficulty and sat up, moving his hand before his nose in a strange manner just as if he were driving away flies. He waved his hand and said something, and seemed to Vasili Andreevich to be calling him. Vasili Andreevich left the cloth unadjusted and went up to the sledge.

"What is it?" he asked. "What are you saying?"

"I'm dy . . . ing, that's what," said Nikita brokenly and with difficulty. "Give what is owing to me to my lad, or to my wife, no matter."

"Why, are you really frozen?" asked Vasili Andreevich.

"I feel it's my death. Forgive me for Christ's sake . . ." said Nikita in a tearful voice, continuing to wave his hand before his face as if driving away flies.

Vasili Andreevich stood silent and motionless for half a minute. Then suddenly, with the same resolution with which he used to strike hands when making a good purchase, he took a step back and turning up his sleeves began raking the snow off Nikita and out of the sledge. Having done this he hurriedly undid his girdle, opened out his fur coat, and having pushed Nikita down, lay down on top of him, covering him not only with his fur coat but with the whole of his body, which glowed with warmth. After pushing the skirts of his coat between Nikita and the sides of the sledge, and holding down its hem with his knees, Vasili Andreevich lay like that face down, with his head pressed against the front of the sledge. Here he no longer heard the horse's movements or the whistling of the wind, but only Nikita's breathing. At first and for a long time Nikita lay motionless; then he sighed deeply and moved.

"There, and you say you are dying! Lie still and get warm, that's our way ..." began Vasili Andreevich.

But to his great surprise he could say no more, for tears came to his eyes and his lower jaw began to quiver rapidly. He stopped speaking and only gulped down the risings in his throat. "Seems I was badly frightened and have gone quite weak," he thought. But this weakness was not only not unpleasant, but gave him a peculiar joy such as he had never felt before.

"That's our way!" he said to himself, experiencing a strange and solemn tenderness. He lay like that for a long time, wiping his eyes on the fur of his coat and tucking under his knee the right skirt, which the wind kept turning up.

But he longed so passionately to tell somebody of his joyful condition that he said: "Nikita!"

"It's comfortable, warm!" came a voice from beneath.

"There, you see, friend, I was going to perish. And you would have been frozen, and I should have ..."

But again his jaws began to quiver and his eyes to fill with tears, and he could say no more.

"Well, never mind," he thought. "I know about myself what I know."

He remained silent and lay like that for a long time.

Nikita kept him warm from below and his fur coats from above. Only his hands, with which he kept his coat-skirts down round Nikita's sides, and his legs which the wind kept uncovering, began to freeze, especially his right hand which had no glove. But he did not think of his legs or of his hands but only of how to warm the peasant who was lying under him. He looked out several

times at Mukhorty and could see that his back was uncovered and the drugget and breeching lying on the
snow, and that he ought to get up and cover him, but he
could not bring himself to leave Nikita and disturb even
for a moment the joyous condition he was in. He no longer felt any kind of terror.

"No fear, we shan't lose him this time!" he said to
himself, referring to his getting the peasant warm with
the same boastfulness with which he spoke of his buying
and selling.

Vasili Andreevich lay in that way for one hour, another, and a third, but he was unconscious of the passage
of time. At first impressions of the snow-storm, the
sledge-shafts, and the horse with the shaft-bow shaking
before his eyes kept passing through his mind; then he
remembered Nikita lying under him, then recollections
of the festival, his wife, the police officer, and the box of
candles began to mingle with these; then again Nikita,
this time lying under that box; then the peasants, customers and traders, and the white walls of his house with its
iron roof with Nikita lying underneath presented themselves to his imagination. Afterwards all these impressions blended into one nothingness. As the colours of the
rainbow unite into one white light, so all these different
impressions mingled into one, and he fell asleep.

For a long time he slept without dreaming, but just
before dawn the visions recommenced. It seemed to him
that he was standing by the box of tapers and that Tik-
hon's wife was asking for a five-kopek taper for the
church fête. He wished to take one out and give it to her,
but his hands would not lift being held tight in his pockets. He wanted to walk round the box but his feet would
not move and his new clean galoshes had grown to the
stone floor, and he could neither lift them nor get his feet
out of the galoshes. Then the taper-box was no longer a
box but a bed, and suddenly Vasili Andreevich saw himself lying in his bed at home. He was lying in his bed and
could not get up. Yet it was necessary for him to get up
because Ivan Matveich, the police officer, would soon

call for him and he had to go with him—either to bargain
for the forest or to put Mukhorty's breeching straight.

He asked his wife: "Nikolaevna,* hasn't he come yet?"
"No, he hasn't," she replied. He heard someone drive up
to the front steps. "It must be him." "No, he's gone past."
"Nikolaevna! I say, Nikolaevna, isn't he here yet?" "No."
He was still lying on his bed and could not get up, but
was always waiting. And this waiting was uncanny and
yet joyful. Then suddenly his joy was completed. He
whom he was expecting came; not Ivan Matveich the police officer, but someone else—yet it was he whom he
had been waiting for. He came and called him; and it was
he who had called him and told him to lie down on Nikita. And Vasili Andreevich was glad that that one had
come for him.

"I'm coming!" he cried joyfully, and that cry awoke
him, but woke him up not at all the same person he had
been when he fell asleep. He tried to get up but could
not, tried to move his arm and could not, to move his leg
and also could not, to turn his head and could not. He
was surprised but not at all disturbed by this. He understood that this was death, and was not at all disturbed by
that either. He remembered that Nikita was lying under
him and that he had got warm and was alive, and it
seemed to him that he was Nikita and Nikita was he, and
that his life was not in himself but in Nikita. He strained
his ears and heard Nikita breathing and even slightly
snoring. "Nikita is alive, so I too am alive!" he said to
himself triumphantly.

And he remembered his money, his shop, his house,
the buying and selling, and Mironov's millions, and it was
hard for him to understand why that man, called Vasili
Brekhunov, had troubled himself with all those things
with which he had been troubled.

"Well, it was because he did not know what the real
thing was," he thought, concerning that Vasili Brekhu-

*A familiar peasant use of the patronymic in place of the Christian
name. A.M.

nov. "He did not know, but now I know and know for sure. Now I know!" And again he heard the voice of the one who had called him before. "I'm coming! Coming!" he responded gladly, and his whole being was filled with joyful emotion. He felt himself free and that nothing could hold him back any longer.

After that Vasili Andreevich neither saw, heard, nor felt anything more in this world.

All around the snow still eddied. The same whirlwinds of snow circled about, covering the dead Vasili Andreevich's fur coat, the shivering Mukhorty, the sledge, now scarcely to be seen, and Nikita lying at the bottom of it, kept warm beneath his dead master.

X

NIKITA AWOKE before daybreak. He was aroused by the cold that had begun to creep down his back. He had dreamt that he was coming from the mill with a load of his master's flour and when crossing the stream had missed the bridge and let the cart get stuck. And he saw that he had crawled under the cart and was trying to lift it by arching his back. But strange to say the cart did not move, it stuck to his back and he could neither lift it nor get out from under it. It was crushing the whole of his loins. And how cold it felt! Evidently he must crawl out. "Have done!" he exclaimed, to whoever was pressing the cart down on him. "Take out the sacks!" But the cart pressed down colder and colder, and then he heard a strange knocking, awoke completely, and remembered everything. The cold cart was his dead and frozen master lying upon him. And the knock was produced by Mukhorty, who had twice struck the sledge with his hoof.

"Andreeich! Eh, Andreeich!* Nikita called cautiously, beginning to realize the truth, and straightening his back.

---

*Again the characteristic peasant use of the patronymic without the Christian name preceding it. A.M.

But Vasili Andreevich did not answer and his stomach and legs were stiff and cold and heavy like iron weights.

"He must have died! May the Kingdom of Heaven be his!" thought Nikita.

He turned his head, dug with his hand through the snow about him and opened his eyes. It was daylight; the wind was whistling as before between the shafts, and the snow was falling in the same way, except that it was no longer driving against the frame of the sledge but silently covered both sledge and horse deeper and deeper, and neither the horse's movements nor his breathing were any longer to be heard.

"He must have frozen too," thought Nikita of Mukhorty, and indeed those hoof knocks against the sledge, which had awakened Nikita, were the last efforts the already numbed Mukhorty had made to keep on his feet before dying.

"O Lord God, it seems Thou art calling me too!" said Nikita. "Thy Holy Will be done. But it's uncanny. . . . Still, a man can't die twice and must die once. If only it would come soon!"

And he again drew in his head, closed his eyes, and became unconscious, fully convinced that now he was certainly and finally dying.

It was not till noon that day that peasants dug Vasili Andreevich and Nikita out of the snow with their shovels, not more than seventy yards from the road and less than half a mile from the village.

The snow had hidden the sledge, but the shafts and the kerchief tied to them were still visible. Mukhorty, buried up to his belly in snow, with the breeching and drugget hanging down, stood all white, his dead head pressed against his frozen throat: icicles hung from his nostrils, his eyes were covered with hoar-frost as though filled with tears, and he had grown so thin in that one night that he was nothing but skin and bone.

Vasili Andreevich was stiff as a frozen carcass, and when they rolled him off Nikita his legs remained apart and his arms stretched out as they had been. His bulging hawk eyes were frozen, and his open mouth under his clipped moustache was full of snow. But Nikita though chilled through was still alive. When he had been brought to, he felt sure that he was already dead and that what was taking place with him was no longer happening in this world but in the next. When he heard the peasants shouting as they dug him out and rolled the frozen body of Vasili Andreevich from off him, he was at first surprised that in the other world peasants should be shouting in the same old way and had the same kind of body, and then when he realized that he was still in this world he was sorry rather than glad, especially when he found that the toes on both his feet were frozen.

Nikita lay in hospital for two months. They cut off three of his toes, but the others recovered so that he was still able to work and went on living for another twenty years, first as a farm-labourer, then in his old age as a watchman. He died at home as he had wished, only this year, under the icons with a lighted taper in his hands. Before he died he asked his wife's forgiveness and forgave her for the cooper. He also took leave of his son and grandchildren, and died sincerely glad that he was relieving his son and daughter-in-law of the burden of having to feed him, and that he was now really passing from this life of which he was weary into that other life which every year and every hour grew clearer and more desirable to him. Whether he is better or worse off there where he awoke after his death, whether he was disappointed or found there what he expected, we shall all soon learn.

AFTERWORD

TOLSTOY's towering reputation no doubt rests primarily on his two great novels, *War and Peace* and *Anna Karenina,* which still rank among the best ever written. However, Tolstoy also excelled at the shorter forms of fiction, four outstanding examples of which are presented in this volume.

Tolstoy began his career as a writer in the 1850s, with a quasiautobiographical trilogy, *Childhood, Boyhood,* and *Youth,* interspersed with stories and sketches based on his experiences in the Russian army, fighting first in the Caucasus and later in the Crimean War. When in late 1855, at the age of twenty-seven, he appeared in St. Petersburg in his officer's uniform, he was feted both as a military hero and as a writer of immense promise.

It was an exciting time for Russians. The loss of the war and the accession of Alexander II (1855–81) brought to the surface multiple impulses toward reform, notably the commitment of the new czar to emancipate the millions of peasant serfs, hitherto the private property of such gentlemen as Tolstoy. The literary world too was beginning to diversify, dividing between those who wanted to use literature as a vehicle of social criticism and a gentry party that cherished art as a manifestation of mankind's eternal striving for the sublime. Count Tolstoy sided with the aristocrats, but with a difference. Tolstoy was never an aesthete. For him fiction was never merely verbal art, however exalted. Throughout his life he insisted on its *moral* responsibility.

By the late 1850s Tolstoy discovered a bitter truth: instant fame can rapidly become instant oblivion. In 1856 he had seemed a fresh voice, but by 1859 he was just another gentleman author, writing about such "eternal" topics as growing up, war, art, and death. The dominant left-leaning critics, demanding exposés of social evils, wrote him off as irrelevant, even a renegade.

There was one "eternal" theme Tolstoy had not yet touched: love. Tolstoy had personal reasons for turning to it now. He was over thirty, and it was time to find himself a wife. Hitherto he had mostly confined himself to erotic relationships with women of the lower classes, including his own serfs. But for three years (1856–59), Tolstoy had been carrying on a tepid romance with a neighboring lady, one Valeria Arseneva. He kept expecting something big called "love" to explode in his soul, but nothing like that happened. He was not stirred by her, and he never proposed, though he had led her to believe that he would.

Nevertheless, Tolstoy decided to pursue the subject of love imaginatively, as a literary theme, and to carry it through to its conclusion, as his rival Turgenev almost never did. He would not debunk the poetry of romance, but he wanted to explore what happened afterward. Tolstoy had not yet experienced marriage, but in "Family Happiness" he would try to imagine what it was like. He would also try a bold experiment: he would present the experience from the *woman's* point of view. And at the same time, with his picture of a marriage that degenerated because of the woman's immaturity, he would show that he had been right in not marrying Valeria.

The first part of "Family Happiness" invokes the typical heroine of a Russian gentry romance, the young girl just awakening to womanhood, fresh, innocent, and ripe for romance. Tolstoy handles masterfully the budding love between his Masha and Sergey Mikhaylych, a considerably older man and her guardian. This first part has been described as a perfect idyll, contrasting with the second, set in the harsher key of realism. In crossing the border beyond the altar, Tolstoy had to choose. He could follow his ideal heroine into an ideal marriage, a marriage not falsified, but simply demonstrating maturation; a good, live, vigorous girl becomes a good, live, vigorous wife and mother. In the great novels, Tolstoy was to treat this pattern beautifully. A second alternative was for the marriage to disintegrate. Like Anna Karenina, Masha might have drifted into adultery with the sexy Italian. So here two great Tolstoyan themes were compressed into one, perhaps causing some short-circuiting. In "Family Happiness," instead of either polar opposite, a "realistic" compromise is reached: a marriage that never regains the closeness of the idyll, but reaches a plateau of serenity and mutual accommodation.

At the time of its publication "Family Happiness" passed unnoticed, and Tolstoy came to hate the story. The apparent failure triggered a moral crisis, anticipating others to come. "'Family Happiness,'" he wrote in his diary, "is a shameful abomination. . . . I am buried as a writer. . . . There is not a live word in the whole thing." Fortunately, this withering judgment has decidedly not stood the test of time; the story has become a recognized classic.

The two decades of the 1860s and 1870s were momentous ones in Tolstoy's life. His marriage to Sofia Behrs in 1862 was followed by two immense creative undertakings, the two great novels. Before completing *Anna Karenina,* however, Tolstoy was in the throes of another moral crisis. More and more he felt that he could not go on living without coming to some conclusion about the meaning of life. What is life for? Why are we here? And especially, how can life have any meaning if it must end in death?

Tolstoy spent years searching for answers to these "accursed" questions. Only in religion, he felt, were these issues addressed squarely, but most religions were fatally

contaminated by supernatural nonsense. Tolstoy therefore undertook to cleanse Christianity of all such "nonsense." The result was a new religion that came to be
called "Tolstoyism," a rational, nonmagic version of
Christianity focused on the *teachings* of Jesus, especially
the doctrine of nonviolent resistance to evil. The princi-
ples of this new religion were expounded in a series of
treatises that Tolstoy considered his most important con-
tribution to humanity, far more valuable than the "trivial," elitist giant novels.

Though the older Tolstoy found little moral justification for most art, he did allow the legitimacy of two
kinds. He approved of a simple, unsophisticated art ac-
cessible to all mankind, and he acknowledged an art de-
signed to "infect" the recipient with morally beneficent
feelings. Therefore, after his "conversion" of the late
1870s, Tolstoy occasionally allowed himself to reactivate
his enormous artistic gifts and write fiction consonant
with Tolstoyism. The three other stories in this book
were all squeezed through this loophole.

The topic of death had long been on Tolstoy's mind,
no doubt the result of a life experience studded with
deaths: his mother (1830), his father (1837), two brothers
(1856, 1860) and other relations, as well as the many fellow soldiers he had seen killed. The theme had already
found expression in fiction in many early stories, such as
"Three Deaths" (1859), and in the two novels. Death was
obviously a basic fact of nature, but still hard to reconcile
with any sense of justice. After the death of his beloved
brother Nikolai, Tolstoy had raged at the Creator, both
for this death and for all deaths. "What is the use of anything when tomorrow the torments of death may begin?" he wrote. He could not accept conventional
Christian notions of personal immortality, though he did
eventually come to believe in a quasi-Buddhist merging
of the soul after death with the infinite One. In "The
Death of Ivan Ilych," his first post-conversion fiction,
Tolstoy would attempt to confront the metaphysical
question of the meaning of death. To this impulse was

added an equally powerful one: Tolstoy's increasing disgust with Russian upper-class society.

The immediate stimulus for the writing of the story was the death from cancer on July 2, 1881, of one Ivan Ilych Mechnikov, a judge in the neighboring city, Tula. Tolstoy learned that in his last days Mechnikov had lamented the fruitlessness of his life. Aha! Tolstoy had long had an aversion for lawyers, and judges were obviously in violation of Christ's commandment "Judge not that ye be not judged." He seized on Mechnikov as a perfect example of the false values by which upper-class Russians lived.

Death is the point of contact between the finite world of being, the physical, on the one hand, and on the other the metaphysical, the infinite and unknown. By taking a character's death as our point of vantage, we can look back into his life and forward into the eternal. In particular, death provides a perspective for assessing life's values. How do they stand up when measured against the infinite?

Note the unexpected design of the story. It *begins* with its temporal conclusion, the fact of Ivan Ilych's death, treated as a news item. The reactions of his fellow officials are a measure of the falseness of their values: how his death will affect positions in the service, especially mine; it is he who is dead and not I; and how tiresome to have to condole with the widow and attend the funeral. All these reactions are evasions, refusals to confront the meaning of death, because to do so would mean to confront the emptiness of their lives. But the thought is subliminally there; it is the voice of God within us. It speaks in a muffled way to Peter Ivanovich during his visit to Ivan Ilych's house, at the sight of his corpse (in Russia it was customary for a body to lie in state at home). "[T]here was in that expression [on the corpse's face] a reproach and a warning to the living. This warning seemed to Peter Ivanovich out of place, or at least not applicable to him." This response is directly parallel to Ivan Ilych's reaction to the famous syllogism:

Caius is a man, all men are mortal, therefore Caius is
mortal—but that was Caius, not me.

Falseness and pretense pervade the whole society. In
the newspaper advertisement Ivan Ilych's widow spoke
of her "profound sorrow," the expected conventional
emotion, whereas in fact she felt mainly relief. During
the "condolence" conversation with Peter Ivanovich it is
clear that her main interest is money. The conversation
takes place in a drawing room filled with *things,* perhaps
among them the curtains Ivan Ilych was hanging when
he suffered the injury that ultimately caused his death.
Tolstoy even gives this scene a humorous touch, as Peter
Ivanovich must contend with the indecorous "rebellious
springs" of the pouffe under him.

The world of false values is eager to deny the moral
significance of death. It is evaded by all the upper-class
characters. The only person to say or do anything genuine is the peasant servant Gerasim, who says, "It's God's
will. We shall all come to it some day."

From the perspective of death, Tolstoy can look back
over Ivan Ilych's whole life, pronouncing a harsh moral
judgment. His life had been "most simple and most ordinary and therefore most terrible" (the word "therefore"
was added by the translator). It had a familiar pattern.
Ivan Ilych was a good fellow, did what was expected of
him, made his way in the service, got married, rose in
rank and affluence. Life seemed pleasant and proper; but
it was terribly empty. It not only had no moral purpose,
there were not even any deep human bonds. His illness
and death show that no one is close, no one really cares.
His marriage had deteriorated to the point of estrangement, and even at its brighter beginning, "conjugal caresses" had been linked in the same sentence with "new
furniture, new crockery, and new linen."

After Ivan Ilych contracts the fatal illness, there follows the fearsome account of the process of dying. It
may seem morbid, but it is necessary for Tolstoy's pur-
poses. A moral struggle takes place. The inexorable reality of approaching death forces Ivan Ilych to face his life

as it is. It is terribly hard to do this. He uses every means of evasion and denial, encouraged by the doctors, who, as always in Tolstoy, are useless, expensive, insensitive frauds. They cannot cure, they cannot even relieve pain, and they will not answer the ultimate question "Will I die?" But the pain grows steadily worse, and Ivan Ilych terrifies the household with his screams. Only in the last hour is there a moral change. Ivan Ilych at last recognizes that his life has been false and senseless. He is reconciled to his death, which he now sees as the beginning of something else. "In place of death there was light."

In the later 1880s Tolstoy became increasingly obsessed with the question of human sexuality. The antithesis that had satisfied him when he wrote the two novels—between good, marital, biologically sanctioned, procreative sex and the bad, adulterous, self-indulgent kind—was no longer acceptable. Though he himself had sired thirteen children, Tolstoy now concluded that sex itself was bad, a relic of the "animal nature" we must all seek to outgrow. He set about embodying these views in "The Kreutzer Sonata."

The story is cast in a form Tolstoy rarely used, one in which a primary narrator (the author?) transmits a story told him orally by a second narrator. Here the inner story is told during a discussion by passengers in a railway compartment. The topic is sex. The views expressed cover a gamut of prevalent attitudes. At one extreme is the old merchant, who maintains that every husband should enforce his wife's virtue by fear, even beatings, though men are permitted occasional lapses (the "double standard"). At the other pole is the smoking lady (smoking is always a bad sign in Tolstoy), who insists that marriage should be based on love; if love is gone, the marriage is defunct and the partners free. Another problem raised is the ambiguous relationship between "love" and "lust." As the inner narrator, Pozdnyshev, puts it, "Spiritual affinity! Identity of ideals! But in that case why go to bed together?"

Here most of the discussants depart, and Pozdnyshev

can relate his sexual history to the primary narrator, a
history Tolstoy considered typical of the Russian upper-
class male. After puberty, the boy begins to masturbate,
perhaps has a homosexual experience, later goes to a
brothel. Sexual release was considered necessary for
health, and some parents even arranged these visits for
their sons.

Only at age thirty did Pozdnyshev decide to get married, although in Tolstoy's view he had been "married"
hundreds of times before. Idyllic stories of romance, perhaps like his own "Family Happiness," between virginal
girls and these sullied men were therefore mendacious.
Pozdnyshev indignantly observes how upper-class girls,
instructed by their mothers, try to enhance their sexual
attractiveness in order to induce men to marry them. The
world of society, he concludes, is no better than a brothel.
Only recently have people come to believe that marriages should be based on love, but in fact this love is
nothing but lust.

Pozdnyshev now begins the vivid account of his court-
ship and marriage. We would surely regard it today as
the ambivalent relationship of two very egotistical indi-
viduals based on sexual passion alone, but Pozdnyshev/
Tolstoy apparently regards it as typical. Sexual relations
makes matters worse. Sexual satiety, Pozdnyshev be-
lieves, makes people quarrelsome and vicious. The relationship degenerates.

The paradox, which Tolstoy regards as a built-in feature of human sexuality, is that the husband, despite an
estrangement from his wife that has become hatred, nevertheless is intensely jealous of her relationship with a
violinist friend. Their duets seem to him like acts of love.
The passionate strains of Beethoven's famous sonata,
played by the two together, arouse intense feelings, not
only in them, but in Pozdnyshev himself. The jealousy is
probably unjustified, but it drives him to commit murder.

Tolstoy manages to insert in Pozdnyshev's diatribes
many other quirks and prejudices about sex (which irritated Dr. Anton Chekhov, among others): sexual inter-

course during pregnancy or lactation is a crime, birth control is a crime, and so forth. It would be gratifying if we could write off these extreme views as those of the crazed Pozdnyshev, a confessed murderer. But alas, Tolstoy appended to the story an afterword not included in this volume in which he takes full responsibility for them. Ideologically, he and Pozdnyshev are one. Tolstoy stresses there his belief that even married couples should try to live together like brother and sister, without sex. To the obvious criticism that if universally followed, this prescription would mean the end of the human race, Tolstoy replied: first, that it was an ideal to be striven for, not an expected reality; and second, that if the ideal were to be attained, it would mean that we had achieved God's mission for us on earth, and there would be no need to continue the species.

In the early 1890s Tolstoy was inspired to compose a new parable on the ever looming question of death. The result was "Master and Man" (1895). As in "The Death of Ivan Ilych," the imminence of death produces in the protagonist a total reassessment of his life. This time the "hero," Vasili Brekhunov, is of the middle class, a merchant. He has ambitions to become a millionaire, and his whole life has been focused on money, on property. His wife is little more than an inescapable appendage, and his son is not so much a live child as "the heir." Brekhunov has enriched himself largely by underhanded deals, overlooking no opportunity for gain. His immediate goal is to purchase some wooded land for much less than it is worth from a commercially naive neighboring gentleman, and it is important to close the deal before he is undercut by other merchants. Hence his haste, his insistence on travelling despite the threatening blizzard.

Brekhunov's companion on his journey, Nikita, is one of Tolstoy's classic good-hearted peasants, though Tolstoy avoids idealizing him beyond credibility. Like most peasants, he has had a hard, poverty-stricken life. In relation to "masters," like Brekhunov, his attitude is one of passive, you're-the-boss acceptance. Vodka has been his weakness, but he has recently vowed to abstain and does so successfully in the story. In relation to death he has a peasant's indifference: the next world, he assumes, is likely to be better than this one, and his death will free space for others. So despite warnings, the two set off on a threatening winter afternoon, into heavy snow and howling wind. Even after getting lost once and by luck finding shelter, Brekhunov insists on starting again.

The great strength of the story is its concreteness, the extraordinary vividness with which Tolstoy evokes the experience—the horse (even the horse has a marked personality), the harness, the sleigh, each man's clothing, each man's thoughts. Tolstoy had powerfully treated the blizzard theme years before, in "The Snowstorm" (1856), but in a very different, youthful spirit—more social, with a happy ending, no deaths, and few thoughts about it. But here, isolation, terrible cold, and a bleak white landscape devoid of any sign of human habitation become not only agents of death but its very image.

Like Ivan Ilych, Brekhunov clings to his own self-focused life until nearly the end, even abandoning Nikita to his fate by riding off on the horse. But when this action proves futile, something happens in him. He returns to Nikita and saves Nikita's life at the expense of his own, by lying down on top of him. Brekhunov passes through three psychological stages. The initial bravado and self-congratulation are intersected by fear. The fear becomes more and more dominant until the third stage, the transformation. Tolstoy avoids giving us an insider's view of what Brekhunov thinks and feels as this third stage begins. We see only that he lies down on Nikita and that tears fill his eyes. Only then are we at last given his thoughts. For the first time he thinks not of "me," but of "you" and "us." Like Ivan Ilych, the emotion he now feels is "joy." Various cloudy fantasies fill his mind, but he continues to feel the presence of Him, the One who called him and ordered him to lie on Nikita. He remembers what used to fill his life, all the buying and selling,

and wonders how he could ever have cared about such
things. "Now I know," he says.

It has been argued that Brekhunov's act of self-
sacrifice is not motivated by Tolstoyan Christian princi-
ples at all, nor by the desire to save another's life, but
only by the wish to escape the terrible fear through
closeness to another human being. If there is nothing
beyond death, then on earth we have only one another.
This essentially atheistic reading may in some ultimate
sense be true of Tolstoy the author, who was indeed
plagued to the end by deep doubts about his God. But it
is not true of the story, which reassuringly offers us a
"He" who calls Brekhunov to perform his salvific act and
renders death easy and joyful.

—Hugh McLean

SELECTED BIBLIOGRAPHY

Other Works by Tolstoy

Autobiographical Trilogy

Childhood (1852)
Boyhood (1854)
Youth (1857)

Stories

"The Raid" (1852), "Notes of a Billiard Marker" (1855), "The Wood-cutting" (1855), "Sevastopol in December" (1855), "Sevastopol in May (1855), "Sevastopol in August, 1855" (1856), "The Snowstorm" (1856), "Two Hussars" (1856), "Reduced to the Ranks" (1856), "Lucerne" (1857), "Albert" (1858), "Three Deaths" (1859), "The Cossacks" (1863), "Polikushka" (1863), "God Sees the Truth but Waits" (1872), "A Prisoner of the Caucasus" (1872), "What Men Live By (1881), "Strider: The Story of a Horse" (1885), "How Much Land Does a Man Need?" (1886), "The Devil" (written 1889–90; published 1911), "Father Sergius" (written 1890–91; published 1911), "After the Ball" (written 1903; published 1911), "Hadji Murad" (written 1896–1905; published 1912), "The Forged Coupon" (written 1889–1904; published 1911)

Novels

War and Peace (1865–69)
Anna Karenina (1874–77)
Resurrection (1899–1900)

Plays

The Power of Darkness (1887)
The Fruits of Enlightenment (1891)
The Living Corpse (written 1899–1900; published 1911)
The Light Shineth in Darkness (published 1911)

Treatises

A Confession (1882), *Union and Translation of the Four Gospels* (1882), *A Critique of Dogmatic Theology* (1882), *What I Believe* (1885), *What Then Must We Do?* (1886), *The Kingdom of God Is Within You* (1890)

Essay

What Is Art? (1898)

Biography and Criticism

Bartlett, Rosamund. *Tolstoy: A Russian Life*. New York: Houghton Mifflin Harcourt, 2011.
Bayley, John. *Tolstoy and the Novel*. New York: The Viking Press, 1966.
Berlin, Isaiah. *The Hedgehog and the Fox*. New York: Simon & Schuster, 1953.
Christian, Reginald F. *Tolstoy: A Critical Introduction*. Cambridge: Cambridge University Press, 1969.
Eikhenbaum, Boris. *The Young Tolstoy*. Ann Arbor, MI: Ardis, 1972.
———. *Tolstoy in the Seventies*. Ann Arbor, MI: Ardis, 1982.
Gifford, Henry. *Leo Tolstoy: A Critical Anthology*. Harmondsworth, England: Penguin, 1971.
Jahn, Gary. *The Death of Ivan Iyich: A Critical Companion*. Evanston, IL: Northwestern University Press, 1999.

———. *The Death of Ivan Iyich: An Interpretation*. New York: Twayne, 1993.

Jones, Malcolm. *New Essays on Tolstoy*. Cambridge: Cambridge University Press, 1978.

Matlaw, Ralph E., ed. *Tolstoy: A Collection of Critical Essays*. Englewood Cliffs, NJ: Prentice-Hall, 1967.

McLean, Hugh, ed. *In the Shade of the Giant: Essays on Tolstoy*. Berkeley: University of California Press, 1989 (essay by John Kopper on "The Kreutzer Sonata").

Orwin, Donna, ed. *A Tolstoy Companion*. Cambridge: Cambridge University Press, 2002.

Poggioli, Renato. *The Oaken Flute*. Cambridge, MA: Harvard University Press, 1975 (essay on "Family Happiness").

Popoff, Alexandra. *Sophia Tolstoy: A Biography*. New York: Free Press, 2010.

Porter, Cathy, trans. *The Diaries of Sofia Tolstoy*. New York: Harper Perennial, 2009.

Rahv, Philip. *Image and Idea*. New York: J. Laughlin, 1957 (essay on "The Death of Ivan Ilych").

Wasiolek, Edward. *Critical Essays on Tolstoy*. Boston: G. K. Hall, 1986.

———. *Tolstoy's Major Fiction*. Chicago: University Of Chicago Press, 1978.

Wilson, A. N. *Tolstoy*. London: Hamish Hamilton, 1988.

Signet Classics

Russia's Greatest Short Fiction

ANTON CHEKHOV: SELECTED STORIES
translated by Ann Dunnigan

Anton Chekhov, a master of both the sentimental and
ironic, is a writer of broad scope and thoughtful insight.
These tales, whether sadly sentimental or pensively bitter, are
the equal of his plays. Included in this volume are:
*The Confession, A Nincompoop, Ninochka—A Love Story,
A Cure for Drinking, The Milksop, In Spring, The Kiss,*
and many more.

DIARY OF A MADMAN & OTHER STORIES
by Nicolai Gogol
translated by Andrew R. MacAndrew

Gogol's great talent was to write both immensely funny and
incredibly moving works. From the biting social
commentary of the title story, to the sad and hilarious
misadventures of *The Nose and The Overcoat*, to the
adventure and romance of *Taras Bulba*, Gogol provides his
readers with thoughtful and entertaining tales.

**Available wherever books are sold or at
signetclassics.com**

facebook.com/signetclassic